GW00738923

The R _____

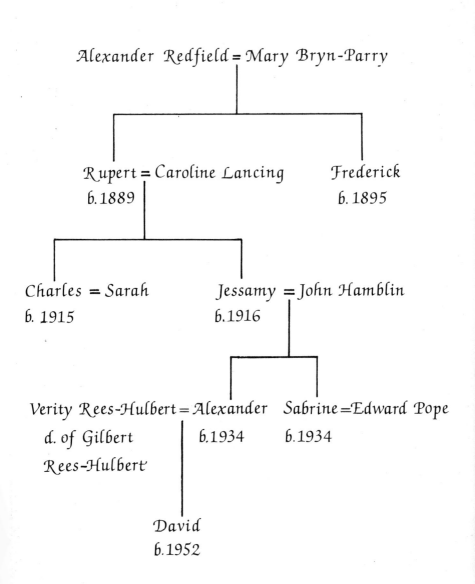

Alexander Redfield = Mary Bryn-Parry

Rupert = Caroline Lancing   Frederick
b. 1889   b. 1895

Charles = Sarah   Jessamy = John Hamblin
b. 1915   b.1916

Verity Rees-Hulbert = Alexander   Sabrine = Edward Pope
d. of Gilbert   b.1934   b.1934
Rees-Hulbert

David
b.1952

NEAREST OF
KIN

Also by Pamela Townley:

THE STONE MAIDEN
WINTER JASMINE
BREATHING SPACE
ROGAN'S MOOR
FOXY LADY
THE IMAGE

PAMELA TOWNLEY

NEAREST OF KIN

NEW ENGLISH LIBRARY

Copyright © 1988 by Pamela Townley

First published in Great Britain in 1988 by
New English Library, Mill Road, Dunton Green, Sevenoaks, Kent.
Editorial office: 47 Bedford Square, London WC1B 3DP

All rights reserved. No part of this publication may
be reproduced or transmitted in any form or by any
means, electronically or mechanically, including
photocopying, recording or any information storage
or retrieval system, without either the prior permission
in writing from the publisher or a licence permitting
restricted copying. In the United Kingdom such licences
are issued by the Copyright Licensing Agency,
33–34 Alfred Place, London WC1E 7DP.

Typeset in Linotron Baskerville by
Rowland Phototypesetting Ltd
Bury St Edmunds, Suffolk
Printed in Great Britain by
St Edmundsbury Press Ltd
Bury St Edmunds, Suffolk

British Library Cataloguing in Publication Data
Townley, Pamela
  Nearest of kin.
  I. Title
  823'.914[F]   PR6070.089

ISBN 0-450-42538-X

for my son, Rogan

and for Gavan,
for Hazel and Olivia,
Tracey, for caring for Rogan,
Carole and Julian,
John Plender for merchant banking,
Harvey Tring and Michael Taylor for aviation,
and for Meepy-Mewl

Health is the greatest blessing,
Contentment the best possession,
A true friend the nearest of kin.

Buddha

BOOK ONE

1960 – 1964

Midsummer 1960

There was an old rowing-boat pulled up against the reeds. The evening sun still smouldered high up in the sky and the river was turning a deep oily silver. It was warm on their backs, the last rays catching at the switching tails of the cows munching contentedly in the meadow and the restless gnats hovering over the creek. On the opposite bank was an old wooden barn, its terracotta roof low-lying against the long green grass and the blue skies sharp behind. A fish splashed in the river. Around them were the sounds and smell of farm and river at the going down of the day. Charles Redfield cast his line again.

David Hamblin watched as in the distance the small biplane looped and circled high in the sky, the faint burr reaching them through the silence.

'I'd love to learn to fly,' he said.

Charles looked up and nodded. 'Great sport.' He lifted his bottle of beer from the grass beside him. 'I wanted to once.' He took a long drink from the bottle, felt the tug on the line, waited for it to tighten.

'Why didn't you?'

He watched as Charles reeled in his line. 'Oh, circumstance,' he said. The hook came clear of the water. 'Well, might as well pack up and go home for supper. They're not biting any more. Sun's got to them as well. Ready to go?' He reached for the hook, pulling the bait free.

But David was not listening. His eyes were screwed up against the light as he stared up into the sky where the plane dipped and swelled. The end of the day gathered in, shaking itself like a nesting bird.

'Whoever's up there's having a great time, Uncle Charles. I'd love that kind of freedom.'

Charles looked at his great-nephew. At eight years old he was a highly accomplished and personable young man, appearing far older than his years. He had taken on a maturity forced upon him by the indifference of his father, the recent lack of a mother, yet David never showed a gloomy nature. He always looked forward. Charles treated him as an equal.

'Yes, I thought so too once, myself,' he said wryly, as he packed up his rod and line, pushing the empty beer bottle back in amongst the paper bags that had held their sandwiches. He fastened the strap of his satchel. 'I even pursued the idea of combining flying with medicine. You know, like they do in Australia. I might have become a flying doctor.'

David looked at him with interest.

'Maybe when I leave school I'll go down to Bower Hill and ask the Bennetts for a job.'

Charles laughed. 'Don't! Take my advice. Try one of the other airfields if you're really keen.' He got to his feet, hefting the satchel over his shoulder. David stood up with him, brushing at the seat of blue cotton shorts, and following the line of his great-uncle's gaze as Charles looked back into the sky. 'It was Max Bennett that I went to when I was interested. He bit my head off, told me to take a running jump.'

'Why?'

'Oh . . .' Charles frowned with recollection, 'for reasons that you'll become aware of when you're older.'

'That's a rotten answer.'

Charles looked into the young face and smiled fondly. 'It is, I know, old chap, but it's all you're going to get for now. Sorry to be so obtuse but you really are too young for the full unexpurgated edition of why the Redfields hate the Bennetts and vice versa.' He put his arm around the boy's shoulders. He regretted the tenor of his words. David was far too bright for such a brush-off, but he would learn the story in the fullness of time, not now. He felt the warmth flow through him as he always did when in contact with the boy, and as he did so he looked down into the clear depths of his eyes. 'You've been like a son to me, David,' he said suddenly.

'It's good of you to say so.'

'Oh, come on now, you can do better than that.'

David glanced down at the ground and then back at his great-uncle. There was feeling in his face, his look direct. 'I feel the same way,' he said, paused a moment, and added, 'About Aunt Sarah too, since mother . . .' he began, and then faltered.

Charles felt a rush of emotion as the conjured image hung in the air between them. Verity's death had been such a shock to them all, mostly to her young son. The boy's eyes had darkened, their expression claiming his heart. 'You still miss her, don't you,' he said softly.

'Very much.'

Charles sighed and held him. He looked up over the field that ran high up to a crest, bordered to one side by Cobbold's Wood. A little brush of wind came up the river, pleating its surface. It folded around them, warm, as they stood together.

'You know you've got us,' he said simply. 'We're always here, always ready to listen, lend a hand. We love you as if you were our own boy. You know that, don't you, David.'

'Yes.' He did. But it was this time of year when the memories caught at him. The wind rushed in the trees, and its breeze was warm, the summer drowsy and the evenings long and deep. On such an evening, when the cool cut into the warmth of evening they had said goodbye. 'Mum . . . I love you.' He had seen the tears in her eyes, her white face in the darkness and held it in his memory as he ran to the dorm. Now it stood there for him, for ever. Those last words, her tragic face. He shook himself free.

'Want to talk about it?'

'No, not really. I miss her, that's all.'

He looked out over the water, a slight crease between his brows, and shoved his hands deep into his pockets. The sun sank in the sky; there was softness all around as the twilight gathered in. The last birds twittered comfortably in the trees. It was hard without a mother and his father had always taught him that men did not cry. A father he had hardly known to date: all his love had been cast on his mother, a mother who had protected and adored him.

Charles, understanding, did not interrupt his thoughts. The two of them stood awhile and gave themselves to the beauty of the evening. High above, the tiny craft banked and headed back over the wood into a western sky suddenly turned as red as fire.

The end of the day was crisp and bright, the breeze strong up above the wisps of cloud just as she had anticipated. Dickie Latimer had primed up her machine and taxied out onto the runway. With the familiar burr of sound she had fled down its length, lifting high up and over the line of trees and out into the brilliance of the open sky, a summer sky so deeply blue that held a muggy warmth against the land below, a midsummer heat. She had seen the cloud gather gently at the horizon, thundercloud an hour or so away, but in between there would be a fresh

13

promising wind with a damp hint of rain. She was right: already the small craft was being buffeted and pummelled around by the weather.

Dickie held her on course. It was perfect when there was a wind. It reminded her of so much, especially California, the early beginnings, the challenging times that had been so exciting. Hard too, but she had never seen hardship as anything more or less than a challenge that drove her onwards towards her goal. Something she had not yet reached.

The little Canuck responded beautifully to the controls. This one was hers; no one else was allowed to care for the first aircraft she had ever owned, a memory of adventure in an empire grown so large it threatened to engulf the past completely. This was her way of remembering the days when she was Dickie Bennett. She needed to; she had her reasons.

Dickie adjusted her goggles comfortably, throttled back and lifted the blunt nose up towards the blue above, the feathered clouds now suffused with magenta to the west, and to the east the darkening sky tightening in readiness. It was going to be a dramatic sunset if it died within the oncoming storm.

The wind was fresh on her face, a trail of woody sweetness in it, the burring of the blue Canuck biplane familiar and relaxing. She pulled the worn stick back in and to the right to dip and turn back towards the wood, and Foxhall. That was her goal.

That was when she saw the fire. And knew instinctively which house it was.

CHAPTER ONE

Max Bennett turned the corner by the old gate and swung the Land-Rover roughly through the gap and onto the stony track leading up to the cottage. He did not need his headlights any more. Ahead, it sat back from the clearing, flames leaping to the thatch. Smoke poured out of its blackened windows, the smell of burning and the harsh crackle of dry wood filling the clear evening air. Beyond the cottage itself, the tall trunks of the beech wood were picked out in livid relief, too close, the sparks leaping towards the tinder-dry carpet of brush and fern.

Max skidded the machine to a halt and leaped down to the ground. A sheet of flame licked out of a bedroom window and caught immediately in the thickly packed straw thatch. The cottage was going to go up quickly. He had been the first to react when the call came through from the airfield, dropping his evening newspaper to stride for the front door of Longbarrow and out into the drive. Bob Lovelock was a friend of his. Any greater significance was lost on him as he spun the wheels of the Land-Rover on the gravel and headed out onto the country lane beyond, past the village and onwards in the direction of the Redfield estate, Foxhall.

Tilly Lovelock saw him almost immediately and came running at him, clutching frantically at his arm.

'My Lesley!' she was crying, her eyes ringed with fear. 'She's still up in the bedroom! My baby! Do something, Mr Bennett, for the love of God . . . !' She pointed a finger at a man lying on the ground. His face was smeared with soot. Two children knelt beside him, holding him down. He was fighting to get back against their pleas. 'Bob's already tried!' she moaned. 'He's been burned ever so bad. The smoke stopped him.' She was sobbing now, shaking. 'He's going to kill himself trying . . . oh God!'

Max's reaction was instantaneous.

'Which room's she in?' His eyes bored into hers, striking

sanity into her hysteria. He grasped her arm. 'Which one? Point! Quickly!'

The woman shook in his grip. 'That one! That one!' she cried, pointing up at the right-hand corner, the opposite side to the burning thatch. 'Oh God, please hurry!'

There was a chance. 'Where's the rain barrel?'

'Over there. By the back door!'

His feet were already running before he had even consciously registered her words. Tearing his jacket from his back he plunged it deep into the dark swirl of water before throwing it over his head. He came round the corner of the building again just as Charles and David came running through the long grass from the direction of the fields beyond the cottage and Home Farm.

Charles was in front of the boy. He saw Max immediately and took in the situation at a glance. For a split second the two men held a look. Then Max, briefing himself on his blind path ahead, pulled the coat down over his forehead and disappeared in through the blazing doorway and into the cottage. Charles watched him go for only a second; both men had reason enough not to be here. The thought passed as he turned.

'Quickly! Let's get anything we can use!' He touched his nephew on the arm and pointed over towards the shed. 'There's bound to be buckets, something, in there.'

Man and boy ran across the clearing, Charles wrenching open the flimsy door to the shed. Inside they found two cow pails, a large wooden bucket from an old well, and a garden hose. 'Thank God!' breathed Charles. 'Though I don't think it's going to be much use to us now . . . here David, take this.' He thrust the bucket at him.

Outside he found the stand pump and pushed the mouth of the hose firmly on. David dunked his bucket into the rainwater barrel and dashed the contents against the burning building.

'It's not going to do much good, Uncle Charles,' he shouted. The licking flames hardly hesitated in their frenetic embrace of the dry building. With their first attempt they realised the futility of their efforts against the fire that now surrounded the cottage.

'Where the hell's that damn fire brigade!' shouted Charles frustratedly as he switched on the hose and played the thin drizzle against the charred walls and windows by the back door. 'This is absolutely hopeless, David!' he called out as the young boy bent and threw the water from his bucket in rapid rhythm. 'We're hardly making any impression at all!'

His voice was almost drowned by the crackling fury of the thatch as it exploded in a shower of sparks above them, the fire leaping out to roar through a gaping black hole in the roof. 'We'd be better helping Max Bennett in some way! Let the building go . . . it's going to anyway! Come on!' He did not say what was on his mind but he had understood what was happening as soon as he saw Max dash in through the door. A quick head count of the desperate Lovelock family clutching at each other in front of their home had told him what he had dreaded. Their small baby was still trapped in the house.

As the two of them rounded the building once more towards the front door, Charles's attention was caught by the man straddling the stile to the west of the cottage and the field that led up to the orchard at Foxhall. He sprang to the ground, agile despite his age.

'There's great-grandfather!' David pointed, and was gone to join him, running across the darkened grass to the figure that now strode forward, the flames lighting up the familiar face. Rupert Redfield was an imposing figure of a man, his yellow-white hair swept back from his forehead, the cold blue hooded eyes missing nothing. His sweeping glance surveyed the cottage, the flames shimmering up against the dark of the night sky that had now fallen, before returning to the boy who now stood talking before him. Rupert gave a brief smile as he listened, his eyes lifting to those of his son, Charles, as his hand came to rest on the boy's shoulder. There was no doubt that between these two, the oldest and the youngest of the Redfield dynasty, there was a friendship.

Charles's attention returned to the windows of the cottage, and the door, still blank, with no sign of Max or the child. He wondered about running inside himself, but realised it could only create more of a hazard for the man inside. Despite their differences, he knew this man was more capable than any of saving the child, if it were possible.

Rupert walked over to join him and once again Charles felt his father's eyes upon him. He addressed him as if there had been no breach, as if they spoke regularly.

'Anybody in there, Charles?' He had caught sight of the weeping woman and her family.

'Yes.' Charles replied in kind. 'A child . . . and Max Bennett.'

'*Bennett?*' The tone had become hard. 'What the hell's he doing here?'

Charles did not look at him. 'Came to help.' He willed the tall figure to reappear in the empty doorway. 'Let's hope he does.' A fresh gust of wind fanned the flames into a heavy roar as they caught both sides of the thatch. Charles tensed. Now it was only a matter of minutes. Sweat broke on his brow. A dark shadow moved at the window.

'There he is! And the child with him!'

'*Lesley!*'

All heads craned forward. Max's silhouette was blurred by the dense acrid smoke that spewed from the window under the eaves. His dark head was bare, in his arms the tiny bulk of the child wrapped in the wet jacket he had worn for protection. His face was blackened and he was shouting inaudibly.

At that moment there was the deafening crackle of breaking wood. The whole staircase inside the front door crumpled and fell, black charred spokes against a sheet of flame that burst out through the door and upwards. Inside the front door an inferno raged. His exit was blocked completely.

They understood and as a man they ran forward, only one remaining to watch, his hand clamped firmly to his great-grandson's shoulder. David felt the extra pressure and stood still as his uncle Charles and Bob Lovelock, recovered enough now to act, and two of the local farmhands arrived in the last few minutes, stood under the window, shielding their eyes to stare upwards at the man above. Max's voice, deafened by the noise and cracking from his smoke-filled lungs, broke through to them. Max's words were still not clear, but the mother had already moved. Pulling a blanket from the back of one of her children, she was already in their midst, thrusting it into their hands.

'Make a drop, he's shouting . . . get a move on!'

Charles cupped a hand to his mouth. Black dense smoke whirled between him and the man above. He shouted with all his strength.

'We've got a blanket! Let the baby go when I shout!'

He grasped the rough grey blanket with both his hands and pulled it tight.

'Now!' he shouted as the others nodded their readiness. 'Drop the baby, Max!'

Bob Lovelock twisted a grip on his corner. A shaft of brilliant light lit the blackness behind Max. Desperately all eyes stared upwards towards the charred window and the figure that leaned outwards, seeing them now as the wind swept the flames and smoke in a swift new direction. The small shape was held in his arms as he braced himself on the window ledge. Tilly Lovelock's hand held back her straggled hair from her face, her eyes glued to the sight above, her lips moving in silent prayer.

Rupert stood behind them in the flickering dark, both hands now holding the boy. His head was briefly bent in thought, though he lifted it to the sound of clanging bells coming up the lane fast from the direction of their village, Foxhall Green. He dismissed it as he turned, his interest captured far more by the man who now stepped out onto the window ledge.

Dickie Latimer had heard the bells too.

She stood at the balcony of her bedroom, framed against the dark by full length pale blue velvet curtains and the recently opened French windows. She was an incongruous sight against the pale elegance, still dressed in scuffed green leather jodhpurs, dusty boots and a slightly crumpled white shirt open at the throat, stains of oil along the long fingers that she now rubbed distractedly with a towel, an unseen smear across her forehead. It highlighted the troubled green of her eyes and the short black hair that was only lightly streaked with grey, her sixty years belied by the forceful vitality that flowed from her.

She had come straight here from the airfield, to her apartments in the west wing of the house, the rooms she had chosen because of the view when they had first bought Longbarrow. It was magnificent, commanding as it did the whole sweep of lawns to the river's edge, the meadow land flat beyond, climbing in the distance up to the Berkshire hills, to the east a Brunel bridge hand-spanning the waist of the river, and to the west . . . she looked over her land towards Sam's Hill. Lights spilled out from the house illuminating the lawns and trees around, but despite the darkness of the summer night the horizon was brilliant. Dark red flooded the backdrop of Cobbold's Wood, crimson lit the crests of the tallest trees fanning up the sky in a swirl of black smoke dotted with a thousand pinpricks of light, the flying sparks visible even from this distance of well over a mile. The night had an electric quality, the blue tension of a summer's night before the thunderstorm breaks.

Dickie felt it coming and shivered slightly, her free hand rubbing her arm as if in comfort. She felt herself compressed into a vision of the past, despite herself, as she stared out towards Foxhall. Once again a small girl ran through the wood, terrified. Cobbold's Wood. She wondered if she would ever really want to own that too. Yes, she would. She had to. To retrace those steps and exorcise the past.

She wanted to turn away but even now the memory lingered and held her. All of her past was there, good and bad. Figures flitted through her memory, her Dad . . . and her brother Sam. The family grouped around the little table in the front room eating their meagre supper. She remembered their hardship, and their love. Love that clutched at the heart and never loosed its hold. Those memories would never fade, that summer of 1913, a golden summer for her and Sam; two children on a hilltop watching the sunrise, and dreaming . . . until both their dreams had been shattered. Her old anger was renewed, the wound opened up again with the reminder of how much a child could suffer. Oak Cottage would burn to the ground, she knew it would, with that thatch. And then there would be nothing left of the past, nothing to remind her. Except her oath, her promise to herself and Sam. And Jim, her Dad. Both dead.

'Dickie?'

She turned to the unexpected voice. Bill Latimer crossed the room towards her. His shoulders were broad and held an athlete's strength, his skin a fading summer tan, his hair though thick, now completely grey.

'Thought I'd find you up here, saw your car in the drive. The kids are home, Jennie too,' he said, referring to Max's wife and children. 'We had a great day in London. You coming down to say "hi"?'

'Well, not right now, I . . .'

She had no need to explain. By now he was right behind her, his arms slipping round her slender waist. 'I missed you . . . Good God, what's that?' He stared over her head to the horizon, hesitated. 'Not Foxhall?'

'No.' He heard the tremor in her voice. 'It's Oak Cottage.'

'Oh, sweetheart.' The strong arms held her closer to him.

She rested her own arms on his. 'Max is there.'

20

'Max?' He looked down into her face with surprise. 'What the hell's he doing there?'

She raised her eyebrows, her gaze still fixed to the brilliant skittering red light that filled the sky. Black clouds oozed in now, closing darkly over the scene. 'I couldn't stop him. But then, maybe I didn't try. I couldn't go, of course. I saw it from the sky at first, called home when I got back to the field. Max answered. I imagine he had reason to go.' She took a breath. 'I hope he's all right.'

'He's a step removed, Dickie. It was still possible for him to go and help them. And as you say, he'd have his reasons. You couldn't have stopped him anyway, even if you'd wanted to. Max is his own man. He wouldn't have stayed away from that.' He followed her gaze, his voice losing itself in thought. 'He'll take care of himself. Don't you worry.'

But she was worried. Her own kin, over there amongst them, helping them. It was like Max not to think of himself, just to take over. She had bred him to be brave, to have courage and by God he had. 'Where angels fear to tread'; the line came to her suddenly. He bowed to no man, and wasn't that exactly what she had always wanted for him? A son just like herself, fulfilling the promise she had made. Her words echoed back to her. 'We have nothing if we haven't our pride. One day I will have money to own land like this. And then no one, not even the Redfields, will be able to use me again in this way or any other . . . *I'll fight those damn Redfields to their graves. God help me, I will destroy him.*' Then she had been vulnerable, her father and brother too weak to fight. Now her son carried her banner, a son who stooped to no one, who was strong enough to stride into their midst and take control. They held no fear for him. Through the press of worry that sat on her heart, she felt a surge of pride. The first raindrops started to patter on the terrace. She smelt the warmth of Bill holding her, the rough hair of his arms under her fingertips, the strong muscles of his chest. She relaxed slightly.

He bent to kiss her forehead. 'That's it, no need to worry, sweetheart . . . besides, I think he's gone to earth.'

An apt phrase considering the man's favourite sport, but still she said: 'Who?'

'Rupert Redfield, of course . . . isn't that who you were thinking of?'

'Partly, yes,' she admitted. 'But why do you say that?'

The rain picked up speed, spattering on the concrete, dark patches spreading on the pale, a torrent, the sound building all around them, damp smells released from summer earth. Her eyes had to search now for the wood, for the fire.

'Ten years, Dickie. You've been ready for him all this time, but nothing's happened.'

'Growing old gracefully? I don't think so, somehow.'

She saw his face again, the way he looked as he bent over her in that sunlit glade, the terrible smile. She tensed in memory.

Bill wrapped his arm around her, gentle but firm, and drew her back. 'Come inside, Dickie, come on . . .'

The patter became a sheet of silver that swept diagonally across the countryside. The heavens cracked open with a dramatic plunge of lightning. They were shaken by a peal of thunder.

He closed the French doors and held her against him.

'Forget him . . .'

Around the clearing the first raindrops punctured the dry bracken like a hail of arrows beating on the leaves. The child dropped from the window, falling, hardly having time to turn in the air before it hit the blanket which sagged slightly even under such a delicate weight.

The men lowered it gently to the ground. Tilly Lovelock ran forward as Charles knelt down beside the child, starting to unwrap the bulky jacket from its tiny frame.

At the gate, the fire engine clanged into the corner and came sweeping up towards them. The firemen leapt to the ground, unravelling hoses at speed, their action, noise and bright colour charging the atmosphere in a space of seconds.

Bill Lovelock twisted a new hold on the blanket.

'Get over here!' he shouted to the men. 'Hurry!'

Above, the windowsill was crumbling under Max's weight. Smoke billowed around him. He was obviously affected by it, an arm covering his face for protection. Rain poured down now, saturating the clearing.

Two firemen grabbed the corners. A ladder was already pushing up towards him, but now there was no time at all. A flame gushed towards him like the mouth of a dragon. Max had no time to decide; he jumped instantly, the blanket as firm as they could make it, but not enough for his weight. He fell heavily, hitting the ground with his hip, the folds of the rug caving in on him as he rolled over with a groan of pain.

Bob bent to help him, his hands outstretched. 'Forget it,' said Max, his voice tainted with pain. 'I'm fine.' He waved his hands away, his eyes on Charles, on the baby. 'How's the baby?'

Bob dropped to one knee. Rain beat on his head, streaming into his eyes. 'I don't know,' he said, his voice a pit of weariness. 'Mr Redfield is doing all he can.' He sighed, his voice tearing. 'I hardly dare look.'

Max touched his hand, but said nothing. He looked over towards the heavily built man who had now unwrapped the hasty swaddling of Max's coat. Once Charles Redfield had been the village doctor, until an error of judgement had put him before the courts. A jail sentence, though short, had seen the end of his career. Now he was a farmer, but in the absence of any legitimate doctor, no one here was going to stop what he was doing now, least of all Max who had jeopardised his own life for the child. It was her they were thinking of now, nothing else. Charles had to save her.

The little face was lifeless, the eyes closed, the baby-pink lips open like a bird expecting nourishment. Charles' body protected her from the storm. She lay as if asleep beneath him, no sign of movement, one cherub cheek pressed against the cloth. No one had noticed his concentrated desperation in those few seconds, not even the half-crazed mother whose eyes were only strained to those closed ones of her child. Now they all looked and saw. Charles' head dropped to his chest. He no longer tried. Between his knees the tiny body lay dormant. His eyes lifted to meet those of the mother. A world of emotion passed between them as the answer was acknowledged.

The woman's cry rent the air. She fell to her knees beside her child, her hands fluttering to gently touch, then fiercely grasp the inert asphyxiated body to her breast. It was a dreadul sight for them all. The men stood silent in helpless shock, listening to the sobs that rose and fell. Behind them, the rain played uselessly against the thatch, a hail of sound. Nobody turned, nobody noticed. Like a circle of standing stones, the men stood, immobile.

The ambulance sped in through the gate. The back doors were opened, the two men jumping out, splashing through puddles. One bent towards the mother, the child swiftly examined then bundled into a blanket, hastened into the back of the ambulance and strapped in. One man climbed in with her and bent instantly over her. The blue light flashed against the scene, brilliantly illuminating the reddened trunks of trees and the faces of those standing beside.

Max had pulled himself painfully to his feet, his hand resting against the trunk of a tree. His clothes were burned, his hair and hands singed, and his lungs rasped with every breath. He was worn out with emotion and a blind resistance to his own pain. Now he knew the fate of the child it seemed to return, swimming through his body with the weight of a dam bursting. He caught his breath as he tried to move his leg. He nearly fell.

A hand caught him. 'Here, let me help.' The voice was one he knew. Charles Redfield held him, steadied him. 'All right?' He looked into the other man's face.

'Yes.'

'I'm so sorry.'

Max nodded. Again their eyes met. Their thoughts were unspoken in that snatched second, but they were as one; hostilities were down, a truce drawn between two men who should have been friends, now united in a common cause of sorrow. They had put all else aside in the hope of saving life but they had failed. This was not a time to remember grievances. Both had assumed their role in this and neither had questioned it. They were cut from the same cloth.

'Better let them see to that hip.' Charles's voice was drawn. 'You'll need care yourself. He had had time to see the other man fall, knew his pain and how he was marshalling his resistance to it.

The ambulance man came over, his forehead creased with concern. The dead child had affected him deeply. He took Max's arm, looked at his leg.

'Hear you fell, sir. How's the leg?'

'Painful.' Max winced as he moved.

'Better come along with us, sir. Leg'll need seeing to. Not to mention a good checkover.'

The stretcher came forward. Max was lifted on, raised to the level of their arms. A tarpaulin was spread over him.

At that moment, they all turned to the shriek of despair that had come from the direction of the ambulance. Rupert Redfield had moved towards the mother leaning over her child, sobbing.

He had thought to say something, to offer some help, condolence.

She had seen his approach, heard his voice address her.

'You bastard!' she screamed suddenly and came down the steps of the ambulance to rush at him. She pushed him away, screaming her grief at him. Rupert, though a big man, was almost knocked off balance by the vehemence of her attack, caught off guard. 'Don't you come near my child! It's all your fault!' Her face was marked with pain. It shocked them all to see how naked her expression was. She saw none of them; her agony was conveyed to Rupert Redfield alone. 'If you'd have been a proper landlord, none of this would have happened. Now my baby's dead . . . my baby's dead . . . you killed her!' She shuddered and clasped her face in her hands.

Rupert started to lift his hands. She screamed again. 'Go! Go away!'

Her husband was by her side immediately, his arms around her shoulders.

'Go, please,' he said.

Rupert did not move, amazed by the request. This was his land.

Charles went quickly over. 'Father,' he said, more sternly. 'Go. Just go now, please.'

Rupert gave him a look, then them. He started to leave, but not before he had caught Max's eye as he was borne forward by the two ambulance men. Max looked straight at him, curiously, before they lifted him inside.

The rain teemed down around him, but Rupert appeared not to notice, his expression unchanged as he strode from the clearing back towards the stile.

The doors were closed, the handle secured. Above, the blue light flashed and with a gently rocking motion the ambulance picked its way over the stones and grass now awash with puddles and out onto the country lane. It headed for the hospital in the nearby town of Foxhall Minster. A flash of lightning lit the sky.

Charles pulled his collar up around his ears and grimaced as the first thunder clap broke overhead. David moved in alongside him.

Charles turned to the boy, almost shouting above the noise. 'Are you all right, David?'

'I'm all right.' His face was pale. Charles would have

preferred him not to have seen what he had seen, but there had been no time for niceties. 'He was a brave man,' he said. 'Wasn't he.'

Charles looked into his face. 'Yes. He always has been.'

'You're alike. Did you know that?'

The simplicity of it snagged at Charles's heart. Children saw so clearly. Of course they were. With what he knew to be true, they would be. He smiled, laid his hand on David's head, his eyes warm. 'Go along now. Want me to see you home?'

'No. I can make it.' He looked worried. 'Uncle Charles . . . ? How come he came to help us . . . if nobody likes him?'

'I don't know. It's just the kind of man he is, I suppose.' He sighed, pushing the wet hair back from his face.

'I don't know. It's just the kind of man he is, I suppose.' He sighed, pushing the wet hair back from his face. 'See you tomorrow, huh?'

'OK.' David turned and ran, following the route his great-grandfather had taken over the stile and up the field towards the lights of Foxhall. Charles watched him go for the moment, frowning, then he turned and looked up at the ruined house, thought of the little child carried away in the ambulance. The policeman was putting away his notebook, the fire engines were starting to pack up, the cottage smouldering now under the sheet of rain, a blackened shell. Charles turned on his heel and headed off home.

The ambulance reached the main road that led from the village out towards the next town. Max had not spoken, and nor did Bob Lovelock. Tilly's soft sobbing filled the tiny space. All of them were too aware of the tiny cargo that rocked gently with every bend of the road.

Max sensed the familiar turn beside the crossroads as they took the opposite direction to his home, Longbarrow. And it was only then as he thought of what he now termed home that the realisation hit him.

He had just watched his birthplace burn to the ground.

CHAPTER TWO

'It can climb, and it can run.' Dickie pushed the dossier across to the other directors on the board of the Bennett Group. 'It's just what I told you it would be. A great aircraft.' She sat back and watched them. 'You doubting Thomases can eat your words.'

The comment was delivered with a smile in her voice. She had been right. Way back in 1955 Pan Am had placed a massive order for the two new aircraft: $265 million for twenty Boeing 707s, and twenty-five Douglas DC-8s. Bennett Air had just taken delivery of their own ten aircraft that morning at a cost to the company of well over fifty million.

George Reilly, their banker at Rees-Hulbert, twisted the photograph round in front of him. Pan Am's inaugural flight of October, 1958, showed the stars lined up in New York to take their places in history, the first 707 overnight flight from New York to Paris, forty de-luxe passengers and seventy-one economy. The day of jet travel had begun. Now they were a part of it.

'I certainly have to hand it to you, Dickie. You had your finger right on the pulse that time. I remember thinking that jets might not even get beyond that 1955 prototype, yet here we are. As you said then, if we'd waited for them to be in service, we'd have been way behind the times. I have to admit I was wrong.'

She released him from his penance. 'You're a banker, George. You had to sound the note of caution whether I took notice of it or not. We were right to follow our instincts, though,' she said, looking over at Bill watching her from the other side of the highly polished table, exchanging a smile with him. He had been there beside her all the way, her moral support. It had been a big decision; they had had to borrow well above their financial resources, taking a gamble on an aircraft not even proven.

Bill took up her lead. 'Yes, well, Bill Boeing's always been at the head of things. We've always gone with him. It was my mole in the company that told us, remember, said it was going to be really innovative. He was a guy I always thought of as being right on target.' He tapped the blunt end of his pencil on the desk. 'The cost-sharing idea worked out as well.' He pointed to the rows of figures on his dossier of which all the others had a copy in front of them.

It had been Dickie who suggested that they put money towards development of the new jets, and subsequently they had backed Boeing, the major aircraft manufacturer, by placing an order to offset the cost of building prototypes. Cost sharing. Boeing were launching new ideas all the time. Paying a little deposit up front helped the manufacturer to cover the cost. The gamble had paid off, but they still had a long way to go to repay the loan. They had taken on lease finance with their merchant bankers, Rees-Hulbert, so that they could buy the giant new aircraft that would be rolled out of their hangars three years after the prototype quick and early. Bennett's had been ready with their cheque books; now they would be able to pay off their debt over a period of years, once delivery had taken place.

Dickie was well pleased with events. 'If you're agreeable, gentlemen, we'll visit Heathrow later in the day and see our new fleet for ourselves. This is quite a moment for us.' She surveyed the faces of the four men around the table. Her board – only Max missing. These were her allies, her friends: George Reilly, the banker, Thomas Fraser, the stockbroker, Anthony Nightingale, the solicitor, and Bill, ex-Air-Force pilot, inventor and long-time partner. All extremely bright in their own particular fields, and loyal to her and her ideas. They would now reap their just reward. 'Jet travel has arrived and we are at the forefront. I believe that with it will come a huge and fruitful market in the next decade. Flying will become an adventure for the man in the street. It is no longer the privilege of the few. It is to him that we now have to appeal.'

Everything had changed over the last three years in readiness for this moment. They had sold off the Connies and the DC-6s and 7s, trimming the fleet down to make way for the new aircraft and to raise capital, retrained their ground staff and made proper preparation at Heathrow with new facilities for both the giant aircraft and for the extra passenger load. The hotel boom had already started as businessmen decentralised their operations to regional offices across the world. Bennett's had already begun building a chain of hotels in major cities throughout the United States and Europe, but also in the holiday spots like the Bahamas and Hawaii. The Americans had the money to travel, Dickie knew that from experience. Their needs were where her market lay.

She pushed back her chair, signifying the meeting was at an end.

'Now, if you'll excuse us, Bill and I must get back to Longbarrow . . .'

Thomas's eyes sharpened in his darkly elegant face. 'Oh yes, how is Max?'

Dickie's expression softened. 'He's all right. He can walk. Hip's not broken, but apparently it's pretty painful.' She squared the papers on her desk, slotted them into a folder. 'He's up already, limping around. The specialist has said he'd like to keep him in for a day or so . . .'

George Reilly raised a cynical eyebrow. He knew Dickie's son, their managing director, an athletic man far too energetic to stay still, certainly not to order. 'And is he staying . . . ?'

'No.' Dickie's look matched his. 'He's discharging himself as soon as we get there. One night in hospital was apparently quite enough for him.'

'I can well believe it,' George managed a laugh. 'Well, it'll be good to have him back in one piece. Could have been worse, after all.'

Dickie drew a slight breath, her eyes flickering up to meet those of Bill. The child. It had hurt her so much to hear of that death last night, imagining the small body, the ordeal of the poor mother. Max had been given a shot to make him sleep by the time they arrived; the first time they would see him was this morning. They had exchanged a brief telephone conversation early, Max insisting that the meeting should go ahead on such an auspicious day. He had brushed away his injuries as nothing; he just wanted to be picked up and taken out. Hospitals held bad memories for him. The Lovelock family had been off limits the evening before, coupled in their tragedy. Dickie had sent a message of condolence, pitifully little under the circumstances. Today, perhaps they could do more.

'Yes, it could have been worse,' she agreed, coming to her feet. She eyed them with a collective glance. 'I'll see you at the airfield. Around five.' She turned her back and walked to the window, a small slender figure in pale linen, somehow even a little lonely. Bill ushered them out swiftly and went over to her. She had an extraordinary capacity to seem both dominant one minute and very feminine, even frail, the next. It was what had drawn him to her so long ago, and still did.

'Do you want a drink, sweetheart? Before we go?'

She smiled gratefully up at him, making her look young again.

'Thanks, Bill.' She reached for his hand.

'That's better. Can't have you weakening, not on a day like this. Celebration is more in order, despite the circumstances,' he added, seeing her face.

She searched his eyes. 'It's just that child , . .'

'I know. I know just how you feel. But Max did all he could. Here, pick you up if nothing else.'

He handed her the glass of champagne. She sipped once, then held the glass as she looked out over Piccadilly. The day was warm outside, the long white net curtains lifting softly in the breeze from the open windows. The sun shone on the dark cap of her hair, striking it with red summer lights amongst the silver, catching the profile of the small face so bold in its determination, the head held high with pride, and the still remarkable green eyes now soft with reflection, a luminous quality to them that had always been her best feature. But it was her manner, the force of her personality and the absolute and inextinguishable courage that had given her her beauty.

Bill took a cigarette from the breast pocket of his blue cotton shirt and lit it, his eyes still on her. It was not that he was himself immune to the tragedy of the child; Bill was cut from a much gentler cloth than his wife, but as much as she was the driving force of the two in business, in times of emotional need his calm strength became enough for both of them, making the perfect partnership that they had both learned to rely on.

There was something in her face that reminded him then of a day forty years ago when he had first seen her; maybe it was the warmth from the sunny summer day outside just beginning, perhaps in the breeze that lilted in around them, a smell in the air, perhaps; it was how memories were formed, a collection of senses that took you back to a time and place, but suddenly he was back there, seeing her for the first time, feeling that combination of emotion and strength that he had first fallen in love with.

'You've come a long way, Dickie,' he said.

She had indeed come a long way. Since their early beginnings, when she with little more than hope and drive had taken her five-year old son Max, one suitcase, a blanket and the Redfields' blood-money, and had taken the ship over to America to start a new beginning, a farm girl of nineteen who had never even set foot outside her home village of Foxhall Green before.

In New York there had followed months of hardship and then the wonderful day of Gerry Oswald's fair when she had had her first ride as a professional, and he had taken her on, jumping from the plane piloted by Bill Latimer for a few dollars a week. Her need to succeed had taken them from the fairground to their first 'fixed base' operation – one plane, one field, in California, ferrying movie stars across to Catalina. In those days anyone with enough ambition and sense of adventure could set up. Dickie had more, a burning need for revenge, more of an aphrodisiac for success than any other emotion, and a sense of business and gut feeling for the public's needs.

Dickie had returned to Foxhall Green wealthy, beautiful and groomed, her new husband Bill Latimer at her side to start her revenge against the family that had wronged her, the Redfields. During the war as a fighter pilot Max had won himself a distinguished reputation, as did Dickie, flying for the ATA, her finger on the button as she saw how the old military aircraft could be bought up for low prices, done up after the war to be sold at a killing.

Her gamble and tactics had paid off. They now owned the biggest domestic fleet in Britain, and their international line had taken off.

'Ready to go?'

She came back to the present. Bill was looking at her, waiting.

'Well, no, actually; there's something I want to do first.' She paused. 'Before we get home.' She looked at her watch briefly. 'Jennie'll have Max back there around lunchtime. I'll be back by then.' Her eyes widened now, encompassing him. 'I have something I want to do alone, Bill. Could you . . . would you mind going on home alone? I'll join you all there for lunch, OK?'

He kissed her. It had to be important. He had learned to respect that need in her through the years.

'Naturally,' he said. 'We'll put yours in the oven.'

It had become a joke between them. She smiled warmly at him as he left the room. Alone, she gave herself to the conversation held between herself and her son just before the board meeting had claimed all of her attention. Now she frowned slightly, remembering:

'What are the Lovelocks going to do, Max?'

'I don't know.' His voice had been strained, even over the distance of the telephone line. 'Tilly was beside herself, distraught. I had a word with Bob, offered him a job with Bennett Air. We can put him in the factory, something, anything. He's a strong fellow and loyal.' He had sighed with memory. 'Nothing's going to make up for their loss. The ride was awful . . . awful . . . Tilly was hysterical the whole way in. They had to sedate her.'

Dickie had held the receiver tighter. 'Poor woman.' And she had had to ask. 'Was Rupert Redfield there?'

She heard his murmur of assent. 'She attacked him. Seems as if he bears some of the responsibility. I don't know to what degree. I imagine he let the house fall to rack and ruin.'

She heard, but said nothing.

Max was still talking. 'An odd man,' he was saying, his voice thoughtful. 'The look on his face when he held her off. Almost . . . contempt.' He paused as if recalling it.

Dickie had not wanted to hear any more. She knew just the look he spoke of. It had been that same contempt for her when he had raped her in 1913. Just another servant girl. Of no consequence at all. Not someone to consider with feeling.

She had wanted to stop talking then, not to think about it for the moment, wanted to be alone with her feelings and memories, but the board members had been drifting in then for the meeting, the men's voices filling the hallway outside her office and about to enter.

She had put the telephone down knowing she had to return, to see for herself, and alone. Now she gave a last look to the reality of her present surroundings. Safety. Solid security. Measured in prime property, family, a huge worldwide business. It gave her the strength to return to her past.

She parked her car at Greatley House, stepping out to look over the view quietly before setting off. Greatley House had once been a part of the Redfield estate, as had Home Farm in the valley beyond, but Rupert Redfield had sold both properties and their surrounding farmland at the end of the nineteen-twenties. What he had not known was that she had just returned from America a wealthy woman, wealthy enough to buy both stretches of land from under his nose. The contracts had been signed before he knew the name of his purchaser. She had known how much it would infuriate him, how it would show him the beginnings of her power and its purpose too; one of the fields that lay up against the wood, Cobbolds Wood, was the very same hill that she and her brother had named for him, Sam's Hill – where they dreamed together of a better life, as children. For sentimental reasons as well as any other, she had retained Greatley House despite buying Longbarrow for the family – and where she now lived in essence. Home Farm had been sold on to Charles Redfield, when his father had thrown him out of the house. It was a nice piece of irony, as was the above-market price she had exacted from him.

She took to the old familiar farm track across the brow of the fields towards Sam's Hill. From there, she skirted the edge of the wood and Home Farm nestled in the valley. She glanced down at the long brick farmhouse, seeing the soft curl of smoke rise from its chimneys against the backdrop of fields and the lane beyond. Someone was home. She did not particularly want to be seen even though for the moment this was still her land. She was about to trespass onto Foxhall territory.

Dickie kept close to the wood as she rounded the last outcrop of trees. She did not hurry, as if she wanted to brace herself against what she was about to see. Hands in pockets, she went forward.

Scots pine surrounded the house, the grass rough outside. It had been built snug and strong, of Cotswold flint and stone with a deep thatched roof and a heavy studded oak door. Now the rafters were exposed and bent, charred. Through them the wide blue sky could now be seen, a perfect blue, streaked with flares of cloud and wisps of grey. Flakes of paint peeled from the walls. The soft wind stirred. Once, this had been home to her.

She stood there a while, alone, thinking of the past, making silent communication with her brother and her father. And then suddenly the wind rattled the catch and the sound brought with it a thousand memories.

It was incredible how she could not forget. As the sound of a wood pigeon cooing in the ash tree at Longbarrow would instantly remind her of being a child and hearing it outside her bedroom window. The seasons touching her skin, the cool October air, or the sudden warm breath of spring caressing a bare shoulder after winter's wool. The memories came flooding back. She closed her eyes, the feeling suddenly strong: a smell, a breeze, a distant dog's barking across a hill, and she was there.

She remembered the sudden warmth of an unexpected October sun, the bubbling of the weekly stew on the stove, and her stepping out to catch the joy of a slumberous autumn day. She remembered the cat's fur under her fingers, how it all happened at once, the hounds bursting through the hedge tan and white against the green, the rush of sound and movement as the Redfield brothers galloped into the clearing beyond the cottage, reining in their horses, sweaty, straining. In the distance she heard again the sound of the huntsman's horn; the fox had gone away. Two hounds had broken from the pack, two horsemen too, and it no longer mattered that the fox was lost. They had a new quarry.

Hooves stamping, backing into her father's neat hedge, the huntsmen's barked commands, the slide of leather through rough hands, the glossy coats of the horses, the well-fed men in immaculately cut pinks, the shining black boots spattered with mud, the jingling of harness, the strong thighs that held the horses to a command, breath clouding the autumn air, her fear. It was all there . . .

'The case will probably go to the coroner's court. Because of the death of the child.'

'They can't prove a thing. I'm above all this sort of thing, Frederick.'

The leaves crunched under their feet. They came from nowhere into the clearing in front of the cottage. It was too late for her to leave unseen, and she was trespassing. Dickie, startled, made a quick decision and stepped down into the front room. She pressed back against the wall.

They came to a halt at the front door. Rupert looked up at the charred timbers. 'Needed pulling down anyway. Never did like this cottage. We'll have it cleared as soon as possible.'

'Rupert, this cottage was in bad repair. You never cared what happened to these people.' Frederick's voice came from beyond his brother's; it was markedly different. He appeared to move closer, almost to the door frame. She held her breath and pressed back further against the wall. Frederick touched the frame, the wood disintegrating under his fingers. 'You're going to be called in for negligence,' he said.

'Oh, I don't think so. That damn Lovelock woman stirred all this up. Told the police faulty wiring had caused the fire. Inspector turned up this morning first thing whilst you were out but even he knew it was a waste of his time.' Rupert gave a short barking laugh. 'And they thought I'd keep them on after that?'

'You'd have dismissed him anyway.'

'Very probably,' he admitted. 'Nuisance value only. Always complaining. I'll go to court if necessary, but I'm not to blame for anything. Tied cottage, they take care of themselves.'

Inside the house, Dickie felt herself steel against the man. Her eyes hardened, hardly believing what she was hearing. She had to restrain herself from stepping out of her hiding-place and confronting him. His brother's gentler voice upbraided him.

'Aren't you forgetting they lost a child in the fire?'

'No, I'm not forgetting that, but neither am I running a charity here.'

'Oh Rupert, for God's sake, you could have offered them alternative accommodation!' Dickie heard the sound of breaking twigs as the two men walked towards the window beside her. 'There's a cottage about to come free,' Frederick was saying. 'Appletree Cottage. They could have had that for the time being.'

'No. I'm telling you I wanted them out.' Her eyes widened. The voice was as close as if he was directly beside her, as if she could feel his breath on her. As she had once before. She held herself still, her eyes following the sound of the voice as it moved to the open window. 'My lawyer tells me I need feel no responsibility for them, and nor do I.'

'You might feel a little when you hear where they've gone.'

Dickie lifted her chin.

'Where?'

Rupert knocked at the stone, a rush of charred timber falling down around him. Dickie leaned in towards the window as they stepped back, their voices fainter.

'Bennett's. She's taken him on.'

There was a silence. 'That woman's a thorn in my side. But very soon she's going to find out what she's up against. I'll deal with her. My way.' He seemed to pause, savouring a thought. 'I won't have some guttersnipe thinking she can outweigh me. No . . . Miss Bennett's got another think coming.' His voice was a murmur.

'Rupert,' Frederick's voice was tired. 'Let it be. She won't like it.'

'Won't like it?' His brother's rough voice was rich with delight. 'Why, Frederick, she started it, she started to fight me. I don't give a damn whether she likes it or not! No one fights me! And we're safe enough, there's nothing she can do to us.' His voice was silky now, laced with venom. 'I'm merely going to give the bitch a run for her money.' Dickie was jarred by the hate in his voice. 'I'm going back now. You coming?'

'Yes, in just a moment.' His voice was coming closer to her as he spoke. Dickie kept very still, her eyes on the open door. He was just outside.

'What are you doing?' The abrupt voice was distant, shouting from a distance away. 'Come on, nothing to see inside.'

Her eyes opened wide. She could even hear Frederick's breathing now, almost in her ear in the silence. His shadow fell across the threshold.

'Be right with you, Rupert. Go on, I'll follow.'

His voice echoed into the room, filling it as if he stood right by her. And then suddenly she saw him. His long, lean frame, casually dressed, the familiar shape of him right there. He had stepped into the dusty room, was looking all around, looking for something. She pressed back into shadow.

'No, I'll wait. God's sake man, I want to talk to you,' Rupert's voice was dark with impatience. 'What are you doing?' He was starting to come back.

'Coming.' Frederick's eyes were on her. She could tell, as his voice swept her, though she could not see him, her head pressed back against the stone wall, her body protruded beyond the door frame. If he had reached out he could have touched her. She did not move a muscle.

The leaves crunched outside as the heavy feet approached. She heard Frederick's breath, sensed him look and reflect. He knew she was there all right. He'd seen her. God, now what –? Would she step out? Rupert was right outside the front door now. What a fool she had been.

'Nothing here, you're right.' The voice was cool, uninterested. She felt the strength of his gaze dissolve. Frederick stepped out through the door frame, brushed his hands together. 'Let's go.'

She opened her mouth, letting the breath flow rapidly out.

Voices receded towards the stile. She crept to the window and watched. Frederick had his hand at his brother's elbow, stooping slightly as they walked, listening to his brother talk. They reached the stile, climbed over. He never looked back.

The clearing was silent again, but she could not move. Had he seen her then? She was absolutely sure that he had, so why had he said nothing to his brother? In her mind, her hate for the two had coupled them into one since coming back here; she was unable to bestow any finer characteristic on Frederick other than the obvious: that he could not have seen her. Over all else ran the override of Rupert's brutality. She was a child again, shaking, vandalised. Why did he hate her so deeply? She had more reason by far to hate him, and she questioned why after all these years she still did, why it would not leave her.

Her thoughts were interrupted by a glimmer of something lying on the floor amongst the blackened tiles. She stepped forward and bent down to pick it up, turning it in her fingers with wonder. It was Sam's posthumous medal from the Great War. Max had played with it. She remembered the day she realised he had grown big enough to reach the mantel and had lost it. She blew the soot from its surface, and almost smiled. But then she heard the echo of Rupert's words, Sam's voice and his kindness, her father telling her after she had been cruelly raped at the age of fourteen that they could not fight aginst the likes of the Redfields. Her father had died old and broken, before his time, her brother too as cannon fodder whilst Rupert Redfield sat well behind the lines, and safe.

As the October breeze skidded and skirted around the house, drifting in to touch her skin, she recalled her promise, her oath. Rupert's hound barked in the distance as he went home. 'We're safe enough.' It brought back all the old helplessness, the subservience and the rage that went with it.

She walked over to the old range, ran a finger over its blackened surface. Years had passed since she stood there cooking, bone tired, hating, Max pulling at her skirts. By the end of this week this would all be no more. Her memories would be taken from her once again by Rupert Redfield. She looked around her, replanting it all in her mind. It was the last time she would stand in this cottage, Oak Cottage, where it all began.

And then she realised why Rupert hated her. She had fought back. That was what Rupert Redfield would never forgive.

CHAPTER THREE

It was all about power.

Rupert sat at his desk, the final papers spread out in front of him. They would be signed today and it would become official. The list of impressive clients would come together: Redfield-Strauss and Rees-Hulbert would become one, merging two powerful merchant banks.

They were going to make a great team. They were already joined by marriage. Rupert's grandson, Alexander, had married Verity Rees-Hulbert, and given Rupert his favoured great-grandson, David. Redfield's had advised a huge soft drinks merchant; Rees-Hulbert's, a brewer. Redfield's advised a chemical giant; Rees-Hulbert's a petroleum king. Redfield's advised a shipping line, and Rees-Hulbert's, the airline and property group, Bennett's.

Rupert sat back comfortably, leaning his broad frame into the leather swivel chair. His gaze wandered out through the windows of his impressive chairman's office to the grey meandering Thames, wide and cloudy beneath and beyond the office building. It was a dismal day but it did not matter. Put together, the two banks would have a much broader mix of clients, an opportunity to do more business. Size equalled power: Rupert's key word. All that was left was the crucial power struggle over who came out on top. The answer was, the more predatory of the two. Rupert saw himself in that role. He had been at school with Gilbert Rees-Hulbert and Gilbert was someone he had always controlled. Soon, he would be running two banks.

He had a look of pure satisfaction on his face, the blue eyes tilted under the satanic pale lids. He tapped a pen against his teeth.

From across the width of the mahogany desk Guy Prudham watched him. Since Rupert's first days in the bank, Guy had been there, as his secretary and now as an official of the bank. Though not yet a director on the board, Guy felt smoothly sure that was just around the corner.

Guy plucked at the knife-edge neatness of his grey trousered knee and leaned forward from his chair, spreading the papers he had just brought for Rupert to sign neatly under the chairman's nose. As if reading his mind, he spoke the words Rupert had been thinking.

'What's Rees-Hulbert like?' he said.

'Gilbert?' Rupert raised a lazy eyebrow. 'Weak.' He touched the papers evenly before him, edge to edge precisely. 'Knew him at school. He always played the fool. His family have owned the bank for three generations but they've never thrown off the nouveau image. May be their client list,' he said narrowly, thinking of the Bennetts. 'Still, Bennett's will be pulling out when they hear this news,' he said.

And that was the peach: what he was going to do to them before they had a chance to swim clear. They'd be sucked down with the ship, well and truly. They were in debt up to their necks. He gave a short chuckle.

Guy levered himself elegantly back into his chair.

'Bennett's pulling out?' he said. 'Could be detrimental to us.' He frowned and shook his head. 'They're good business, we could serve them all right. Why would they want to go?'

'They will, believe me.' Rupert was not ready to divulge his personal feelings to this man. 'And we don't need them. Better off without them in fact. Got to be some casualties in a merger, don't you know.' He pursed his lips thoughtfully, his mind moving on. 'There's still a whole array of good pickings at Rees-Hulbert's. Couple of bright boys on the board. Family are stupid, of course, except for my great-grandson, David, which bodes well for us. We can have our way.' He gave a quick nod at Guy. 'They'll bring in a fresh injection of ideas and capital. We'll be on top from the start, precisely for that reason: they need us more than we need them. Money always wants class more than class wants money, though the two are good bed-fellows.' He laughed, thinking of how eagerly Gilbert had approved Verity and Alexander's youthful marriage. David, his great-grandson, had balls enough to match him, the only one in the family. That marriage had paved the way for this merger. Clever Alexander; he didn't like his grandson, how could he with his own red-blooded way of thinking; but despite the fact that he was admittedly homosexual he had proved himself both in bed it seemed, and in the bank. The appalling discovery that his own bloodline was perverted had its advantages; Rupert had married him off to Verity at the age of seventeen. Verity was common as muck, just like her father. All brass and arse. But very rich, and an only child.

Rupert had conveniently forgotten his own great-grandfather's not so auspicious beginnings as a horse-breeder.

'What's the pecking order?' Guy said bluntly.

'Oh, I reckon I can do a deal in which I get to be chief executive. Allow the old man, Roland, to be chairman. He's got one foot in the grave, but it'll look good. We'll have the psychological edge. He'll retire in two years' time and then I'll take control of the whole thing. We just have to find a way to keep Gilbert underfoot.'

'There's only one way to keep Gilbert out. And that's on the basis that you own slightly more shares and his father's retired.'

'Precisely. Then I can really put the boot in.'

Guy thought a moment. 'How are you going to get hold of more shares, Rupert? We'll have even distribution, won't we?'

'Yes, well that might pose a slight problem, but I don't think so. I have a feeling that the Rees-Hulberts might want to sell some shares.' He pursed his lips, and looked at the ceiling. 'They've got too many eggs in one basket, so the reason they wanted to throw away their independence in the first place and sell out to us was so that they could get some capital of their own.' He nodded, drew in a breath. 'We'll be standing by ready to buy them up.'

Guy had another thought. A directorship was on his mind; maybe now. He picked at an imaginary thread on his trousered knee.

'Are the directors of each becoming directors of both?'

'Ideally, yes.' Rupert rubbed at his chin. 'Though I expect there'll be a few casualties. Some are bound to get hoofed out.' It was highly political, a pyschological guessing game, a power struggle where the strongest survived. 'We'll skim what we want from both boards, and the rest we'll let go.'

'No new directors coming in then?'

'No.' He had his answer. Rupert leaned back in his chair toying with a pencil. 'And also I thought we might leave both banks where they are at the moment.'

'We're not planning a move?' That surprised him even out of his own thoughts. 'It's a recipe for trouble, Rupert. We'll have the right hand not knowing what the left hand is doing.'

'Yes, that's right, but not trouble, Guy.' His eyes glinted

coldly. 'Just keeping them in the dark. Basically, we will go on doing what we want here at Head Office. They won't know what's going on. We'll simply use their capital and profit desirably. The combined group will have a greater ability to compete in the market, a greater ability to make bigger loans. Together we will represent probably one of the best, if not the best, client list in the City . . . in the league table of who's who in the banking business.'

'And the name?' An important factor, as the more powerful submerged the weaker.

Rupert gave a cold smile. 'Redfield's.'

CHAPTER FOUR

Late summer 1960

'I thought you should be the first to know.'

'I had no idea there was a connection.' She got up from her desk and went over to the window. From this side they overlooked the stream of evening traffic as it edged its way down Piccadilly. Across the road, a well-heeled couple stepped out of the Ritz to enter their taxi, obviously heading for the theatre or dinner, or maybe they were just out to view the bright lights of the West End on a warm evening. She rubbed the back of her neck; she should have known.

George came across to join her. 'Gilbert Rees-Hulbert is an old friend of Rupert's. They went to school together, were in the Hussars together. Daughter married his grandson.' He ran a hand over his head, smoothing his hair. 'It's fairly common knowledge in the City.'

'Not to me.' She folded her arms. Surprising she had never known of the connection when she knew so much. Redfield-Strauss and the Rees-Hulbert bank about to merge. 'God, I don't want to deal with those charlatans,' she said. 'I'm deeply unhappy about this, George. Especially at this time.' The green eyes looked round into his. 'We've just taken on new financial obligations with a bank we trust.' The extra loan put them in a temporarily vulnerable position. 'Rupert Redfield is head of Redfield-Strauss. He could instruct you to make life difficult for us, George.'

The man chewed at his lip. 'I'm afraid he already has.'

'What?'

'Made life difficult. You see, whilst the business you did with us was quite separate, the loan is not.' He cleared his throat. 'Redfield's have asked for an ad hoc committee to be set up whilst the formal merger document is being drafted; no major loan worth more than half a million to take place without the full decision of the committee. The merger should take four to six weeks until consummation; the shareholders have to approve the transaction of course.'

'Obviously Rupert Redfield is on this committee.'

George looked thoughtful. 'He's heading it, yes.'

Dickie gave an exasperated sigh as she turned away from the window. 'Then of course we're not going to get it, George. He's going to screw it up for us, for certain.'

George's eyes followed her as she crossed the room. Dickie was elegantly dressed today in grey cashmere, the customary pearls at her throat. He spread his hands. 'Oh, I don't think there's that much cause to worry. The very worst he can do, because the company is in some difficulty now, is to demand a higher rate of interest. You're a very good client. He's not the only one to make this decision. They're sitting this evening as a matter of fact, going over all the bank's business together. I have asked one of my partners to telephone me here if there are any things we should know.'

She turned at the end of the room, underneath the photograph that showed her as a young woman out in California, triumphant beside her first Curtiss Jenny. 'It's just now, George. Just as we've started to pay off the debt for the new fleet. It's taken all our resources. The new loan puts us right over the top. We can easily repay it in time, but . . .'

'Oh yes, I know that. You'd probably only need a short-term loan, perhaps six months to three years. Not very long. Of course that can be sorted out . . . you're known to be a very good client . . .'

'We're very beholden to you. More so than ever. We've invested so deeply.'

He saw the concern in her eyes. 'Dickie,' he said. 'You're quite safe. Look, I don't know your social problems with the man, but primarily he's a businessman. Now Bennett's is a viable concern, one of the Rees-Hulbert client list that we are very proud of.' He lifted a hand briefly, before pushing it back into the pocket of his trousers. 'Gilbert has never been very involved with the bank,' he went on. 'I think he really prefers the polo field, but he still knows what's going on. He knows your value to the bank. Rupert, whatever his feelings about you as you say, could not expose his hand without showing the decision was an emotional one, not a business one, and that simply wouldn't wash. Whatever you think of him, Dickie, he has a sound board of directors and an excellent client list; Redfield's are one of the oldest established banks in the city. They didn't get like that by letting emotion interfere with their decision-making.' He watched her move behind her desk and let herself down slowly into her chair. She sat back, but her eyes were not on him. 'As far as Rees-Hulbert are concerned,' he said, crossing the room to stand behind the elegant Sheraton chair placed across from her desk, 'they have made a good decision. We have very different client lists to Redfield's and we could do well together. There are some very bright lads on our side, a lot of experience, age and respect on theirs. It could work wonders. You'd do well to be a part of it.'

She looked up at him then, green eyes vibrant. 'No, George. Only out of respect for you would I stay, for your judgement and friendship, and even so . . .'

'Dickie, I . . .'

But she was not listening, her mind already moving on.

She thought about the ad hoc committee sitting at that moment in judgement. 'Why weren't you on this committee, George? You're a director . . .'

'Well, it was just a temporary selection. It all happened rather suddenly actually, last few days whilst I've been in LA talking to Wiley regarding the financing over there. Don't suppose they felt it was necessary to call me back particularly; they have plenty of able people on the board.'

She felt the nagging worry increase immediately. 'Seems like it may have been rushed through a bit, doesn't it?'

He sat down. 'Oh no, I don't think so. Once these things have been decided they can go through quite quickly.'

The telephone rang on the desk beside her. She stretched out her left hand to pick up the receiver. 'Well, we're in difficulty just now, George. It's a crucial moment. I'm not happy at all that this has happened in just this very week.' She spoke into the receiver, her eyes swivelling to those of her colleague. 'Yes, he's here.' She held out the receiver to him. 'It's for you, the bank.'

She tried not to worry as she stood up, pulling the grey cashmere cardigan down over her hips. She crossed the room, stood again at the window, watching the traffic, thinning out now, the lights in the last of the windows opposite going out, leaving only those working late. That feeling inside was pinching her nerves, and would not go away. She tried not to listen to George's voice in the background, monosyllabic mostly; 'yes', 'no', 'I see'. She took a long breath, looked up at the night sky, purpling twilight softened by the glow of the city beneath, the black spires against it. 'Yes, all right, thanks for letting me know, Dan. I'll see you in the morning.'

She swung round, said nothing. George sat back in his chair slowly, his face more troubled than she had ever seen it. He looked years older in those few minutes. 'It's happened, hasn't it?' she said quietly.

He shook his head as if he could not understand. 'I find it hard to believe. Dickie, you know, in certain circumstances a bank can be quite harsh in its decision about whether to, say, put more money into a company that's run into debt, or to help it over a difficult patch.' He lifted his hand then let it drop back to his knee, his eyes staring distantly at the carpet. Now they lifted to hers. 'Or whether to pull the rug out from under it.' She saw the expression in his eyes, and knew which had happened to them. 'Dan had the devil's own fight this evening, he said. The obvious thing to do and the sensible thing to do was to put more money in to help you out: it's common practice.' He shook his head, his voice slower. 'But Rupert, for some reason, is making waves. He wants to pull the rug out from under you.' She clenched her jaw as she heard. 'Dan told me something else, too.'

She raised her eyebrows, waiting.

'It would appear that he has already started to apply pressure to the individuals involved in Bennett's to sell their assets now that they're in trouble, and they know they can't get a decent price for them. I believe he wants them to sell to a company he's involved in without actually revealing it to them. It's quite broadly known that Rupert plays that sort of game, and it's also accepted. Legal, but nasty.'

'Then he could put the shares back on the market.'

He folded his arms, spread his legs slightly. 'Not necessarily shares. We're now fundamentally sound, we've just got a temporary cash flow problem. He's blocked the extra loan, Dickie, and you need it right now.' His brown eyes glanced up at her. 'He wants to put a receiver in. The receiver will go in to recover the bank's original loan basically, and to do that, what he would do is to sell off the assets of the company. Now Rupert knows it could be broken up by the receiver, he knows all the good things it's got and might well get some company he's secretly involved in to buy all the choice pieces. Not only will he remove the company from under your nose, but he will have a maintenance and transport company of his own which he might then indeed be able to float on the stock exchange or sell on to somebody else. The whole thing would be a nice financial coup.'

'And a slap in the face for me.'

He nodded, lowering his head. 'Yes.'

'And he's able to do that?' She walked slowly back until she was standing just before him. She no longer looked worried, he realised as he looked up into her face. More, her eyes had taken on a dangerous light.

'I'm afraid so,' he said. Unless we can find help elsewhere, it'll be the end of Bennett's. That million you needed to tide you over was essential. I'm really sorry,' he said. 'You were right. Maybe he did indeed time this when he knew I would be away, knowing I would have objected, but without my voice there, he pushed it through. He must be a very convincing talker,' he went on, his head shaking slightly.

'Oh, he is . . .' she murmured.

'It was all over before Dan realised what had happened. It would appear that Rupert had the green light right from the start. It seems Gilbert is hand in glove with him.'

'So that's how he did it . . . well, we'll play him at his own game.'

'You'll have to pull out of Rees-Hulbert. I've got good friends in other banks,' he said, seeing the light harden in her eyes. She was ready to fight the man now, fair and square or otherwise.

Dickie sat down on the edge of the desk in front of him.

'You're obviously not going to let him win.'

'No, we're not giving in.' She looked him straight in the eyes. 'But I'm going to have to ask you to come in with us, George. I need your help, need you with us all the time. You can no longer work for them and for us. You have to sever your connections.'

'There'll be no need,' he said evenly. He had been a casualty of the merger. 'I've been sacked.'

A dawn wind swirled around the corners of the old Gothic buildings. It was not yet sun-up, a few pale stars were still visible. The City was cool and quiet, not a light to be seen. The Rolls crossed smoothly over London Bridge.

In the back, Dickie leaned back into the cream leather, momentarily deep in thought. George Reilly sat in the front, apparently deep in the *Financial Times*. Dickie was not fooled. He had not changed his eyeline for the last five minutes. She was pleased with her old friend; he had advised her well and she had listened. It was why they were here, driving into London at five a.m. on an autumn morning when most people were asleep in their beds. The City was a network of spies, the bush telegraph a rapid conveyer of both gossip and fact. This was a meeting in which the players were to remain under cover until the decision had been reached. If it were to be negative, all parties could walk away as if it had never taken place. The tinted glass of the hired Rolls enhanced that security. Just until she was sure, and then . . .

The young man beside her finished reading the last page of the report. The Bennett Group was not new to him, but the catalogue of their endeavours to date, both private and public, and their far-reaching ideas for the future made excellent reading. They were an innovative company, backing their hunches, good at repaying their loans to date. He could not understand why Redfield's were being so hard on them. It had to be personal, there could be no other reason that he could see. Through a third party he had thoroughly checked out Bennett's once he had heard from George Reilly that they were looking for a new merchant bank to carry them. The reports had all been favourable, and George had always been a bright and trusted friend. He liked what he saw and he liked the excitement of a challenge. He felt that this woman sitting beside him would not lead him astray. The Bennett fleet was expanding and he wanted to be a part of it.

He re-straightened the papers in his hands. 'Very impressive,' he said. 'Everything you have done to date has been successful.' His voice was deep and confident. A very bright young man, George had said, an ideas man. You'll like him.

'And . . . ?'

He smiled. 'I cannot see why Redfield's would try to push you under.'

'Can't you?' Her eyes held his. 'I'm sure you've done your homework. Therefore you've got to know it's personal.'

'Yes. You must tell me one day.'

'One day.' They were approaching the office. She came straight to the point. 'Can we count on Hammond's, Philip?'

He was as blunt as her. 'You can, yes.'

He held out his hand. She took it as George's eyes moved on to the next page. She saw the corner of his mouth lift in a smile. They were back on the road again. She had not thought they

47

would be ruined by Rupert's move; she was sure that nor had Rupert believed it either. They were too good a proposition to be left out in the cold for too long. He had just wanted to let them know he was after them; firing a warning shot across the bows, letting them know his power. Well, she knew now. Bennett's was not going to go under and into the jaws of Rupert Redfield and nor was she.

She was ready for him now.

The Rolls sped on towards the bank.

CHAPTER FIVE

Christmas 1960

'Most merchant banks in the City would turn you down, you know.'

'Yes,' said the man, 'but I'm asking you.'

Paul Riley looked across the huge mahogany desk at the chairman of Redfield's and his smile was confident. He knew that Rupert Redfield was his man. It was one of the oldest games in banking. Where there was power and money, there was corruption, and two of like mind would find each other. For businesses that were dubious, that might go bust overnight, there was always a place to go. And a price to pay.

'It looks pretty suspect.' Rupert pushed the papers away and leaned back in his chair. The complacent smile left the man's face. Had he heard wrong? Beside the chairman, the company secretary, Guy Prudham, folded his fingers like a steeple as he watched the game unfold. 'I'm not interested in lending money on things which have something dubious about them,' Rupert was saying. 'Such as this.' He flicked at the papers before him on the desk.

Paul Riley recovered his composure. 'Oh come on, how about a kickback. We would provide you with some quid pro quo, some alternative.' The intercom rang on Rupert's desk. He leaned forward, pressing the button down to listen as the man continued to speak. 'For the sake of argument,' he was saying, 'a commission paid into a Swiss bank.'

Rupert was interested, but he did not show it. He appeared not even to hear the man's words. 'Yes . . . ?' he said into the mouthpiece. 'What is it?'

'Your grandson is waiting outside to see you.' The secretary's voice sounded into the room. 'Shall I send him in?'

'Yes. I'm almost through here.' He flipped down the switch, the meeting over. Paul Riley wanted to finance the building of an office block in a semi-derelict area of the city. He was a known, and crooked, property entrepreneur. Everybody in the city was fighting shy of him, and the man was sweating. Rupert saw that and smiled to himself. It was a good chance to grease his own pocket. He had already studied the map set out before him. There were still families living in rundown houses within the designated spot, also an ancient and rather beautiful church almost hidden amongst the debris of a once elegant area. He knew too there was a preservation order on the church, a letter going out from the City Planners that night to stop its demolition. Paul Riley could take care of that if he gave him the go-ahead. Rupert knew it had to happen tonight, by tomorrow the church would remain intact by order. That would put paid to Paul Riley's plans. The man needed him badly. He had nowhere else to go.

'You're in very deep water, Mr Riley,' he said, closing the folder before him. 'One per cent overall to me personally, and ten per cent of the company doing the development, and we'll go along with you.'

Paul Riley shifted in his chair, laying his hands along its wooden arms. He watched Rupert's face for a clue to the man's feelings as the chairman pushed the closed folder across the desk towards him.

'That's very steep,' he said, playing for time.

'There is no negotiation.' Rupert's face was impassive. The door opened behind the man. Guy turned sharply to look, and smiled. Alexander came in, his eyes directed to his grandfather. Rupert ignored him. Paul Riley sought for words.

'I know about the Order,' said Rupert quietly, without looking up.

Paul Riley knew then that he was cornered. He nodded slowly. 'All right,' he said at last.

'Good.' Rupert looked up then and caught Alexander's eye. He motioned him to a chair. 'Mr Prudham will deal with this. Set up the details. Good day.' He pushed his glasses more firmly against the bridge of his nose, giving the man merely a quick, hard stare as Paul Riley stood and left the room, Guy Prudham following behind.

Rupert called him as he reached the door. 'Guy . . .'

The elegantly dressed figure turned, an eyebrow arched in query.

'Prop Finance,' said Rupert, for his assistant's ear alone. Alexander, settled already into a chair, looked from one face to the other. Guy Prudham seemed to understand though. He nodded once, and was gone.

'So,' said Rupert, as the door closed. 'How are you getting along, Alexander?' His grandfather leaned back in his chair again, the blue eyes boring into him. The question seemed innocuous enough to Alexander though briefly he wondered what or who was Prop Finance. He had never heard of it, or seen reference to it in the Redfield ledgers.

'Very well. I enjoy it here, as you know.'

'I know you do. I want you to do something for me, Alexander.' Rupert looked into the face that watched him, a reflection of his own suspicious nature there, but that was all. At twenty-six years old, his grandson was not like him, either in his sexual tastes or his looks. Alexander was slight; dark blond curls topping a face of almost transparently olive skin, veins showing at his temples and in the hands now lightly crossed in his lap, giving him a look of fragility. It was deceptive. Though he was good-looking in an effeminate way, his eyes showed him for what he was; cold, heavy-lidded and moody, they were as ice-grey and bottomless as a winter sea. Rupert stared into their chilly depths a moment longer, thinking; they could never be friends, certainly after the loveless marriage into which he had forced his grandson at such an early age, before the tongues started to wag. It had been for the family's good, but he did not expect Alexander to understand that. Privately, he despised the boy, but he could still be useful to him. He tapped his fingers on the desk. 'You'll know of course that Bennett's have pulled out and gone over to Hammond's,' he began.

Alexander nodded. He had heard rumours of the boardroom scuffle over Bennett's and of his grandfather's hard line on their loan, though not the story in full. He had heard too how Hammond's had pulled them back on top, much to Rupert's chagrin. Alexander knew how Rupert hated Dickie Bennett, and it had to be that that had motivated him to try and close them down. It certainly had not been good banking business. He wondered now how he was to be involved.

'They were in the process of buying a maintenance company for their fleet when they left us,' Rupert went on. 'Maintenance and spare parts for their aircraft. A company called Bramway. I happen to know that the foreman of their Union is about to step down. Illness in the family or some such,' he said, moving his heavy hand dismissively from the table at the irrelevance of it. He lifted his chin and stared into the middle distance as if thinking. 'I know just the man to take his place. His name is

Mick Davie, and I want you to negotiate with him, Alexander.'
Now his eyes swung across to meet those of the other man. 'I
want him to cause trouble for the Bennetts, and I don't want to
be seen to be a part of it. You will act as my intermediary, on my
instructions. Do you understand, Alexander?'

He understood perfectly.

CHAPTER SIX

Dickie lay awake listening to the comfortable hum of the house. It was still early, the first light of day only just stealing through the gap between the floor-length curtains. It was quiet with the family gone. Max had flown over the day before to join Jennie and the kids with his in-laws in California. She would miss them all this Christmas, the children growing up at last. She realised how much she had grown used to the whole family living here together at Longbarrow, the noise and untidiness of children and their friends a daily pattern. Just her and Bill alone; it was almost too quiet, but good in its way. She smiled at the thought that crossed her mind – like the old days – and remembering them fondly looked down at the man sleeping beside her.

The familiar face was deeply lined now around the eyes and mouth but in sleep the lines seemed to soften bringing back a youthful innocence, the set of his mouth showing the gentleness that was an inherent part of the man himself. Gentle, yet strong when he needed to be. That was Bill. He had been the right man for her to marry, though she might not have thought it at first. She had been young then, hot-headed, determined, bent on revenge. Bill had been her lover and partner, but marriage had simply been an easy path to respectability, and – because it had seemed the right thing to do at the time. Also, he had always been a good lover, suiting her temperament, touching hidden passions and chords in her that she had never expected anyone to find. He moved in his sleep as she watched him and remembered the power he had to move her at those times. That had never changed, even now, at their age. His arm, thrown across the sheet, was strong and brown, the fingers of his hand resting on her hip. Her eyes softened. It was he who had surprisingly taught her to mellow, but to mellow with strength in a more level and compassionate way than that of youth. His quiet strength, which she had not seen at first, had become so essential to her she wondered now how she would have managed without Bill. With all the wisdom of hindsight she knew how much she loved him, had loved and needed him all along, how they fitted together just right, like pieces of a puzzle. He had known that from the start, of course, had stuck by her, convincing her to first trust him and then love him back. Thank God he had. Forty years would have been a long time alone without his friendship to guide her, for that was what it was based upon, like all the best, most lasting love affairs.

However, with the scenarios that were now flowing into her mind in these reflective hours before the day started, there came the dart of memory, the one thing that Bill had never mellowed, the one thing that never truly left her mind. And now, Philip Hammond had pulled them back from the brink of possible disaster. The company was strong again, but was it safe? The recent message had left its mark on her. Rupert Redfield was not giving up. She thought of the man and frowned. He would be angry that they had won; he would be looking for another way to strike. The thought made her restless, lancing the warmth of her memories. She could no longer stay in bed.

Dickie lifted back the sheets to slip from the bed. Bill's hand stopped her, his arm going around her waist.

'Where are you going? Don't get up yet.'

She lay back and looked into his face, his eyes still closed, but the strength in the arms that now held her showing he had been lying awake too.

'I thought you were asleep,' she said softly.

'Not me. I've been lying here listening to you thinking.'

He smiled, and she laughed. 'You know me so well.'

'Of course. Come here.' They did not talk about the thing that was on her mind. He knew; but instead he pulled her close.

She moved into his arms. He held her, kissed her forehead. The tension that had begun in her moments before melted away. 'I was just thinking how quiet it was without the children,' she said. 'I miss them, don't you?'

'Oh, I don't know.' His voice was warm. 'I think it's kinda nice to be alone.'

She heard the note and looked into his eyes. They held a light she knew. 'Bill . . . !' She pushed gently at his bare chest. He had never lost the California habit of sleeping nude, despite the chill of English winter.

He held her fast, kissing her on the mouth. 'You're still the only girl that made me feel this way, Dickie,' he said, his body moving closer to hers, so she could feel its message. 'Still beautiful . . .' his voice roughened, softened, looking at her. 'Most forty-year-olds would give their eye teeth to look the way you do.'

Her green eyes became smoky in response, her slender legs moving against the roughness of his. He felt good, strong, wonderfully, warmly familiar. 'You're so corny!' she teased.

'But right . . . aren't I!' His hands pushed back the sheet smoothly from her waist, pushed up the sheer silk nightgown she wore, over the narrow hips, the curve of her waist hardly thickened despite her sixty-one years, to her breasts. 'You never used to wear a nightgown . . . remember, California, those long beautiful nights,' he persuaded, bringing back the pictures as the nightgown slid from her shoulders, the ribbons undone. 'Remember by the fire, the first night I loved you . . .' He bent to kiss her breasts, gently. 'You're just as beautiful now, as you were then . . . to me, oh Dickie . . .'

His words evoked so much, the California nights, the stars studding the darkness of the sky, the perfume of the desert wind stroking over them. She felt his kisses on her skin, his lips soft and warm on her breasts and she sighed, her hands stroking his head. Her fingers ran down over his shoulders and her eyes glowed as his hands moved down, stroking gently at first, then more urgently as his need for her built. Soon, she was touching him too, the deeply sensual woman he had first discovered, her movements fluid and feline. She knew him oh so well.

Bill groaned with pleasure. She was soft and beautiful, brushing her skin against the soft hair of his chest as he felt the answering stir in her.

He looked into her eyes, finding them radiant with desire for him.

'I'm so glad I found you,' he said. 'You're my life, Dickie.' His soul was in his eyes. She could hardly bear to see so much, and yet she needed it from him, that ability to lay himself bare for her. It was how he had won her. She pulled his face to hers to kiss him and felt him hard against her. She sighed against his mouth.

Bill felt the blood race through him in a surge. She was bone and flesh sensual to him. He wanted to feel her, deep inside her, strong against her delicacy, hard against her tenderness. Her pale skin darkened under the press of his fingers. She was like a flower opening to him as he pushed into her.

Her murmurs became cries, soft and erotic. There were no years of age as they fell away, back to the two of them in their twenties. Their love-making had not diminished. Her skin was flushed and damp as she moved beneath him, urging him onwards with her sound and smell. From the narrow opening of the bedroom window came a slight breeze moving across them, cooling his perspiration like a silver knife upon his skin. Her breath rushed upon the air. Deep inside she was warm and moist and the sensation too much for him.

'Dickie,' he said. 'I can't hold on.'

'Come,' she said. 'I'm so near, too.'

She cried out as he did, his pleasure heightening the moment for her. She throbbed around him as he exploded into her, an exquisite pain into a heavenly flood of release.

His strength ebbed from him like a tide. He laid his cheek against her rose-damp breast as he had always done, his eyes closing, and held her beneath him, thoughts drifting together; comfortable.

Max stepped out of the beach house onto the sun-bright deck and went quickly down the wooden steps onto the sand. He felt the sun bite into his skin immediately. The beach was almost deserted, the salt freshness of the ocean skimming in the wind; a typical California day. He looked down at the familiar beach, hesitating for a moment; his family had not yet seen him. He wanted to observe them, feel for a moment. The memories danced around him. This was like a second home for him, where he had begun his childhood, to where he had returned with his first wife . . . Melanie.

At the edge of the waves, Jennie sat on the sand, surrounded by children, in a prettily cut floral one-piece bathing suit, her red-gold hair casually knotted up on her head. Beside her a huge umbrella shaded a large towel spread out on the sand. Max recognised the tallow-haired grandson of Wiley Fairfax, the family's long-time business partner here in the States. Robbie came running from the sea, followed by Kay, the surf flying up around their ankles, their laughter borne on the wind. The two were both outgoing, like young animals. There was no sign of his son, Jim. Max shielded his eyes from the sun and checked the heads bobbing in the waves. No sign. He looked up the beach.

Jim was there, walking in the wet gleam of sand at the water's edge, alone, his hands pushed down into the pockets of cut-off shorts, his dark head looking down at his toes, neither to left or right as he flicked the sand with his feet. He had not seen him either, and Max took a moment to study his son. The kid was fourteen now, adolescent, gangly and awkward, but not just with the awkwardness of that age – no, it was more than that. Jim's trouble ran deep, pyschologically so. Max frowned as he watched his son kick the sand and as he did so, look up to see him standing there on the steps of the deck. He saw the boy's eyes, so like his own, flash with recognition, but not the happiness Max wanted to see as he lifted his hand to wave to his son. Jim just stood still, his eyes from that distance angry, lonely; hurt.

The look was Melanie's. Max shook himself inwardly to rid his mind of the shock, the swift jolting memory of his first wife, dark and serene, lying in his arms as the blue light of the ambulance flashed on the rubble around them that had once been their California home. The earthquake had been swift and merciless and he had not been there to protect them. He had been at a party down on the coast. One never knew until one lost how late realisation could come in life. He had driven like a maniac once the rumblings had started, but he had been too late. Melanie's arms had been thrown around their son, saving his life. He saw the boy now look towards the group on the beach and back to him, his eyes darkly accusing. Yes, Jim blamed him for the tragedy. In some corner of his mind his father's absence and his mother's own sacrifice had fused together in his young mind, causing him endless problems of guilt and pain culminating in nightmares, bad school reports, truancy – all the signs of a disturbed mind. Max could not get through to him, Jim just shut him out. His marriage the following year to Jennie McVey had not helped either. Jim had never accepted what he saw as an interloper. Strangely, the only two who actually had any rapport with him were his grandmother, Dickie, and his half-sister, Kay. Kay, untouched by grief herself, forced it out of him by meeting him head on, not through bullying, but through the life and spirit that was particularly her. She was full of life, bright and strong, a laughing, responsive child, as now, seeing him.

'Daddy!'

Her voice cut through his thoughts. Jennie was turning to look, her face smiling already. She was getting to her feet, but

Kay was running, flying from the sea towards him, her long brown legs kicking up the spray around her, her eyes on him. There was no more time to reflect further on Jim, watching his half-sister now with disdainful amusement. Max came down the steps to greet her.

Kay got to him first, throwing her lithe body into his arms, still boyish at nine years old.

'Hey . . . !' Max caught her round the waist and lifted her up against him. 'How's my girl?'

'Great, Daddy . . . want to see me surf?'

She looked California-healthy, blush brown, her chestnut curls tinted with light, freckles abundant on her skin, her sea-green eyes clear and happy. She smelt of salt and sand and warm sun. He hugged her, and let her down.

'Of course . . . later. Want to talk to Mummy first, OK?'

'OK.' She ran off to join Robbie, waiting by the water's edge, more interested in the lively girl than in his counterpart of similar age. Max saw him look briefly up the beach towards Jim, now coming slowly towards them, and dismiss him. His eyes were soon back on Kay, running down the beach again.

Max lifted a hand to wave at the lad.

'Hi, Robbie . . .'

A hand lifted back, a grin split the happy face, and then Kay was bounding back through the water with a scream and a splash as she fell over and he fell with her.

Jennie had been content to wait for her children to greet their father, but Jim was taking too long. Max came down the sand towards her, the affectionate smile that he had had for Kay still in his eyes. Jennie registered the slight limp, a legacy from the day of the fire, knowing that he would always have it now. Then he was kissing her, taking her lovingly into his arms.

'Hello, sweetheart . . . missed you.'

'Me too.' She laid her face against his shoulder. Kay and Robbie's happy laughter floated up from the sea, but behind them Jim came to a halt, watching their embrace. It turned something in his stomach to see them like this; she was so unlike his mother, so red where his mother was so soft and dark. He turned on his heel and left them, feeling left out and hated. He was sure they did not even notice him go, and for the moment they did not.

CHAPTER SEVEN

July 1961

As the London to Oxford express came hurtling by, a whoosh of sound, they narrowed their eyes against the blast, hair flying as they pressed back against the low bridge that crossed the river. The train flew into the distance.

'Where is it?'

Kay was already jumping over the tracks to look.

'Somewhere here. I saw it go.' She searched amongst the stones eagerly, bent down. 'Here it is . . . wow!' She held the American quarter in her fingers and stared at it. *'Look at this!'* Her voice was awed.

Robbie and Jim ran over. Jim took it. Kay squeezed in to stare at the coin. It was completely flat.

'Yeah, isn't that great?' Robbie's smiling eyes crinkled into a grin of pleasure. He had shown them something.

'Huh! I can do something better than that.' Jim stood away from them all. 'Come on. I'll show you.' He ran to the edge of the bank and grabbed a tuft of grass as he let himself slide back down. 'Come *on* . . . !'

They went after him. Jim was the one the other children, particularly his sister Kay, looked up to, which was unfortunate because his tricks generally ran towards the unpleasant. He had learned to hang out with the village boys despite Max and Jennie's disapproval, and with them he had learned to smoke and drink. Jim was going to initiate his sister, and their American friend, Robbie Fairfax. Jim was jealous of him; until now he had them under his control. Robbie had turned out to be quite as much a leader, only good fun too, and he was the same age as Jim. He was always going on about America ever since he had come to stay for the summer. Robbie was suntanned and easy and he had great stories to tell. Jim had noticed his other friends starting to look up to him. Jim was about to change all that.

Kay tagged along in their wake as they scrambled under the perimeter fence and down towards the summer house at the end of the orchard. Her long gangly legs wriggled under the hedge as they followed Jim, who did not want them to be seen from the windows of Greatley House. She came up the other side and took her place between the boys; now nearly ten years old and precociously pretty, her blue eyes shot with green, apple-soft skin and chestnut hair. Robbie stood alongside her. They had crowded in single file into the narrow space behind the shed, hemmed in by the scratchy laurel hedge and the damp wood. There was a musty rotten smell of leaves and darkness. They were all silent as Jim reached his fingers along the grimy windowsill.

'Ah, here they are.'

He pulled the stubs down, pushed one in his pocket and the other in his mouth. There was a box of matches there too. He rattled its contents before opening it, and fitting the match to the side. It flared alive and he held the flame to the stub and began to drag on it. It was lit. Jim narrowed his eyes and exhaled a stream of pungent smoke.

'Where did you get them?' Kay's eyes were wide and admiring.

'From Dad's study.' He drew in with sophistication. 'Here.'

Kay took it, looked at it and fitted it to her pursed lips. She drew gingerly.

'Deeper than that,' said Jim.

Kay drew deeper, and held it in her fingers as she blew out slowly.

Beside her, Robbie was conscious of the moment, though not so much of the cigarettes, which he had seen often before back home; he was more conscious of the pearl of light on her lip where the sun filtered through the density of leaves above and dappled them all with its light, of the soft swell of her russet cheeks and glowing eyes, the straight little slope of her nose and the softly brushed brows and tousled dark red hair, glinting alongside him so close he could touch.

His thoughts were interrupted by the stomach-cramping cough. Kay was bent right over, coughing hard, almost retching.

'For Christ's sake,' Jim hissed. 'Do you want the whole world down here?' He grabbed the butt from her fingers, clicking his tongue with annoyance. 'Can't even smoke a little cigarette. This thing's almost finished,' he said. 'Don't suppose anyone else wants a go . . . no, you're not having it.' He held it to him as Kay reached out for it.

'Let me have another go.' She was not put off. Robbie looked admiring.

'Uh-uh.'

Robbie intervened. 'I'll finish it.' Somehow he did not want her to try again, but for quite separate reasons to those of Jim. He wanted to show off to her. As she had stretched out her arm, her warm shoulder had brushed against his and he had felt its flavour run through him.

Jim's eyes narrowed; he handed it over slowly. Robbie lifted the cigarette to his lips and drew.

As he breathed out on the plume of smoke, he talked. 'Hey, you know what this reminds me of?' The others waited. 'This time last year I went on a camping trip with my folks. My Dad likes to camp, says living rough is good for us, thinks we all live too easy these days. So, anyway, one of my friends at this camp and me, we went down by the river. There'd been a scavenging coyote the night before in camp. We thought we knew where it hung out, on the other side of this river. It was swollen with flood water, but Dan . . . that's my friend,' he said, pulling on the cigarette again. 'Well, he kind of dared me, and well you know how it is with a dare. You gotta take it! I had to dive into this ice-cold river,' he said, diving with his hand, his eyes shadowed against the smoke of the cigarette butt he now held expertly between his lips, 'swim right across. I found that goddamn bad coyote and I cut off its head, just like Dan had dared me to, and I swam right back with its head on my shoulder . . . !'

Robbie stole a look at Kay.

'Ugh!' she said and looked away. Robbie felt discomfited; she was not impressed at all. She had folded her arms and looked disgusted. 'I think that's cruel.' He looked straight down at her.

'You like cats?'

'Yes.' The eyes flashed up at him.

'Well, coyotes kill cats.'

Kay said nothing.

Robbie watched her. 'One of the girls there was scared. I did it for her too,' he said. 'If you'd been scared, I'd have done it for you.'

Kay swung her shoulders slightly and still said nothing. Jim watched, and felt a little tingle in the air. Something different was going on here; his sister was reacting quite differently to this boy. She had gone silent.

Robbie threw the butt to the ground, ignoring her now. He twisted the toe of his shoe against it, pushing it in amongst the damp leaves. Jim watched silently; he did not know what a coyote was and he was not about to ask. Robbie's competitive spirit made him sulk alone. No one noticed.

'Did you cut off his head alive?' Kay had recovered now.

'No!' Robbie laughed and stuck his hands in his pockets. 'Course not. I couldn't catch him, could I? No, I shot him first.'

'Your Dad lets you shoot?'

'Sure. We grow up fast in the States!' He grinned and winked at Kay, giving her a long look. Kay's eyes widened and then she sort of twisted her head a little and started to become absorbed in a leaf that was hanging down in front of her. Jim was fascinated despite himself.

He leaned back against the corner of the summer house. He looked down at Robbie from under his lids and spoke sharply.

'Can you drink?'

'Sure.'

'You been out with a girl?'

Robbie chuckled.

'You *haven't* been out with a girl.' Jim smiled.

'And you have?'

'Yeah.' Now he had all their attention.

'*Who?*' asked Kay.

'Dinah Champion in the village.' Kay looked up. She was one of the girls from school. 'She met me behind the church hall last week. She let me touch her.' His eyes were dark and knowing. 'I'm meeting her again this weekend before we go back to school. She's made me a promise!' He laughed.

Robbie thought a moment. 'I've been cattle rustling,' he said. 'Out riding with my friends. We put them back again later though. You been cattle rustling?'

Jim kicked at the leaves. 'Doesn't happen here.'

Kay spoke without thinking. 'Yes it does.' She was on Robbie's side. 'Poachers have been in the fields all around here, there's plenty of cattle rustling if you wanted to do it.'

'That's not true.' Jim sneered at her. 'Baby's making it up to be clever.'

'It *is* true,' she said indignantly.

'Oh yeah?' He slid round the corner of the shed and stood over her. 'And how would you know?'

'Well, I . . .' Suddenly she was bewildered. Frederick Redfield was her friend; their conversations her secret. It was he who had told her about the poachers, but she could not tell Jim that. She knew instinctively she could not. There was something between them and the Redfields who lived beyond the wood, something that told her everyone would be very angry if they knew who her friend was, her friend whom she had met in the village one day after school last summer term; a friend who understood her, shared thoughts with her, laughed with her and told her stories whilst she waited for the bus home. A friend who told her she had laughing green eyes, and that she had spirit she should never let go of, just like her grandmother. But she could not talk about him, and so she closed her mouth and just stared silently at her brother's accusing face, her cheeks pinkening.

'Well,' he said again. 'How would you know? Answer me!'

'I don't,' she muttered unhappily.

'You see!' Jim's voice was triumphant. 'What did I tell you? She's . . .'

The clanging of the brass gong startled them all. It was the way Jennie called them back from their adventures on these long summer days.

Jim pulled a piece of chewing-gum from his pocket as the kids straightened up and started to push their way out of their private meeting-place behind the summer house.

'Here!' he said, pulling at their arms. He had split it into three. Each of them took a piece. 'Removes all traces,' he said knowingly.

They trooped out into the sunshine, chewing on the minty gum. Jim sauntered out behind them. Ahead, on the flagged patio of Greatley House, Jennie stood, the gong in one hand, shielding her eyes from the sun as she looked out over the surrounding fields. Their grandmother's hideaway house had never been sold; it was where the family now spent many summer weekends with her. Jennie smiled as she saw them, and laid the gong to one side.

'Hi, kids,' she said as they trailed across the lawn towards her. 'Jim, your father's going up to town. Go and get tidied up, would you, sweetheart. He wants you to go too!'

63

'Oh God,' Jim muttered under his breath. He did not want to go.

Jennie sat down on the steps. 'And what have you been up to? Having fun?'

They nodded. A rug was laid out on the lawn beside her mother. Kay went over and sat down on it, curling up her legs against the soft wool.

'We were discussing the best cricketers of the season, Aunt Jennie,' said Robbie, smiling at her.

Jennie nodded. She reached up to Jim as he came over, straightening his collar and brushing her fingers through his dark curls. Jim pulled away slightly, but she was not bothered. She had long been used to his ways. 'Don't you want to go, Jim?' she asked, a little sternly.

Jim raised his eyebrows. He had been planning to meet his friends from the village and steal from the sweet shop later. Old Mrs Evans never noticed until too late. He knew there was nothing he could say either. Jennie was uncompromising. She always followed his father's wishes.

Max stepped out of the French doors onto the terrace. He was in a short-sleeved blue cotton shirt and jeans. 'It's OK, you can come like that, Jim. We're not getting dressed up on a hot day like this.' He walked over and stood above at the head of the terrace steps. 'Thought we'd run down to the airfield after-wards. Take up one of the new planes.'

Jim's lack of response was hidden as Kay came to her knees. 'Can I come?' Her eyes had brightened at the prospect.

Max smiled at his daughter. 'No, sorry, darling. You're too young. Jim is the one with the privileges at the moment, he's the one who has to learn the business. One day he'll be running it.'

Jim's look said that he considered it an endurance rather than a privilege, but nobody saw as he shielded his resentment with downcast eyes. He felt the pressure put on him to follow his father into the airline business, without even being consulted as to his feelings. Max had not walked into riches; he had worked for them and now he was passing on the fruits of his labours to his son. He had automatically expected him to want to join with him. His hand fell to Jim's shoulder. It was firm and heavy. To Jim, it felt like a dead weight he had to carry; he wanted to jerk it off him, to turn and shout. Instead he stood there looking expressionless.

Max looked down at Robbie. 'You want a game of cricket when we get back?'

'Sure!'

'OK. We'll be leaving in an hour, back around six.'

'Want a race, Kay?' Robbie knew her. She jumped to her feet, the gleam from her eyes spreading to her face. The two of them were never disappointed for long. 'I'll beat you!' she said laughing.

'No you won't.' He laid a hand on his bent knee, ready. Robbie looked over at her. The sun touched her hair and made it glow a deep dark red, the wind softly ruffling it over her summer-dusky shoulders. Her long brown legs had a silvery glisten out here in the sunlight where the delicate blonde hairs just softened her skin. He turned away to stare ahead of him. 'Give us the countdown, Uncle Max.' Jim ran up alongside the two of them, bending ready.

'Right . . . on your marks, get set . . . GO!'

Kay was off, her laughter trailing out behind her like a long scarf. Robbie pummelled ahead, Jim in close pursuit of the two of them. They headed for the top field and Sam's Hill. Kay ran like a gazelle. The remaining family watched them go. Jennie laughed and exchanged a smile of happiness with Max.

'She's a real tomboy,' she said.

'Uh-huh, but she won't be for ever,' said Max. He shouted after them. 'Remember we're leaving within the hour.'

He chuckled softly, watching them go, his arm falling around his wife's shoulders.

'Are you all right, darling?'

'I'm fine.' Her smile was soft.

They had reached the edge of the woods. Jim ran ahead towards their favourite swinging-tree. 'Race you to the top,' he said.

They both began to scramble upwards. 'If I win you have to do another dare,' he shouted, breathing heavily as he fought to beat her rapid climb. Kay was smaller and lighter and had no fear at all as she grasped at the branches and launched herself upwards towards the swaying leaves of the beech high up against the blue of the sky. Robbie was at the foot of the tree, watching. He had no head for heights. As they climbed up he could see the branches already beginning to bend under their weight.

'Watch out,' he called. 'You're going to break them!'

Neither wanted to lose. They were still eagerly climbing, half-laughing as they strove together to be first. But Jim had found the better side of the tree, the branches like a stepladder. Hand over hand he went up as far as he could go. Kay swung easily up beneath him, catching him. And then he felt the green bough split under his weight.

'Whoops . . . ! Kay, stop, that's as high as we can go. I won!'

'That's not fair.' She came up alongside him, her arms entwined around the green bark. 'I can climb higher still. I'm lighter.'

'I won, Kay. You've got to do another dare.' He started to slide swiftly back down again, stepping onto the boughs that creaked under his weight.

He jumped to the floor of the wood and dusted off his hands. Kay came down the other side. 'What's the dare?'

'You two are crazy!' Robbie looked from one to the other. 'That was really dangerous. Did you hear that branch breaking. I could see from here, the whole tree was bending over.'

Kay laughed. 'What's the dare!' She brushed her hands across her chest.

'Dare you to go into the woods.'

'I dare.'

'Deep in the woods where the bogeyman is. All by yourself.'

Kay swallowed nervously. She had to do it.

'Double dare.' She shook hands on it.

'You've got to go so we can't see you any more.' Jim pointed through the tall open beeches of the wood towards the centre. The acid green fingers of the beech trees spread high above them, shifting and swaying in the wind, forming a protective canopy of sheer green, the sunlight dappling through as they moved gently to and fro. It was quiet as they listened, the roof rustling against the sky. Cobbold's Wood was very beautiful, the trees tall and lean, but further in the vegetation of bushes became dense. She had never been that far. The woods were the one thing she was frightened of. She had always felt it was too quiet, a damp dripping quiet, the moisture held there where the sunlight never went.

But they dared each other all the time; no one had ever broken it yet. She bit her lip. There was someone in there; they all knew the story. No one said anything really but from somewhere had come the story that something bad had once

66

happened to Dickie, something bad, really bad. The woods were scary; Jim knew that.

He grinned at her. 'You don't dare. You've got to give me your Cliff Richard record.' Kay only had two records: Cliff Richard and Elvis Presley, both equally dear. She danced alone to them when no one was around.

'I do dare,' she said, challenged. 'You'll see.'

She started walking down the grassy path towards the centre. Brambles and fern criss-crossed her way and she stepped over them. Beyond, the trees grew closer. She knew the wood went on and on. Somewhere, far over on the other side, it opened out again onto Foxhall Manor. One could reach that house by the river footpath, but it was private and no one ever went that way.

She pushed aside the branches, the ferns against her legs damp and clinging.

'Go until you can't see us.' Already his voice was fading. 'We'll count to five hundred.'

She turned once and saw both their faces, pale moons watching between the trees, and then, heart beating loudly, she pressed on.

CHAPTER EIGHT

Inside the cool, elegant drawing-room, Dickie had stood and watched the children run across the fields in the distance. She had heard their shouts of delight and smiled. She patted the hair at the nape of her neck, seeming thoughtful, and unusually for her, nervous. Her eyes strayed often to the clock on the mantelpiece that now showed one minute past one.

The door bell rang in the distance. She turned her head towards it, but did not move immediately. She heard her new housekeeper cross the hall to answer it. There was a murmur of voices. The door shut, and the footsteps came across towards the drawing-room. Only then did she turn, cough slightly, her hand to her mouth, and cross the room to meet her visitor.

The door opened.

'Katherine.' Dickie went forward, at ease now she had arrived, to take her hand. The two of them were of similar height. Katherine Haslett leaned forward to kiss her cheek and then the two of them stood back. Dickie's eyes were admiring. 'You haven't changed.'

'And nor have you.'

Katherine held herself well, despite her seventy-odd years, with no stoop. Her eyes were still clear and brown and warm. They were direct, no fear there, just gentleness. Her skin was that of some old women who have had a lifetime of good skin, a soft olive against the silver of her hair that waved close to her head in a light perm. Her features were slender and well balanced; she had almost an Italian look. She wore dark green silk in blouse and skirt, a bow at her throat, and a matching jacket with plum silk frogging thrown casually over her shoulders. She wore her clothes with style as she had always done. Katherine was a striking woman, still beautiful, with the air of one who had always commandeered attention in a highly feminine way.

'Come and sit down,' said Dickie gently. 'Tell me what has

been happening to you. It's been so long.' She still held her hand as she drew her into the room. 'Why did you lose touch? There was no need, you know.'

'I know.' Katherine's voice was gentle. She had a quiet dignity, as did Dickie. She allowed herself to be led to the long cream sofa beside the open bay windows. Dickie had laid out a tray of sherry. They sat together. 'It was Henry,' she said, and Dickie nodded.

The two of them bore a strange history. It was she, Katherine, Lady Haslett, who had been Frederick Redfield's lover for a quarter of a century, yet in all that time she had remained married to her husband, Henry. She had had two sons from an earlier marriage, her first husband killed in the Great War, and a daughter, Melanie, from her marriage to Henry. It was Melanie, lovely sensual Melanie, who had first inflamed the heart of Charles Redfield, but it had been Dickie's son, Max, who had captured her own heart. From the first time she had set eyes on him she had adored him, and with their marriage had taken Dickie and Katherine, both lovers of Frederick but in so, so different ways, into a strange friendship.

With Melanie's tragic death, the Haslett family had sold up their home and left to join her son abroad, Henry a bitter man, and Katherine a desperately sad mother. It had ended her affair with Frederick and her relationship with the Bennetts. Henry had sworn hatred for Max, somehow seeming to see him as to blame for the tragedy, and forbidden Katherine ever to see them again. Katherine had not seen her grandson Jim since an early visit to California when he was a baby.

'I came to talk to you, Dickie,' said Katherine. 'To tell you some things.' Her eyes were gentle. 'Enough has gone by, enough hatred, enough time.' She paused. 'Henry's dead.'

'Oh, I'm so sorry.'

Katherine went on after a moment. 'The last years weren't easy, you know. He wasn't well.' She remembered them briefly, the accusations, the atmospheres, the invalid she had had to care for, the invalid so full of hatred and pain. She had chosen her bed though, and she had stayed until the end. 'Death was a release, I think for all of us. He forbade me to come back, you know,' she said, looking at the other woman then. 'I've so longed to . . . there's so much here that's a part of me . . .'

She looked away, towards the French windows behind the sofa.

'So much I had to forego.'

'Yes. I know.'

'You knew,' she said. 'About Frederick?'

'Yes.' Dickie could not remember how she had first heard, but she had known.

Katherine nodded. 'I'm glad. But it's not him I came back for. I'd like to see Jim, if . . .'

'Of course.' Dickie leaned forward, covering her hand with her own.

The sound of distant shouts, the kick of a football, cut up through the quiet of the day. 'Is that the children?' asked Katherine, her hand on the back of the sofa, ready to look. One of them screamed with laughter. Yells and shouts followed.

'Yes,' said Dickie. 'That's Jim. You'll want to see him right away, I've no doubt. He's a good-looking boy, a fine boy, the image of his parents. It's been very difficult for him, Katherine. I'm afraid he still has nightmares about the earthquake. He missed her dreadfully at first. As did we all. She was such a lovely girl . . .' Katherine's eyes sharpened with the memory of a conjured image, her daughter. Dickie started to stand. 'I'll go and call him . . .'

'No, wait.' Katherine stretched out her hand, golden bangles falling back against the dark green silk. 'I'm longing to see him, of course, to hear all about him. But first, I want to talk to you.'

Kay was deep inside the wood. It was not so scary after all. At the centre of the wood the summer sun still found entry and poured down in shafts of brilliant light. The foliage was lustrous and green and the leaves high above were a glittering pale green and diaphanous, making a leafy temple for the soft mossy floor of the wood. The shadows were dappled with sunlight, and underneath the carpet of fallen acorns and twigs, the earth was soft and spongy. Ahead she heard the gentle sound of water. She had found the spring where it bubbled from the ground and idled over the shiny stones towards the mother river, silvery and cool.

Kay bent at its edge and dipped her hands in to feel it. It was very soft. Birds twittered high above against the wood's silence. She felt as if she were in a secret world, and very brave. Jim would have to do some really good dares for her after this. She thought back to the moment when she had backed down in front of him. He would hold that against her, call her a weed – but there really was nothing she could have said. As she knelt there, fingers in the cool water, she thought of last summer, and her friend, Frederick.

It had been a bad day at school, bullied by one of the older girls, Dinah Champion, the very girl her brother, Jim, was keen on. They had had a fight out in the field at break. Kay had won; that gave her some satisfaction at least – she had always been a good scrapper, learned it from Jim himself. But the result had not been good. Dinah was a sneak. She had told the headmistress it had been Kay who started it. The punishment had been extreme – the head, Miss Grey, had taken the chrysalis of her Privet Moth and thrown it away, out of the classroom window. She had not shown her feelings but it had been a terrible loss for her. She had been so proud of her find, had longed for the moment when the hard shell would break and the beautiful moth appear.

Down at the bus-stop in the village an old man had stumbled up by the bridge over the river, dropping his stick. Kay, forgetting her problems for the moment, had run over to help him back to his feet. It had been the start of something special – for both of them. Funny to think of someone Dickie's age being her friend, but there it was. His face had been kind, and she had liked the way his dark blue eyes crinkled with laughter, sleepy eyes. They had watched the river together as it flowed under the bridge, just talking, whilst she waited for the bus home. He had noticed the torn ribbon on her plait, the dried mud on her dress, and the tiny scratch on her cheek. More than that, he had noticed her hurt pride. Without knowing how it had happened, Kay, generally quite private despite her outward-going nature, was telling him the whole story. And how she had won. It had made the old man chuckle. He had called her quite a scrapper, just like her grandmother – it was then he had told her just how alike they were. And he was funny too. She had liked him, asked him his name – he seemed to know hers; well, it was written on her satchel – and when the bus had come along she had asked if he was often down in the village, and he had said he was. They would meet again, he said, and they had. Quite often, just to talk about things. Frederick listened, and Kay had so much to say. He had told her always to listen to her heart in life and go after the things she wanted, and she would rarely go wrong. Kay thought that was good advice.

The thrashing sound from the ferns somewhere close by began to catch her attention. She had been about to drink from the brook, but now lifted her head to look. Her eyes peered into the distance beyond, her ears listening sharply for the sound again.

There it was. And a little cry of pain, the sound of an animal in distress. She could even see the ferns move. She jumped over the brook straight away and moved quickly at first and then more slowly so as not to scare whatever it was as she came closer. She stopped, waiting, as the ferns stood still. A moment later, and now much, much nearer, she heard the desperate scrabbling and a whimper of agony. Now she could even see the flash of red.

Kay's eyes were wide, trained on the spot as she moved closer, crouching slightly, her bare legs scratched by the thick undergrowth. At the base of one of the trees she saw it clearly for the first time and it saw her, but it could not run away, its round eyes terrified, imprisoned by its fear and pain.

The fox had its back leg caught in a gin trap. The evil black teeth were clamped tight, shearing the fur to the bone. Blood was everywhere, all over the creature's mouth, down its white breast and paws. Its leg was dangling uselessly, crushed by the cruel machinations of the trap. Its scrabbling to be free had done nothing to release it. Now, even as she watched, it turned its head and bit frantically at the damaged leg.

For a moment she could not move, horrified by what she saw. Then she knew somehow she had to get the poor thing loose. She went forward gently, talking like she might to a kitten or domestic pet.

'Come on, now, come on. I'm not going to hurt you, poor little thing. Don't be scared . . .'

The fox backed away, pulling its leg, its fear of her overcoming pain. It did not cry out, though the leg must have been agonising as it pulled away on the chain of the trap. It could go no further, its eyes rolled in its head and its lip snarled back over its long white teeth.

Kay felt tears in her eyes for what it was doing to itself. She did not mean to hurt it but by going closer she was terrifying it more. If only it understood. She had to help it. Its teeth were like fangs, bared at her, blood spattered on its gums. She cooed softly at it as she closed in, conscious only that she had somehow to grab its ruff to hold its head away, and then force open the vicious iron jaws of the trap.

The fox strained away. Kay's eyes were huge as she came within its reach, seeing the damp sweat on its fur, the agony in its eyes. She reached out a hand for its neck, the fox pulled. She had it. It wriggled and wrenched to be free.

'Don't, don't,' she said urgently. 'I'm going to help you, I'm going to help you. Don't fight, please little fox.'

It was very strong, too strong for her. Desperately, she held on, trying to force at the edges of the steel trap with one hand. It was impossible. Her fingers pulled at the long black teeth and the fox panicked under her, wriggling free. She lost the grip on its neck, immediately using both hands to pull and pull on the teeth of the trap. The fox did not bite her as she had expected, the teeth were opening . . . just . . . it was such a strain, oh . . .

'What the hell are you doing?'

Kay jumped as though she had been struck. She let go of everything and reeled back against the ground as the gloved hand caught her shoulder.

'I said, what are you doing here?'

Kay lay on the ground and looked up at him. She could not answer. The man was enormous, a terrifying sight. The fox dragged the trap and pulled the chain through the undergrowth, away from them both. Kay stared upwards to where the man's face stood out, blackened with smeared mud, a dark hat on his head, only the eyes blazing down on her. He had a gun over his shoulder. It seemed to take all her strength to tear her eyes away from it. She had met one of the poachers. Now he would kill her too.

'I . . . I . . .'

He bent over her, let the gun down to the ground. 'You're trespassing. Who are you? Speak!'

'K – Kay . . . B – Bennett . . .' She inched backwards on her bottom, ready to run. 'Are . . . are you a poacher?'

The man drew in a deep breath; his eyes became dangerous. He looked into her green green eyes, saw her terror, the skirt that had ridden back on her long young legs.

He reached down.

She screamed. Screamed loud, loud, loud . . . 'Let go of me!' She fought her way up, twisting, twisting against the gloved leather hand that caught her, held her. 'JIM! JIM! Help, Robbie! *Help!*'

'Kay! Kay!' The voices echoed each other. The boys would rescue her. 'Kay, where are you?'

The man's grip loosened as he turned his head to the voices.

Kay was on her feet and gone, running, as fast as she could. Away over the brushes and undergrowth, flying through the brambles, not looking, just breathlessly running. The bogeyman. The bogeyman.

The gunshot was like a crack in the wood. The birds scattered in the trees above. Kay stumbled, gasped, and almost fell. Brushing her hair from her eyes she turned, just once and swiftly. The big man was bending to the trap, opening it with ease. He pulled the limp fox from its prison, no longer in agony, and tossed it over his shoulder. Its wide mouth lolled open against his back. He turned and looked at her, moving the gun under his arm. Even from here she could feel the blaze in those eyes.

Her heart thudded in her chest. He was going to shoot her too, like the fox. A little cry escaped her as she took off again, her legs propelling her forward, her hands outstretched to ward off the twigs and greenery that branched across her path.

'Kay!'

'Robbie, I'm here! Over here!'

Ahead, she saw them. At last she saw them. Her back felt seared with heat where she awaited the bullet that was sure to come from the bogeyman as she ran towards her friend. His blond hair was falling in his eyes, his eyes fearful, searching for her. Jim came too, both running forwards.

'Kay, what happened?'

She reached them both, fell sobbing into Robbie's arms. Sobbing with fear.

'Why did you scream?' His arm held her. He looked beyond into the depths of the now silent wood and could see nothing. The birds twittered back on to their lofty perches.

She was breathing heavily, her lungs bursting. Eventually she slid her arms from him and turned. 'There!'

But there was nothing. He had gone. Suddenly she wasn't grown up and brave at all. The wood was frightening. She had known it would be. She was cold and scared. Scared, she started to hurry ahead. 'Let's go!' she called to them still hanging back and looking. 'Come on. I saw the bogeyman, Robbie, I saw him!'

They looked, curious, trying to see. Kay would not stay.

She would never come here again. She ran, not stopping till she reached the swinging-tree and the lovely sight of Sam's Hill beyond. She ran out into the open and fell upon the cool grass, her head on her arms. She would never go in there again.

On the opposite side of the wood, Rupert Redfield walked out into the open, climbing through the wire fence. He set off at a steady pace in the direction of Foxhall Manor.

Dickie looked quizzically at her guest. She felt warmly towards this woman, despite her association with Frederick Redfield. She, alone of all the great landowners in the area, had welcomed the Bennetts into her home. She had always treated Dickie with kindness and respect, and when her father, Jim Bennett for whom the young Jim had been named, had been made homeless by Rupert Redfield, she had instantly found him a place to live in the grounds of her own ancestral home, Menderley.

'I wanted to be reunited with you,' Katherine was saying. 'Not only because of Jim, but because it may be the last time.' She laid her hands on her lap, tilting her head slightly in reflection. 'I'm shortly going back to America next week, you see, to live with my son. I'm an old woman, and well . . .' She lifted her hands in explanation and brought them down again. She looked then at Dickie. 'And also I wanted to warn you.'

'To warn me?'

'How are things between you and the Redfields?'

'Much the same,' she said cautiously. 'Why?' The question did not seem strange; everybody knew there was animosity between them, though not why. It had never been in anybody's interests to say why, on either side.

Katherine leaned forward, laying her hand on Dickie's. Her voice was very soft. 'Give up the fight, Dickie.'

Dickie sighed. 'Katherine, listen to me. You don't understand.'

'Oh, but I do.'

'No, no.' She took the other woman's hand in her own. 'You don't. There's so much, so much,' she said sadly, her green eyes brilliant, 'that I cannot say to you.' So much that had to do with the man she, too, thought she had loved, Frederick Redfield. 'Oh, of course there have been times I've felt I'd like to give up,

75

but I never have.' She took another breath. 'It's not just me any more either, it's him. He won't let it go.'

'You mean Rupert,' she said quietly.

'Yes. Rupert,' Dickie said slowly. 'But Katherine, I have reason to hate not just him, but them.'

'By them, you mean my Frederick.'

'Katherine, I . . .'

'No, listen.' She lifted her hand. 'I have to tell you a story, Dickie, a story that might help you to understand. You see,' she began, 'he never meant you any harm. He loved you. He probably still does.' Katherine's voice was gentle, almost dreamy. 'All through our love affair of over twenty years, my dear, I knew I only ever came second to you. And Caroline. Well he loved her, yes, but she was merely a substitute when he could not have you.'

Dickie was stunned, staring at the woman before her as she paused, her dark eyes warm with caring. She could not speak.

'Poor Frederick,' Katherine was saying. 'The day he took you weakened him for the rest of his life. Yes, you see, I know all about it. I loved Frederick. It was I who took him into the wood to seduce him, to give him the love he had never had. He really was a beautiful lover,' she said smiling in memory, 'but I never had his heart.' She looked back towards Dickie, her expression rueful. 'He told me that day what he had done to you. Do you know that he sincerely thought you were co-operating, that you loved him too? He could not resist you.' Dickie's head was spinning, the memories back with her, how she had lain there on the floor of the wood as Rupert had moved off her and the sunlight had been full in her eyes. And there had stood Frederick, the man she had believed herself in love with, and he was coming down over her, whispering.

Dickie took a deep breath. In any other circumstances would she have . . . her thoughts were broken by Katherine's voice.

'Oh, I know it all sounds wild now, but that's Frederick. Foolish, romantic, very influenced by others. I do think he's stronger now,' she said, shaking her head. 'But that day in the woods . . .' she looked back into Dickie's eyes. 'Well, he told me you didn't stop him and he could not stop himself.'

Silence fell between them. Dickie sat there, unmoving. She could not have stopped him. She had been brutalised, terrified by Rupert. And yes, she had thought herself in love with

76

Frederick. What a terrible mistake he had made, they had both made, and paid for it all their lives.

'I would have left Henry,' Katherine said then. 'Had he asked me. But he never did. There had only ever been one woman for him.' She gave a soft laugh. 'I don't know if you've ever noticed it, but there's a stone maiden in the gardens at Foxhall. He likened you to her. He said when the sun came up in the morning and she was gilded with light, he could never see the statue without thinking of you.'

'Stop!' It was a soft cry from Dickie, forced out of her. 'Don't say any more.' She lowered her head. 'I know the statue.' How well she did. It was upon the statue that she had made her oath as she carried her heavy baby in the heat of the summer, working so hard in the kitchens of Foxhall, burdened by her memories, her shame of being poor and defenceless, her illegitimate child weighing her down through those long, sweltering days; her oath to destroy them all. To think he had likened her to it too.

'Dickie, I didn't mean to come here and hurt you,' she said. 'Only to say, keep your anger for the one who deserves it. Rupert. It's not only you who has suffered at his hands. Frederick has too; all that family. He influenced them all. Even Caroline, before the Great War. Being the person he is, he swept her away from Frederick, married her, then used her to get what he wanted from Frederick. You do know that Alexander, their father, disinherited Rupert in favour of Frederick?'

Dickie tried to recover. She looked up, running her hand over her cheek. 'No, I didn't,' she said. 'Why on earth would he do that?'

'Because of you.'

'Me?'

'Yes. He found out about it, what they had done to you. Rupert couldn't have cared less and told him so. He threw it in the old man's face. He was marrying Caroline Lancing, and he thought he was secure. He was cocky, and he laughed at Alexander's concern for you. He knew about the child, you see.'

'Good heavens.'

'Alexander left a will disinheriting Rupert completely. When Rupert found out, he used Caroline to pry the estate back from Frederick.' She nodded slowly. 'And Caroline was no innocent party either,' she said drily. 'In her way she used Frederick too, she used his love for her.'

'I see,' Dickie said slowly. A lawnmower started up in the distance, bringing her back to the present. She blinked and looked out into the sun that filled the terrace, the soft pink of the roses nodding against the stone. This was all so strange, so much part of the past. She felt disoriented, vulnerable, as if the strength of her defences had been stripped from her. And it had taken this gentle old woman to do it.

'You see what I am saying, Dickie,' she went on. 'Don't hate him. I would not have loved a selfish, cruel man. He is not that. Try to forgive him. Keep your hatred for the one that matters. Rupert. I know how he hates you, that's all. I've heard him with my own ears, talking to Henry. He swore revenge on you. Not only for being successful when he had merely thought of you as, you'll forgive me, a servant, but because you were the direct cause of his disinheritance, nearly losing him everything that he was due to possess. No one's ever had so much power over Rupert,' she said coolly. 'It's not something he would *ever* forgive. Think on that and never underestimate him. I'm not a vengeful woman, Dickie, but I consider myself your friend if I may. Just don't give him the opening. As for the others, they are innocents . . . Frederick, Charles, poor Jessamy . . .'

Yes, Jessamy, Rupert Redfield's beautiful, tragic daughter. Dickie gave a deep sigh. And that was the problem. It was no longer just her revenge; she had told Max and Max carried his mother's pain in his heart. She remembered Jessamy, and what her own son had done to her in retaliation.

'I find it hard to believe all this,' she said at last.

'Well, believe it you must. It is the truth.'

She shook her head lightly, picked up her glass in both hands.

'Katherine, it carries its own impetus, revenge. You cannot isolate it.' She remembered Bill, how he had said that to her. It was so true.

'You can stop it,' she urged.

'No.' Her voice was even sad. 'I don't see how. You said yourself that Rupert will not let it rest. Until he dies, or until I have Foxhall as I once promised my father and my brother, it will go on. I cannot stop it. I'm not even sure I want to.'

Katherine saw the expression on her face. 'Well,' she said, picking up her own glass too. 'I can see how you feel. We're not alike, Dickie. I could never take revenge, but then . . . maybe if

78

I had more of your spirit I would have made Frederick love me and marry me.'

'Katherine.' Dickie took her hand in her own. 'You have colossal spirit. You're the woman I would most have wanted to be. You have warmth and love.'

'And loss.'

'We both have that. We've both lost and won, in our ways. We both have our families, you have your sons now. I have my children here, my grandchildren, Longbarrow, I'm still happy. Come on,' she said, 'let me take you outside to meet them. Stop this morbid talk. I've heard what you've told me and I'm grateful, but it's time now to think of the future, not the past . . .'

Katherine put down her glass and smiled sweetly. The warmth lit her eyes giving her the great beauty for which she had been renowned in her youth. 'I'd like that.'

The two women stood. Dickie leaned forward and embraced her. Katherine was right, she was different. She knew as she straightened again with a smile and looked her old friend straight in the eye that even more now she could not let the feud die. She had to take Foxhall for herself, to take the one thing Rupert needed the most, to prove he was no longer any threat to her or to her family.

'Now,' said Katherine as they walked back through the room together. 'Tell me what has been happening with your business . . .'

Out on the terrace, Kay sat on the wall in shock. She had returned, running across the fields, the sunshine and fresh air dispelling the fears and closeness of the wood, almost as if it had been a dream, some terrible nightmare. She had not stopped to think about it as she headed back to safety, thinking to reflect on it once she was safe back at her grandmother's house. She had heard more or less everything they had said, their words drifting out to her and her eyes growing huge as she heard the story.

She ran quickly across the terrace and in through the French doors towards the narrow wooden staircase that curved downwards flooded with sunshine. She slipped quickly up the stairs as the murmur of voices grew louder as they reached the drawing-room door. *Jim's grandmother, Katherine.* She knew her name, had put two and two together. She wanted to see her, appalled at what she had heard. Still too young to fully comprehend the extent of it, she understood the basics of the story fully. She was truly shocked that it had been her friend, Frederick, who had done something to her grandmother, hurt her so much as to make her hate the Redfields as the whole family knew she did. They never discussed it, it was taboo. Now, *she* knew. It made no difference to her friendship with him; he was every bit as gentle and kind as the soft voice had said he was. She knew that too. She understood how easy it would be to love him, especially when he had been young and handsome. Thoughts whirled around her head as the two women came out, slowly walking together. They passed down the hall at the foot of the stairs, heading for the terrace and the brilliant sunshine. Kay crouched down behind the banister.

'. . . everybody flies now,' her grandmother was saying. 'Pop stars, presidents, mothers, hairdressers. It's all very different now, one has to move with the times. We've had a man in space, we've had skyjackings, and we have the jet age . . .'

They moved out of sight as they turned together onto the terrace. The other woman had looked gracious and kind, very thin but elegantly so. Kay clambered up the rest of the stairs and down the corridor to Jim's bedroom. The sound of music beat out from his transistor beyond the closed door. He had come on here ahead of her and gone straight up to his room.

'Jim! Jim!' She knocked urgently and pushed the door open.

Jim was sitting by the window, listening to the music. He had his feet up on the window seat, a book resting on his knees. He seemed absorbed.

'Jim!'

He turned to look at her. 'What?'

Kay came across the room to his side. She leaned across him to the open window and looked out. They were there, crossing to the chairs that were placed out on the small terrace.

'What are you doing, Kay?' said Jim, almost with annoyance. She was squashing his book against his knees.

She looked back at him, her face glowing. 'There!' she said, pointing.

'Where?' he asked, sitting up to look out of the window. Dickie was standing, the other woman, a stranger, sitting down, smoothing her skirt underneath her with care. He shrugged. 'I don't see anything.'

Kay pulled at his arm. 'Yes, you do,' she said. 'That woman.'

She nodded at him, eyes bright. She was not about to tell him the story, but she wanted him to know who the woman with the white hair was. Her half-brother Jim had always been unhappy, difficult with others though never with her. She had not let him. She had always felt a little sorry for him. Now everything would be all right. She felt proud of her knowledge.

'What about her?' Jim looked down at the elegant woman, her silver hair shining in the sun.

'She's come to see you!'

'Me? Why?'

'She's your grandmother, Jim.'

Dickie stood looking out over the lawn, listening to the sound of Max's motor mower at the side of the house. The smell of the grass caught at her nostrils. She looked at Katherine. 'Are you going to see Frederick?'

Katherine shook her head. 'Not now. It's a different world now. I want him to remember me as I was, young and well . . .'

'Beautiful. You still are, Katherine. True beauty never dies.'

'Thank you.' She smiled. 'But no, I won't be seeing Frederick. I did not come here to see him, but to see . . .'

Her eyes had caught sight of the boy who stood at the French windows staring down the length of the terrace at them. There was something about him, something in the eyes, in the way he held himself. Her eyes misted.

'That's not . . . ?'

Dickie turned to the note in her voice. 'Yes, that's Jim.'

She had no need to call him. Jim was starting to walk towards them. Katherine's eyes did not leave him. She was already rising slowly from her chair, the half-smile on her face. Dickie bent to help her, holding her elbow, feeling the slight tremor of her body.

Someone to love. Someone like his mother. He was scared and excited. Maybe Kay had been wrong, maybe it wasn't true. But he had found himself running from his room, down the stairs, only coming to a halt as he found himself out on the terrace, the old woman coming to her feet, smiling at him.

He was tall, fifteen, a young man, but the sudden shy look in his eyes, the tilt of his head and the curve of his mouth, were all Melanie. 'Oh!' she cried, a little sob in her throat. 'Is it really you, Jim?'

Her arms went out. Dickie stood back. Jim was coming

forward, his face showing all his feelings. The woman's smile, her soft eyes, those arms widening for him, the shape of her face, they were all his mother.

He felt the choke catch him as suddenly he was moving into her embrace. It was true. In each there was the reflection of Melanie whom they had loved so dearly, causing Jim, at least, to resent the woman who he wrongly felt had tried to replace her, Jennie.

Jim bent his head to her shoulder. 'Why did you stay away so long?'

In answer, she merely hugged him tight. As tight as she was able.

Dickie turned and left them as quietly as she could.

Upstairs, Kay drew away from the window. She let out a sigh and went to find her mother.

Jennie was in her bedroom, brushing her hands over the bedspread to straighten the creases.

Kay went across to her and looped her arms around her. 'Mum?'

'Yes, darling?' Jennie put her arms around her daughter.

'I heard Granny talking . . .'

'Oh?' Kay seemed unusually troubled.

'It was about her and the Redfields, Rupert and Frederick. Jim's grandmother's come . . .'

'Has she?' Jennie's eyes lifted quickly to hers.

'Yes, and they were talking about what happened to Granny. I was lying on the wall outside. I couldn't help but hear. Mum,' she said, 'will you explain it to me? It all sounded so . . . awful.'

Jennie understood then. She knew the story well. She regarded her daughter's troubled face for just a moment.

'Yes, of course I will,' she said then. She had always been straight with the children. 'But whatever you heard, and whatever I tell you, I want you to promise to forget it afterwards, certainly not to talk about it to anyone else. Promise?' She lifted her chin with her hand.

Kay nodded.

Jennie sat down gently on the side of the bed with her and started to talk. She told her the story as kindly as she was able, knowing that whatever the child had heard it would only have been in snatches, to become distorted in her mind. Much better that even if she were still too young to know the real horror of what happened, she should hear from someone she trusted a palatable version of the truth. Jennie was a very smart woman. She knew better than to try and close a young and enquiring mind.

Kay heard the story in silence. She was calm and sensible, grateful for her mother's honesty. She did not feel any hate towards the Redfields as her father might have done so many years before when he had first heard the truth. For the first time, carefully told, the story that had created so much hatred and revenge between the two families was met with compassion. It was a beginning.

Kay left her mother and went back to her room. She leaned on the windowsill, knees on her own window seat as she had done as a child. But today she was no longer a child. She looked out. The terrace was empty now, Jim and his grandmother gone to some corner of the estate to catch up on those long missed years, lonely years. Kay remembered the terrible man in the wood, the same one who had done those things to Granny. She knew who he was now. She had learned some things today too, about her friend Frederick. She decided it made no difference; he was her friend anyway. She looked out at the empty lawns, the midsummer sky, the gardens where she had toddled after her brother, played hide and seek and tag, fought and rolled in the grass, played cricket and swum in the creek. Today it had all been so different. It had changed suddenly, a little scarily. The boys had chased her, her mother had confided in her. Kay knew then herself that she had grown up. She would never feel quite like a child again.

CHAPTER NINE

'Christ, not again.'

Charles Redfield stood at the gate of the field. It was empty. The cattle rustlers had pulled down the hedge to make it look as if the cattle had forced their way through. The prize Aberdeen Angus herd had gone.

Frederick bent over the earth. He squatted down and touched the disguised tyre tracks, the mud churned on the ditch alongside the lane. 'Poachers. I wish we could prove who they are.' He looked down the empty lane as if hoping to see evidence.

'The rewards don't seem to be making any difference, do they?' Charles looked across at his uncle. Frederick ran a hand over his chin. He was still a handsome man, lean, the dark sleepy blue eyes crinkled now as he pondered the problem.

'No,' he answered. 'Don't suppose they will either. Wouldn't be worth it for any local to give the game away. The rustlers'll be locals themselves, I don't doubt. Well,' he looked up into the grey morning sky, 'I'll be cancelling my plans now for the Brigadiere.'

'What?'

'I was going to ship the cattle by freight over to Ireland and Europe. Going to use one of the new Bennett planes. The Brigadiere. It's a modified jet trainer they've converted,' he explained. 'Very useful.'

'Does Father know about this?'

'No.' Frederick gave him a level look. He folded his arms loosely and planted his feet squarely on the stubby grass. 'I decided a while ago to make my own decisions regarding the farm. Round about the time you decided to change your profession,' he said drily. 'Otherwise I would not be helping you with your own farm. Rupert's interests have never included farming. Obviously he leaves estate decisions to me. I decided that the Bennett operation was a good one,' he said, looking down first at the toe of his boot and then up towards the lane.

'They've been carrying bloodstock in their converted aircraft for other farms. They seem to turn a profit. And our breeding bulls are, or were,' he added, looking back to Charles, 'the best around here.'

'I see.' He followed his uncle as he went through the gate, and shut it behind them. 'Well, what do we do now?'

'Plenty to do this morning. Joe's coming over to your place with the seed drill once he's finished up there.' He tipped his head in the direction of the puttering tractor. 'Might as well get down to your dairy now. I'll give you a hand with the milking, then we'll go down into the village, ask a few questions, but I don't think we'll get anywhere.'

He walked ahead up the lane. Charles fell in beside him.

'How's everything up at the Manor?' He pushed his hands deep into the pockets of his jacket.

'Much the same,' the older man replied. 'Alexander's doing well at Redfield's. Moving up the ladder. Doesn't come here at all in termtime, except when Rupert summons him for something or other,' he added in an aside. 'Only appears when David's here, and then not that often. But then you'll know that from the lad himself.'

'Yes.' Charles shook his head. 'I'm afraid I do. No woman on the horizon then?'

It was Frederick who shook his head this time. 'No. But then you and I both know that's unlikely.' He glanced meaningfully at his nephew. It was fairly common knowledge that Alexander was another way inclined, or had been at one time. It was a fairly good bet also that he had seen a profitable marriage in Verity Rees-Hulbert. Rupert had talked about a merger with the wealthy Rees-Hulbert bank for some time before Alexander's courtship of the only child of the chairman's only son. Verity was an obvious choice. Cut from the same cloth as his grandfather, Frederick thought, Alexander had one eye on the main chance. He, like everyone else, had no idea of the real circumstances of the marriage.

Charles gave a wry smile, and chewed his lip. 'True,' he said drily. 'I'm glad David doesn't realise it. It's bad enough having an absentee father without all the other as well. How about Jessamy?'

Frederick frowned. 'Jessamy seems absolutely uninterested in anything and everything. It's a crying shame. You remember how beautiful she used to be.' He looked upon a lovely memory in his mind, his eyes warming. 'She was so lovely, that girl. You remember the day she got married?' His dark blue eyes were soft and smiling as he looked at the younger man.

'Yes, I do. I always thought my sister was more beautiful than any girl I'd ever seen, except perhaps, Melanie Haslett. They were similar.'

'Yes,' the older man said it more slowly. 'Indeed they were.'

There were too many memories, far too many, for both men. A silence fell between them as they paced over the brow of the hill and down the lane the other side, turning onto the track that led through to the Home Farm fields.

Charles knew all too well his sister Jessamy's problem. And his uncle's. He stole a look at him, wondering if the man thought of the past right now. He certainly was quiet all of a sudden. It would have been the perfect moment for them to talk about it all, alone out here in the early morning with no one to listen or disturb them, but it had to come from Frederick. He was privy to the knowledge simply through curiosity and not through a confidence. He'd read it all in David Biddy's notes when he had taken on the partnership in the village medical practice, quite against David Biddy's dictates. He had gained unlawful knowledge of his own family and of the Bennetts, and made his own conclusions.

He remembered that night now, the breeze touching his face as they came out into the open field. It spun up fresh and sweet from the valley and the river beyond. This was his land now. Then he had been young and eager and inquisitive, the bottle of brandy by his side, the goose-neck lamp bright over the accumulated papers. He remembered the glow of the mahogany desk in the pool of light, the worn leather, his hands tightening on the pages as he had read. That night was as clear to him in smell as in sense and sound: the warmth of the lamp on the back of his hand, the sharpness of Mrs Biggs' lavender polish, the light crackle of paper as he read on. And on, the sounds in the room so loud, but strangely he had not heard the return of David's car, so that he had been caught heart pounding, palms damp, as he slammed papers back into filing cabinets, twisted the key and hid it before David's amiable old face and crumpled figure appeared in the doorway, his hand reaching out for the brandy flask to drink a late night cup with a familiarity born of shared understanding and exhaustion.

86

Biddy had said he would make a fine young doctor, once the village had taken to him. Under the older man's firm and fond tuition he had done just that, until his fatal mistake. Now the knowledge sat with him, as uncomfortably as any eavesdropper. He knew about the blood tie with the Bennetts; knew, as the man did himself, what Max Bennett was to him; knew every time he looked into those Redfield-blue eyes, which he himself, by some strange fate, had not inherited. He knew too, what plagued his own sister, Jessamy. Was he the only one party to the full story? It was a heavy load to carry, one that he would like to have shared with his uncle, Frederick. But it was not to be.

'You going to the Cunninghams' ball next week?' The innocuous question broke into Charles's conscious. They were not the words he had hoped to hear, though in his heart he had known Frederick would never discuss it. He was of a generation that kept feelings a very private matter. He fell in with the conversation and glossed over his memories.

'No. Not my sort of thing. Not yours either, is it?'

'Not really! Rupert's going. Asked me to go along. Try to persuade Jessamy, I think.'

'Yes, that'd be good.'

They walked down the slope towards the out-buildings to the side of the farm. It was laid out in the valley. As he always did on coming home, Charles admired the rich russet brick, the eaves painted a dark emerald green against the tiled roof, faded now by the sun of the years to a sharp terracotta red. Above, the sky was a cerulean blue, unpatched by cloud, the trees around the dwelling a deep olive green, and the grass on the lawn softly freckled with daisies. The countryside was still, the early sun catching the blond tail of Leah's pony in the field alongside the house. Though Sarah's daughter from her first marriage hardly came home these days, preferring to spend time with a circle of young friends in London, when she did return she liked to know that Brandy still remembered her. So he remained a fixture, munching contentedly on the grass.

Beyond lay the barn, and the dairy. As they clumped down the hill together, he could smell the slight tinge of creosote on the air from the wood he had treated the day before. The tiled roof was thick with green lichen. Eventually it would pull down the tiles. It needed repairing. It all took money, money which he didn't have. His father had cut him off without a penny after his 'demise'. Charles sighed inwardly as he opened the gate and they went through into the concrete yard.

'You're staying for breakfast, I take it.'

'Love to. How's Sarah?'

'Marvellous,' replied Charles, his smile saying it all for him. 'I'm a lucky man.' But a small frown was in his eyes as he entered the dairy ahead of Frederick. He thought of her visit yesterday to the doctor. They were trying so hard still; at thirty-nine there was no reason why she should not conceive. Some people popped them out like peas. Why couldn't they . . . ? And now the news that they wanted to run tests on him.

Frederick, entering the cool dark of the dairy behind him, saw the quick frown and thought he understood the reason. He knew they had been trying for a child for over ten years, a brother or sister for Sarah's little girl, Leah, would have been a wonderful addition to their perfect marriage. They were a splendid couple, his nephew a man he was extremely proud to know, upright and decent, and now married to a woman just as fine who had proved her strength by standing beside him throughout that awful court case. And that strength had become love for both of them. They deserved so much the happiness of a child, but life was strange. Charles had been right about his own thoughts; as they had walked down over the fields Frederick had been reflecting sorrowfully on his own life. Charles's own mother, dead now these many years from a stroke, had been the spiritual love of his youth, never consummated. Rupert had seen to that, taking her under his physical spell as he had done with so many women. It was only in later years that he had discovered the lady was not deserving of such gallant devotion. She had wrested his inheritance from him by playing on his love for her, just as surely as if she had stolen it outright.

There had been only two women who had borne his physical love, much as for Charles there had been first Melanie Haslett who eventually married Max Bennett; she had been the love of his loins but never possessed, and then there had been Sarah, a gentler subtler more sensual love, one that had become companionship and friendship, the best kind. Katherine Haslett had been that to Frederick: wife of a local landowner, Sir Henry; a dark and sensual woman, and his mistress and his friend for nearly thirty years, and the other . . . the one that had obsessed him . . . that was a different story. Only once, and in such bizarre circumstances.

The spectre rose to haunt him time and time again: that lovely oval face so snow-white against the tumbling black hair, the green underwater eyes that had dragged him into their depths as she writhed beneath his brother in the sunlit glade. She had not cried out, but her eyes called to him and he had found himself dismounting from his horse, walking forward as his brother dressed himself . . . to save her . . . ? He had not. She had not moved, just lain there and he had misunderstood the message in her eyes, but not his own. He had wanted her, more than anything in his life. It was a feeling of the deepest, most compelling desire, perhaps even love, and all else had been thrown aside as he laid himself down over her . . . and she had not stopped him.

He shook his head now as he stood and waited for Charles, in conversation now with Ken, the young lad who was hand-milking the herd for him. He tried to rid himself of the vision of her, so technicolour now from repetition. He had not realised then, as he did when the mists of passion had cleared, that she had been too terrified to move. He had raped her just as surely as had his brother. He was just as guilty. Within months he had set eyes on the eligible Caroline Lancing and transferred the guilt into a lifetime of devoted love to his brother's wife, a woman totally unattainable. The three of them drifted in his mind's eye now. Not all so different in appearance, but wholly different as women. Caroline Redfield, alcoholic, and fragile as bone china; Katherine Haslett, earthy and warm as the autumn leaves in which they had first made their bed; Dickie Bennett, strong and sensual as a sultry midsummer's day.

His emotions filled his eyes. He had never married, circum-stance had judged it that way. He never would now; he had loved and been loved, but the final bond of marriage and children had eluded him. It was why he felt so compassionate towards his nephew. He too, would have been the perfect family man, but life was never what you expected.

CHAPTER TEN

July, 1961

'The strike could not have come at a worse time, frankly. It's our first venture into a new realm and one which I had wished to see pay off handsomely.'

The strike was imminent, the men angling for more pay, whilst others in the work force abiding by union rules stood around on full pay with nothing to do. 'It's union rules, I'm afraid,' she said.

Max threw down his pen and folded his arms. He stretched out his damaged right leg and flexed it, feeling the shoot of pain in his hip.

'Union rules,' he went on, not looking at his mother. 'Pity we didn't take a leaf out of Coastline's book.' Except for the pilots' association, Coastline had no unions to spoil the alacrity of its service: mechanics frequently dropped their wrenches to help move customers' baggage out to the waiting-room. Such things counted. The nature of air transport was changing and the new travellers noticed such easy cooperation with approval.

Dickie sat quietly across the board-room table from her son. She knew his physical pain was adding to his irritation. 'This is not America,' she said.

'No, more's the pity. It says something about the British mentality though, doesn't it . . . ?'

Max's initiation into business had been the American way, where all were equal.

'You should have known better, Max.'

'Oh, hell,' he said, rubbing his thigh and looking immediately to her. 'I cannot believe that my getting down on the shop floor to help out at a moment of crisis could have blown up into this catastrophe. It's simply the British inertia. None of them want to work.'

No one was allowed to cross the line and lend a hand to another and Max, management and therefore elitist, had stepped in to help out at a moment of crisis as the other workers had looked on. A row had erupted and Max had furiously sacked the man who should have been there that day and was subsequently found sleeping at home. Max had thrown aside rules and got down on the shop floor to work on one of the engines. The truth was that he had enjoyed it, that fact only making him angrier than ever. Max was a physical man and missed manual involvement at management level. Now the men were threatening a walkout.

'Well, what do you suggest,' asked Dickie, watching the blue anger burn in his eyes, the dark brows knotted in thought. Her eyes caught those of Bill across the table from her. So far he had said little, just listening as was his way.

'I think we should take drastic measures.' Max's glance swept to both of them.

'Such as?'

'Shut down the factory and show the men what it would be like to be out of work.'

'I don't agree.' Bill leaned forward. He had never wanted them to stretch themselves this far financially anyway. 'We had little personal knowledge of this area, construction, engineering, shipping, etcetera before we took it on. Bramway is a new scope for us, their ways ways we don't know yet, men new to us and us to them. You stepped out of line, Max. Should have trod more gentle.' He patted the air to emphasise his point.

Max opened his hands wide.

'Sure,' went on Bill. 'I understand why you did it, and with our own guys of course there wouldn't have been any trouble, but we don't know this foreman, do we . . . He's the one we've got to sit down with, the one who's stirring it up for us. And then,' his forehead creased as he sat back. 'The men in all the other companies in the group have already threatened to go on a sympathetic strike of their own, should we not reinstate this man *and* up their wages . . .'

Max's hands rested on the table. 'That would mean a serious breakdown in our companies right across the board, including Bennett Air.' A spiral of sunlight caught the dust in the air, flooding the surface of the table between them as the clouds drifted in the noonday sky. 'We simply cannot afford that right now,' he said. 'We're just breaking through with our expansion plans and linking up good routes with the USA. Competition are hot on our tail. We've stepped ahead with our DC-8s and 707s; its given us our financial clout. We can't lose that lead.'

'We have to work this one out with him somehow then,' said Dickie.

'What do you suggest?' Max looked at her. 'Sit down with the bastard. Reason with him? He doesn't know the meaning of the word.' He tapped his pencil gently against the mahogany surface, his eyes now on the pool of sunshine.

'We have to.'

Max shook his head, the dark face autocratic. 'Force is better than reason here. You haven't dealt with the man, Mother. I have. He's after our blood.' He felt it, knew somehow the man wanted trouble. He was convinced of it. 'No amount of reason in the world will stop him now he's tasted power. The men are right behind him too.' He pursed his lips. 'Pity they're not our men, as you say, Bill.'

Dickie raised her eyebrows, her voice dry. 'Well, it's irrelevant. Our man or theirs, they're all going to stand together now. It's the union rule, whether we like it or not. We're going to have to sit down and work it out over the table.'

'Do you want to set up a meeting with him?'

'I think so, yes.'

Max rubbed at his mouth. 'All right, but I'm running out of patience. Let's set it up for next Tuesday, that'll give me time to collect any information I might need, make sure all the board members are available and for you to prepare yourself for the fight ahead.' He raised an eyebrow, his eyes lit with the faintest of amused smiles. His mother's power of persuasive battle was legendary. Dickie eyed him speculatively.

'We don't need all the board members, Max. I can handle this man alone if needs be. You never know, we may formulate an understanding quite easily.'

'You know that's not true.' He stood up, straightening his tie. I need to be there at least. For whatever reason, Mick Davie is after our blood personally. I'm sure he'd like to wipe our noses in it across our boardroom table . . .'

The meeting had broken up. Dickie returned to her office and sat in the high swivel armchair behind her desk. She moved it gently beneath her, a thought sticking in her head. Was it possible they had been led into this deliberately? Bramway's was sound, she knew that, had had it thoroughly investigated, but what of its employees? She was a woman who had lived by her guts and wits and instinct. They told her something was wrong. Max had felt it too. She stretched across her tooled leather desk, picked up the telephone and asked her secretary to get hold of a number. It was no good. Katherine had asked her to stop the fight, but Rupert simply would not give up. She was sure he had to be at the bottom of this. She was going to get someone on the inside to look out for them. If he was out to trip them up, she would find out.

David leaned down and pulled the farm gate shut behind them. He lifted the old iron latch and slid it home over the wooden post. Rupert waited for him, Warrior still dancing on his feet even after the long ride over the Berkshire hills. They had had a good day together. He held the bay's head in as he turned on the spot.

'Whoa, boy, whoa!'

He was proud of his great-grandson. Flushed from the ride, his damp shoulders strong under the light aertex shirt, he was an extremely able youth. At nine years old, he had a good seat and loved horses, was able to make them do whatever he wanted for him, the sure sign of a fine horseman.

David grinned at his great-grandfather as he joined him. 'Looks like Warrior wants another day out, sir.'

Rupert wheeled the animal round. 'Never knows when to quit, that's all.' They fell in together with easy camaraderie, Rupert leaning down to pat the horse's sweating neck. His arms were muscled and strong, browned from the sun in his short-sleeved shirt. His head was bare, the yellow-white hair that crowned his head still thick, giving him the appearance of a younger man, despite the leathery dark skin. His blue eyes under white brows were as sharp as they had ever been. 'Did you have a bet on the two thirty?'

'Yes. I've got a sixpence each way treble on the first two horses coupled with Fine and Dandy.'

'Fine and Dandy!' Rupert retorted. 'You don't know your arse from your elbow!' David laughed; it was a familiar argument. 'He'll never make it. No, Early Bird's the one. Wait and see.'

Their hooves rang against the cobbles as they hit the stable yard, echoing around the buildings. 'I'll lay you a bet on who's right then,' countered David.

'Another sixpence?'

'You're on!'

They leaned across and shook hands on it. Rupert roared

with laughter. He enjoyed himself immensely with the boy. 'We'll go in and watch when we've rubbed these two down. Enjoying the farm are you, David?'

'Yes, sir.' David reined in. 'Uncle Frederick's been clueing me up on farming procedures. We're going to get the harvest in this afternoon. He said I could help if I wanted; I like the physical work.' He slid to the ground.

'Christ, not going to become a farmer, are you?'

'No, sir.' He stroked Danton's bony nose with affection. 'I'd like to run a racing stable.'

'*Would* you indeed!' Rupert's voice was tinged with admiration. David certainly had a way with horses, the inner strength that both animals and humans respected, and the intelligence to do well in his own business. 'Well,' he said. 'Keep on as you are and you may well get your wish!' He dropped to the ground, checked his watch. 'Nearly time for that race. Let's get these fellows rubbed down and out in the field. Hello, Frederick, come to get your helper?'

'No. Something's happened.' He came quickly across to them. 'We've been waiting for you to get back.' Both faces turned towards him. 'It's Jessamy, Rupert. She's very ill. I think you'd both better come inside.'

The shock of Jessamy's sudden illness the previous afternoon had affected the family deeply. All except Rupert: he had other things on his mind. Now, in the stillness of the early morning as the family lay sleeping, Rupert put down the telephone in his study with a smile on his face. He leaned his elbows on the desk, his blue eyes distant with pleasure, and rubbed briefly at his chin with his fingers. Mick Davie had done his job well. The Bennetts were worried now – they had discovered there was no way out, no negotiation. Mick had them blocked at every turn, his men behind him. They had even called him into a board meeting and tried to talk some reason into him. Mick had laughed over the telephone with the telling of it. Rupert had his measure: bullies could be bullied, it just depended on the pecking order. Mick's laugh, though nasty, had just the right trace of subservience in it. Rupert liked that, liked someone to know their place.

He leaned back in his chair, swivelling it to face out over the view of Foxhall's lawns, a tranquil scene. What was the next stage for the Bennetts? He gave a short laugh. Their new factory would be forced to close, commitments would be broken; they would have to borrow again to rebuild their loss. And he would be waiting. Did they think they could outwit him? Surely not. But then they did not know his need. They were new to the game, whereas it was in his blood; the need to win. The Redfields had been bankers for three generations, landowners long before that. What were they, the Bennetts? First-generation money, common workers before that – his workers. A cold look came into his eyes as he looked out across his land. Now they dared to try and match him, land for land and pound for pound. They did not know their place. He would teach them a salutary lesson. Upstarts.

The view over the river to the hills beyond was quite magnificent, and on this summer morning a soft light bathed the house and its surrounding stone terrace in a mellow air that seemed unique in its calm beauty. Foxhall Manor was a truly outstanding home, and it was this facet that he gave himself to for this moment, pleasured by the news that he had just received.

Foxhall Manor was of medieval design, mullioned, leaded windows set into stone and weathered wood, its lovely lines gracing the slope of land that led down to the banks of the Thames, framed to one side by a substantial beechwood and to the rest by acres of tranquil parkland beyond which a further three hundred acres were set to agriculture and cattle.

It had been Rupert himself, early in the twenties, who had sold off their village property in a bid for money, and in order to expand the guest and family living quarters of the house. And how had the family repaid him? He had given them everything, every opportunity, and they had thrown it away. His hands squeezed a little tighter on the arms of his chair. What a useless bunch. Jessamy, his daughter, had thrown away her beauty, wasted it, and he did not even know why. Since her marriage, and the children, the twins – Sabrine and Alexander – she just seemed to have given up. It could not have been the death of her husband John, a weak individual if ever there was one. No. Rupert shook his head. It had been something else. Jessamy's dark, blue-eyed beauty, the lovely pale skin, had been reputed in their social circle. And now look at her. Her greying fragility was nothing to do with the cancer that was now eating her away upstairs. A car drawing up outside caught his attention. He leaned forward . . . Charles. Both his children, how disappointing they had been to him. Charles, his son and heir, hardly worth consideration. He had shamed the family name with that episode in court, struck off the medical register for performing an illegal abortion. What a fool, a humanitarian fool. And then he had had to compound it by marrying not only a divorcee, but a Jewish one to boot. His children had never understood, though he had tried to impart it to them – blood was everything, name was everything – let no man take it from you. He himself had been married as society had decreed he should, to Caroline, the third daughter of the Earl of Lancing, owner then of Longbarrow. And there was the abiding hate in him. Longbarrow should rightfully have been his. He had meant it to be. Old man Lancing knew that, and had sold it right under his nose to that woman – a house quite as beautiful as Foxhall, quite as grand, though of a more graceful line. It presided over the valley below it, and the river and the meadows around in much the same way as the house in which he now sat. There were only two things in life that mattered to Rupert: inheritance and power. That woman had nearly cost him both. And now she presumed to take more. Well, let her see herself wriggle her way out of the strike that was now crippling them. Rupert gave a harsh laugh and swung back around in his chair, his hands still pressed to the curved wooden arms.

A woman whom he had taken in a forest one brief October morning. To him, it had meant nothing, but she had affected his life adversely ever since. He still could not believe that his own father, Alexander, would disinherit him for something so trivial as a silly misdemeanour. His father had seen it differently. It had only been Caroline's cooperation and his own sleight of hand that had changed all that, and Frederick his brother coughing up willingly all that was his anyway by right. Still, the brief moment when he had faced the loss of everything that meant anything to him, Foxhall, had had its effect on him, a massive impact. It had driven him to accumulate as much money as he could, and equally he had never forgiven the source of his father's anger.

He heard the front door slam in the distance and the sound of his son's footsteps cross the hall and climb the stairs up to Jessamy's room. Charles had not bothered to come in and greet him; there was still too much antagonism between them. It had only been Frederick's intervention and Jessamy's request that her brother come home to be with her now, plus of course

Charles's surprisingly strong stance on the issue, that had forced him to allow the return of his son – and his wife – at this time. So be it. He was not concerned any more, one way or the other. What was far more pressing was the other matter. There was still that thorn in his side. He heard the rain start to patter on the flagstones outside and turned to watch. He would not rest until he had pulled it out.

CHAPTER ELEVEN

The rain poured down outside with the sound of hot fat. Charles walked to the window. The room was humid and quiet. The net curtains lifted with the breeze.

'Frightful weather,' he said. 'It's going to flatten all the crops. Thank God we got the harvest in early. One thing that is predictable in this country is that the weather is not.'

He stared out at the teeming rain. A river ran down the gulley into the guttering beyond Jessamy's window, and drummed onto the roof of an outhouse below.

'Charles?'

He turned. 'Yes?'

She was sitting up against her pillows staring at him. The defeat had gone out of her eyes and she seemed almost well again, though her face was sunken, painfully thin, and her skin a stretched yellow-white. Her dark blue eyes looked huge.

'I've got something I must tell you. Please, would you come here?'

He went across and sat down, waiting.

She pulled at the white patterned bedspread. 'Charles, I've never told anyone this. It's almost like a confession.' Her laugh was hollow. 'You won't judge me harshly, I know. Please, will you listen?'

'Of course. Tell me.'

'It's about my wedding day. You see, just before my marriage to John, there was someone, someone . . .' She hesitated, the admission dreadfully painful, harder to put into words than she had imagined, especially to the brother whom she had loved so dearly. 'I loved someone,' she said. 'And that day I . . . I knew, I just knew somehow I had to . . . have him . . .' her voice trailed, 'and so I,' she sighed heavily, '. . . so I got dressed and ran from the house, out to the fields. He was there.' She halted, her face taking on a glow of memory, a dreadful sadness mingled with it. She did not go on, her mouth staying open as if in wonder.

'Jessamy darling, if it's about Max Bennett, I already know.' He covered her paper-thin hands with his own; he had to save her this agony.

Jessamy was startled. 'But, how could you? I told no one!'

Charles drew in a breath. He held fast to her hand. 'You remember I worked for David Biddy. One night I opened the files on our family. Perhaps it was very wrong of me but there were things I had to find out. Your file was in there, sweetheart. I read it all,' he said gently. 'I know the full truth of what happened.'

Jessamy let out a sigh of relief, her eyes brilliant as they rested on his. 'And you don't judge me? You understand everything?'

'Yes.'

Her huge eyes filled with tears. 'Oh, Charles, it's been such a strain not telling them . . .'

'It's all right,' he said softly. 'Nobody needs to know, Jess. There's no need to unburden yourself any more unless you want to. Save your strength. I know the whole story from start to finish. There's no need to belabour yourself. It wasn't so bad.'

'Oh yes, it was, it was! It was awful!' The guilt she had borne. Her own brother. The children could have been mad! She had given them that legacy . . . her own children. Hadn't she suffered over the years as she had looked for any sign of madness? Had she seen it? In her cold son, Alexander, and her crazy daughter, Sabrine? *Was* she crazy, or was she just temperamental? Now she had gone away and she, Jessamy, would never know what course that wildness in her would take. She was to blame. She was to blame for whatever Sabrine might do. That was why, when they had been young, very young, children, she had gone into the nursery, to Sabrine's cot, and seen those deep eyes staring up at her making her all too aware of her guilt. She had lifted the child's pillow, grasping it in her hands, blotting out that gaze, and . . . and . . .

She saw the scene again. A sob escaped her throat.

'Oh God!' She closed her eyes. 'What an awful woman I am. What an awful mother I've been! Will she ever forgive me?'

'Darling.' Charles put his arms around her and held her close. 'Of *course* she'll forgive you, it's not so awful at all, quite understandable. I know and I forgive you.'

'You know it all?' she murmured against his chest. '. . . and you forgive me? Charles?' she said, her voice soft with meaning. '. . . do you think they'll be all right?'

'Yes, I do.' He stroked the back of her dark head. 'Of course I do.'

Jessamy let out a great sigh. He let her go and she rested back against the pillows. 'Then maybe,' she said slowly, her eyes on him again, calmer now. 'Just maybe, there's a hope for me in heaven. It's been a dreadful life, Charles, living a lie. But I did love him. I still do,' she added almost inaudibly, turning her face against the cool of her pillow. She was quiet for a moment as he held her hand. 'I'm grateful that you know everything, Charles,' she said at last, her voice more even. 'It makes it easier to ask you this.' She turned her face back to look at him. 'Will you do something for me?'

'Whatever I can.'

'Get Max Bennett to come here. I want to see him again before I die.'

He shook his head. 'I don't know if he'll come, Jess.'

'Just . . . please try.' She squeezed his hand. 'And Sabrine, try to get her to forgive me and come home. That's all I want. To see them both again before I die. To ask them to forgive me.'

He bent down to kiss her. 'I'll do what I can, but it won't be easy.'

Mick Davie saw him coming. He was in the midst of a group of men standing outside the huge factory doors when Max's car drove up. An ugly buzz ran through the crowd. Mick looked over and saw him, and his eyes hardened.

'No trouble, lads,' he said. 'So the mountain comes to Mohammed. And alone. No trouble,' he murmured again as a body of men surged forward. 'Bad press when the man's alone.'

There were over one hundred men picketing, men who had families, children to support. They had had a bad summer. They had listened to Mick Davie tell them to hold out for more pay, despite the offers they were getting. The man who had been sacked was in Mick's pocket; a wrecker, he refused to return to work without the demands of his union being met. It was now a far greater issue than that of the previous weeks. The men were in a dangerous mood.

Max did not hesitate. This man did not frighten him. They had heard the news that morning. Mick Davie was trying to close the yard. Suddenly, Max was more angry than he had been in years. All this they had tried to build, all their hard work, and now the weeks of gentle negotiation favoured by the board, but they were up against a wrecking bastard; he had known it from the start. He was tired of playing pussyfoot with this idiot. Max had got in behind the wheel of his car and driven straight down to the factory, all guns blazing, ready to do battle. A man like Mick Davie was a slug to be squashed under a stone. He had nothing to lose any more, ready to use his bare fists if needs be.

He hardly noticed the surge of men as he strode forward, the crowd of angry faces parting reluctantly, aware of the power of the man. Ahead of him, Mick Davie stood on the steps of the building. He was a burly man with sharp eyes, fat cheeks, a thin turned-down mouth and huge shoulders hunched over, his hands enormous and a protruding beer gut. His dark hair was carefully combed low down over his forehead, and his eyebrows raised quizzically as if in permanent surprise. He was young, ambitious and not about to let them off the hook. He was a man who boasted frequently about his industrial relations prowess.

In the first week of the strike the craftsmen had voted to return to work, but Davie and his stewards had refused to obey national union orders to call off the walkout until their member had been reinstated. Then there had been the pay settlement. He had heard one or two of the men grumbling, wanting to get back to work, but he had squashed them down with a ring of louder voices, hired voices.

He took a step down and onto the ground to face Max.

'Call it off, Davie.'

'Well now, Mr Bennett. I don't remember calling a meeting . . .'

'There was no meeting. I've come to talk some sense into you, the way I know. The way you understand . . .'

Mick Davie saw the hands fisted at his sides, the look in his eyes. He was safe here on his territory. The man was a fool, playing right into his hands. The press would love it.

'I don't think I do understand. I reckon I'm doing a good job for my workers.'

'You want trouble, don't you, Davie . . .'

'There'll certainly be trouble unless we get a pay settlement,' he warned. 'Any further conflict could cost you orders worth hundreds of thousands of pounds, Mr Bennett, so I should watch your mouth if I were you. You know what we want, and it stands. Or you fall . . . !'

Max's piercing eyes burned him through. Behind their foreman's bulk his supporters watched silently. 'A fifteen per cent pay demand is ridiculous,' said Max. 'It'd break us. We've offered you a pay rise of eight per cent per man. You're a wrecker, Davie, an activist. You want us to fail just to prove some evil plan of your own. Now what is it you're up to? Just plain power or something else . . . ?'

Davie's greasy eyes narrowed. 'Fighting talk, Mr Bennett. And I'm not the man to cross.' He was annoyed at the suggestion that he was a wrecker, despite the threat to more than a thousand jobs. He was an ambitious man, who hoped to become a national union figure; here in the Bramway engineering yard he would prove his leadership. He jagged a finger at Max's face. 'Listen here. The leadership of my union are right-wingers. That's why I turned down the rise. It's the most undemocratic union in Britain, but I'm thinking about my men . . .'

'You're thinking about yourself.' Max stood his ground, his shoulders squared. 'A fresh strike would undoubtedly sound the death knell of this factory. Is that what you want, despite our excellent pay offers to you? Is that what you want?' he shouted, throwing his arm wide to include the men standing around them. 'You've got families. Some of you know me, you know we've always been fair to you. Good conditions, good wages, are you going to listen to him . . . or us . . . for let me tell you,' he said in a more deadly voice, his eyes drilling into them all. 'Listen to him and you'll go down with him, and he'll move on, leaving you with what . . . ?' His eyes swept the crowd. 'Nothing, that's what . . . and I'm tired of negotiating with your bully boy. I intend to do what I wanted to do with him in the beginning. Yes, I'll play your game, Davie,' he said. 'Go ahead, close the factory. Our last offer was your only offer. If that's what you want to do to these men, go ahead and do it. They'll lose, and you'll gain . . . whatever it is that you're after . . .'

He turned once more to look at the men. 'Now. My offer is a good one, in your hearts you'll know that. I'm sure you all want to get back to work. So do it. Disregard this man, he wants to wreck this yard . . .'

''Ere, now you watch it, son . . .'

Max's voice was cool against the bluster of the man. 'Don't

let him do it . . .' He turned on his heel and left them standing. He had seen Bob Lovelock's face in the crowd, caught his eye. It was up to him now; he was their only hope. They had about a week left before they ran out of time.

CHAPTER TWELVE

Bob Lovelock leaned against the public bar of the Jolly Waterman. Dilys was polishing glasses. She stretched up to fit them back on the rack above the bar and saw him watching her. She gave him a wink.

'What's yours going to be, luv?'

She laid her hands on the bar and smiled at him.

Bob Lovelock came back to the present and saw the smile.

'Oh, whisky, straight please . . . make it a double.'

'Like that, is it!' she said, still flirting. She cast her eyes at him one last time before turning to push the glass up under the nozzle of Johnnie Walker.

Bob stood up straight again and briefly looked around him. Normally, he might have given the odd quip back to her. She was pretty enough in a clichéd busty barmaid way, but he had not been looking at her tonight, merely through her. There was a lot on his mind, a lot that worried him. The factory for one, the Bennetts for another. Dickie had called him in when it had first all broken out down at the yard, asked him to help if he could. He would have. He was primarily a loyal man, despite now being a union man. He had to stay out with his mates, but he owed her and Max first, most of all Max. After what he had done.

The drink came across the bar to him, and this time he missed her smile completely as he counted out the change. Dilys got the message and moved on to another customer at the far end of the bar, leaving Bob with his whisky. The image of little Lesley floated in his mind. That bastard Redfield. He took a deep swig of his whisky, clasped his hands and stared down at them propped against the polished wood.

'Bob . . .'

He turned his face up to the voice. Ted Collins stood beside him, swaying slightly on his feet. It was obvious he had already had one too many.

'Evening, Bob!' He grinned, the smile splitting his reddened face. It was already shiny with sweat, his eyes made a brighter blue by the bloodshot whites. His check shirt was open at the neck showing the thick red-brown neck, the sleeves rolled up to reveal the massive biceps. Ted was a thickset middle-aged family man, not usually a drinker, usually a good worker. He was one of the shop stewards at the factory.

Bob indicated the bar. 'Have a drink?' he said, wondering about the wisdom of it.

'Yeah . . .' Ted threw a matey arm around his shoulders. The big hand patted him. 'Same as you . . .' Bob lifted a hand to call Dilys. 'You're a good lad, Bob . . . good lad . . .' He fell into a quieter mood.

Bob nodded. 'Whisky, Dilys . . . double . . .'

The two seemed reflective. Ted took a deep breath, about to speak, then thought better of it. He stared at Dilys's straining fine cotton blouse as she reached up again. It was a warm muggy night; warm weather always made him randy. His eyes drank her in; though he had never been unfaithful to Mandy, he could look, couldn't he?

Dilys turned again. 'Thanks, darling,' he said.

'Where's it going to end, Ted?'

'What?' He was still smiling crookedly at a patently un-interested Dilys as Bob phrased the words. He turned towards the other man, lifting the glass. 'Cheers, mate . . .' He drank. 'Aah . . . Where's *what* going to end?'

'The strike, man. What do you think? What's going on?' Bob was angry. He wanted the work. The offer was fair, but it was being blocked for some reason. His divided loyalties were tearing him up, for two pins he'd walk out and find another job. Tilly was after him too, telling him to get off his arse and do something for Miss Bennett to help her out of the fix. He was losing money too.

'Oh, yeah . . .' Ted stared off into the middle distance. A pall of depression seemed to settle on his heavy shoulders. 'It's a mess, son, a real mess. Wish I wasn't any part of it . . .'

'But you are . . . isn't there something you can do?'

'With Mick?' Ted gave a short barking laugh. 'He's got it in for them, hasn't he? What am *I* going to do about that?'

The back of Bob's neck prickled. This was it. He turned to Ted. 'Got it in for them?' he said slowly. 'In what way . . . ?'

Ted's bleary eyes snapped into consciousness again for just a moment. 'Shouldn't have said that . . .' he said, draining the glass. 'Forget what I said, Bob . . . want another?' He lifted a finger to call the barmaid back again. 'Two more,' he indicated.

Bob was like a gundog on the scent.

'Oh come on, Ted . . . you can talk to me.'

'You're in with them. I thought I heard . . .'

'You thought wrong. I'm a *union* man. Now tell me, what's up with Davie and the Bennetts? Maybe I can help . . . see things more clearly like, eh?' He drank his drink carefully and stared ahead, his manner casual, as if he didn't really care one way or the other. 'It's obviously bothering you, mate.'

'As a matter of fact, you're right.' Ted pulled his fresh drink towards him, his head dropping forward, so that his expression resembled a bloodhound. He sighed deeply. 'It's really got to me now, you know, and Mandy's giving me hell.'

'Tilly too,' Bob offered. Though obviously not for the same reason. He waited. The man was becoming drunk and maudlin.

'This afternoon,' he began. 'What happened at the factory. I thought Mick was going to hit him.'

'Mick wouldn't do that. He's far too smart.'

''s right. He is, too smart for his own good. For our good. Christ, man, you've gotta keep this between you and me, but . . .' and here he came closer, his sweaty face pressed up against Bob's, his blue eyes deeply troubled, darting around them. 'He's been paid to start trouble,' he whispered hoarsely. 'That's it. He got me in his bloody confidence . . . what can I do?' Bob held his breath. 'Too tempting to refuse, that was what,' he went on. 'A cut of the purse for my help. Helped him stir things up, didn't I?' He shook his head. 'I got family troubles, you see, Bob . . . Mandy . . .' He stopped there for a moment, his face twisting slightly as if he was about to break down. Bob felt acutely embarrassed but stopped himself doing anything, moving a muscle. He was about to hear. Ted seemed to tail off though.

'I'm sorry to hear that, Ted,' he prompted.

'Yeah . . .' He came back to the conversation. 'The money's helped, of course. Helped to . . . oh, I don't know, I feel such a bastard taking it,' he said all in a rush. 'The man's always been good to us, always been fair. I'm jammed in a corner, that I am. That's why I'm doing this . . .' He turned the glass in his hand, gave another cynical laugh. 'Ted, the family man . . . huh! That's what they think of me . . . and all around me me workmates are suffering, sat in their front rooms, me with 'em, sharing their supper 'cos I'm a mate and out of work too, and all the time . . .' He let it hang in the air. 'I've got a bad conscience, that I have.' He drank a deep draught of whisky. 'Dunno if I can stand much more . . .'

Bob pursed his lips, his brown eyes strong with an understanding of the situation. He was sharp now, now he knew the truth. No more wondering, just a few more prompts.

'You know they're going to lose the whole company, don't you?' he said.

Ted looked up, his eyes worried. 'Why?'

'Why do you think? Mick knows it. They need the money, just like us. They're not capitalists, Ted. He's one of us, Max Bennett. So's she. Started just like we did. You know he saved my kid.'

'He didn't . . .'

'He did. That's what done that limp to him. You seen it.' He took a drink, his memory casting itself back painfully. 'Risked his own life,' he said.

'And Mick said . . .' Now there was real anger there. His conscience could no longer stand it. That put the lid on it.

'Bennett's a good man, Bob. Offering a decent living. The others think so too. Mick Davie's an animal . . . bought by the highest bidder; that's all . . . I'd like to do something to him . . .' He breathed deeply again. 'But it's union, it's union that stops me. D'you understand that?'

He looked at Bob for help. Bob gave a sigh of his own, a deep frown creased between his eyes. He could give none. He already knew what he was going to do, his mind made up. There was no question of disloyalty to the man, though *he* had already been disloyal to them by taking the bribe and misdirecting them. One paid the penalty for such, thought Bob, watching the tortured mind of the shop steward. Ted was already paying his.

Just one more thing. 'I understand, Ted,' he said, picking up his glass to drain it, ready to go. 'Any idea who paid Mick?'

'No idea.' Ted was drifting in an unhappy world of his own. 'No idea at all. Didn't tell me that.'

Bob straightened. 'Well, it'll sort out. I've got to be going. I'll see you, Ted.'

'Don't want one for the road?'

'Uh-uh.' Bob shook his head. 'I promised Tilly . . .'

He touched him quickly on the shoulder and left the bar. As he reached the door, he saw that Ted had hardly moved. He would be doing him a favour too with what he was about to do. It was Sunday, but he knew Mrs Latimer would want to hear this news right away.

Dickie put down the telephone. She sat for a while at her desk, her fingers rubbing over her forehead, hardly seeing the room around her.

Bob had brought the news they had been waiting for. And just in time. A few more days and they would have been forced to close, with far-reaching consequences for the business, far the worst part of which would have been their vulnerability. *He* knew that, it was what he was aiming for. She could almost read the way his mind worked. She felt suddenly cold: he had almost succeeded.

Well, not now. She gathered herself again, knowing the solution as she reached out once more for the telephone and dialled. They themselves would bribe the foreman, tell him of their knowledge. He was a man who would play both sides. Once the strike was defused, they would expose him for what he was: they would not stay loyal to any promises they might make to him beforehand. There were no codes of decency with a man like that.

Nor with the man who had paid him in the first place to stir up trouble for them. For just the briefest of moments her mind dwelt on him, but her brief feeling of weakness was now overtaken by strength: she was never better than when she was fighting back. She would deal with Rupert Redfield. First, she had to save her company from the brink of defeat.

'Are you ready to go?' she asked him.

Max came down the stairs pulling himself into his charcoal-grey jacket. Dickie was already standing in the hall ready for him in a scarlet linen suit, a loose black bow at the throat of her white silk shirt.

'Ready,' he said in answer, shooting the cuffs of his suit. He held the front door open for her. 'Is everything prepared?'

She went through and out into the cool of the wet summer day. 'It's all set up,' she said. It had not worked out quite as they had expected; though perhaps this way was even better. He had not taken their bribe, but he had admitted everything and in quite a nasty fashion too, thinking himself to be alone with her.

'Good.' He put a hand to her back. 'Let's go then.'

The car was waiting at the foot of the steps. Max was driving to the Southampton factory where Mick Davie still held control of the striking work force.

He put the Rolls into gear and turned out of Longbarrow's drive.

The men were milling outside as they drove up. Once they were recognised the murmuring grew louder, some abusive, some angry. Max helped his mother from the car and lifted his hand to them.

'It's a Monday morning,' he said quietly to those closest. 'A Monday morning when you could have been working. Earning money. Now I've made a good offer to you all. Do you still think he's right?'

The murmurs rose and fell around him. Someone shook a fist. One or two looked thoughtful. The strike had gone on too long, Bennett's second offer had been a good one. Many had wanted to vote, call a ballot on going back to work, but the ballot idea had been thrown out.

'Let's go inside,' said Max. 'Come on, come on. Let us through.'

He held his mother's arm and went up the steps into the reception area. From here, another flight of iron steps led up to the suite of offices that lined the side of the huge engineering factory for aeroplane parts. At the top of the steps he paused and turned, looking down at the sea of faces.

'Where's Mick Davie?' he shouted.

'Here, Bennett.' The thickset man walked forward slowly into the centre of the men. He had been waiting beyond the half-finished and idle machinery, hidden by a clique of his hangers-on. Now he stood aggressively, the smile on his face. 'What can I do for you?'

Max did not answer for the moment. He leaned his hands on the rail, Dickie beside him, and looked out over the faces below. There seemed to be hundreds of them, waiting.

'Are you all here?'

'Yes, we're all here,' one shouted. His hands were pushed into his pockets. He came forward a pace and lifted his hand. 'Get on with it, Bennett, if you've anything to say.'

'All right . . . I'm going to say just this,' he began. 'Now, I'm aware that many of you would like to have returned to work after our second offer . . . I'm also aware,' he said against the grumbles that started again, 'that you felt unable to do so out of loyalty to your union. Fair enough, but in the case of this man, a very misplaced loyalty, I'm afraid . . . as you are about to find out . . .' He lifted his hand to their previously unseen partner at the other side of the factory. The heads turned to see Bob Lovelock standing there on a small platform. Bob lifted his hand. The men's murmurs began again only this time in curiosity.

Max looked all around him again. He spoke quietly. 'Bob, who you know, and I believe many of you like and respect, came down with me this weekend . . . to the factory. You are about to see why . . . all right, Bob, let her go . . .'

Bob turned to a switch on the wall. The static crackled from four loudspeakers set at the corners of the massive hall. Heads on the shop floor twisted and turned to see what was happening. The static popped and crackled and then was drowned out by the voice that every one to a man recognised.

'Yes, that's true, but what of it? Comes to the same thing in the end.'

'I just want to hear you say it.' Dickie's voice was lighter against the static.

The overbearing manner of the foreman came across on the loudspeakers.

'All right, seeing it's just you and me. I'll say it. You've got some good spies in my camp and I'd like to know who they are. But whoever they are they'll do you no good, Miss Bennett; you can't prove a thing . . .'

'Can't I?'

'No. Because it's just you and me, not even a third party. Maybe I did get a little . . . *remuneration* . . . yes!'

'How much *were* you paid to set up this strike, Mr Davie?'

'How *much* . . . ?' There was a round of rich laughter. 'Now that would be telling, wouldn't it, but . . . a substantial amount, very substantial! And the longer I spin it out, the more I get . . .' He couldn't help crowing.

'You know you're breaking the yard. Very soon we're going to have to close it. All your men are going to be without jobs. Don't you care, Mr Davie?'

'Why should I care?'

Ugly murmurs grew in the hall. The men turned and ringed

around him. Mick Davie stood in their midst, a changed man now, sweating, grey . . .

'It's *you* gotta care . . .' Another cosy laugh. 'Once this yard is closed, it's going to affect all your businesses right across the board. This ain't the only thing that's going to close, the whole of Bennett's is going to break up, and I know you've got a loan out on it. Yes, you see, I know a lot about you . . .'

'So you're trying to finish Bennett's, are you? You alone?'

'No.' His voice held a lazy sneer. 'Not me alone.'

'The man who's paying you.'

'That's right!'

'Who is he?'

'You should know that . . .'

A pause . . .

There was silence from the hall beneath as all listened. By Max's side Dickie stood erect and cool. Mick Davie's eyes glanced around for an exit. He was hemmed in on all sides.

The tape crackled and went on . . .

'Well, perhaps I do know, and you're not going to tell me, but that doesn't matter quite so much, as why. For money alone?'

'And other things.'

'Because it makes you look good to be in power . . . despite the fact that these men have loyally supported you, thinking you to be honest and right, these men who have wives and families . . . and they have put their trust in you . . . that means nothing . . . ?'

'Not so much, no.'

'How do you think they're going to feel when they find out?'

'They *never will*!'

In the hall, the murmured growls erupted into shouts. 'Get him . . . get the bastard . . .'

'No, wait,' shouted Max from above. 'Let it finish . . .'

Dickie's voice came over again. Down below, the men crowded their overseer in ugly mood.

'Just one last thing then. *Do* you think personally that our last offer was a good one?'

There was the sound of a chair scraping on the floor. The weight of the man's breath as he stood, his face closer to the mike.

'I thought the *first* offer was a good one! Good-day, Miss Bennett!'

Over the roars below, her voice came over steadily.

'Will you stop the strike, Mr Davie?'

'No. And you cannot prove a thing . . . !' Another laugh. A door slammed.

The tape crackled loudly, the hiss of recording suddenly gone. It was over.

'Lynch him . . . the BASTARD . . . !'

Angry faces thronged him. Mick Davie looked terrified as they clutched at his vest and arms.

'Stop! Stop a minute.'

Max lifted a hand. He turned towards his mother.

'You can go on home now. The driver'll take you.'

She did not like his mood.

'Max, they'll destroy him.'

'I'll take care of it. Go on.'

'No . . . I can't let you do this.' She looked first at her son, then at her husband. Both men were silent, rigid. 'Bill?'

Bill's normally gentle eyes were stern. They flicked over her. He shook his head. 'It's going to happen anyway, I can't stop it.' He saw her expression; he *wouldn't* stop it. Briefly, his eyes closed. Then he opened them again. 'I'll be here,' he said, as if by way of answer. 'I'll see you to the car.'

'I can go alone,' she said; not wasting more time she turned and walked swiftly down the stairs.

Max did not turn. The men watched her go. Mick stood, held by the crowd. There was terror on his face, amidst a desperate defiance. He had seen the exchange; though brief, he sensed its significance.

'You can't do anything to me,' he shouted up at them, throwing off the hands that held him with a curse.

'You bloody bastard . . . lay into him . . .' Voices punctuated the roar that pulsed around him again.

Max turned his back. 'Give them two minutes.'

Bill stayed him with his hand. 'Max, they'll kill him.'

Max's piercing blue eyes met his. They were full of cold anger. 'Not quite . . . and he'll talk.' He walked back into the office.

Behind him, Bill hesitated, then gave the nod to Bob Lovelock. At the edge of the throng, Bob stood back.

'OK,' he said. 'He's all yours.' He strode from the room and up the steps to join Max and Bill. Behind him, the pack crowded Mick with a jostle of shouts and jeers. Bill saw the man go down.

There was silence in the small glassed office until the two

minutes were up. Max signalled Bob with a look and a nod. He walked outside and shouted to the men to bring him up.

Mick stood in the doorway. He had a split lip, eyes that were already beginning to swell, his nose was smashed across his face and blood smeared from his nostrils. He lifted the back of his hand to his face, clutching at his ribs with his other arm.

Max showed neither compassion nor pleasure. 'Who was it?'

'Can't say.'

'OK, out you go.'

'No, wait . . .' Mick held up a hand. 'I'll tell you.' He drew a breath. 'It was Grandpa's messenger boy,' he said scathingly. 'Couldn't even do the job himself . . .' He looked down and spat.

Max regarded him coldly. '*Grandpa*? Let me hear you say the name, Davie.'

Mick eyed him back from under his brows. 'Redfield,' he growled. 'I'll be finished now with him . . .'

Max's eyes had grown bitter at the name. 'You're finished anyway,' he said. 'Get out.'

He listened to the man stumble down the steps. He stood from the desk, cast a meaningful glance at Bill and came around the edge of the desk to walk outside on to the platform. He came down the steps into the throng of men. Mick was nowhere to be seen. In the quiet a distant car motor started up, revved, and roared away out of the yard.

Max looked at all the faces. One of the men in the semi-circle around him raised his voice as if for all of them.

'A bastard, Mr Bennett . . . well rid of him . . .'

Max looked towards the man, unsmiling. 'You speak for everybody, do you?'

'Aye . . .' The assenting jumble of voices rose as the men shuffled, agreeing.

Max lifted his chin, silent a moment. 'You think the fault lies only with him,' he said. 'Look at yourselves . . .' The smiles of seconds ago fell away. Shame picked out the faces of the few. 'Now we know where your priorities lay,' he went on. 'You let a pig like that rule you for six weeks, despite what we offered . . .' He paused for a moment to let it sink in. 'You owe us,' he said, 'all of you. Bob, you're foreman.'

Without a further look he turned on his heel and walked out into the new sunshine. Bill was already standing there, looking out at the day. He fell into step beside the younger man, surprised by the change in his face as he left the men. Lines of tension, sadness, pain. The anger gone leaving him drained of it. 'A near thing,' he said. 'Let's get home.'

'Yes,' said Bill. And thought of Dickie.

She was waiting, as he had known she would be, in the peaceful serenity of their bedroom, not standing at the window as he had imagined she might be, but sitting at the small yew-wood writing desk in the alcove. She seemed busy, writing.

She put down her pen as he came into the room and shut the door, her eyes on him immediately. He knew then that her concentration had been a cover; she had been waiting for his return, unable to relax fully until he was there.

'What happened?'

He went across to her and stood a couple of yards away, looking down at her, his hands pushed into his pockets. His eyes held her face, looking up at him. He saw the same vulnerability there that he had seen in Max. These two were so alike.

'What we expected. Man got a bloody nose. Should have got more, in my opinion.' He raised an eyebrow. 'That's an end of it now. Company's back on course; Bob's in charge. Max gave the men a piece of his mind before we left. They needed it. I saw his face – thing that hurt him most was their disloyalty, but . . .' he shook his head matter-of-factly, 'they're union men. They do as they're told. That's the union rule . . .' He was about to turn.

Her eyes sharpened, changing with her emotion. 'Bob . . .' Her voice stopped him. 'Did he admit it . . . who it was?'

'Oh, yeah . . .' He gave a small laugh and turned back to her. 'He sure did.'

'Rupert Redfield,' she said, her voice lower.

'His grandson actually,' he said. 'Grandpa's messenger boy is what he called him. Alexander. He was sent to do the dirty work.'

'He wouldn't soil his hands with something so demeaning as this,' she said, understanding as she stared away into the middle distance.

'That's about the size of it. A real bastard, that one.' He came over and touched her gently, stroking her hair. 'Honey, you're gonna have to show this fella you mean business.'

She felt his familiar strength flow into her. She took his hand into hers as he laid it on her shoulder.

'Yes,' she said. 'Yes, I am, aren't I.'

CHAPTER THIRTEEN

Sabrine Hamblin wandered along the minstrels' gallery that overlooked the drawing-room at Foxhall. Down below a huge fire burned in the stone fireplace at the head of the room, despite the summer's day, for this vast room with its walls of stone two feet deep, held a chill even on the warmest of days. The girl that looked down into the room had a stunning Snow White beauty that seven years in the California sunshine had not changed at all. Her face still held the porcelain-white loveliness it always had, a deceptive calm in it that was only defeated by the challenge in her eyes. Wide, midnight-blue eyes that held a wilful, almost wild light, her dark eyebrows arching precociously above. Sabrine was extraordinary to look at, but headstrong and spoilt, used to being adored. Men fell in love with what they saw, and not the girl beneath. Sabrine had a cold heart, and there was only one person that mattered to her.

Her uncle Charles's request to come home to be with her mother had actually suited her plans at the time, and so she had come. Otherwise she would probably not have bothered. There was little between her and her mother; she hated her mother's listlessness which she saw as weakness. Sabrine gravitated to others as manipulative as herself, seeing them as a challenge – and that included her grandfather for whom she had a soft spot, though even that relationship had not stood in her way once Hollywood beckoned. In seven years there she had become a star, with Edward, her English actor husband, trailing in her wake. It was apt; she had never seen him as anything more than a stepping stone. She had found far more men out there in the sun to have fun with, the only trouble being that now Edward had found out. They had had a terrible row, just as the call home had come from Charles. And so she had come, for a little breathing space. And to let Edward miss her, apologise to *her*!

Of course, surprises never worked out the way you expected. She had arrived home unannounced, meaning to surprise them, and found the whole family at church. She had forgotten the ghastly Sunday ritual. She had heard from the butler that her mother alone was home, and sleeping. Sabrine had dismissed him and wandered upstairs, in no hurry to get to her mother, the apparent reason for her return. Jessamy could sleep all day for all she cared. Bored, she slid her hand along the banister watching as the maid came across the room towards the fire, kneeled down and started to sweep the ash into a dustpan. Unseen, Sabrine watched her for a moment, as she bustled back to plump up the cushions of the long sofas that framed the fireplace. Then she went on to flip a duster over her grandmother's grand piano, stopping to gaze out of the long, leaded windows that overlooked the lawns outside. It was odd to be such a silent spectator, but not unpleasant. Sabrine hoped she might do something she was not supposed to, giving her a voyeur's thrill, but the girl did not. After only a few seconds' concentrated viewing as if deep in a world of her own, she resumed her work with diligence, dusting and plumping like a robot.

Sabrine moved away, her fingers trailing off the bevelled carving of the banister and pushing aside the heavy green velvet curtain that led to the wing of bedrooms on the east side of the house. She pushed open the door of her mother's bedroom and went in.

It was silent, a window open to the day; the maids had already been in here to clean up whilst the family were out. A bird sang in a tree outside the window. A fresh breeze curled into the room. Jessamy lay in the bed, sleeping as if she were dead to the world.

Sabrine sighed, crossing first to the window to look out over the Italian garden below, and then back into the room. It was so quiet; deadly. After the excitement and colour she had experienced in LA, it was like another world here. And she had not seen Max Bennett yet. She recalled the last time she had been home, how she had stationed herself in the village coffee shop, certain that the beauty she possessed which had opened doors to anything she wanted would not be lost on him. And she wanted him, she had done ever since she was . . . well, about twenty and she had seen him catch her mother's eye in church. How they had looked at each other, and how she, Sabrine, had looked at him. He was the epitome of the handsome man; dashing, daring, a war hero, and even more – taboo in her household. It was perfect; titillating. To say that he had become an obsession for her in the intervening years would not be far off the truth. This time, *this time*, she thought with a glow of desire inside her that sparked in her dark blue eyes, she would get him. Some way, somehow! Her beauty was even more now than it had been before, and she was experienced, oh so experienced in bed. He would fall for her the way so many others had. The slow smile curved her lips upwards. Despite the diligence of her time in that damn little coffee shop, last time she had been unsuccessful. She had driven past the gates of Longbarrow, slowly through the village, past the church, but she had not seen his distinctive black Rolls-Royce anywhere, nor the dark head and powerful shoulders that had made her blood rush to her temples, and her skin tingle with want. Well, she would get all these boring reunion greetings over, then she would take herself off to the village. This time, she was not going back without tracking him down.

The smile of pleasure was still in her eyes as she sat down at her mother's dressing-table. The glass top was spotless, little on its surface of interest. A gilt triple mirror reflected the petulance in her face, the white angora sweater and pearl and diamond drop earrings; a present from Edward. There were two photographs in art deco silver frames, a glass tray containing some hair pins, a small pot of face powder and a used postage stamp. Sabrine picked up the photographs: Jessamy sat with the twins on her knee, dressed in their christening robes. There was no expression on her face, the black and white photograph faded a little, so that the three of them appeared slightly out of focus and unreal. The other smaller photograph was a soft brown sepia study of two angelic children sitting on the small stone pillars in front of the fish pond at the bottom of the Foxhall gardens. Jessamy and Charles held hands and smiled for the camera. She had been beautiful. Sabrine stared into her mother's early face for a moment.

She replaced the picture slowly, her eyes still on it and picked up the silver-backed hairbrush, pulling it slowly through her hair. Her hand reached down and pulled open the narrow middle drawer of the fruitwood dressing-table. The gilt handles clinked delicately. A lipstick rolled to the front of the drawer. Sabrine picked it up and unscrewed the cap. It was too dark for her, a deep plummy red. Sabrine liked pale pink. She dropped the lipstick back and pushed the drawer. It stuck. Sabrine wriggled it free, wondering at the obstruction. She bent down, put her hand into the back and pulled it. The drawer came free, as did the cache of make-up pushed to the back of the drawer.

Sabrine's interest was alight now. Her mother had never bothered with her appearance, and yet old photographs had shown her to be a beauty. This make-up was old. She never wore any nowadays. Sabrine put her hand in and touched some of it; creamy powders and soft rouges, pretty lipsticks. Sabrine felt into the back of the drawer for more. Her fingers found the edge of leather. Both hands reached in and pulled it forward. The jewellery box was locked. It did not take very much more time for Sabrine to find the key in the top right-hand drawer of the dressing-table. The bunch of tiny keys hanging on a hook inside the drawer were like a clue to Jessamy's secret life. Sabrine tried them one by one and the lid sprang open as she tried the fourth of many.

On the top blue-velvet tray lay Jessamy's extravagant jewellery collection. Sabrine was breathless. Her father, John, had been wealthy, she knew, but what she did not know was his generosity to her mother. These jewels were fabulous: a long diamond pin curved around two tiny brilliant feathers, a convex enamel brooch in an exquisite blue, studded with diamonds like stars in a night sky; an array of beautiful rings, one after the other, all of them worth a small fortune; gold-linked bracelets set with emeralds and rubies and diamonds, and perhaps the most beautiful of all, a necklace of diamonds and rubies. Sabrine drew it out slowly, gazing at it draped in her hands. She found the clasp and laid it around her neck, touched the jewels into place. They glittered like cold fire in the soft light of the room, Sabrine marvelling at the glow they gave her. What a find! What else was hidden in the compartment beneath?

She lifted the first tray and looked beneath, searching further. She was disappointed. There was no more jewellery in this deeper section, only a few pieces of paper, a sealed en-velope, the glue weakened with age. She lifted them out, looked and dropped them back in, her other hand lifting the tray to replace it. The pieces of paper separated, the edge of an old newspaper cutting showing a photograph and article.

Idly, Sabrine lifted it out. She unfolded the article. It was quite lengthy: 'War Hero Returns to Foxhall Green'.

Her heart quickened as her eyes did a scan and took in the content. The photograph was of Max Bennett. Eyes pained but strong, he stared out at her, his hand leaning on a crutch, his leg bandaged, and some sort of dressing on the side of his face. He looked piratical; dark and handsome in his Air Force uniform. The article praised him for his heroics.

Sabrine was hardly breathing now, her fingers tight on the edges of the paper. She held it before her, her eyes alight. What was this doing here, hidden by Jessamy? She stared out ahead over the rim of the winged gilt mirror and through the opened window. She remembered how upset her mother had been when she asked about Max Bennett, how her mother had in the end shown little opposition to her going to California, how she had forbidden her to talk about him. She had thought it was the 'feud'; everybody knew about that though not why it had all started; no one would discuss it. Now, she knew in her heart there was much, much more to it than that as far as her silent mother was concerned.

Her eyes lit on the badly glued envelope. It had been opened before and resealed; it would be again. She pulled it carefully open and pulled out the slip of paper inside.

The poem was very revealing and rather good. In four poignant verses Jessamy poured out the story of their love.

Sabrine had not known at all what she was going to find and it was shocking. She did not move as she read, and read again. Her mother was in love with Max Bennett: that much she had suspected. Not that they had made love, one day, one summer; her parents' wedding day.

Sabrine was still sitting there as her mother stirred in bed an hour later. Jessamy coughed and opened her eyes. Sabrine faced her in her own bedroom mirror. Her face was bright with anger.

Jessamy sat up in bed, against the pillows. She looked startled at the sight of her daughter in the mirror.

'Sabrine? I didn't know you were home.' She gave a faint smile, ready for their habitual embrace. 'Thank you for coming back, darling.'

The new kindness in her mother's voice sickened Sabrine. She stared at her.

'Why, whatever's the matter? You look as if you're ill, Sabrine.'

And then she saw the box in front of her, knew immediately that something was wrong. She pointed to the dressing-table.

'Whatever's that doing out?'

She had not looked at her daughter. Her thoughts were on the box, and its contents. She threw back the sheets, slowly slid her body round, an urgent strength returning to her. Sabrine screwed round in her seat.

'Is this what you're looking for?' She waved the photo in the air.

'Sabrine!' She stopped and stared. 'Where did you get that?'

'You know perfectly well.' She stood up and faced her mother.

'So this is your secret, is it!' she said. 'A secret passion for Max Bennett!'

'Sabrine. Give me that photograph.' She reached out.

'No. Not until I know more, mother.'

'I do not have to stand for this, Sabrine. Now give me that and get out of my room.'

Jessamy was on her feet. She came around the bed and advanced on her taller daughter, her hand out, her hair loose around her shoulders. Sabrine held the photo away, stronger, more agile, more determined. This was a moment she had never expected. Her mother was transformed in her anger, out of control. Their confrontation had come.

Sabrine taunted her. 'You may not have got him,' she said, 'But I'm going to. Do you hear that, mother. You can't keep me away now. I'm twenty-seven. I can do what I like. I'm going to have Max Bennett, married or not. I'll succeed where you failed . . .'

Jessamy raised her voice.

'Don't be a little whore, Sabrine. And a fool as well. Max Bennett is not for you. Leave him alone!'

'So you can pine over him some more? I know all about you. I read the clipping, your pathetic poem. You never stood a chance with a man like that. He'd have wanted a beautiful woman, *look* how you let yourself go all your life. Look at you!'

'Sabrine. For the last time. I forbid a liaison between you.' She held out her hand, palm flat. 'Give me the photograph.'

'What! You're jealous, that's all,' Sabrine shouted back defiantly. 'All right, have your photograph . . .' She threw it to the floor, torn in two. 'I'm going to have the man.'

Jessamy cried aloud and bent for the pieces, her nightdress a pool around her, holding them in her hands, her face white.

'You little fool . . .' She was standing slowly now. 'Not

beautiful? I was far more beautiful than you,' she said through gritted teeth, her eyes flashing. 'You're so vulgar and obvious. Half the men in the country wanted me,' she said. 'But I didn't want them.' She advanced on her daughter. 'You've asked for this, Sabrine, and now you're going to get it. He was my life, no, you listen . . .' She grabbed her arm with a feverish grip. 'I had Max Bennett . . . I was beautiful enough to entice him against his desires. I went out to find him in the fields.' Her nostrils flared as she breathed deeply, her eyes wild. 'He couldn't resist. He was beautiful too. He knew we were made for each other . . .'

Sabrine turned her head away.

'No . . . you listen! I've carried the burden through my life. Now it's ended, you can share this, Sabrine. *Max Bennett is your father. . .*'

Charles walked out onto the airfield at Bower Hill. He had been told by one of the ground engineers where to find Max Bennett. He rounded the corner of the wooden building and looked out over the open field. He shielded his eyes from the glare of the sun and saw him.

Max was standing by the nose of an old Lockheed Star-fighter, in conversation with a man in overalls, wiping his hands on a rag. They were in deep discussion and did not notice initially as Charles strode across the distance of grass towards them.

From about ten to fifteen yards away, Max suddenly noticed him. He dismissed the man in a moment and advanced a few steps towards Charles.

Charles slowed to a halt. He looked into the man's face, the blue eyes so strangely disconcerting, and felt that old twinge of recognition that he did whenever he came close to Max, but there was no responding interest in Max's eyes. Charles remembered the night of the fire. There had been some communication there then; he wondered if there would be now despite their differences.

'Can I have a moment of your time?'

Max said nothing.

'This is important, believe me,' he said, his voice quiet against the still summer air. 'Otherwise I would not have come.'

'I can believe that.'

'I'll come straight to the point then. My sister, Jessamy,' he said, wondering why he felt the need to explain who she was when the man knew so well, 'is dying of cancer. She has asked for you. I know the whole story, and I know why. There are no secrets between us. Will you come? It's her last request,' he finished.

The light in Max's eyes grew deeper as he spoke. His feelings towards Jessamy had haunted him for much of his life. Like any youth, he could not forget the initial penetration of his first woman. The smells, the colours, the air, they all came back to him now as if they were new, her body and her face looking at him, demanding that he love her.

He shook his head. The last thing he wanted to do was to see her. He did not want to go near Foxhall. It would serve no purpose. He would not do that to either of them. What was done was done. Also, the recent strike had hurt his family, still angered him. This man, despite his obvious lack of involvement, was still a Redfield. The thought showed in his eyes as he answered him.

'No,' he said, at last. 'I'm afraid not. You must know why.'

Charles, hurt by his sister's agony, was not feeling rational. 'You're a bastard,' he said slowly. 'Do you know that? A real bastard. The woman is dying, Max, and you have to resurrect some old and stupid grievance at a moment like this and throw it in her face . . .'

'I'm sorry.'

'You're *sorry*!' It seemed to antagonise him even more. 'I'd like to fight you, you bastard . . .'

He swung round suddenly, his fists up, shoulders squared, a powerful man protecting someone he loved, and took a step forward.

Max instinctively put up his hands and tried to parry the blow he thought was coming. Off-balance he stepped back quickly onto his bad leg. The hip gave way; he could not hold the position and stumbled, almost falling.

He righted himself quickly, but almost as quickly the fire had gone out of Charles. He saw what had happened and remembered the night of the fire, why he had limped since. He remembered the heroics of this very same man who now stood before him, unafraid.

He almost threw his hands to his sides.

'I'm not going to fight a cripple,' he said. His eyes burned with dislike. 'I hope in time you're ashamed of yourself.'

Charles felt the legacy of hate in him as he drove furiously all the way back to Foxhall. It was still there, embedded like a shaft of steel, as he climbed the stairs and approached her door. He could not avoid this; he knew she would be waiting.

He said nothing as he crossed the room towards her. She appeared to be sleeping, but as he approached her eyes came open.

The question was in her eyes. He shook his head, and saw the resignation settle over her features. She had lost them both; for good. First one, and now the other. She turned away to look out through the open window without a sound, and after a moment she closed her eyes again.

Now he knew she had given up completely.

CHAPTER FOURTEEN

Early August 1961

Rupert Redfield watched the funeral cortège leave the hearse, watched the men take the easy weight onto their shoulders. At the end of her life, Jessamy had been skin and bone, featherlight. The way she had given up, given in, made him angrier than anything she had ever done. He did not accept that the cancer that had riddled her bones should have killed her so early; Redfields had more fight than that.

He stood back from the path watching as the casket came towards him, out from under the trees at the edge of the village green and into the sunlight. It was a beautiful day, a perfect English summer's day; a soft breeze coming off the river. Cut down in the prime of life – he knew the vicar would say that. It was untrue. Her prime of life had been her wedding day, a day similar to this one. Early that morning in 1933 he had caught sight of her, gazing out over the fields of Foxhall, the radiance and wonder glowing in her transforming her beautiful face into something unreal. He had never seen such beauty, and had stepped back into the shadows of the landing upstairs just to keep his eyes on her. And now.

He took a deep breath, and flexed his shoulders, watching as the procession came slowly forward, the family members downcast in its wake. Despite his seventy-odd years, he still stood straighter than any of them. Damn fools; had they no pride. No need to slouch like that just because they were in mourning – it was the time to hold the head up, show strength. He made a sign of 'shoulders back' to Alexander, who accompanied his sister, Sabrine, immediately behind the coffin. Alexander caught his eye. Even from this distance the cold eyes looked strange and veiled, though his chin came up at the silent order. Goddamn little poof, thought Rupert. God, what have I bred. And Sabrine . . . beautiful, fabulous Sabrine, more beautiful even than her mother had been. She had the Lancing women's porcelain fragility, and the Redfields' grace. Yet, what had she done with it? She was cheap. Her beauty could have given her real power, the one thing Rupert admired, but instead she had abused it. He had heard of the drinking, the raucous temperamental scenes, the very public slanging matches she had with her husband, the men who she had slept with and who talked laughingly about her behind her back, Sabrine's sexual prowess legendary now. He heard it all from those who chose to report – out of 'friendship' – back to him. Friends – it was a way to rub his nose in it, to show he might be invincible, but that his family were not. How they let him down, what a poor show. Now, poor cuckolded stupid Edward had found out – the last to know, of course. Alexander thought he could curry favour by sneaking on the private conversations he had held with his sister. He was so wrong; Rupert held no respect for him at all, in fact the reverse, but he did not tell him so, because in fact Alexander was useful to him, someone who needed him and whom he could manipulate, as he had already proved. That a cold hate sat in the young man's eyes when he came to his grandfather to talk to him, was neither here nor there. He had nothing save his tittle-tattle to offer. Well, the one who held the power was the one in control, and Alexander would never have that power, he would see to that. Rupert knew how badly he wanted those shares that he dangled like a carrot above his grandson's head. The day he gave them to him would be the day Alexander gained his own strength. So he would never have them, but the promise was there, as long as he did what he was told, and he had done all right so far, but primarily it meant finding a way to the Bennetts, a way to destroy them. That brought the memory of his recent defeat.

No one would have guessed what it was that was on his mind as he stepped forward to take his place in the slow-moving procession, but it was not on the solemnity of the day. Mick Davie had come blubbering to him, his ugly face swollen and purpling, telling him what they had done to him. Rupert had listened, silent, and had then thrown him out, having first asked whether he had admitted their participation in the strike. The man had not wanted to admit it, but in that alone Rupert had read the truth. She knew. Thinking about it afterwards, it did not bother him, in fact it was the only aspect that pleased him. That her company was not now in ruins, nor in his hands, made him bilious. He had expected to ruin her. He had nearly succeeded. In time, he would. He had lost this round only.

He took his place alongside his son, Charles, hardly giving a glance his way. His son was too disappointing to him, with neither the grace and bearing of his family, nor their ideals. Alongside him, he saw the wife, pious Sarah, her blonde hair pulled back into a bun, her face veiled, giving him a sidelong look. She did not like him, he knew that, but it was irrelevant. Another thought had taken place in his head as he walked behind the erect figure of his granddaughter. She had not given him five minutes alone with her since her return. That was unusual. Even now, aware that he was behind her, she had not glanced at him at all, just stared straight ahead. In another, it might have been the overwhelming emotion of the day, but not her. He knew his Sabrine, rather too well in fact. Like recognised like. They had been very close, or at least until she had swanned off to Hollywood and cheapened herself in the process. There was something affecting her; he would find out what after the service perhaps.

For a moment, the sun caught the brass handles of the coffin, glinting as the trees above swayed and shifted in the breeze. Rupert remembered her beauty again. What a shame, what a goddamned waste. He gave himself to the memory of her as she was. The mournful music swelled out of the dark belly of the church as they crossed the stone flags into the cool shadows and out of the sunlight. It was more real now. He felt the weight of unhappiness that lay over all the faces around him as they slid into their pews, and wished they would all cheer up. It depressed him, and disconcertingly he suddenly felt a strong wave of loneliness rush through him. He turned away from the sea of faces sitting, settling – to break the feeling, and his eyes caught those of David.

The boy was waiting at the edge of the pew for him, hair brushed neatly, and wearing a new grey suit, the cool brown eyes concerned for him. He alone had noticed. Rupert felt an immediate warmth for the boy: he was so likeable, strong too. Here was a Redfield indeed that they could all be proud of. The thought was refreshing. But from the loins of that wet Alexander. How did he do it? He smiled to let the boy know he acknowledged his look, and went towards him, back down the aisle a pace; he did not need to sit in the front pew today. He would sit with someone he cared for.

David stood back to let his great-grandfather in ahead of him, and was rewarded with a pat on the head. Rupert eased himself in, determined not to show the strain the years were taking on him, and sat down heavily beside the stone pillar dissecting the third pew from the front. David came in beside him, and knelt.

Rupert looked down fondly on the back of the neat head. The service began.

The day had passed with interminable slowness; the lawyer taking his time to read the extensive will that Jessamy had left behind. Rupert stared thoughtfully into the depths of his brandy glass. Frederick had been talking to him for some time; he had hardly heard a word. The reading of Jessamy's will had been a surprise to them all. None more than her daughter, Sabrine. He raised an eyebrow in her direction, where she sat in a blue armchair by the fireside. She had been the recipient of one hundred thousand pounds, and all of her mother's jewellery. Jessamy had been worth far more than any of them knew.

'. . . did you hear what I said, Rupert?'

'No, sorry I . . . I was miles away. What was it, Frederick?'

Frederick studied the absorption in his brother's face and followed his glance over to Sabrine as he spoke.

'I said, Sabrine seems quite taken aback by all this, doesn't she?'

'Yes, well I don't think any of us realised just how much John took care of Jessamy's needs. He must have left her everything.' Sabrine placed the jewellery box on her knee and was staring at it.

Frederick frowned at Rupert. 'No . . . I don't mean the money, Rupert. I mean . . . losing her mother.'

Sabrine stood up, the box in the crook of her arm, and turned to walk silently from the room, looking at no one. It was most unlike her. She generally tried to win everybody before she left a room, never slipped out quietly.

'Rubbish,' said Rupert, putting down his brandy glass on the mantelpiece. 'Sabrine never gave a fig for Jessamy. The two of them simply did not hit it off, from the word 'go', that's all. Excuse me, Frederick.' And he brushed past his brother to follow Sabrine from the room. He caught up with her just outside the drawing-room door and heading for the stairs.

'Sabrine, wait!'

She had her hand on the newel post, her foot on the first step. She turned to the sound of his voice. She had not spoken at length to him since her return. Luckily, there had not been a moment. She remembered that scene with her mother. So much of this had been his fault. If not for him and his high-handed attitude their lives would have all been so different. She had not forgiven him. In many ways her judgement was as much against herself as him. They were too alike; the recognition had made it all the more painful and bitter.

'What do you want?'

He came up beside her. 'What is the matter with you, Sabrine? Why are you acting like this? At least now tell me. Now your mother's gone . . . surely whatever it was she told you that drove us apart you can tell me now?'

She looked down at his face. She felt none of the old emotion she had as a child, like to like, laughing over their unified sense of power. He had lost her the one thing she had wanted most. The revenge Max Bennett had taken on his mother's account was revenge on them all.

'My mother told me everything . . . *everything*, the day I returned,' she said. All except the part that he did not know. Not yet, anyway. She narrowed her eyes. She could hurt him, if he was not careful. *'The things you did to that woman.'*

His own eyes darkened, 'Oh, *that* . . . you mean,' he nodded. 'The Bennett woman . . . *that's* what's the matter! Is that it? You can't mean it, it was so trivial! Listen,' he said, leaning forward and trying to cover her hand with his, to find her withdraw it immediately, 'I'm *not* the ogre you think, Sabrine.' His rough voice was persuasive. 'It always takes two . . . I expect you've found that out by now . . .' She drew in a breath, her eyes cold. She would not be drawn into similarities of character with him ever again. 'That woman, she wanted it,' he said. 'I wouldn't have been able to . . . take her, otherwise, now would I? *Sabrine* . . .'

'I wonder who you're trying to convince.'

'What do you mean?'

'Grandfather, you don't pull the wool over my eyes,' she said wearily. 'You're cheap. If you'd been a woman, you'd have sold yourself to the highest bidder. You've no integral pride, no decency. Money and gain are your gods. That's the legacy you've given us. You wouldn't mind who you hurt . . .'

'Like you, you mean,' he said coldly.

She looked back at him. 'Possibly,' she said, her voice even. 'We are alike, it's true, much as I hate to admit it. But I'm

128

better off in my way, through the experience of seeing you make your mistakes first-hand.' Her eyes hardened. 'At least I know what I am. I *can* be honest about that. I don't think you even know just how much everybody hates you and sees through you for what you've done . . .'

He had sensed something ominous; now he knew he was right. He felt it coming.

'You've ruined all our lives,' she said. 'And now you're going to pay in loneliness. As you said to me once, "As ye sow, so shall ye reap". I think it fits now, don't you?'

She made ready to go up the stairs. That quip about loneliness. He caught her arm quickly in a grip that hurt her.

'Let go of me!'

'No.' His voice was as unpleasant as hers now, cold and daunting. 'You've said what you want to say, Sabrine, and I've no doubt by the tone of it that you've been saving it up a long time. Knowing you as I do, it does me little damage . . .' He saw the fire and the threat in her eyes, but he did not care. 'What I want is to know what's in your mind.' He stared her down, sure now of his hold over her. 'Alexander told me, you said something to him . . . something about your mother?'

'Oh, *Alexander*,' she said. 'He always played both sides.'

'Yes, that's why I know. I'm not letting you go until you tell me. *Tell me, Sabrine* .. . !' He sensed the words would unlock a door for him, a door to the secret of Jessamy. A terrible secret, yes, it had to be that. But he must know. 'I must know,' he said, repeating his thoughts. 'What made her change? Do you know, you little bitch? I'll bet you do.'

Sabrine tossed her head and pulled at her arm. They were on fighting terms now.

'Yes, I do!' she said, her eyes starting to blaze. 'If you want to know so badly!' She shook her arm free with frustration. She pulled in a breath. '*All right* . . . you remember when I last came home, that Christmas?'

'Yes.' He was still now, not a flicker. Staring hard.

Sabrine measured her words as she leaned forward over the banister. Her eyes were cruel. 'Well, grandfather . . . I fell in love . . . or thought I did . . .'

He moved his head ever so slightly sideways, his eyes still trained on her. 'What does that have to do with her?'

'Everything,' she breathed. 'You see, the man I was attracted to was one of the reasons I came back this time. No, not just for mother,' she said, seeing his look. 'I'm sure you, of *all* people, realised that . . . but for *me*.' She stabbed at her chest, her eyes brilliant. 'But what I found out was, the man I had fallen for . . . *was my own father* . . . yes, that's what she told me!' she said. 'It was *Max Bennett* . . . !'

With a sob in her voice, she ran up the stairs and along the landing to her old bedroom, slamming the door behind her.

In the silence of his study, Rupert stood alone. He did not move, but his mind was in torment. He refused to accept what it was telling him. He had to be wrong. She could not possibly have meant it. She was lying. She had to be.

It was many moments before he had the strength to move, his breathing calmer. His eyes were on the silver frame on his desk, its back to him, its edge gleaming in the light from the window. He could not trust himself to remember them clearly in his mind's eye, the two of them.

Forcing himself forward, as if wading through the worst of nightmares he went round the corner of his desk and into the bay, sitting heavily into his chair. He did not look at first, but then slowly lifted up his eyes to look into the faces of the twins, their photograph taken summers ago, close together, smiling; very clear.

Alexander. Fair, pale, the Redfield colouring, a Redfield through and through, almost a replica of Frederick, except for the winter-green eyes. No Redfield had green eyes . . . but, yes, he remembered the Hamblin family at Jessamy's wedding. Green eyes, the same green.

He felt the prickle of heat in his scalp. And Sabrine. Oh, Sabrine, that dark, dramatic face, those dancing, observant eyes, deeper, darker than the Redfield blue, but that black hair, their expression, and yes, their blue . . . there was something . . . was there . . . wasn't there . . . ?

He leaned back with a deep sigh, the perspiration popping all over him. He stared at the ceiling, remembering that goddamn man Bennett at times seen in the village. He recalled the dark smooth head, the straight shoulders and the set of him, the pride. Sabrine had that pride.

Ah, but she could have got it from them. After all, this, if it was true – because he knew what had happened now and he had to face it, to face what they had done to him – was not the first time. Their blood had mixed before, that could be it . . . it could have found a way through, making them look so much alike. But that face, the dark bold look as the man had beheld his own; he remembered it from just last week, across the high street, was so very much like hers, so very much in his memory . . . he looked once again from a distance into the face that laughed back at him from across the desk. Yes, the likeness was there.

What had they done to him? *What had they done!* True or false, he would say nothing. His pride would stop any acknowledgement of this. He put his head in his hands, appalled and shaken. Sabrine was right.

CHAPTER FIFTEEN

August 1963

'We need to talk seriously about the package-holiday market. Coastline's doing very good business with charter in the States,' he said, mentioning their American subsidiary. 'Americans deal so well with holiday traffic. Their priorities are sun, sand, sea and sex . . .'

'In that order?' joked Philip Hammond, relaxing in his white slatted chair. His laughter reached to the other men.

'Not necessarily,' Max smiled. 'What I want to put across to you is this . . . Las Vegas and Miami lead all destinations and jets are constantly en route to the Caribbean every winter. We've offered fourteen to twenty-one day excursions between California and Hawaii, New York and Puerto Rico, New York to Miami, Los Angeles-San Francisco to Vegas, and they're being snapped up. Now we need to think about doing the same here.'

The Bennett directors sat out on the terrace of the London penthouse. A huge umbrella-striped awning shielded them from the rays of the hot afternoon sun. A jug of iced tea sat on a tray in the centre of the white table. Dickie wore a cornflower-blue summer dress, sprigged with daisies. A soft tan warmed her skin, and her hair still shone darkly in the sun. She looked considerably younger than her sixty-three years. 'What if we don't have enough charter passengers to fill a plane?' she said.

'We'll simply switch them into the empty seats of a scheduled airliner.' Max lifted the jug and poured himself a tall glass of tea, the ice cubes chinking. He put his fingers in and lifted out the leaf of mint that had floated into his glass.

'I've had an idea,' he said. 'Tell me what you think of this.'

He took a sip and put down the glass. 'What we want are the young travellers. Now originally it was the "jet set", the fashionable people who were our passengers for the glamorous routes – no longer. Young people studying in Europe don't have much money and they don't need frills. We don't need to pamper them; what they want is to *get here*.' He tapped his finger on the table. 'They can turn up on spec. "Stand by", we would

132

call it. Travel fast, travel light. Cheap flights with bare essentials only if they're prepared to stand by at the airport. Mass migration. We'll offer bargain youth fares to those willing to wait till the last minute for unsold seats.' He lifted his hands. 'That way we're covered for those seats. We'll sell them, I know we will.' He looked at Bill and then at Philip Hammond, George Reilly and back to Dickie. 'What do you think?'

She looked doubtful. 'I don't know, Max. We've always had the image of a quality, caring airline. The best. Won't this cheapen us? And besides, I'm not sure you're right about selling those last seats. We could be left with egg on our faces.'

'We'll still be a quality airline,' he said. 'But there's no harm in making the sixties a decade of youth. It seems to me it's already happening.'

'And what about the package-holiday market?' she said.

'We'll go for more routes to Europe, more holidays, more profit.'

'Only a tiny margin of profit on each holiday, Max.' She leaned back in her chair. The sun caught her eyes. She narrowed her eyes against the glare. 'And what if the oil price goes up. We'll be left with unused aircraft. We'd have to have many more aeroplanes to cover the extra passengers. We'd be left with unfilled seats.'

'Exactly what I'm saying. That's where stand-by comes in every time. Lots of kids would be ready to get straight on board with light baggage for a good price, the chance of a holiday they've never been able to afford before.' He looked into her eyes. 'I think we should expedite this for next summer's holiday traffic.'

'But if we expand the holiday business, we cannot keep the prices high on each holiday. We'd have to go for mass market appeal, so we'd already be lowering our prices. Where's the profit?'

'Well.' He rested his elbows on the table before him. 'I think we could capture a bigger market by dramatically reducing the prices of each holiday, taking only a small profit on each but having many more holidays for sale.'

She shook her head. 'I think you're wrong. There are too many loopholes, too many imponderables. Only this time two years ago, don't forget, we put ourselves in a vulnerable position and look what happened,' she said, memory of the strike and its repercussions still far too fresh in her mind. 'I'm all for security now. That was a close call.' She looked worried for a moment. 'I think we'd be in trouble if we did a huge scale reorganisation like this. As I said, the oil price, for one . . . everything's strung together. What if it didn't work, if your stand-by idea didn't catch on. We don't know that it will, do we. There's no prototype.'

'I don't think it's too risky.' Philip Hammond's voice was smooth. He was the perfect banker in lightweight silk suit and tie, despite the day. He personally would never fly package. He had already been away for the summer on a comfortable first-class flight to the sun.

'I do.' She turned her face briefly towards him, sitting to her right. 'That's my opinion.'

Max pursed his lips and looked deeply at her. 'You know,' he said slowly. 'If we'd taken such an attitude in 1955 when the prototype of the 707 came out, we would not be where we are today. We are number one, Mother. Everybody knows that. They'll follow our lead . . . the kids *will* fly us, because of our reputation, and not only kids. We took a gamble then and we were right. I think we should play the hunch and take a gamble now.' He paused. 'You put me in the hot seat.' Dickie eyed him; after the strike was over she had given him the chair, seeing it as the right time.

'But it's not only you that'll get burned.'

Their eyes met and held. 'Still,' he said at last. 'I feel that I am right. I'd like to go ahead.' His voice was firm. 'Gentlemen, how do you feel about this?' He sat back and looked around the table.

Hammond had already seen which way the wind blew. 'I have to go with you, Max.'

'Good. George?'

Reilly looked first at Dickie, then at him. 'I have to agree with your mother, Max. Hang fire. It's early days yet.'

'All right. Bill?' he said, blue eyes level. 'Yours is the decider.'

Bill had been quiet throughout, listening as was his way. He looked to the future and spoke the words she had never thought to hear.

'Sorry, Dickie. I'm going with Max. I think he's right.'

Dickie walked down over the lawns towards the riverbank. Black Scotch firs rode up against the evening sky, framing the cool lines of Longbarrow.

She sat down at the river's edge, remembering yesterday. They had walked here together, she and Bill. She looked out over the river. Now he had gone over to New York to check on their operation over there, to start the ball rolling on the stand-by project; the project on which he had sided with Max instead of her. He had always been an ideas man.

She stood up, thinking about the family as she walked along towards the towpath. She had spent time with them in the last week, watched them and thought about that last meeting with the board. Maybe Max and Bill had been right to take the gamble; things did change. Maybe she would mellow, go on a cruise with Bill. She smiled as she thought of his parting suggestion before he had flown off. She lifted her head, remembering how it had been, as she looked out over the river.

It had been a beautiful day; cold, clean, the wind rushing and rustling, the river paddling by, a nimbus of cloud reflected on its surface.

'I never thought I'd see the day, Bill,' she had said.

He had been walking beside her, deep in thought, enjoying her by his side. At her words he had turned, stopped to look at her. His face was gentle but there was a strength there in his eyes.

'I told you once it would come. I couldn't always side with you, sweetheart, though I might want to.' His voice had been a little sad, but firm. 'Forward thinking, Dickie. It's always been your way. Give the young ones a chance; they have the ideas, the finger on the pulse. Do you regret handing the company over to Max?'

'No.' She had looked up at him. A blustery wind chivvied the river along. Bill's grey hair was ruffled, his lean face still handsome. 'I just never thought you would oppose me, that's all. It gave me quite a shock.'

'And having thought about it, do you think I was so wrong?'

'Oh, I don't know. As I said . . . oh well you know what I said . . .' She looked towards the river and then up into his eyes. Somehow today, on a lovely day like this, she wanted to forget business. She wanted just to stroll with Bill, arm in arm. 'Come on, let's walk,' she said, fitting her arm into his.

His eyes had softened in the way she had always loved. He was the gentlest man she had ever known; that's why this sudden show of obstinacy had surprised her. Or maybe he had just been right, and she was wrong. He had kissed the top of her head and turned her on to the path with him, feeling the early September sun on their skins.

'You know,' he had said, drawing her arm in closer against him. 'Maybe it's time for us to have time to ourselves. Do something together . . .' She had looked up, a curious look on her face.

'Such as what?'

'Oh, I don't know. Go on a world cruise. Buy a retirement home, let Max and the family run riot at Longbarrow . . .'

'A retirement home? Me? You need your head testing!'

'A holiday then.'

'A *package* holiday perhaps . . .'

'Dickie . . .' He stopped; pulled her into his arms. 'Come on. Just a holiday. The two of us . . .'

She felt his strength come through to her; Bill had always wanted her to get away, to hand over to Max and spend more time relaxing with him, enjoying more of a tranquil life. But no, she was not ready yet.

'Maybe next year,' she said. 'I still have a lot to do.'

'You won't let go easily, will you?' he had said gently.

'No I won't. And if I remember rightly, it's one of the things you used to say you loved about me!' she teased, laughing up at him.

His arms had reaffirmed their hold, his voice fond. 'Well, I guess I can't expect you to change now!'

'No, you can't!'

He chuckled, bent and kissed her softly, the wind riffling through their hair, wrapping itself around them. She felt the warmth of his body through the heavy wool sweater, his smell familiar, and his arms around her comforting. Her eyes closed, the sun on her face; at that moment she could have stayed in his arms for ever.

But she had let him go without changing her mind. A woman's prerogative to do so, but she hardly ever did. She made decisions. Maybe this was one time she should give in.

She took one last look across the river, to the cows in the meadows beyond, and thought of Bill working now in New York. There was something about the day, something fresh and new, that made her want to change. It would be exciting to take a cruise, a romantic cruise.

CHAPTER SIXTEEN

December 1963

'I'm catching the flight to New York first thing. I'll be checking into the Bennett Imperial,' he said. Their newest hotel had just reached completion on New York's fashionable Fifth Avenue. 'I'll call you from there. Just a couple of days in New York and I'll be home at the weekend.'

He stood at the window of the Presidential Suite. The Chicago Imperial was just as grand as its New York sister, perhaps a little more flavour to it; the New York hotel was less on atmosphere and more on luxury.

'Bill?'

'Yes, sweetheart.'

The line crackled with static. 'I want you to know something. Let's take that cruise.'

'You mean it! Damn it, I can't hear.' He turned away from the window, pressing the receiver to his ear. 'Dickie, are you still there?'

'Yes, I mean it.' Her voice travelled faintly across the wire. 'I've already booked it for Christmas. I've left it until now to surprise you. It's my Christmas present to you. Max is coping excellently. You were right. It is time for us to put our feet up and take a break together. We never have, have we?' The holiday she had picked was a Christmas cruise to see the northern lights. She pictured the two of them like a couple of young lovers standing at the rail of the ship. Looking at the icebergs and the stars. A new wardrobe, that was what she needed now. Suddenly she felt as giddy as a young girl on a first date. 'Bill?' There was still something that she had to say to him.

But the line had gone dead. 'Bill?' She tapped at the receiver rest. 'Oh, damn.' She put down the receiver slowly, lifted it again, about to redial the hotel. But then she had another idea. She would fly out to New York tonight, book in to the Bennett Imperial and surprise him.

*

It was mid-morning, the conditions terrible as Midwest's DC-8 from Chicago edged its way through rain, sleet and snow towards La Guardia Airport. Above New Jersey, the aircraft was still under its own navigational system as it dove down through the driving weather ready to come in on ground control. It crossed into the New York area and radioed in:

'Midwest 824 approaching La Guardia at 5,000 feet.'

High above New York city, Bill rubbed the moisture from his window with the tips of his fingers. He looked out of the aeroplane window through a break in the cloud at the snow covering the city. It looked like a picture out of a fairy tale. It was a beautiful sight. He settled himself comfortably, his seat back upright and his belt tightened. A soft smile lay in his eyes. Two days in one of his favourite cities and then he would be home again. The fairyland city lay twinkling beneath him. They would be landing any moment now.

On a street in Brooklyn, a man stood on the corner, rubbing his hands to keep warm. Christmas trees were stacked up beside him against the wall. Icicles hung from the gutter above. It was cold, but the snow sparkled and the people hurried by. A white Christmas. 'Give 'em what they want, God,' he said jokingly. Bing Crosby crooned it out from a radio across the street. The festive spirit was in the air, yule logs and glad tidings, holly berries and a warm hearth. He waved his arm at a passer-by.

'Cheapest trees. Best you'll get. Take a look . . .'

No sale. Still, he wasn't doing badly. Soon he'd make enough to go home to his wife and kids. He stamped his feet and shouted again.

The air traffic controller at Newark watched his radar scope as he brought the STA's inward Flight 266 from Los Angeles home again. He eased her in gently. And then he saw something entirely unexpected. He leaned forward and stared, realising.

He picked up his microphone.

'Jet traffic off to your right now at three o'clock one mile.'

High above, the STA pilot flying blind through a maelstrom of bad weather, acknowledged him.

The air controller saw the blip closing on him across his scope.

He shouted into the mike:

'States Air 266 . . . turn further left . . . !'

Bill closed his magazine and folded his arms as the DC-8

cruised down. He hoped Dickie had got his message at Long-barrow. He had missed Bennett Air's flight from Chicago because of a traffic snarl-up. Midwest had been the next best thing. He chuckled; she'd probably kill him. Bill dreamed on, thinking of those early days when they had worked so hard to build together; now they would relax together. Max would take care of the business and he would have Dickie all to himself.

At Newark the controller watched his radar scope helplessly. He had received no answer to his call, and he could not get through to La Guardia quickly enough. There was nothing he could do but watch the screen. The two blips continued towards each other. A second passed. They met; two blips became one. STA's signal was gone. The other headed north for an agonising eight miles. Then there was nothing.

The explosion ripped through the plane. The plane started to fall rapidly. Bill gripped his seat. All around him people started to scream. Dickie! Bright memories flashed through his mind, her smile, her eyes, he saw them standing on the ship together, arms around each other, just as she had. He knew it would never happen now.

The DC-8 fell out of the sky, crashing into the row of Brooklyn houses. Bodies, fuselage and fuel were scattered wide over the snowy streets. The fuel caught and burst into shards of flame, igniting cars on the street and blowing them to pieces. The man selling Christmas trees was killed instantly, the snow stained crimson with his blood and that of other passers-by. There were screams and cries from the twisted fuselage. Ambulances and fire engines were already howling their way towards the wreckage.

One small boy was thrown into the snow just barely alive. Two policemen hurried over as they heard his weak cries. They wrapped him gently but swiftly into their coats, dousing the flames, rolling him in the snow. Borne in a stretcher he was hurried to the back of the waiting ambulance. Bodies lay strewn across the pavement in their path, blackened, twisted and torn. So far there had been only one survivor.

In New York, Dickie crossed the terminal building. She wore a new black Chanel suit and the pearls Bill had given her for their first anniversary. She smiled as she joined the others waiting for the arrival of the Bennett 707 from Chicago.

The passengers filtered down to the last few. In her hurry,

she had not bothered to check the passenger list. Frowning now, the smile dying on her face, she went over to one of her agents, asking her to check on Mr Latimer.

The girl was back in no time.

'Mr Latimer was not on the flight, ma'am. Apparently he got held up in traffic. I think he would have caught the Midwest flight shortly afterwards.'

Dickie gave a wry smile. She would have something to say about that. He was due any moment then. She went back to the barrier to wait, her eyes on the door.

The tannoy crackled into life. Dickie heard its message. Before it had finished she was already running desperately through the startled crowds.

September 1964

'Father?'

Alexander Hamblin looked up from his desk as the boy came round the door.

'Come in, David.'

David walked across the room towards him. Alexander put down his pen and sat back, surveying his son. David was dressed in his school uniform; he looked older than his twelve years.

'Uncle Charles is here. I just came to say goodbye.'

'Ah yes.' Alexander pushed back his chair and stood up. He had come back to Foxhall for the last few days of his son's holiday. 'How's the summer been for you. All right?'

David nodded. He felt like a stranger with this man he hardly saw, yet despite Alexander's lack of interest in him, there was a cold sort of caring there for him. 'Great-grandfather taught me to jump. He says I've got a good seat. Aunt Sarah and Uncle Charles said they'll come and take me out on the first leave-out.' He had spent most of the summer down at Home Farm with them.

'Good. Don't mind if I can't make it, then?'

'No. If you're busy, it's OK with me. I understand.'

Alexander turned sharply, looking for sarcasm. There was none, just those frank brown eyes regarding him. 'I'll see you at Christmas. Perhaps we'll see more of each other then.'

'Yes.'

'Well, goodbye then, David.'

He came around the desk and proffered his hand. The young boy took it in a firm, warm grip. 'Goodbye, Father.'

He turned smartly and left the room. Alexander walked slowly to the window and stood there, watching, as Charles closed the boot on his trunk. David stood on the gravel beside Sarah, her hand around his shoulder. Alexander wondered how much of a mother Charles's wife was to David. They never talked about his real mother. Out in the sunshine, the boy stepped into the car, followed by Sarah. Charles climbed into the driver's seat and Rupert stood back on the curved steps, ready to wave, Frederick beside him.

The car drew away down the drive, the boy waving from the back window. Rupert and Frederick turned and came back inside. Alexander still stood at the window and watched the car as it disappeared down the long drive through Foxhall's park land towards the lane beyond.

The door opened.

'Watching him go?' Rupert came in, his eyes on his grandson. He had reached seventy-five now and was beginning to feel his age. He sat down in the tapestried Gainsborough chair by the window. 'Fine boy, Alexander.'

'Yes. I didn't feel like coming out. We said our goodbyes in here.'

'Quite, quite, I understand. Emotional moment. Still,' he wrinkled his forehead. 'Seems to love school. Good games-player, bright boy, well-mannered, independent. You must be proud.'

'Oh, yes, I am. I only wish I could spend more time with him,' he said as he returned to sit behind the desk. His voice was careful. 'But I find myself so busy at the bank these days.'

'Absolutely. And Charles and Sarah are quite taken with looking after him, it seems. Actually I wanted to talk to you, Alexander. About the bank.'

He took his pipe from his pocket, and his leather pouch of tobacco. Alexander's eyes were veiled as he watched him.

He sat back and waited, one arm lying on the desk top, the pen threading and re-threading through his fingers.

'Yes.' Rupert puffed his pipe alight. The aroma filled Alexander's nostrils. He hated it. Rupert put the pouch back in his pocket. 'I'm very impressed by the way you're handling things up there, I have to say,' he started. 'Very diligent. People speak highly of you, so Guy Prudham tells me.' Alexander felt a cold laugh inside him. He and Guy had been allies since the start. 'Since poor Verity's death,' he said, looking down, 'I know it's been hard for you. But I expect in time you'll get over it, find another wife . . .'

Alexander could not believe what he was hearing. Did the old man think homosexuality was a disease, something that you could cure?

'And you've got your fine boy. Alexander, I've made a decision over the last couple of years,' he said, looking ahead of him and not at his grandson. 'I'm getting on a bit now, had my share of tragedy just as you have. I don't feel much like running the bank any longer. I want you to do it,' he said. Now Rupert's blue eyes were trained on him, as strong as ever as he spoke. 'Officially.'

Alexander could hardly believe it. 'Thank you,' he said. 'A great honour.'

'Of course,' Rupert went on. 'You have your wife's shares. She left them to you, and so you won't be needing any more from me.'

Alexander felt himself harden; there had to be a sting in the tail. Without majority shares, or even a large whack of the action, he might as well be nothing. Shares gave him the power and the clout, without them he was a eunuch. Rupert knew that, the bastard. Why bark when you've got a dog to do it. He was giving him all and nothing; shares would give him freedom and that was one thing Rupert was not about to bequeath. For a moment he had tasted it, before Rupert had slammed the door. The man would never change.

'I'll give you authority,' he was saying. 'Tell them on Monday. How does that sound?'

It sounded like nothing. He already ran the bank. 'Very good.'

'Fine, fine.' The genial note, however, was leaving his voice. 'I'm going to take you into my confidence now, Alexander, because I want you to do a little job for me in return.' Across the room, their eyes met. 'You may have heard stories about the past, my past, from one source or another. You may have wondered why I've always hated the Bennett family, especially that woman.'

Alexander was alert now, his mind as clear as a bell on a summer's day. His past was off the hook, here was his future.

'Well, I'm going to tell you why. My father, Alexander,

disinherited me because of her. Took away everything that was rightfully mine.' His voice darkened with it. 'I managed to regain it. And all because of something so trivial. You know how it is when you're young, kitchen maids, village girls . . . they all want it, proud of it mostly if you're from the big house. This one fought back. Decided to try and ruin me. Practically did. A kitchen maid.' He nodded slowly. 'Frederick and me, we raped her in Cobbold's Wood. We were out hunting and she got cheeky. So I showed her what was what, thought nothing of it afterwards, why should I? That was my mistake,' he growled. 'That little upstart came after me. Came back here with her confounded airline and set up here to embarrass and humiliate me.'

He turned round in his chair now and pulled himself to his feet. She had saved her company from defeat after the strike. She had won that one; he had found no opening since – she was too aware of him now – but there had to be one. 'I may be old, but I haven't finished yet. Before I'm dead I'll break her. I've nearly got her once or twice, but she's slippery as an eel . . .' His voice trailed off, seeing her face, those green eyes laughing at him. He walked to the fireplace and stared at Alexander.

'I'm giving you the chairmanship on one condition, Alexander. You find that weakness, find the link and break her. Get her, Alexander, and you can have my shares.'

She looked out over the fields beyond the lawn. The dog roses were out, the meadow high with buttercups. In the fields the hay bales were stacked high on the iron carts, handles resting on the ground, waiting for the tractors to come and lift them away. She missed haymaking. Now she remembered the fun of it, remembered the tales her father had once told her. A plane swooped in the distance; Jim, one of the family. Yes, time did move on. It was almost a year since Bill had died. She felt suddenly old and alone.

He had been the unsung hero: a gentle man, fair but strong; an anchor for her, a father for Max, a grandfather for the children and a rational business partner; a calming influence on the many temperaments and personalities. To her he had been stability, someone who gentled her headstrong ways as once her own father had done. He had opposed her at the very end, as one day long before he had warned her he would do, and she had seen him in another light. She had taken him for granted all

143

of her life, his being there for her, and now he no longer was. She remembered how irritated she had been at first with him for voting against her on the cheap travel thing. How trivial it seemed and how little it mattered now. She felt the loss of her old friend more keenly than any business deal. And they had never found his body; that was the hardest part of all. She could not even mourn him properly.

She returned to her painting, trying to immerse herself in the brushwork of colour. She had come back to Greatley House permanently now, somehow needing solitude. Bill was right; it was the children who saw the future. It was their turn now. Hers to guide them only. She would let Max take the helm.

On her low stool she sat, apparently absorbed as Max came round the corner of the white Georgian house looking for her. She wore a faded pink and green hat pulled down over her face like a cloche to shield her eyes from the sun. Her dress was a rose-print shirtwaister, her legs bare, her feet in sandals. She sat on the front lawn beside a bank of rhododendrons and azaleas looking out through the orchard to the laburnum trees and the mowed garden beyond. She looked ready for an artist's brush herself.

She was in a world of her own. He came up beside her and sat on the grass, his arms looped around his knees. He said nothing for the moment.

She looked down at him and smiled. There was grey in his hair.

'What are you doing here?'

'Just came to check on you.' He plucked at a blade of grass. 'What were you thinking of?'

'Bill.'

'I thought you might be.' He looked into the distance beyond them. 'Feel like talking?'

She said nothing, but her thoughts flooded her mind. She was glad of his presence, of his understanding. She laid down her brush with a sigh.

'You know, darling,' she began. 'I've found it hard to reach happiness. I'm a taxing woman, I suppose. Men that I liked didn't like the competitive sort; my type of woman generally goes for a gentler, more humorous man able to let all the challenge and drive ride over them with a tolerant calm.' She smiled wryly. 'Trouble is, I never could abide that sort of man. I'd permanently be trying to make him react, get a little bit of fire out of him, you know!' She laughed at herself. 'I'd soon be bored.' She sighed a little. 'On the other hand a man who likes a challenge would probably prefer to be the driving force in the family. He wouldn't want a fight on his own hearth. He'd prefer a soft feminine woman who would tell him he was wonderful whether he was or not, tell him he was a brilliant man and let him preen. A good cook and a perfect mother.' She shook her head at that. 'I never fell into either category, and neither did Bill. He wasn't at all the walkover he might have seemed at times.'

'I never thought he was.'

They listened for a moment to the birds chirruping in the trees around the orchard. This house had been their first real home in England after all those hard adventurous years in California, hard but exciting. She had always led the way, and he had always given her her head. That was his strength.

She spoke again; gentler. 'I found as much happiness as was possible for me with Bill. You see, I don't think I was made for true happiness. Some of us aren't. When you have a driving force inside you, contentment is beyond you, I think. With Bill, I came as close as I was ever likely to get to contentment, and I never knew it. Fighting, fighting, all the way.' She shook her head sadly. She had been brave all of her life, fought for everything. 'I never stopped to think, Max. He kept telling me to slow down, to relax. And now . . .'

'Mother.' He took her hand in her lap. 'You made him very happy.'

She looked out over the lawns. 'Did I?'

'You did. He told me.'

She turned back to him. She had always been strong; she would not change now. Yet he had never seen her face so vulnerable.

'When?' she said.

'In Chicago. A couple of nights before . . .' He saw her look. 'It was regarding the meeting. He knew you were upset.' His voice was comforting, his hand still holding hers. 'He told me he could not have been happier, through bad times as well as good, than with the life you gave him. He recited to me that old Buddhist poem. You know the one?

> Health is the greatest blessing,
> Contentment the best possession,
> A true friend the nearest of kin.

That said more than anything about your life together. You were his true friend, nearer than kin to him.'

Dickie bent her head. She had come full circle. The pain was behind her now, but her lifelong companion had gone. She felt shadowed by her thoughts. A long time ago she had thought herself in love yet it had been Bill with whom she had spent over forty years of her life and truly loved. She wondered whether he even knew that.

'I never told him just how much I loved him.'

'I think he knew.'

She took a deep breath. 'I was going to go on a cruise with him, Max. I was going to give up fighting.'

Above them, the clouds sailed across a robin's-egg blue sky. A skylark sang in the field up by Sam's Hill. It was a gentle day.

'You still can,' he said.

She nodded. 'I'd like to be alone for a bit now please, darling.'

'Fine.' He got to his feet, bent and kissed her. 'You know where we are. Longbarrow's your home.' She did not look at him, felt only the disturbance of air as he left her, alone.

Dickie stared off across the lawns for a moment, quiet now, the hot afternoon still. The birds gently sang their isolated song. She closed her eyes, bent her head, and cried.

BOOK TWO

1968 – 1976

CHAPTER SEVENTEEN

Summer, 1968

Kay came running, half-flying, down the long staircase into the hall, still pulling herself into a beige cotton-knit sweater. This was to be a special day. No more school, no more greasy tasteless food and rubbery puddings, no more hurrying from lesson to lesson, no more bells ringing their summons to behave. She was home, and free, and Dickie had made her a special promise.

Beyond the woodblocked hall the dining-room doors stood open, the rest of the family already assembled, the hum of noise and clatter of plates and laughter drifting out into the hall. It was a sunny day already, the light pouring in across the newly decorated walls in green trelliswork on white, the matching Sheraton mahogany table and chairs polished to a deep glow. Her father's back was towards her.

'The Jumbo is a superb aircraft. Two and a half times more passengers than the biggest 707s and DC-8s. Tall as a five-storey building, passengers nine abreast. Every place on earth is available within twenty hours; quite a feat. We're taking a trip on the new Concorde this week, your mother and I,' he announced as Kay came in, leaning to kiss her father quickly on the cheek before going to her place.

'Morning, everyone.' She sat down. 'I'm starved.' She reached out for the milk to pour on her cornflakes and caught Dickie's eye across the table. She winked at her. Kay grinned back conspiratorially.

Max looked at his daughter. She had laid her hands in her lap, the clear sea-green eyes fixed on him. They were beautiful eyes, honest and strong, framed by the glowing dark red hair that fell to just below her ears. Her skin was fresh and young.

'Well,' he said, admiring his daughter. 'We're going to have to decide what you're going to do now you've left school. Your mother and I thought of La Place in Switzerland. I hear good reports, and then perhaps you might think about doing the Season next year, and we're . . .'

'Finishing school!' she interrupted, horrified. 'The Season! Absolutely not, Daddy! Not for me. I want to learn to fly this summer.'

'Well, you can fly in the holidays, darling,' said Max at last. 'I've no objection to that. You'd probably make a good pilot. Your grandmother was.' Dickie looked up at him.

'Is.' Kay corrected.

Max smiled. 'Is.'

Kay did not smile; instead she looked reflective, a little sad. 'Dad, you don't understand, do you. I don't want to get into a marriage market like my friends. That's all they think about, the holidays and boys.'

Max wrinkled his brow. 'Is that so bad?' His smile was crooked.

'Not, I suppose, for them, but I want to be a pilot. To join Bennett Air. I've got some good ideas that could be of value. I'd hate to be like them. I'd go mad being social all the time. I want to fly. Why won't you take me seriously?'

'You're still too young to make such decisions, Kay,' he said.

'I am not,' she said hotly. 'At my age Dickie had had you, and she was planning to go halfway across the world, to America. I know the story . . . look what she did!'

'That was then,' he said, passing his empty coffee cup up the table to Jennie for a refill. 'And this is now. She had to, she had no option.' He did not look to see Dickie's expression at the end of the table. 'You're in a privileged position, something to be taken advantage of. Things would have been quite different had your grandmother been in the same boat.' Dickie sat stony-faced looking at her son, hardly believing the blatant sexism in his words; but this was between father and daughter. She concealed her feelings with difficulty. Kay answered for her.

'That's not true, and you know it,' she argued. 'So don't try to say that. Dickie would have been the way she is whatever had happened. She loves a challenge, and so do I. I want to fly like she did, challenge the elements and myself.' Beyond her, Dickie still sat in silence, though a thoughtful look came into her eyes as she looked from one to the other. 'I'd like to test myself,' she went on, 'to do speed trials or competitions. Maybe be the first female pilot to break a record that hasn't been conquered yet. I'd like to be the first, Dad. I'd like to be the one to *win*!'

Dead silence followed her speech. Dickie still held a cup in her hand, watching Kay. Max regarded her flushed face, the green-gold eyes bright and potent; bold eyes. She had all the spirit and the obstinacy of her grandmother. He was taken aback by the similarity all of a sudden. He had grown up with that look, knew exactly what it meant.

'Kay,' he said quietly. 'I understand what you're saying, don't think that I don't, but you're wrong about your grand-mother. She had no choice.' He ignored the look his mother threw at him. 'You have . . . now, I would like you to take advantage of the privileges you have. Start to meet some people, go to a few parties, meet some young men. I want you to mix. Maybe later we can talk about the company. You could do anything you want for the next two years, Kay. Get out and see the world.' He wanted to be able to pamper his only daughter. 'Please me in this, Kay, would you?'

'Oh, Daddy,' she sighed. 'Don't do this to me. I want to be involved, not cast off like some silly empty-headed girl to get married, have two point five children and live in the country going to coffee mornings.' What had happened to her dreams of that morning, her freedom to fly those beautiful machines, to have the respect that her father was affording her brother – but not her.

Max looked up the table at Jennie. Jim silently watched the interchange like a tennis match. 'Is that what you think your mother does?' he asked her.

'More or less . . . yes.'

'Darling, I do a lot more than that,' she said gently. 'There's the Young Conservatives for a start, the village committee . . .'

'Oh,' said an exasperated Kay. 'Don't you see, Mum. I want to achieve something for myself, something to be really proud of. Not to have it all handed to me on a plate.'

'You don't want to be married?' she said, passing the coffee back down the table.

'Certainly. One day. If I fall in love.'

Jennie looked at her lovely daughter. The summer sun caught the back of her shining hair filling it with red-gold lights. She was long and slender, a girl who would fall in love. And men with her.

'I need something to challenge me,' she was saying to her father again. 'Not just to lie down and die.' Jennie's eyes were worried as she met those of her husband at the head of the table. Was that how their daughter saw marriage? What an indictment if so. 'Let me start at Bower Hill!'

'Well, next year, all right. You go off to finishing school this autumn, and next year, we'll see.' Dickie's cup went noisily back into its saucer. As Max's eyes flew to her, she cleared her throat, her expression hard to read. She held his look, but said nothing.

'Daddd . . .'

'That's all, Kay.'

Kay pushed back her chair, her splendid appetite gone. 'I'm going outside,' she said. She stood up.

'Kay, sit down. I didn't say you could leave the table.' Max pointed at her empty chair. 'Finish your breakfast and remember your manners.'

'Manners, manners. What is this?' she said. 'What's happening to you? All these social graces. What are we, Redfield clones suddenly?'

'*Kay!*' Jennie looked startled. 'Apologise. You know how your grandmother feels about them.'

'Oh, hell,' she said. 'Why does it go on . . . ?'

She walked from the room. Max watched her leave, unable to stop her. High-spirited, hot-tempered Kay. She had always stood up for herself.

She turned the corner into the hall and went down the passageway towards the back door. They heard the door open and close. Max wiped his mouth, crumpled his napkin to the table and pushed back his own chair. He stood up and went around the table, following her exit. He passed his wife. Jennie put out a hand to his arm, her eyes spelling both a warning and a request. Max patted her shoulder and left the room. Behind him, Dickie left her chair and stared out across the empty lawn, her eyes distant as a thought entered her mind.

Kay stood by the back wall looking out over the fields.

She heard the footsteps in the hall, and the back door opening. She did not move, or run away. Max came across to her, smoking. She steeled herself.

But he said nothing for the moment, just looked out over the fields beside her. They stood a while quietly.

'I remember the first day I took you to school,' he said at last, his voice sudden, but gentle. 'You wouldn't let me hold your hand. As soon as we got there you ran in. You never looked back. I felt as if a piece of my heart was breaking. Always so independent, my little girl.'

'Oh, Dad!' She turned to look up into his dear face. She saw the love and the pride there. She put her arms around him.

'I only want the best for you, Kay,' he said.

'Oh, Daddy, don't!' she said, her eyes starting with tears. 'Don't appeal to my conscience.' Her naturally warm heart could not stand it. 'Don't you see?' she said, her arms dropping from his waist. 'I have to find out for myself. Otherwise I'll never learn. You can't fight all my battles for me.'

She turned and ran off down the steps towards the fields beyond. Max watched her go. She was right enough. That was what he wanted, to fight her battles for her, never wanting her to be hurt. He felt a tightness in his chest as he watched the figure running through the long grass towards the meadows. He could not protect her for ever. Kay wanted to make her own mistakes, to discover her own world for herself. When the slight figure was no more, he turned and went back into the house, to find that Dickie had left the dining-room.

Kay threw herself onto the grass, and lay listening to the hum of the earth. A bee buzzed idly nearby, the grass moved in the breeze. Across the field, the barley waved in the wind like underwater hair, shifting and breathing, the wind like a sea wind strafing the barley to blow and bluster. It was a glorious day, the soft white clouds lay way, way up against a blue sky, the river lay dappled and glimmering. The wind came in great billowing whirls and snatches, like a spring wind, pagan and promising, the grass as thick as a badger's coat.

Kay rolled over onto her stomach and looked out across the meadows. Beyond the grounds of Longbarrow they were flat right up to the reeds of the river. It was a day to lean against the wooden gatepost down by the towpath, feel the wind whipping, smell the river and the touch of the sun, like fingers on winter skin. Against the horizon the fields dipped down into the lilac mystery of the valleys, misted and quiet against the wood beyond. There was an extraordinary light in the Thames valley here beside the river, maybe because the river was constantly moving and changing. A fish leaped against the surface of the eddying river, a bird sang in the shadow of a passing cloud. In the distance a train rattled closer and the doves cooed. The smell of the earthwas deep with summer; she was aware of breathing it in with delight. Kay felt herself at a crossroads: spoilt, wanting to be strong, wanting to be free, wanting something, feeling weak. The wind was powerful, the sun hot on her back. She bent her face down to the crook of her arm, the skin there suddenly unexpectedly degrees warmer and soft as a child's lips. She closed her eyes like a cat.

'Hello . . . !'

She looked up, squinting through the sun. The silver-dark crest of Dickie's head was framed against the blue sky.

'Thought I'd know where to find you.' She sat down beside her granddaughter. 'Have some of this,' she handed her the coffee she had brought with her. Kay sat up and took it from her, tasting the strong black French coffee that her grandmother preferred.

Dickie watched her pretty strong-willed granddaughter, affection in her eyes and a smile on her lips.

'Why don't they understand, Dickie?'

'Understand what? You ought to take life more easily, Kay. Don't get yourself in such a sweat.'

Kay finished the coffee, felt the taste in her mouth linger. She wanted a cigarette; Dad didn't allow them to smoke. She pulled the crumpled pack from her back pocket, book matches tucked in its side, and lit up. The smell was sweet on the air. The sun burned her back; she felt the beads of perspiration around her hairline.

Kay watched her grandmother. 'Now *you're* being evasive,' she said.

'Hey, Kay,' she said. 'I don't want to get into a pitched battle over this. Do you?'

'No, sorry.' She pulled at the daisies, started to thread them. 'I don't know,' she said. 'I'm not sure where to start, if Daddy won't even take me seriously . . .'

She shrugged. 'Come and learn to fly with me,' she said simply.

Kay's eyes flew up to her face.

'After what Daddy said!?'

'Even more. I take life as it comes, Kay. So should you. You wanted to come up earlier. What's changed?'

'Nothing!' she said, shaking her head, her eyes starting to glow. 'Except that . . . well, I thought you were just going to take me up today for fun.'

'I was,' her grandmother said drily. 'But I've changed my

mind. I'm going to teach you instead.' She looked casually up at the sky.

'Dickie . . . !' Kay's face split in a smile. 'That's the best news I could have had!'

Dickie laughed and stood up. 'Don't get too excited. I'm going to be a hard judge on you, Kay. You'll have to measure up, don't forget that.' She raised a warning finger. 'Well, I'm going down to the airfield. I'll see you there in one hour exactly.' She turned away, then back. 'Just one thing, though,' she said, looking at the glow on the girl's face. 'You'd better be sure this is what you want to do. You've got to work hard, get ready to prove to your father that you mean it. Only then will he realise what you're made of. You've got to be very good, Kay, a damn good pilot, by the time I've finished with you. Your father's a harder taskmaster than me. Take the next hour to think about it, and only come down if you're ready to take on everything that this will mean . . .'

She gave her a deep look, blew her a kiss, and strolled off towards the house.

Kay climbed to her feet, dusted off the seat of her trousers watching her grandmother for a moment, then started out on the towpath that led to the village. She knew what Dickie meant. She was taking sides, against her own son. Kay had to prove them both right; Dickie was putting that trust in her. But she would be good, she knew she would. She had to be. She felt the wind on her face with delight, and pulled herself out of the cotton sweater to knot it casually around her neck, leaving her arms bare beyond her white tee-shirt.

On the other side of the river, a horse came cantering fast. She watched the rider with interest. He was very good, still and strong, as one with the horse. Whilst giving the appearance of letting the horse have its head, he was obviously still in control. It was the perfect sort of day for horse and rider. She stopped to watch him for a moment as he cantered on towards the distant fields bypassing the village, envious of his unity with his animal. They were two who understood each other.

The towpath branched into two at the village and went over towards the old bridge or alongside the river towards Greatley House and Cobbold's Wood. She took the path towards Greatley. As she walked along she saw him again. The horse-man had reined in his horse and had stopped to talk to someone else walking down the field towards him. She recognised the other man immediately. Frederick. The land belonging to Greatley ran down to the water's edge. Dickie had kept a rowing-boat there, tucked in amongst the reeds, for when all of them went over for the day, so that they could row up river for a picnic. Kay went over to it, untied the rope and climbed in, pushing herself away with one of the oars. She was soon rowing in easy strong strokes over to the other side.

'Frederick!'

The horseman had gone when she arrived. She felt a little sorry, thought she would like to have met him, but Frederick was still there, turning to go back up the field. He heard her call, and turned back, shielding his eyes from the sun to see who was calling him.

'I saw you from the towpath,' she said. 'I was out for a walk.'

'I haven't seen you for a while. Where have you been? Away at school?'

'Yes, but it's all over now.' And that brought her back immediately to the breakfast-table conversation of that morning. The glow left her eyes. She stared away up the hill of Redfield land to where the men were working in the distance.

'What are they doing?'

'You *have* been away a long time,' he said wryly. 'That's a combine harvester. We're going to have a good crop this year.' He frowned against the light as they stood watching together, listening to the purr of the machine against the day. It was peaceful here. She had been right to come.

'Can you tell in advance whether a crop's going to turn out well, Frederick?'

'More or less. Farmer's instinct,' he said. 'Always follow instinct, and you'll never go wrong. People make mistakes when they try to go after what they think is right for them and don't listen to what instinct tells them . . . where if they listened to what was up here,' he said tapping first his head and then his heart, 'and in here . . . they'd be better off . . .'

'Yes, I know,' she said slow and thoughtful.

He looked at her. 'What's wrong, Kay?'

'Oh, nothing,' she said, as the promise from Dickie took shape in her mind. Was she ready to fight her father?

'Here,' he said, 'hold on a moment.' He lifted an arm and shouted. 'Joe! Joe!' He waved at the man in the harvester. He switched off the engine and leaned out of the cab, screwing up his face to listen. Frederick cupped his hand to his mouth and took a step up the field. 'I'm just going off for half an hour. I'll be back shortly. Tell David, would you? He's coming back in a moment to help out!' he shouted.

The man lifted a thumb in assent. He switched on the motor and the machine rumbled back into life. It jerked into movement and then moved on slowly and surely as it had done before.

'Right,' said Frederick warmly. 'I'm all yours. Let's walk, shall we?' He indicated the way back towards the village, away from Foxhall, lifting his stick to point. 'Then you can tell me as we go.'

They started out. Ahead were the Berkshire Downs, the grass waving, the untreated crops dotted with poppies. Summer made the land pregnant and blowzy. The path was bleached, whitened with heat and light, the grass dusty by the ditches. It had been a long, hot summer.

She wondered how to explain. It was more a feeling than anything. Putting into words her problems would sound only petty, yet they were not at all. To her, they were very real.

She tried to tell him as well as she could. 'And you see he means well,' she finished, 'but the life he wants for me is not what I want.'

'What do you want?'

'Oh, challenge, variety, adventure. To do something worthwhile, to work and achieve something. To use my talents. I've always loved the open air.' She stretched out her arms and breathed in deeply, looking up at the sky. 'I'd love to fly. They expected Jim to want to fly and run the company, but it's what I want to do. I love planes, I'd love to build my own.'

'Then why don't you?'

'What, build my own plane?'

'Yes. Kay, there's only one life. You have to go out and prove yourself in it.' He thought of his own life, his own lack of action. 'Don't wait for things to come to you. Make them happen. If you're interested enough I think you can do whatever you want, don't you? If building a plane is what you really feel you want to do, do it . . . build it, enter it in a competition. Don't they have kits, things like that?' he puzzled.

'Yes, they do . . .' Her eyes were bright, but distant, a slow smile starting on her lips.

'Well, then, if I were you, I'd look into it.' He scratched at the dusty ground with the tip of his walking stick. 'And no time like the present, if you ask me. You've got all summer now . . . and your father seems to have handed you an opportunity on a plate. You're never going to be so well off again . . . you're living at home, all bills paid, and the time to do anything you want . . . now, if you were to utilise that time learning about flying, looking into this kit business, why at the end of the summer when it was time for your father to send you away, he just might think differently, if you were to *prove* just how interested you are in his business . . . don't you think?'

He looked into her face with a smile. She needed to go after whatever it was that she wanted. He could see her problem; the Bennetts had climbed the social ladder and her father only wanted what was best for her. He had assumed his son would work, but that his daughter would simply marry well into a family he could be proud of. He was about to be proved wrong in his assumptions. Kay had her grandmother's verve, her spirit, and her need. Adversity would only strengthen her, and she was obstinate, just like Dickie. The green eyes flashed now, both with humour and design. She was Dickie all over again.

He laughed. 'Well! Are you going to let him stop you?'

'No.' She grinned up at him, pushing her hands into the pockets of her corduroys. 'I'm not.' The wind whipped the hair around her face.

'Do you think you could build your own plane, Kay?'

'I expect so. I've never thought about it seriously until now. Dickie started all this you know. Put the idea in my head. She promised to help me. She said she'd take me flying.'

A shadow crossed the old man's face, but was gone just as quickly. Kay knew why now, but never mentioned the story she had heard; it was irrelevant to their particular friendship. 'Yes,' he said approvingly, 'I can see her doing that, but I expect she knew the idea was yours, really. Don't you think?'

Kay started to smile at that; she leaned up and gave him a big kiss on the cheek.

'What was that for?'

'Oh, for being my friend. 'Bye now, Frederick. See you later.' She started to run.

The emotion warmed him. He lifted a hand. 'Where are you going?'

She reached the bank, and stepped back into the boat. 'To learn to fly, of course!'

158

CHAPTER EIGHTEEN

Late summer 1968

It was crack of dawn. Kay stirred in her sleep.

'Kay!'

Her eyes opened. Dickie was leaning over her, whispering in her ear and shaking her gently awake. She woke up immediately.

'Is it time?'

'Yes. Come on. I'll wait down in the lane. I left the car there on purpose.' First thing on a quiet summer morning a car engine would wake the dead.

As Dickie left the room Kay was already jumping from the bed and pulling off her flower-sprigged nightdress. It was Jennie's vain attempt to curb her tomboy daughter. Kay much preferred to sleep in the nude or in pyjamas.

She pulled on her jeans and a shirt, grabbed a heavy jacket and her tennis shoes and was gone from the room, pulling the door gently behind her and leaving the curtains closed. Her parents would think she was lying in and leave her until mid-morning. By then, it would all be history. The house was quiet and sleeping; she passed the grandfather clock in her father's study, ticking gently away. Five a.m. She was filled with excitement as she stepped out into the early day and closed the big front door behind her.

Clouds sailed across a soft blue sky. The river was like glass. Dew lay on the grass, the sun picking out drops that glimmered and shook in the thick grass down by the river; the meadow was silver in the shadows by the trees, lying in a soft early morning mist. The skylarks sang. Kay, her jacket under her arm, ran down the drive and out onto the lane.

Dickie was there, waiting, the inevitable flask of coffee beside her.

'Here, pour me a cup while I coast this thing down the hill.'

Kay settled in beside her into the low-slung seat and poured the coffee. Gently, they slid off down the hill; towards the bottom, Dickie let her into gear, far enough away now not to be heard.

'Hold tight,' she said. 'Here we go.' They drove off down the narrow lanes, heading for the airfield at Bower Hill.

Max had bought an old Stearman, a plane that Dickie had flown during the 1930s. It was Kay's favourite. For her, the thrill of open-cockpit flying was far greater than that of the newer lithe little jets.

She ran her hand lovingly over the old biplane. The Stearman was already standing out on the runway; Dickie had the cowling up priming the engine. Around them the first of the ground engineers were starting work, wheeling the aeroplanes out for the daily inspection, priming others ready for charter. The grease, the smells, the flapping of the canvas by the hangar, all were like life and breath to her.

'I'll do it for you this once, Kay,' said Dickie, her head re-appearing as she fastened the cowling.

'That's like riding a horse and having a groom,' she said. 'I want to know all about it myself. I'm not Jim, you know.' Jim was well-known at the airfield for pulling rank, stepping into the cockpit ready to go with no preliminaries on his part.

Dickie came alongside, wiping her hands on the rag. She laid her hand on the wing. 'You want to run before you can walk, Kay,' she said, her brow furrowed with humour. She had been teaching her for the last few weeks. 'I knew this morning you'd want to go up quickly, that's all. Stop fighting and be a good girl, huh?'

Dickie was right. This morning Kay was going to have the thrill of flying solo for the first time. She was exhilarated at the thought both of being alone and with the challenge of the machine under her control. It was a splendid morning for it, fresh and clear. She could hardly wait.

'It's your first time. Think you can handle it?' Dickie's tone was more serious now. Kay was good, perhaps potentially a very good flyer, but it took more than mechanical know-how to become a pilot. Many other factors came into play on a solo flight.

'Yes,' she said simply. She climbed in and strapped herself in, five straps to buckle on the harness. The DI, the daily inspection, had been done, but still she thought her way through it as if she had done it herself. A good pilot would do no less. Virtually everything on the aeroplane that moved had to be checked to make sure that it had not been damaged and worked properly. She pulled the stick back now and the elevators went up, pushed it forward and the elevators went down; they were the controlled surface on the back of each side of the rudder. Next she checked the ailerons, the control surfaces of the wings that caused the rotating movement whereby the wing went up and down on the centre of the axis of the aircraft. They were operating smoothly. Each move was vitally important: when the stick was pulled backwards the elevator on the tail would go down, thus creating the air pressure which would push the tail down and the nose up so that the aeroplane could climb.

Dickie had already inspected the undercarriage and the wing root mountings. She had pulled the levers under the cowling, pouring petrol into the carburettor to flood it. Now, as Kay's ground engineer, she would turn the engine over with the throttle shut for four compressions by four pulls of the propeller.

'Off contact.' Ignition switches off, the petrol sucked in.

'Off and closed.' Kay repeated the confirmation.

Dickie pulled the propeller through four times. 'Set and contact.'

'Set and contact.' Kay cracked open the throttle slightly, making contact with the ignition.

Dickie pulled the propeller through once more. The engine roared into life. Kay kept professionally cool, though the adrenalin raced through her as she thought of the moment that was ahead of her as she became airborne for the first time alone. She ran the engine for four minutes to get the oil flowing, and to warm the engine. Then she revved it up to eighteen hundred revs, testing the ignition system. She ran the second ignition; the mag drop was 250 rpm; too high. She revved up the engine to full revs to try and clear it. If it did not clear, she would have to postpone her trip. Hopefully, it was just a bit of muck on the sparking plug.

'Come on,' she whispered under her breath. 'Don't let me down . . .'

The engine throbbed through the little craft. The tactic worked: the mag drop climbing to just under 100 rpm at 1800 revs. Delighted, she did a thumbs-up to Dickie.

Dickie lifted her hand and moved away, clear of the wing. Her hair was blown wildly by the propeller, her shirt and trousers billowing. And then Kay was away, turning, trundling along towards the runway she was to use.

She held back, ready, waiting, the engine straining as if held on an invisible catapult and then as she released the brakes, it was as if the catapult had snapped and she was off, hurtling down the little runway, heading for the trees at the edge of the field, and then away and up, lifting, lifting . . . and she was flying alone, at last.

Her earphones were radioed up and drowned the outside sound. As the plane lifted the air temperature dropped. It was cold, really crisp; wonderful. She pulled on the stick and veered off to the right, swinging back over the airfield and heading out west. The air rushed by her, colder as she climbed, the draught buffeting her little machine quite steadily as she reached one hundred miles an hour and held her steady.

She could see away in the distance that Dickie had gone up too, her little red and white Piper Cub balanced on the wind. Kay watched her for a moment as she went into a loop. Kay longed to do aerobatics herself. Maybe she could try just one. She went for a stall turn, cutting the throttle back until it could not go up any more. The plane went slower and slower, lost its lift and immediately started to fall. Her heart was left behind. Quickly, she pushed the engine up again and pulled it out of the fall. She had been flying 'by the seat of her pants', not watching the instruments constantly, because she had a feel for the plane. She could gauge the speed by the feel of the controls: faster, the controls became stiffer; slower, they were more sloppy. She glanced at her instrument panel to check her air speed; she was sliding up out of the turn with not enough bank. She gave it a bit of left rudder, turning into the turn a bit more, and balanced out.

She emerged through a curtain of early-morning mist into brilliant blue sky above the hills, the air so clear she could distinguish sheep grazing on tiny tablecloths of green pasture. She felt a sense of pure exhilaration. There was no pleasure in life that compared with the joy of coming through clouds into crystal-clear sky and seeing the hills and valleys all spread out below; no pleasure like that solitude.

She stayed up for well over an hour, feeling the ruffle of the wind on her skin, curving and tipping and straightening out again, climbing and diving, playing with the machine as skilfully as she was able. It responded beautifully, soaring to her command, dropping so that she felt the tickle in her stomach before recapturing the lift again.

Finally, she brought the nose round and headed for the runway. Dickie had told her an hour and no more. Max was likely to be at the airfield at any time after eight a.m., and if the first thing he saw was Kay cartwheeling through the skies without any prior knowledge he would ban her from flying, perhaps for good. Dickie felt the time would come when Max would accept Kay's ability with a palatable, if not inescapable, recognition, and that time was not yet. The early ground engineers had been sworn to secrecy, and they understood and admired the girl for her pluck and determination. Nor would they ever think to argue with the boss. Dickie was anxious not to upset Max, not for herself but for Kay's sake.

Kay saw Dickie's aircraft back on the ground and wanted to make her own landing as perfect as possible.

'Clear to finals. Clear to fly in.' The radio clattered with static. 'Oscar whisky rejoining from the north east.' Interference chequered the line. 'QNH 1006 above sea level . . . runway 26.'

She would make it a nice long gentle landing, stopping just by the seventh marker. She gave herself a point, and tested her approach, cut the engine and prepared to fake a landing, just to prove she could do it and take off again safely. She watched her air speed, took the plane to the point of stalling, coming low, slower and slower till it dropped onto the ground from a couple of feet.

She was a tiny bit too fast. The plane bounced slightly and she had lift-up again. The second time was perfect, the right angle, the right speed, the plane dropping gently to the ground to land smoothly.

She was filing her flight plan as Dickie appeared beside the wing.

'Great landing,' she said as Kay stepped out. 'First one wasn't so hot though. You were too eager.'

She climbed down and pulled off her goggles and helmet, shaking her hair free. 'Were you watching! How did I do?'

'You did beautifully.' Dickie gave her a hug. 'Did you see what I meant about the first time? You're concentrating so hard on the technical. Wait until you go up again. Next time it'll be like being in love!'

'I'm in love already,' she grinned. Her eyes glowed and her

cheeks were warm, her lips parted with the pleasure that flying had given her.

Dickie's fond smile became more serious as she looked into her granddaughter's happy face.

'Kay, did you try aerobatics on your own?'

She looked guilty. 'Yes.'

'Don't. You're not experienced enough yet. Flying's a dangerous sport. Now, I want you to just practise cutting your engine and gliding down into a field on your own, just as if the engine had gone. You need to get that perfect first before you start arsing around on your own. Is that clear?'

'Yes.' She felt the shame sweep through her. It was certainly not professional to take chances as she had done. She had a lot to learn after all. 'I'm sorry, Dickie, it was so tempting.'

'OK,' her voice was gentler. 'You'll need to practise that often once you're a pilot, and you're going to be a damn fine one!' She smiled at the light that caught in Kay's eyes. 'I watched you, Kay. You're a natural, but aerobatics are for later. And, when I'm with you.' She put an arm around her. 'Come on. It's time for breakfast. They'll be wondering where we are.'

It was early autumn, six more frustrating weeks, before she was able to talk about trying for her pilot's licence, taking official flying lessons. It was the eve of her seventeenth birthday. Dickie had come over for the day to discuss setting up a fair the following summer, out on their airfield. They were thinking of closing down the domestic side even further now that the international network was so huge, and the domestic line, such as it was, was to run out of Heathrow and other regional airports. Bower Hill was to be kept for private use only. The fair was to be a way of both saying a nostalgic goodbye to the past, and creating publicity for the way the Bennett Group was developing.

Kay sat down at the dining-room table with the rest of them. Dickie had long since left Kay to fly on her own. She had taken to the air with the natural ease her grandmother had guessed at, and much of her time too had been taken up with the drawing-board. They had kept that to themselves too.

Now Kay leaned over the table with interest. 'A barnstorming fair! How wonderful!' she enthused. 'Like they used to in the old days? With aerobatics and rides and picnics, things like that?'

'Hopefully,' agreed her father. 'Though we'd have to dig up some more biplanes if that were the case. We haven't enough to make it a genuine barnstorming fair.'

'We were thinking of having a couple of air races too,' said Dickie. 'In each category of aircraft.'

'Are you going to race, Dickie?' she asked.

'Yes,' she smiled. 'Of course I will. Flying was always the best part of the business to me.'

'Yes,' said Kay slowly. 'I can understand that!' Across the table from her, Dickie mentally braced herself. 'How about an air race for novice aircraft?' Kay suggested to her father.

Max looked at his daughter with interest. 'Novice aircraft? How do you mean?'

They were all looking at her. 'Well,' she said. 'People building their own aircraft – from kits – that would really bring back the flavour of the past, wouldn't it? Let me show you what I mean.'

She pushed back her chair and went quickly across to the sideboard. Bending down, she opened one of the cupboard doors and pulled out the long tube-shaped plan. Back at the table she unfolded it, Dickie taking two corners at her side and securing them with salt and pepper pots. On her side, Kay weighed down the corners with a couple of books.

'How about this?' She sat back as Max and Dickie leaned forward. Max raised an eyebrow and viewed it upside down. He inspected the design closely. 'This is very good, Kay. Very interesting. Whose is it?' He turned it around towards him to look more closely at detail; pushed it over towards Dickie, who smiled. The design had been all Kay's idea.

'Mine.' Max looked up as she pulled her chair closer to her father. It was her own modification of a standard kit.

'Yours?'

'Yes.' She waited no longer. 'There's a competition at Mill Field next year for the best homebuilt aircraft, and for aerobatics. It covers biplanes, open and cabin accommodation, small jets and monoplanes. I've had a look for the right kit plane and I think this is it. I reckon it'll take around 1,400 working hours to prepare, that is around twenty-three weeks at sixty working hours. It'd be ready in plenty of time for the summer. It would fly at around 180 mph on a 200 hp piston engine, and climb at 2,100 feet per minute. It'd be ideal for displays. If the design was successful, we could market it, especially if I win in it . . .'

'Wait, wait, *wait!*' Max lifted his hand in the air to stop her. 'You? Flying in one of these deathtraps?'

'Shame on you, Daddy. How many times have I heard you say that flying's quite safe in the hands of a skilled pilot. Just because something's exhilarating doesn't make it dangerous,' she said, echoing his own words. 'Aerobatics are not even dangerous correctly performed. Performed by idiots, walking across a street is dangerous. Isn't that what you've always told us?' She gave him a small grin. 'Besides,' she went on. 'It depends on what you're doing and how you're doing it. I'm no idiot. I wouldn't suggest this if I didn't think I could pull it off.'

'Where did you learn to draw like this?'

'I've been studying manuals all summer,' she said coolly, not looking at Dickie. 'At night in my bedroom, first thing in the morning. And I've been talking to some of the engineers at the field. They showed me all about how an engine works. I've watched them taking them to pieces, long before you get down there.'

Dickie gave her a quick look, one that held an amused respect. 'Max,' she said. 'This design is really very good. Here, take a look at this,' she said, pointing at the line. 'Kay, I'm proud of you,' she told her. 'How Bill would have enjoyed this.' The final drawings were new even to her.

Max studied the design once more and then looked up, leaning on his elbows. He surveyed his daughter. 'Does that mean what I think it means?'

'Yes, Daddy,' she said evenly. 'You can't send me away now.'

'Oh, can't I?'

'Dad, I want to fly for a living. I want to build this kit. I know you think I'm young, but I'm not going to change. I'm old enough now to enter the competition at Mill Field, and I'd like you to give serious consideration to running the same sort of race at Bower Hill, and letting me enter it. I'm sure I could have a good go at winning.'

Max nodded. 'The kit is good, I have to give you that. The idea to have them race is a good one too. How about a compromise? Your grandmother flies your design, and my ground staff build it.'

'Stop stalling, Daddy. I'm going to build it.'

'Kay, you don't even know how to fly!'

Kay looked over at Dickie. She looked at her son.

'She does, Max. I've been teaching her.'

Max was stunned into momentary silence.

Dickie hid a smile.

'Now, wait a minute.' Max raised his hands. His brow was dark with anger. 'You've encouraged her? Kay,' he said, turning to her, his voice cold. 'Do you mean to say you've been flying all summer?'

'Yes.'

'At sixteen? Below the age limit?' His eyes were angry as he looked up at his mother. 'And you've been teaching her to fly?'

'It was that or let her try somewhere else. You have to admit she had the best teacher around. In my estimation anyway.'

'And the ground staff were in on this. My God, I'm going to . . .'

'Max.' Dickie's voice was reasoning. 'They didn't know she was sixteen. Just that it was to be a surprise for all of you.'

'It bloody well is that.' Max's look was stern. 'Do you realise how dangerous this mad idea of yours has been? She could have been killed, mother.'

Dickie's eyes were cool and challenging. 'It wasn't too dangerous for you. You started before sixteen. And I taught you too.'

Max flung her a look and turned back to his daughter.

'Kay. No more flying. And you're not going to race. That's all.'

'You can't stop me, Daddy.'

'I can indeed.'

'Daddy,' she said softly. 'Look, I'll fly with or without your permission. Don't you see that? I can get my licence now, go to another field. I'd rather get it here.' She leaned forward. 'I know you could stop me, but look at it this way. I know about it now, I love it, it's in my blood as Dickie says. I've proved how serious I am, proved I can do it . . . *I can fly!*' she exclaimed, her face glorious with the memory of it. 'Sooner or later you're going to have to face the fact that flying is all that interests me. I'd rather do it with your blessing, but if not –' She spoke in an urgent whisper. 'Dad. I love flying. Won't you back me up?'

Jennie put her hands on Max's shoulders.

'Darling,' she said to Kay. 'Take it slowly. There's so much of life ahead, so much for you to experience. Don't try to have it all at once.'

Kay came to her feet. 'Mum,' she said. 'How would you have reacted if someone had said that to you at my age . . . ?' She pushed the chair into the table.

'Kay, stop,' said her father, twisting round in his chair. 'Now, hear me out. I realise how much it means to you, but it doesn't mean that now I know about it and what you've admittedly accomplished I'm going to sanction it. Is that clear?'

'Yes.' She stood at the door, waiting, the fire burning in her eyes, transforming her as the words she wanted to say stayed captured inside her. The energy blazed out of her, like a fire.

'I shall talk this over with your mother and see what we both think. Then we shall give you our answer on the subject.'

Jennie sat down in her place alongside Max as Kay left the room. Max shook his head.

'You know,' he said half to himself. 'I was reminding her the other day of the first day I took her to school. I held her hand all the way, but as we got there she let go, walked straight in. I watched her but she never looked back. She was so ready to find out, she had such curiosity.' He looked into his wife's eyes. 'She's a tomboy now, but that's going to change very soon. I'm proud of her, though it may not seem that way to her right now. She's as pigheaded as anyone of near seventeen can be. But what's going to happen when she becomes a woman, when she realises her own beauty?'

They had all seen that fiery streak of independence, the passion in her that made the green eyes burn. She was still a girl, unconscious of her own self, but brave and courageous, her warmth free and emotional, and with a real sense of love. Max knew what vulnerability lay underneath that tough little tomboy exterior; once that was shed and the woman emerged, he feared for her. '. . . There's going to be trouble then,' he murmured.

'And you've been actively encouraging it,' he accused his mother.

'You can't tie her down,' said Dickie flatly. She had been standing back from them at the side of the room. Now she looked directly at her son. 'Kay's a free spirit. She has to find out. There's nothing you can do about it, Max, except support her.'

*

It was a rainy day, a Sunday. The old classroom was quite different now that the other boys had all gone home on a leave-out. The wooden desk was inscribed with the names of previous occupants from generations before. David Hamblin was taking the entrance exam to Andover. He had asked to swap his last year at Eton for a year at Andover, the prestigious school near Boston, Massachusetts. A friend of his had gone there, written to say that America was great. David fully believed him. America was an open land, a land of great opportunity, a land where one could travel unfettered by convention or class, where one could succeed on ability and nothing else. David was a loner, and an individual. America was where he wanted to be.

The questions were on subjects he had never even heard of. He felt bound to fail, but what he did not know was that boys were not necessarily assessed on answers but on their ability to handle the questions, as they might handle life. It was a school for rich, very bright children, with a reputation for real brilliance. Students of thirteen were known to do advanced calculus set for twenty-six-year-old young men. It was also for athletes, and David was one of those. Andover School wanted genius, it wanted very special young men. It was a pass card to anywhere. The future right-hand men to presidents, heads of companies, heirs to massive fortunes sat side by side in its classrooms and played on its fields: Rockefellers, Kennedys mixed with boys from the mid-west towns, towns where their one claim to fame was that one of their own had reached Andover.

David left the classroom and went outside. Charles and Sarah were talking to one of the masters. They broke away and came towards him.

'All over?'

He nodded. 'Let's go.' He still had the rest of the day to enjoy at Windsor: a walk along the riverbank, and one of Sarah's picnic teas.

'How do you think you did?'

'Impossible questions. I did my best.'

'I'm sure you did.' They reached the car, and Charles turned. 'America's a great place. You've made the right decision, David. If you get into Andover, your life will change dramatically. You'll broaden your horizons, that's for sure.'

'It was something I wanted to mention, actually.' He looked

directly at his uncle. 'Would it be all right if I went to stay with Aunt Sabrine in the holidays? Save coming back here. I'd like California, I know.'

'Sabrine?' Charles repeated. Sarah looked a little surprised.

'I didn't know you'd been in contact with her, David,' she said.

'Oh yes, we've become quite good friends.'

'Have you?' She would not have thought Sabrine would have been an automatic choice for friendship, yet young David had an eye for people.

'We got along very well at grandmother's funeral. She's started up a stud farm, just up the coast from Malibu where she used to live. She seems really interested, says she's a successful breeder of Arabians now, between films. I'd rather like to go along and give her a hand.'

Charles unlocked the car door and looked briefly at his wife.

'Has she said she would like that?'

'Actually, yes. What do you think?' he asked them both. 'Do you think father'll go along with it?'

'I don't know,' said Charles. 'We'd better put it to him, don't you think?' He looked at Sarah.

'Yes, of course,' she said. She gave David a gentle hug. He was one of her own now and she would miss him. She did not want either of them to see how sad she felt at losing him. Sarah had never held anyone back from what they wanted. She hid her feelings with a light remark. 'Come on, let's go and have that picnic before the day's all gone.'

CHAPTER NINETEEN

The last stroke brought her cleanly to the edge of the pool. Thirty lengths. Her fingers found the tiled edge and her head broke free of the water, smooth as a seal. Kay pulled in a deep breath. She felt strong and healthy. She swam to the steps and pulled herself out, her thoughts far away.

'Well, you've certainly grown up!' She heard the soft laugh, and her eyes flew up. 'Jennie said I'd find you out here.'

Robbie Fairfax was back. Handsome, yet with the same mischievous sparkle in his eye. He had sat down beside the pool, so quietly she had not heard him come. She wondered how long he had been watching her. She had swum naked at one point. She blushed foolishly. 'Robbie, what are you doing here?'

His blond hair was smoothed back from his forehead, his eyes fringed by their pale lashes were very sensual and his mouth was set in a crooked smile, his gaze admiring. He had always been her hero, since childhood, since that day at the railway line. She did not recall much else about the day now, except the two things that stood out: her terror of the woods, and this handsome youth that now sat beside her, his eyes teasing and his manner deliberately casual. 'Birthday surprise,' he said, eyeing her. 'I remember your skinny little legs when you were climbing up and down those trees,' he said. 'I bet I was the first guy to see how pretty they were going to get.'

His eyes slipped down her body. Mentally she tried to cover herself. Her tiny white bikini left little to the imagination. She picked up her towel.

He laughed. 'Shy, Kay? You never were. I remember you always being so bold. I guess not now, huh?'

Robbie grinned, showing gleaming white teeth. He was a live wire, a devil. Bright, sharp, endearing, never one to be pinned down by anyone or anything, he planned to be footloose all his life. He was always up to tricks, always in trouble, always at the forefront of every activity. Kay thought she had never seen anyone quite so handsome. She tried to be serious, to change the air that he had created.

'You didn't come just to see me,' she said at last. 'What are you doing over here, Robbie? No one knew you were coming, did they?' She looked over towards the house. The doors stood open to the warmth of the day already. It was late September but the temperature had unexpectedly hit the eighties. Kay had taken advantage of the early hours of the day to do her lengths in the new swimming-pool, built down by the side of the house. A yew hedge framed it to one side, giving it an intimacy. An intimacy that made her uncomfortable today, alone here with Robbie. She could sense the masculinity about him, feeling the mocking light in his blue eyes resting on her exposed skin. Robbie was not like the English boys she knew; he was the type to take what he wanted when he wanted. He was a little dangerous.

She stood, and his eyes followed her. 'Nope. Thought I'd pay a surprise visit,' he said. 'I'm up at Oxford studying PPE. You're going to be my home from home for the next few years, do you know that?'

'No. I didn't,' she said drily. 'Do my parents know that?' She poured herself a glass of lemonade at the poolside trolley. She poured one for him too.

'Sure,' he said easily, stretching his long legs out and leaning on his arm. 'They invited me. Thanks,' he added, taking the drink. He took a deep swallow, put the glass down on the tiles, and sat up cross-legged. He looked around briefly, and put his hand into his tee-shirt pocket. He pulled out a plastic wallet, lifted it up to show her.

'Smoke?'

She stared, knowing suddenly. 'Heavens, no.' He shrugged, started to roll the joint with long, expert fingers. He licked the paper carefully and lit up with satisfaction. His eyes creased into shadows, like a well-sunned cat. Kay watched, fascinated.

'Want to try?' he said, handing it to her, his voice breaking with the drag of smoke.

'Not right now,' she said looking at the house.

'Jim would,' he said nonchalantly.

'Jim? Does he smoke that!' Her eyes absorbed the new idea.

'Sure. What do you think he was in training for down behind your summer house all those years ago? Jim's got all the right ideas. You always used to be ready for any challenge too,' he said, cocking an eyebrow at her, the blue eyes smouldering now with the effect of the drug.

'I still am,' she said. She was no longer the child of yester-year. 'For the things that interest me.'

'Show me.' His movement was unexpected and sudden, the alert blue eyes raking her. He had leaned forward fast and taken her hands into his, pulling her towards him. She felt the heat of his skin jump through the palms of her hands like a shock. They were strong hands, demanding, used to getting their way.

Kay did not know quite how to take him. She wished she had been prepared for this. She broke away.

'I'm a little cold. I'm just going to go in and change.'

She ran back up the short flight of steps towards the side terrace of the house, his soft laughter following her indoors. She flew up the stairs, feeling naked from his laughter.

Along the corridor she went quickly into her room. There she stripped off her wet bathing suit, and pulled on knickers, cotton shorts and striped tee-shirt. She felt more comfortable immediately, and sat on the bed for a moment, thinking. Then, drawn to him despite herself, she went over to her bedroom window and looked out.

He was standing beside the pool. He pulled off his jeans and shirt, strode round to the deep end and executed a perfect racing dive, swam underwater to the far end and then kicked off, floating easily on his back, stroking rhythmically back down towards the shallow end again.

Halfway, he looked up as if he sensed her there. Kay drew back, but she had seen again that glimmer on his lips, the light fencing with her in his eyes. She heard again that taunting laugh, felt his long fingers hard on her skin. Robbie disturbed her, in a way she had not previously experienced. She felt that perhaps she did not even like him very much, but it did not seem to matter.

'You come on like a dream, peaches and cream, lips like strawberry wine . . .'

The music drifted out on the night air. It was the last party of the summer, down by the beach. The young crowd had piled into their cars and driven down through the soft warm evening to the New Forest. One of Jim's friends lived there. With the spontaneity of teenagers, they had decided to make use of the sudden heatwave and hold Kay's seventeenth birthday party on the marshy flats beyond his house. She had driven down in Robbie's Lotus, hair flashing around her face in the breeze. They had sung along to all the latest songs about being sixteen and young love, every song lauding their youth and freedom to love and have fun. There was Elvis Presley by the beach and long, hot, days. It had been their summer.

Kay listened to the song as she leaned against the only tree that had survived amongst the scrub bushes up from the dunes. It was a bare, hardy cypress, the only tree that could stand the strong winter winds that tore over this same open land a few months from now, permanently leaning inland after years of lashing sea gales. Now, the night was still. The others had gone off for a swim. The light from the fire was warm, the sound of the distant waves crashing, girls squealing. Kay did not want to swim tonight; she did not want to giggle with the other girls. She felt reflective and mellow. On the far side of the fire, she could see Robbie reclining against the ground, a girl sitting beside him. She was laughing easily, her blonde hair bright against the glow of the flames. She was making it clear she liked him, thought Kay. Robbie had that effect on girls. He was hard to pin down and consequently they were all over him, trying to be the one. She knew this one would never succeed: she was trying far too hard. She turned away towards the sound of the sea.

'Hi!'

She turned to the voice. Robbie stood there, his face dark from his summer tan, his hair crested silver in the light of the moon. His white teeth shone in a ready grin. 'Is this tree taken?'

'No. Of course not.' She moved over slightly, letting him move in beside her. She studied him. 'Not smoking tonight?' she asked caustically.

He looked into her eyes. 'Not at the moment. Want a drink?' He passed her the half-empty bottle of cheap red wine.

She took it, looked at it for a moment.

'You know,' he said, looking out over the marshy heath around them. 'Jennie and your Dad did their romancing just down the road from here. My folks rented a house for the summer, by the sea, and your mom's family all used to come over. I think they were all pretty startled by the English weather.'

She smiled. 'After California, I can imagine. Did you come too?'

'Just about! I don't remember much about it though, except

that apparently Max was the first guy to handle all of us. We hero-worshipped him, or rather Jennie's brothers did. I was only a baby. They didn't play their usual tricks on him, anyway.'

Kay drank from the bottle and handed it back to him. He didn't seem quite so bad now he wasn't teasing, being more friendly, but he still made her feel awkward. Her parents had allowed her to stay out late with Robbie. He was considered family. Safe. If they only knew. She looked back at him. Cool, lean and handsome with that devil-may-care sparkle. Most of the girls had an eye for her good-looking family friend.

'Yeah,' he said. 'Your Dad was quite a guy. Jennie didn't have a chance! She was hard to catch but he had no trouble. They say once you meet the right one it just all falls into place.' His eyes were warm on her. 'Do you think that's true?'

'I don't know,' she said softly. Being with him made her feel warm and uncomfortable both at the same time, but she did not want to move away.

She took the bottle he offered her and drank again. It made her mellow. 'I hadn't really thought about it. It'll just happen, I expect.'

'I expect so too. You're a very beautiful girl, Kay . . .' His fingers touched her face. Her eyes were smoky and sensual, half smiling as she looked at him in the light of the fire. Her body moved slightly to the music that played on around them. Robbie felt the familiar stirrings inside him.

'Do you think so?' she said, her face tilted and her lips parted. Her arms were behind her, leaning against the trunk of the tree, and her breasts outlined against the distant silver line of the sea.

'Can I be the first to wish you happy birthday?'

She nodded. His hand stole around the back of her neck and pulled her to him. She proffered her cheek. Robbie pressed his mouth to hers.

For a moment she was startled, then she felt the thrill run through her. She pulled herself away and turned, ran down the path through the dunes towards the sea. Robbie stood a moment, watching, the taste of her still on his lips. She wore tiny shorts and a sweatshirt that dwarfed her. She was all legs, her red-brown hair ruffled by the breeze, and the green eyes alive in her sunbrown face as she turned to see him closing on her. She cried out, laughing, and ran harder. Robbie was hard on her heels. He almost caught her bare flying legs in a rugger tackle just as she reached the top of the dunes, but a smooth heel was all he felt, slipping from his grasp. She was gone, running down the slope towards the sea, her laughter trailing out behind her. Robbie picked himself up and threw himself down the slope after her, caught her and grabbed her to him.

Beneath him, Kay wriggled and laughed as he pulled at her sweatshirt. She was provocative without even knowing it, thinking this still a game, like the ones she had played with them all as children. He would show her. He reached for her mouth again. The waves licked in and caught them, and then he threw her into the waves, falling in with her. He felt her warmth, the musky smell and incredible softness of her. She intoxicated him.

'Oh, Kay,' he groaned and buried his face in her. Held her tighter, brought his face down to taste the salt on her skin, on her lips. Suddenly, it was not a game. He saw her eyes, felt the passion in her stir.

And swiftly she had broken free. She was gone, back up the beach. Running, running.

Robbie ran after her.

The shaft of light fell across the woodblocked floor outside her mother's cosy little room. Kay knocked softly and stepped forward, pushing on the door. 'Mum . . . ?'

Jennie was half asleep, her reading glasses balanced on the end of her nose, and a new hardback novel open on her knees, her slim hand holding the place as sleep threatened to overtake her. She turned with a gentle smile for her daughter. 'Darling . . . did you have a lovely party?'

'Yes, thank you, Mum, it was . . . Mum, can I talk to you a moment?'

'But of course, honey.' She closed the book and laid it aside on the table. 'Come and sit down here.' She indicated the small button-back chair beside her, but it was to her feet that Kay sank, curling up against her knees the way she had as a child.

'Mum,' she began. 'What's love like? I mean, how does it feel?'

So that was it. 'Well,' she said slowly, 'it's pretty wonderful. I fell in love with your father the first moment I saw him. But it's not always easy to tell the difference between love and infatuation, especially when you're very young. Why do you ask?'

'Love makes you feel happy though, doesn't it? You and Daddy have always been happy. It's been easy for you.'

Jennie thought back. Not necessarily, not always easy. She pulled her daughter closer. 'What's brought this on, darling? Did you meet someone nice at the party?'

'No.' Kay thought for a moment. 'Not really. There isn't anyone, Mum. I'm just interested.'

'Good night!'

She waved her hand happily to them all as they left the pub, and stumbled against Robbie, losing her balance. 'Whoops!' she giggled. 'Must have been a step there.'

Robbie steadied her in his arms, winked at the chap at the bar, who grinned and gestured behind her back. With Robbie's arm firmly around her waist, they stepped out into the street.

Kay laughed happily as she looked up into his face. It was fun being with him. By streetlight Robbie looked even more handsome, his eyes dark and glowing, his suntanned face softly blurred by the rain as they walked away from the Bull alone together. It had been a wonderful evening. They had gone on a pub crawl with all his friends. He was very popular wherever they went, with the girls too, ones who had quite obviously gone out with him and would still like to. They had studied Kay closely, she knew. But Robbie was a rolling stone. No one would ever pin him down and he was so carefree about it that none seemed to take offence. She was just happy to be with him.

He led her round the corner of the high-walled buildings in the direction of his rooms. She knew where they were going and wanted to be taken there. She felt a quiver of excitement and a lush feeling of abandonment she had never felt before; all her inhibitions seemed numbed and she felt relaxed, with no sense of caution at all. All she wanted was for Robbie's warm strong arm to hold her for ever the way he was doing, and to feel his kiss again. With a flood of feeling that coursed all the way up through her limbs she remembered that brief kiss on the marshes, and how his arms had tightened around her, how demanding and strong his hands had felt as they pulled her to him, that dark look of wanting in his eyes. The need for him seemed to sweep into her temples making her dizzy. She did not seem in control at all, and nor did she want to be. Robbie was leading her back to his rooms and that was exactly where she wanted to be.

'Are you all right?' He pulled her a little closer, kissing her rain-soaked forehead.

'Yes. I'm fine!' They rounded the corner and went in through the high gates.

The rain suddenly became a torrent, a wind whipping in from behind them and whirling the rain into gusts. 'Come on!' he said. 'We're going to get soaked!' He grabbed her hand and ran her across the grass quadrangle towards the door at the opposite side. In his wake, Kay felt as if she were flying along, towed by a determined Robbie. She still had the taste of aniseed in her mouth; she had never had so much to drink before and Robbie and his friends had plied her with drink after drink. After the first two she had lost count of the other milky-aniseed Pernods.

Up the stone-dark stairs, quiet and old, the rain still gushing down at the open doorway behind them, but now they were dry and their footsteps resounding as he led her down a tall unlit corridor to a door at the end. He opened it and ushered her in.

'Here we are. My home, madame. Well, what do you think?'

Kay went in. The medium-sized room had old and dark furniture: a couple of leather chairs piled with books, cushions everywhere, a table, a big wooden window seat and a high window that overlooked the quad outside. It was cosy, and in front of the fireplace was a three-bar fire which he was now turning on. The bars started to glow a dim red.

'It's very nice,' she said, still standing.

At the other side of the room, Robbie laughed. 'Not much, but it's mine as they say. Get your coat off; you must be soaked.' He was bending down to a plug as he spoke, disappearing behind a chair.

Kay pulled off her coat and let it drop over the arm of the chair. Her legs were bare, and underneath the thin coat her dress was wet too. She had not closed the buttons of her coat as they had made their mad dash back here. She wiped at it with her hands, pushed back the wet tangle of her hair from her face. A soft light came on in the corner and the opening strains of a pop ballad. Kay felt herself relax, smiling inside at the haunting music as she went over to the window and sat on the hard wooden seat. She pulled her feet up as many must have done before her and looked out over the dark, rain-lashed grass. Soft lights poured from the many windows. Christchurch was a beautiful college, one of the oldest. She felt as if it was the best evening of her life.

Robbie had crossed the room without her hearing. Now he was sitting beside her, his warm eyes resting on her, an intimate light in their depths. Admiring. She held his look, waiting for him to kiss her. She raised her face slightly, feeling her eyelids heavy, her skin warm. His hands reached out towards her. She parted her lips.

His fingers touched the skirt of her dress. 'You're soaking wet,' he said. 'You should get that dress off. I could dry it by the fire.'

'Yes,' she murmured. Her fingers found the buttons at the neck, fumbling slightly. She smiled at him. 'I'd love a bath.'

'Why don't you . . . I'll go and run it for you. You can borrow my dressing-gown and change in there. Hand me out your dress when you're ready. I'll dry it off for you.'

'All right.' Robbie left her; she heard his footsteps cross the hall, the sound of gushing water starting to fill a bath.

She slid her legs over onto the floor and stood up. It seemed hard to do. She wobbled slightly, and steadied herself against the wall. She put her hand to her mouth to stop herself giggling again. She felt very silly. She took a step forward to the chair, reaching out her hand to hold it. Robbie came back into the room, his eyes looking directly for her.

'Ready?'

She nodded.

'I'll just get my dressing-gown. Bath's across there.' He pointed across the hall, and went away across the room again into an adjoining room. His bedroom.

Kay crossed to the door. And then she saw the little table just beside it. There was a tray there, an old battered tin tray, and on it stood a half-bottle of whisky, a small fat candle and a box of matches. Robbie's seduction gear. She gave a little laugh to herself, and picked them up, tucking them into her arms as she went across the hall.

The bathroom was huge, white tiles and ghastly orange paint reflected in the glare of a blazing strip light. It hurt her eyes. The water blasted from the tap with all the strength and noise of Niagara Falls into a yellow rust-stained bath. Hand over her eyes, she quickly doused the light and carried her candle over to the ledge by the tiny window. She placed it there, lit it, and stood back. Much better. She pulled off her dress, bent to turn off the water, the room blissfully quiet. With satisfaction, she pulled off her flimsy cotton underwear, stepped into the bath and slid down into the warm water, briefly closing her eyes. She came up again, took the bottle of whisky, unscrewed the cap and tipped her head back.

'Kay? Kay? Are you ready?'

There was no answer. He knew what state she was in. God knows, wasn't it just what he had wanted? But perhaps she had fallen in the bath. He pushed gently on the door. It opened.

The room was transformed, dim with a peachy glow. At first he could not see her. The light was thrown from the candle, like stained glass in a soft pattern over the room. It lit the edges of the window, the black glass pearled with the continuing rain-storm outside. Inside was silence, except for the drip of the tap into the still water like the sound in an underground cave. The room was not hot, but steamy, there was a distant smell of damp in the air. The water moved softly. A swirl in the dark.

'Kay?'

He saw her then. A smoky brown silhouette in the bath, her hair knotted on her head, her knee breaking the water. He could see the smile on her face, feel the warmth of her eyes.

'Robbie, come here.'

Her voice was different, slightly slurred. He saw the bottle. Her eyes glowed in the dark. He went closer. Her body was spectacular. She pulled herself up from the water as he turned away, her arms around his neck. There was whisky on her breath.

'Kiss me, Robbie. Love me . . .'

Her lips lifted to his. She was beautiful, feminine, a glorious body available to him. His hands tightened on her wrists. He bent his head. The sweep of her warm lips brushed his, their sexuality unmistakable. For a moment his head burned with her, her scent, the softness of her skin, those fabulous eyes drawing him in. He groaned and took her in his arms for just a second, as she arched up to him.

She felt the warmth of his skin through his thin shirt, the roughness of his jeans against her thighs. It was heaven.

'Kay, you're drunk.'

'I found your whisky.'

He had tried to get her drunk, and succeeded. Suddenly, he felt like a real heel. This was Kay. She was special, not like the others. 'I'm not going to touch you, Kay. You'll thank me tomorrow for this,' he said.

'I won't. I'll thank you for making me a woman!' she slurred slightly, and the soft giggle was not a child's, it was a sensual ripple along his spine. The words were only those of a child: a child who knew no wrong. Kay was naïve and drunk. He could take advantage of her, or – and Robbie did not know where he, the great cocksman, found his strength – he could deny her. As she leaned in against him, her head against his shoulder, submissive, as gently as he was able he untangled the languorous arms from around his neck and reached for the towel.

'Here, let me help you out.'

She climbed into his arms, like a Venus rising from the waves, her body long and beautifully drawn. The water broke around her as she rose, reverberating against his ears within the hum of steamy dark silence.

She drooped gently against him, gauche little Kay. He wrapped her in the towel, the love he suddenly felt for her overwhelming.

'I thought you loved me,' she said sleepily. 'I thought you wanted me.'

'I do love you, Kay, that's why . . .' he said, knowing the truth now. He rubbed her back gently. If she had been anyone else, they would already be in bed together.

'I'm sleepy, Robbie.'

He pulled his dressing-gown around her, tying the belt at her waist, and then led her across the hall, through his room and into the bedroom. He had turned down the bed earlier. Now he felt shame as he remembered his thoughts. She had been so willing it had destroyed him. He slid the gown from her shoulders, and tried not to look as he tucked the glorious and naked body into his bed. He would sleep on the horsehair sofa. Hadn't he done that often enough before, with a girl wrapped in his arms too, after an exhausted night of love? He knew how to love, how to please. If only Kay had known that. He had a reputation for it.

'I'm sorry, Kay, please try to understand,' He started to explain.

Soft breathing came from the bed. He leaned over. She had not heard. Already she was sleeping, her profile graceful against the worn white pillow, her hair strewn darkly across it.

He pushed his clothes from the old cane-back chair beside the bed and sat down, straightening the sheet across her shoulder. He watched her for a moment.

She slept on, and had never seemed more beautiful. He remembered a thousand things, an aeroplane kit, a flash of long legs, the laughter at the top of the tree when they had been climbing that summer they were still children, the down on her cheek as they had stood close behind the summer house, the sun in her hair suddenly, the flash of those eyes as if in a glimpse of some early primaeval knowledge.

She was his Kay. So precious. He had nearly abused her beauty. He stood up, kissed her gently and left the room.

Robbie almost laughed at his honourable behaviour as he grabbed the old rug from the cupboard in the sitting-room, pulled off his shoes and trousers and eased himself onto the hard springs of the old sofa. In a few hours he would wake her, sober her with black coffee and get her over the wall in the dark.

His need for her burned in him as he reached for his cigarettes. He did not want her like this, drunk because of some underhand bet with his friends. It had cheapened her, made him ashamed. He wanted her sober, loving him too. He pulled the blanket over his chest, smoked his cigarette and lay awake in the dark, waiting for the early hours of morning. He could not hold out much longer.

CHAPTER TWENTY

Early summer, 1969

It had been no contest. Rupert had objected to letting David go to America but Alexander had agreed, and David had been accepted for the summer course.

The day was hot and still. An aeroplane cruised high overhead. On the summer air the school choir sang, the windows of the classroom open to the day.

A small wind disturbed the boughs of the cherry tree, a cloud of pink blossom floating downwards. The petals drifted to land on the sleeping form of the boy who lay in the grass beneath.

David woke as the soft blossom touched his face. Up above, through the rustling boughs, the sky was blue without a cloud, the sun warm on his skin. All his senses came aware as he listened to the choir singing, felt the light velvet brush of the petals as the wind lifted them gently once more, the perfume still with him, the sun closing his lashes as he breathed in. It was the first truly sensual experience of his life. David felt warm and golden. It was not yet time for his class. He had gone to sleep under the tree in the warmth of the sun. Now he lay and listened peacefully.

The music was finishing, there was movement, the scraping of chairs. The doors opened, the class emerging ready to play. David hardly noticed; he was separate from them, as if he had come alive for the first time.

'Dave, hey, *Dave.*'

The blond giant hung over him, footed him lightly in the side.

'We're going to hang out down at the girls' school. You coming?'

David squinted upwards. 'No. I've got some reading to do.'

The other boy laughed. 'I don't think you're going to get much reading done.' He squatted down beside David, tipping the wink in the direction of the edge of the playing-field. David rolled over onto his side and followed the line of his gaze. The girl stood under the trees on the far side, her hair signalling her like a banner. He knew exactly who she was. His friend chuckled. 'Lucky bastard! She won't look at any of us. She sure likes you. Well, so long, and good luck!'

The group gathered together, murmuring as they went off across the fields towards town, their deep voices punctured with bursts of meaningful laughter. Diagonally, across the field, she came. Quite slowly, her hair lifting out on the breeze. David watched her for a moment, his dark eyes absorbing her intensely at first, and then as if he had all the time in the world, he lay back, arms behind his head, and waited.

He smelled the warm scent of her as she settled herself down beside him, not shop-bought perfume like many of the girls, but natural skin. She said nothing.

David opened one eye and looked up. She was watching him, her long white-blonde hair framing her, her skin like palest gold.

'It's a nice day for the beach,' she said at last. David said nothing. 'I thought I'd go down.' She eyed him, very conscious of his brown eyes studying her behind their lashes. 'Would you like to come?' she finished softly. 'There's going to be a full moon tonight.'

'With the others?' He shook his head and closed his eyes against the heat of the sun. 'No, thanks.' They always went together, a whole group of them. It was not for him, the girls giggling on the sand, the boys rough-housing around them, too eager; the best athlete, the best . . .

'No, alone. Just you and me.' She licked her lips.

David opened his eyes again. The look he gave her made her cheeks flush and she dropped her eyes, plucking at a blade of grass. Not for long. When they opened again, their pale blue had deepened. David was very still, his eyes ran down over her breasts and back up to her face. The white silk hair waved in the wind and her lips were full, like palest peach.

He had a class, but . . .

'All right . . .' He sat up, coming closer to her. She could smell the slight muskiness from his skin after lying in the sun, the crush of grass mingling with it. It made her feel heady; she had wanted him so badly.

He took her hand in his as he stood up. 'Let's go, then.' He did not waste time. She came to her feet beside him, touching his shoulder.

'My car's over there,' she said, pointing at the parking lot. The chrome on the new long red American sports car glittered in the sunlight.

David shook his head, ran a hand over the blond hair, now cropped closer to his head. 'No. We'll go in mine.'

They watched the sea in silence. The moon spread a gleam across it, the waves phosphorescent as they tumbled onto the shore, licking the sand before they pulled out again slowly. They felt the rhythm, sitting side by side on the worn red leather seat in the front of his van. They had swum all afternoon, talked a little, drunk the cold beer she had brought and hamburgers cooked in the little town just up beyond the dunes. They felt salty and burnt and easy. The beer tasted good.

Her feet were up on the dashboard, slender golden legs in tattered cut-off shorts, ending in old plimsolls. Her hair was silver in the ocean light. She tossed it back over her shoulders and drank the last of her beer, then placed the can between her feet.

'Ever had an older woman, David?' she asked suddenly into the silence that had sprung between them. Her eyes caught his across the divide.

'You're not much older than me. Only two years.'

'It's a major amount where I come from.'

'Yeah?'

'Yeah!' She laughed lightly. The music of it, and maybe the tension too, caught at him, and he laughed with her. She saw him: dark, teeth white in the shadows, his hair like a crest of gold; saw the power of his lean muscles, the long strong legs parted as he sat so relaxed. Her eyes strayed upwards. Her laughter still giggled through her, but it was helpless and nervous. She wanted badly to reach out for him, for him to reach for her, to feel his strength on her. Their laughter died as he saw the look in her.

'I never had any woman,' he said.

She felt herself hold her breath as he came closer. Her eyes went dark and wide, the shadow of his face covered hers, and she felt all at once enclosed in him, his arms a band around her, his lips so warm. Her eyes closed swiftly.

David pulled away, his fingers finding the buttons of her clothes as if with practised ease. The girl felt the need to say something: it was as if he was born to it. But she was proud, she was his first.

'Never had a woman, David?' she breathed, her skin trembling as his fingers brushed over her. 'Well, when's your birthday . . .' she said, a half-laugh in her voice, as her senses fell apart, her bones weakening.

'This month', he lied.

'Happy birthday!' she said, and laughed no more. His lips were against her skin, her head tipped back and she drew in a long breath as he found her, a dusting of silver hair where the last button of her shorts came undone. He slid them from under her, the pool of her navel all that was dark against the lovely long lean shape of her, white-pale, almost albino, her long hair stretching fine and silky down to her buttocks. David took her in with pleasure, sensing what was to come. And then he bent his head to her, and listened to her cries.

In the dunes, he had his first girl. In his van parked behind the dunes, with the sound of the ocean bathing them. Afterwards they shared a cigarette, and he held her in his arms. She was soft and very slender, her hair trailing like mist across him as she slept. David smoked the cigarette and held her. He went over the feeling in his memory, every detail clear. It was glorious.

At Bower Hill, the brand new test plane swept over the land, dipping and rising high into the early dawn. The light was beautiful and the airfield deserted and grey, the morning pearly.

A collection of people stood and watched as the plane roared by again, blasting them in a gust of wind. The small aircraft climbed swiftly and once high in the sky looped over on its back, causing them to watch open-mouthed. The pilot pulled out smoothly, flew straight for a moment and climbing slightly again went into a perfect tumble turn, spiralling downwards over the fields.

'Damn that boy. She's not safe,' said Max. 'Much too flimsy.'

Dickie watched, a smile etched onto her face. 'Well, he seems to be managing it all right.'

He had planned his aerial display well. Flying straight, a dive . . . into a loop, out of the loop, stall turn, forward, tumble turn and back, soaring magnificently up into the clouds over their heads as if in perfect pleasure, and then with a deep throaty roar in the early morning, the small craft banked into the turn and flipped over onto its back to fly along upside down.

'Oh, my God!' Jennie put her hands to her face. 'Is he safe, Max?'

Max's frown had been replaced by a definite look of interest, and a dawning pride. He seemed to be handling the machine beautifully. 'He's doing all right.'

'Don't be so ungenerous,' said Dickie. There was laughter in her voice. 'That was a perfect display. Good as I've ever done.' She chuckled, pleased. It had been a long time since anyone in the family had taken to the air like this. It had all been business, business. It did her good. Up above them, the plane had righted itself and was now banking in rhythmic turns. The pilot was playing with the sky like a fish in a pool. 'I never knew he enjoyed it so much,' said Max. 'I was wrong about him.' His son had always seemed to him so uninterested in flying.

'I'll still have a few words to say to him when he gets down. That homemade's not strong enough to stand up to too much of that. I should have tested it first.'

Dickie smiled, and watched as the pilot brought the tiny craft smoothly back down towards the airfield. In the end, Max had given over the now empty hangar at the end of the airfield for the ground engineers and Dickie to build Kay's kit plane for her. She had given in to this under pressure, with the promise of building her own next time round, and helping out at weekends under Jim and Dickie's supervision. This was the first time the family had seen her out of the hangar and she was a neat little aircraft. However, Max's proviso had been that he would go over her once she was completed and Dickie would test her.

The whole family was gathered on the runway as the plane came in for a touchdown. Max walked forward a pace as it coasted to a stop, its nose swerving to point out over them. His face was grim. Brilliant as the display had been, it had also been foolhardy. He was ready to read the riot act.

The cockpit door opened and the pilot stepped out onto the wing.

Max came around the nose and stared upward.

'Jim . . . what the hell do you think you're doing? Get down here at once.'

The pilot whipped off his helmet. Kay shook her gold chestnut hair free and laughed happily.

'What do you think, Dad? Didn't I handle her well? Now you'll let me enter the competition, won't you?'

'Good God, Kay, you little fool!' he said.

'Oh, Dad!' She jumped down and faced them, her face exhilarated. 'I knew if I asked you to come down and watch you'd never let me fly her, so I thought this was the best way to let you see. I'm sorry, it's the only way I knew . . .'

'Don't you think she's good?' Dickie's voice came from across the grass. Her eyes smiled knowingly at Max.

Max was struggling with mixed emotions. He was trying hard not to show the feelings of pride overtaking his feeling of fury and fear. She was a damn good pilot, made for it. He was immensely proud of her. She was like a young animal, unafraid. Obstinate too. Beneath the glow in her eyes, there was something more. As she had pulled her hat from her head, she had been ready for the inevitable confrontation but her eyes had said she was not going to back down.

It was Dickie who broke the ice. 'She wasn't just good, she was amazing,' she said, going forward to hold her grand-daughter in her arms. 'You were very, very good, Kay. I am proud of you. Mind you, it's not surprising. It's in your blood!' She laughed. 'And I have taught you!' The girl had the same ruthlessness as her, she had enjoyed it enormously whilst remaining coldly skilful. It was the challenge of precision over machine, of being one and wrestling with the dangers and excitements of air, far far more dangerous than anything that could be achieved on land. This she understood so well, it had been her way too. Fighting for what she believed in, no one had stopped her either. Kay, in her way, was doing just the same. Their eyes met, so similar. Dickie pulled her close and kissed her. 'What a girl you are, after my own heart!'

Kay was laughing in her arms. 'Thank you, Dickie!' There were tears standing in her eyes as she drew away. And looked towards her father.

'Dad, can I join now?'

Dickie looked at him too, her green eyes brilliant with humour.

Max stood and watched them. 'No. I'm grounding you for the rest of the summer.'

Kay paled. 'But I . . .'

'Enough, Kay.' Her father's voice was cold. 'It was foolhardy and dangerous, but more than that I'd already told you "no". You have to learn some time, Kay, where you stop.'

'But you saw,' she said desolately, pointing at the sky.

'It makes no difference.' He turned. 'Now let's go home to breakfast.'

CHAPTER TWENTY-ONE

Alexander Hamblin walked into the foyer of the Redfield-Strauss bank. Today he was coming as their future chairman, and they did not yet know it. It was his secret. He looked about him with an acquisitive air as he strode the spotless hall.

The commissionaire's desk was directly ahead of him, a mahogany plinth carved and set weightily, a centrepiece to the elaborate space all around it. The great hall was carpeted in deep green, the walls lined with carved mahogany panels. To one side a roped-in area fronted spacious and comfortable armchairs and sofas in button-back oxblood leather, and an elegant deep red Persian rug lay stretched across the carpet between. A Nibbs grandfather clock stood to one side, and set against the panelled walls were softly-lit and sombre paintings, all originals, some very valuable. A glass-fronted showcase displayed silver trophies, and on the top was an arrangement of fresh flowers. Windows, veiled with net, gave onto the busy street outside, where one could look out but not in. The commissionaire was uniformed and hatted in green with a plum and gold crest on his pocket and braided cap. He gave a half-salute as he recognised the man who had just entered, and continued talking with studied politeness to the client of the bank who stood before him.

Alexander returned the gesture with just the slightest nod of his head as he strode down the carpeted hallway towards the lift. He was fascinated by the possibilities of banking already. Power. It was what he craved. And this was where he would find it. From today he would run this bank single-handed, command this air of opulence all for himself.

He pressed the bell for the lift and considered his future. Alexander had something of the same self-preservative streak as his sister Sabrine. Through her adolescent hands and through those of his cohorts at school, he had learned to suffer. He had also learned to hide from them all the extent of his extremely sharp mind. It had been his secret. He had hidden it with cunning; learning to be devious and highly manipulative was the only way to survive the humiliations heaped on him. No one had ever given him any credence. He had lived in the shadows of brighter creatures: the school hero, who had made him bend to his will so often in return for his protection; his half-crazy but so utterly beautiful sister, Sabrine, who had played with him as her mood took her; his grandfather, Rupert, an autocratic bully who had forced him to marry despite his own, entirely homosexual inclinations. Now he would come into his own. Here, with the quiet and cold facts and figures he was getting exactly what he had always wanted: since his first foothold on the first rung of the ladder he had known it. His grandfather had shown no interest in the bank, just the occasional foray to line his personal account and then off to lunch or to play polo or socialise. His grandfather had let slip the reins of his empire; now the two of them would come together, he and the bank, natural partners.

It was like coming home. This was where all wrongs would be righted. Rather than using Redfield's for his own petty cash like his grandfather, he would build it once again into the most respected bank in the city, as his namesake Alexander Redfield had done. He would be ruthless. He would discard all those who did not pull their weight and those who had used it for their own personal gain. And in the end that would include Rupert. He would get his own back on the man who had made them kneel on cold stone floors to say their prayers; on a mother, now dead, who had called them devil's children; on a sister who had laughed at him.

The lift arrived, the doors softly whispering open. Alexander stepped inside. The doors shut behind him as he pressed the button for the fourth floor. He turned towards the back of the lift, the whole of which was mirrored. He brushed at the immaculate cut of his new suit and shook himself free of the memories, free of the past. This was a new beginning. His shoes shone, his nails were manicured. He looked at the face that stared back at him. He cut a slender and elegant figure. Dark-blond curls topped a face of almost-transparent olive skin, veins showing at his temples and in his hands giving him a look of fragility. He was good-looking in an effeminate way, but his eyes were cold, heavy lidded and moody. They were definitely unusual, ice-grey with flecks of green, and bottomless, like a cold winter sea. He stared into their chilly depths a moment longer, thinking, then looked away. The lift purred to a stop. He would make them suffer, make them all pay.

He had made a rapid climb in the last fifteen years. From acceptance credits he had gone to mergers and acquisitions, and then to corporate finance, learning about takeovers and such. There, Alexander's agile brain had begun to tick a little faster. Guy Prudham, his grandfather's right-hand man, had guided him through investments, and then through banking, and his knowledge and schooling were complete. Within a very short period of time, Alexander had known how much he would enjoy the entrepreneurial deals that he would soon be making, saw the wonderfully devious things a clever banker could do. It was the first chance he had ever had to apply his quicksilver and meticulous brain. He had been brought up to play behind the scenes. Now he saw the bank and the City around it as his own private playground where he would pull those strings.

He remembered a night just over five years ago. He had stayed late at the office, a host of answers of vague questions in his head. He had gone along the corridor and down to the chairman's suite. Soft overhead lights painted circles on the green carpet at intervals, one flooding the panelled door to the chairman's private office. He had opened the door and gone in.

He had stood for a moment looking at his grandfather's desk, a gloomy bare monolith in a huge room painted in bare outlines by the lights across the waters of the Thames.

He had gone over and looked out, enjoying what he saw. Then, after a moment's silent reflection, turned and switched on a low table lamp illuminating the spotless desktop. He had sat down and tried the first drawer.

His long fingers had stretched in and lifted out a sheaf of papers with care. He had leafed through them, not disturbing their lie just in case his grandfather had a sense of such things. They were disappointing. He put them back in. The other drawers were all locked. Then his eyes had caught at a flap that pulled out to the left side of the desk. His fingers stroked under it, and then pulled. It slid out smoothly. Just another surface for writing on. But no, was it? Another tug. It slid out a fraction more. In the dark recess behind was the glint of a key.

Alexander had felt his pulses quicken. He had taken the key and instantly tried all the drawers. All were still locked, except one.

Assorted papers were in this drawer, and very little of them interested him. Bank business, loans, a list of the board and their family connections and backgrounds, even their characters. Alexander had read that swiftly, finding it of some interest. And then he had seen the telex.

It had been very brief: confirming that a further twenty thousand pounds had been transferred into the account of Prop Finance (UK) Limited. It came from Jersey.

Alexander had sat back, and read it again.

He had felt the tug of discovery at last. It was a personal fund. He had heard of pay-offs for services rendered. Normally, funds would be transferred to a Swiss banking account, or to Guernsey, or indeed . . . Jersey. He had chuckled, and swung forward on the big leather chair again. He had known it.

And so had Guy. The realisation had come to him all at once. He had picked up the list of directors again. All family members, cousins, nephews, brothers, taking their place beside direct family, even husbands of female Redfields; family members stretching back to his great-grandfather's family, the Bryn-Parrys. Added recently had been the family members of the Rees-Hulberts, not too many of them, or anyway not quite as diverse as the Redfield tentacles. But there had been one exception. Guy Prudham had been the first real outsider to get a seat on the board.

Alexander had put down the list and taken off the glasses he had started wearing. He had slipped them into his breast pocket and leaned back again in the swing chair, his hands clasped on his chest.

Guy Prudham. Alexander began to laugh. He remembered that flicker of the eyes on their first meeting and he had been so busy thinking about the bank that he had missed it. Guy, who had taken such pains to school him in the ways of the bank, a man who obviously loved the bank himself. Guy had stood on the sidelines, probably a long time an outcast in his own mind and only recently at nearly sixty made a director. And unmarried. Alexander nodded slowly. Guy had been very clever, he had kept it quiet, but Alexander knew. Had Rupert known of his proclivities he would have been instantly sacked. As it was Guy was probably a party to all of Rupert's sidelines. Alexander was sure of it. For the first time he was glad of his initiation into homosexuality at school. Guy would tell him everything in time, there was no question about it. They were two of a kind, ready to share; neither ready to expose the other with so much at stake. He knew now what Guy had subtly been trying to tell him, waiting for him to find out, right from his first day, that he saw in Alexander a future chairman involved to the hilt, with a need to conquer, and he saw himself as that chairman's mentor, and therefore partner.

He might have done nothing with the information had Rupert not teased him with those shares and chairmanship back in 1964, but it had made him angry. Five years. He had marked a target mentally in his mind. 1969. In five years he would be in control. That was now.

Alexander strode down the corridor towards the boardroom. He had not gained immediate authority, despite Rupert's promise in 1964; the chairman's seat had merely been kept warm for him. Today he would take it. Rupert had effectively given him nothing; nothing that was not rightfully his. He had to prove himself, to fight for his position. It would be different if he had had a decent slice of the shareholding, but as yet he did not. He had not yet found an opening that would inflict any lasting harm on the Bennett Group, professionally or personally, though he had made a few bids against companies they were interested in. He knew that was not what Rupert was after; his grandfather wanted more, much more than that. And he had heard the worst of news. Guy, his confidant, had warned him; Gilbert Rees-Hulbert, his wife's ineffectual father, though not actively partaking in the running of the bank, still kept his ear to the ground. He had mentioned in Guy's hearing that he was very concerned about the lack of home life that his grandson was getting, no mother to care for him and his father permanently up in London either at the house or at the bank. No interest taken in his future career. He was considering stepping in to take a hand in the situation by leaving his whole and substantial wealth to the young man. *Shares*. The word rang like a bell in Alexander's head as he turned the corner into the spacious and elegant room that overlooked the Thames. He had assumed those shares would be in his power, relied on it. To be bypassed in favour of his son was not something he had contemplated. Damn them both, those two old men. They had him powerless in a cleft stick; by pleasing one he could not please the other.

The news had given him the necessary catalyst. He had been so involved in securing his position in Redfield's that he had given little time to David. He had made an immediate move, acquiescing in his request to go to America, and on to Sabrine. The next time the boy spoke to his grandfather Gilbert, he would hear everything he wanted him to hear. Follow up with a few visits from the two of them to the Rees-Hulbert seat in Kent, and Gilbert would soon change his mind. Alexander felt he could easily outsmart his father-in-law; his own grandfather was another matter entirely but at least there was one thing he could be sure of: Rupert was not acting from any altruistic motive as far as his grandson was concerned. He merely wanted a Redfield in the hot seat so that the Rees-Hulbert family did not gain too much control.

Not that they could anyway, thought Alexander, as he crossed the softly carpeted room towards the chairman's armchair, central under the imposing oil painting of the bank's early premises. He laid down his papers before him on the desk and took his place. Scattered around the room were members of the board; obscure Bryn-Parry offspring, weak cousins and husbands of Redfield womenfolk, weak by nature of their position, and the useless heads of the Rees-Hulbert clan, none of them with muscle enough to combat him. There was only one difference between them: the Rees-Hulbert contingent had all been given the power of shares.

Alexander gave them all a scathing glance as he tapped his papers into place. Guy Prudham, taking his seat beside him, felt that he knew what might take place today. He had carefully nurtured this young man, helping him to slip simply and naturally into the place he now held. The news he had given him regarding Gilbert's worries over his grandson's future had taken effect. It was as much in his interest as in his protégé's that Gilbert and Rupert should bequeath their combined power to Alexander. And, therefore, to himself, as mentor.

He leaned forward slightly, a mocking smile in his eyes.

'Good morning,' he said softly. 'Did you sort it out?' he asked pointedly.

'Well enough for now, I think.' Alexander hardly looked his way. His face was cold, as he surveyed his papers. 'A little more to come.'

'I thought so,' Guy murmured, the smile moving to the corners of his mouth. He leaned back comfortably as he spoke. 'This I've got to see.'

Alexander raised his eyebrow, gave him a quick look. Guy

returned it, *en rapport*. He felt himself an observer as Alexander looked up at the assembled room and spoke:

'Gentlemen, shall we get down to the business of the day?'

Heads turned, conversations were wrapped up as they moved towards the horse-shoe-shaped mahogany desk, lit softly by a massive chandelier. In the old days business had been done in gentlemanly fashion, the boardroom set up like a country-house drawing-room, a good fire lit in the marble fireplace, comfortable chairs and an atmosphere of bonhomie and informality. Times had changed, though not a great deal; the shape of the boardroom table did not allow for there to be an obvious head, though there could be little doubt in their minds as to who it was today.

Towards the end of the last year, Alexander had ended up running the bank through sheer force of personality, inventiveness and capability. He had more or less taken control, with everybody turning to him for advice. He was the person who had generated the new ideas. He was the person who had new inventive thoughts about how to finance transactions. He was a whiz-kid, a young whiz-kid who was always at the forefront of everything that was happening in the City. The older members were proud of him. Consequently he had become the acknowledged dynamo of the bank, even though until now he had not been chairman – acknowledged, that is, by all except one or two, and now he was about to deal them out. Earlier in the year, he had set up Redfield Investment Trust, an offshoot of the bank. He had gone to the public and invited them to put money into it and then embarked on a series of spectacular deals. There was now no doubting his ability; the investment trust was his baby. Since its advent, he was securing a profit for himself at the expense of other people, buying and selling shares on the stock market. He had done a lot of deals not only for himself but for the bank that were receiving a large amount of public attention and were very exciting. His own bank now recognised him as a force. Guy Prudham's senses were correct: Alexander was about to test his power for the first time.

Alexander surveyed all the faces around him as they took their places. He did not waste time.

'Right,' he said, leaning forward, and clasping his hands together. 'I've called this meeting today because I've got one or two good ideas I want to put to you. I believe we can really spruce up the bank.' His cold eyes lanced into all of them. 'I think we've got an old-fashioned image. Now, there's a new market in London that I expect you've all become aware of – the Eurobond market.' The Eurobond market was an international market in bonds which were basically loans sold on the stock exchange. A company would issue them much like IOUs, and then trade on the stock exchange. The market to his mind was developing well; a lot of stringent regulations in the United States meant that it happened to pay American companies to come and borrow dollars from Europe. There were also plenty of investors like Swiss banks who were happy to buy dollar bonds. 'It's a new and very fast-growing market,' he went on. 'A new area of activity we should definitely get involved in. A very interesting area. Now,' he said, emphasising with his hands, his voice slightly lower, 'most of the other British merchant banks haven't noticed how fast it's growing. Let's get into it and make some money issuing bonds, encouraging American companies to come and raise money through the Eurobond market in London.'

Robert Hewdon-Vassar shifted in his chair. He was one of Rupert's oldest cronies – and a director of the Jersey company Prop Finance. He shook his head, tapping his heavy fingers against the table. 'No, Alexander,' he said definitely. 'This is a quite dreadful idea. American nobodies. Forget it. We've always done very well.'

Alexander felt a surge of cold anger. The pomposity of the man infuriated him; he had not even given the idea the respect of consideration. Or him. He drew his eyes from the man and looked around. One or two others were nodding their heads in agreement.

'Any other comments?' he said, no emotion betraying his voice.

'American dollars,' said another. 'It's a good idea. A great idea. I was wondering when we'd get into it.' Others looked in his direction.

Alexander's eyes rested on the youngest of the Rees-Hulberts; Johnnie, Verity's cousin. Smart as a whip, a handsome lad, still very much a junior, but singularly rich. He made a mental note. His eyes roved back to Hewdon-Vassar, now glaring at the lad.

Robert Hewdon-Vassar was very much the old guard, with no truck for youth. Age said everything in his book. 'Well, you may well say that,' he said, 'but this new market is unregulated.

Nobody controls the way it works. It's a free-booting black market basically. We don't want to get involved in that.'

Alexander spoke into the silence that followed. 'I think we do,' he said. 'We could establish Redfield's in a new international money market. The City lost a lot of its international business during the war when sterling ceased to be an important currency. I think we could re-establish ourselves,' he went on, his eyes taking them all in now. 'Carve a place in this new market as the City starts to develop its international business again. We could deal well in foreign currencies. Britain, after all, is suffering still from the exchange controls introduced before and during the war. We need something like this to revitalise us.'

The others were looking at him now. Beside him, Guy Prudham nodded his head at his wisdom. Alexander had a gut instinct for this sort of thing, and whether they liked it or not, he was dynamic and mostly right. He was genuinely talented and extraordinarily bright. Around them, that feeling started to grow.

Hewdon-Vassar sensed it. 'No, no,' he said, slapping the arm of his chair. 'You're wrong. We've always done things our way. One way. It's always been good enough.'

Alexander spoke carefully, agreeing. 'Precisely. That is my point. We have a bit of a reputation for being old-fashioned, as I said earlier. My feeling is that we should inject some new young ideas, forward-thinking ideas. They're not lightweight,' he said, changing the tenor of his voice. 'This is a very positive new opening.'

'I disagree, Alexander,' the older man said. 'I think Rupert would too.'

It was rudely put. Beside Alexander, Guy felt the confrontation whip up between them. This was no longer much to do with banking business, much more to do with who held the authority. Robert Hewdon-Vassar quite obviously felt himself to be in charge; he was directly challenging him for the seat he had more or less held by proxy since Rupert's departure. Guy leaned onto the desk before him, making a steeple of his fingers, thumbs under his chin. He pursed his lips and blew out gently, his eyes alert. The moment had come.

'My grandfather,' said Alexander slowly, 'has left this one to me, Robert. Use the telephone if you wish. Ask him.'

'No need for that.' Robert Hewdon-Vassar's deep voice held

confidence, a sliver of a laugh; ridicule. 'I think we should simply put it to the vote. Don't you, gentlemen?'

'Vote?' Alexander leaned back in his chair, his eyes directed on the man. 'I don't think we need to do that, Robert, but if you wish . . .' His voice was silk. He let a pause hang in the air, his wintry eyes holding him. Now he smiled slowly. 'If you wish.' He looked around him. The faces at the table looked back at him; a few dropped their glances, not strong enough for Alexander's stare. 'Well, gentlemen?' he said. 'It's most unusual, but . . .' he opened his hands, 'it seems to have become necessary. All those in favour of joining the Eurobond market say aye.'

The voices murmured their assent, first a group, then under Alexander's intense gaze, singly. Robert Hewdon-Vassar raised his head, the smile gone from his eyes. It was suddenly clear that the vote had swung across the dividing line, enough people were going with Alexander. They were all looking at him. Out with the old, in with the new. He had thought himself the mainstay of the bank, but to them he was merely as old as the armchair he was sitting in and equally fusty. He had misjudged the situation terribly. Suddenly from somewhere had sprung a new bank, one he was not a part of. He had treated Alexander like a young puppy who should be thrashed; it had been a mistake. He tried one last tack.

'I cannot go along with this,' he said. 'This is a resigning issue.' They would not let him go. Apart from Rupert, he *was* the bank.

Alexander nodded. 'I accept your resignation.'

Robert Hewdon-Vassar stared at him in disbelief. The others watched in silent fascination. He had thought himself a part of the institution, the bank itself. He had thought himself indispensable. He had thought himself secure. None of them said a word, titillated by their own fragile security as one of their number squirmed and went under. They saw the sweat break out on his forehead, the knowledge travel across his eyes. He pushed back his chair and stood up. Still, nothing was said. Behind the steeple of his fingers, Guy had not moved, though his eyes danced their delight. The boy had pulled it off. He alone knew the truth: Alexander had nothing to substantiate his position; only his own need. He had proved himself the worthy successor.

Robert Hewdon-Vassar reached down for his file, gathering

it to him. He turned away. He was not going to demean himself with argument.

Alexander's voice split the air like a whip.

'Before you go, I should like the keys to your office, Robert.'

Hewdon-Vassar turned back swiftly, his face paling, to see Alexander holding out his hand. In his office were all the files relating to the business deals that he had done with bank money. Many of them were in correlation with Rupert, but many were not. He had been Rupert's closest confidant, apart from Guy Prudham, and Rupert had left it to him to see the deals through in many cases. He had not been above creaming off a fair share in the process. He needed to tidy up before Alexander got in there.

'I'll give them to you later.'

'Now.' Alexander's eyes were those of a snake. He did not retrieve his hand.

The sea of faces looked expectant. There was no real way out. Everyone knew he carried his keys around with him like those of a keeper. His fingers fished in his trouser pocket. His only hope now was that as a Redfield, Alexander would keep faith with the family and not divulge what he had found. He threw them onto the desk so that they slid towards the centre, ignoring the outstretched hand. Alexander smiled. As Robert Hewdon-Vassar turned and stiffly walked from the room he was gathering them up, dropping them to the table before him for all to see and remember, and talking again, having hardly altered his pace.

'Just one more thing before lunch. I plan to open a new film investment fund for wealthy European investors to take stakes in new productions of the major American studios.' All eyes held his. 'We'll be calling it Central Film Investments. The film business is a growth industry, and with the new Euro market established we can chase millions of dollars for new clients. I've already got Daniel Pelham lining up Columbia to put one million dollars into their three film epics for the next couple of years and another million into two productions with Twentieth Century.' He paused and looked from one to another. He had their attention.

'It will be a unique deal for European investors. Central Films will get in on the ground floor of new productions, earning profits at the same levels as the studios.'

Johnnie was the one to speak up again. Youth had knowledge

of the film industry. 'Alexander, correct me if I'm wrong, but . . . don't the big studios drive a hard bargain over outside finance? I mean, I thought they liked to take their share before outside investors like ourselves had a look-in.'

'Normally that's true,' Alexander agreed smoothly. 'But in this case they can see the sense in our taking a slice of the action. They must do, because they have agreed in all but signature.' He did not add that his sister Sabrine was heavily involved with senior production executives in both houses; it had been easy for her to extract promises for favours returned, exclusively of course. 'The studios are willing to share the profit,' he finished, 'so that they can finance higher output.' Sabrine or no, he thought to himself, it was he who had put the finishing touches to an exciting deal, he who with his quicksilver brain and rich elegance had convinced them he was right.

'When do you aim to do this, Alexander?' Lawrence Bryn-Parry was speaking, a middle-aged, stolid director of the board, a distant cousin and a weak, easily influenced man.

'First we have to raise the readies,' he replied. 'Central will be incorporated in a tax haven to minimise tax liability.' And where you get your cut, thought Guy to himself with amusement – just like his grandfather.

'We will own ten per cent of Central, and a minimum investment in the new vehicle will probably be £20,000 but if everything goes well we could seek a public listing for the shares. The big studios guarantee distribution. I think we should do quite profitably,' he finished, closing his pen and feeding it back into his breast pocket. 'Any more business?'

It was at an end. None of them had anything to say. They all shook their heads. 'No.'

'Good.' His smile was brief. 'Then good-day, gentlemen.' He was already standing, the meeting ended. He was the first to leave the room. Tall, slim and elegant as always, he strode out alone, the keys dangling from his long fingers, leaving no doubt as to who was in charge from now on.

'Alexander?'

Hewdon-Vassar was waiting in the corridor as he had expected he might be. The cold smile took him in.

'I'd like a private word.'

'I'll talk to you later, Robert.'

He walked on down the hall. Later, he would have the information he was seeking. Robert Hewdon-Vassar would be ready to talk to save his own neck, filling in without fully realising it all the gaps that Alexander might not have discovered. It had been Guy Prudham who had told him initially about Robert, a jealous Guy Prudham involved in a certain number of deals with his grandfather but not party to them all, not considered equal enough, not one of the old school tie like Robert Hewdon-Vassar. Alexander meant *him* to sweat a little.

He fitted the longest key to the lock and entered Robert's office, locking the door behind him. Rupert's grandson might not at first have been considered of any consequence or threat but he could be sure that he was now. They would all be talking about him. Let them. He had been fed by his hatred of the man and what he had put him through. Now he sought retribution for those years of pain.

He went over to Hewdon-Vassar's desk and sat down in the well-worn deep leather chair. He unlocked the drawer and reached in. He thought of the years, the long long years when he had been pushed around by so many. No more. Guy had told him where the files were held. He pulled out the files and started to read.

Deeds to a house and fifty acres of land in southern Italy, two beaches, and a private yacht. Good God, he had not known about that. He rubbed a finger across his top lip. How interesting that Rupert should keep it quiet – and who lived there, a mistress? His grandfather had had frequent trips abroad. Alexander felt the amusement rise. Obviously a pay-off and by whom? Mafia? Probably.

A numbered Swiss account. Ah, now that was more expected. The details were listed further in the file on very helpful telexes, privately sent by Robert Hewdon-Vassar. One point on the value of transactions; two points. Ten to one hundred thousand per deal; dubious deals, not ones that would lose the bank money, oh no, but shady, yes very shady indeed. That was where the villa came from.

The Jersey company, Prop Finance (UK) Limited. Every limited company in the country had to file reports at Companies House and say who owned it. At Companies House Alexander knew this particular company would be filed and registered with a Mr Gluckstein, eighty per cent of the share capital owned by this Gluckstein and Co Ltd, twenty per cent owned by Prop Finance (UK) Limited and that would be the end of the line – the same for the Luxembourg deal.

As he leafed through the folder there was more. Rupert had persuaded people in the bank to lend money to finance all of his pet projects. Meantime he had profited personally because of the backhanders on every deal. There were plenty more: an art gallery in the West End, bought and now leased out exorbitantly to a record store and carpet shop, an old church with a preservation order and a string of tenanted terraced houses demolished overnight to make way for an elaborate new development. All the details lovingly filed. None of it known to his fellow directors.

Soon Alexander was smiling broadly. There was no longer much he did not know, just a few questions here and there to link it all together. By now Robert Hewdon-Vassar would be a wreck. He would not know what Alexander knew or did not know, or what he was going to do with it. But one thing he could be sure of if he had assessed the man at all was that he would talk. It would not take much to fill in the gaps.

Alexander finished reading, crossed over to the door and unlocked it. He returned to the desk and pressed the bell for Hewdon-Vassar's secretary.

'Send Mr Hewdon-Vassar in now, please, Shirley.'

He sat back and smiled as the door opened.

CHAPTER TWENTY-TWO

The lane was empty. In the distance a car roared softly and began to climb the hill. The high beeches in the wood waved gently in the breeze, the border of rhododendrons dying now at the end of June.

The car appeared, flying into the far end of the lane, the driver double de-clutching expertly for the favourite of her left-hand bends taken at speed. Down the straight under the trees she slowed. This avenue always took her breath away with its beauty.

Kay was coming back from the airfield. From here, the fields could be glimpsed stretching out over the Chilterns, the purple hills glassy in the far distance under a noon haze. There was a gap in the hedge where the leaves were lashing and thrusting as though the wind had caught them alone, silvery and flaying. These bushes were always in movement, for as long as she could remember, a memory from far childhood when she had gone out driving in her father's open two-seater, held tight but gently on her mother's safe lap, the wind streaming through her hair and into her eyes. This corner at the end of the beechwood avenue was the strongest memory. Kay could not recall when she had first noticed how the wind always caught it, but caught it it always had, never changing through still hot summer or snow-banked winter.

She stopped the car now and listened, a last moment alone before home. Despite Max's warning, she still went down to the airfield, to be amongst the aircraft; he could not stop her. She climbed out and leaned against the hot red bonnet of her car, facing the hedge. The breeze came through, lifting her hair off her face and neck. Kay closed her eyes. There must have been a wind tunnel here snaking through the hills and down along the valleys and up over the grassy cow-studded fields to finish here at this bank of softly tossing beechy-green. The sound was magical, lonely and sweet. She bent in and drew her pack from the car, lit a cigarette, drew in the smoke and gave herself to the feeling. A bird wittered. And then there was silence. Kay became lost in thought.

She heard another car coming from the direction of Long-barrow. It climbed the hill ahead swiftly. It was probably Jim. Sounded like his new high-powered motor. Kay opened her eyes, alert. If he should find her here like this he might stop, guessing where she had been. She did not want him to know. She ditched the cigarette, climbed back into the car and was gone with a little roar and a spurt of dry earth. Jim flew past her; waved a hand. She headed for home.

Olivia Charleswood stepped off the mid-morning train from London. Slender and brown, her black hair fell in a shade around her face. She wore a burnt orange fringed Indian dress with a saffron yellow underskirt which almost reached her ankles, tiny beads strung across her forehead, silver rings on her fingers and her toenails painted every shade of the rainbow.

Olivia was a child of the sixties, gentle and peaceful. She loved Jim Bennett, had for many months, content to live quietly in his shadow. She made him feel strong, which was in itself a novelty. In a way, she was almost old-fashioned in the way she loved him and let him lead, but Olivia's strength lay deep, where Jim could not see it. He saw himself as the strong one because she allowed it to be that way.

Jim came striding through the passengers to greet her, his eyes searching too. She saw him first and raised a hand, hitching the suede bag higher onto her shoulder.

'*Jim . . . !*'

'You made it . . . !'

He came over and took her into his arms. They had met at an outdoor rock concert that summer, smoked hash together, sitting on her blanket, and she had listened to him. Olivia was submissive; before her, Jim felt that the only thing so far that had truly been his and nobody else's was his grandmother, Katherine. But even her visit into his life had been fleeting. They had heard that same summer that she had died in Connecticut. Now there was Olivia.

He set her down and looked into the big, absorbing eyes.

'I've missed you,' she said quietly. 'Two whole days. How are your family?'

Around them, the passengers moved to and fro, doors slammed and the whistle blew for the train to pull out again. Jim hardly heard; his arms still around her waist, he thought about the family at breakfast, chattering on and on about bloody aircraft.

'They're all right,' he said ungracefully. 'I get no thanks for what I do though, you know, Olivia. They just use me, take me for granted. I don't think Dad knows the half of what I put into that damn company in time and effort. He just expects me to be there, clocking in on time, keeping the seat warm for the rest of them. Some days I practically run things on my own, you know! He doesn't come in, flying his precious aeroplanes, expecting me to run the show. And now Kay . . .'

'Kay?' She looked puzzled. He loosed his hands from her and started to walk out as the train pulled away. He shoved his hands in his pockets, her beside him in step.

'Yes. Would you believe it? Last year, Dad said she couldn't join the company, and now she does this damn foolhardy venture, taking a new homebuilt up for the first time, has them all assembled on the field, and when she comes down what does he do? . . . he reads her the riot act, but I just know she's going to get her way in the end. She's so pig-headed; just like him. They don't know what I'm worth.'

'Oh, Jim,' she said soothingly. 'Of course he knows what you're worth. He's made you a director of the firm, put you in a position of authority.' They walked past the ticket collector together, through the archway and out into the sun of the lane beyond. 'He knows, he's proud of you. From what you've told me of him, he's just not a man to show it too easily. Don't forget how hard it was for him. He means to give it all to you because he loves you. You're his children. Both of you . . .'

He looked down into her face and laughed. 'You just don't understand, Olivia. She doesn't deserve it the way I do. He used to get me up at that damn office when I was just a kid. I wanted to play, but oh no, not for me. I had to learn the business, didn't I?' He held open the door of his new open-top MGB for her to step into.

She did not for the moment. 'Well, yes,' she said. 'And so you know a lot more about the business than she does. That puts you in a strong position. I don't see what bothers you. But perhaps, if you are that upset, you should consider doing something of your own . . . outside the family. Prove to them what you're made of. I know you can do it, maybe that way you would too.' She kissed him and smiled.

He smiled down at her. 'Olivia?' he said suddenly. 'Do you want to get married?'

She seemed to hear the words late, like an echo.

'Did you say . . . ?'

'Yes.' His voice was stronger now. 'Do you?' He lifted his head up.

'I . . . I'm not sure, I . . . do you want to?' She was puzzled. He had never said he loved her.

'Yes, of course. Otherwise I wouldn't ask you.' He felt her eyes on him, touched the small pulse that beat in her throat. 'Will you marry me, Olivia. I've got money, a good job I'm never going to lose whatever other course I pursue,' he said wryly. 'We'll buy a little mews house up in London. I've already seen one I like. Well, what do you say?'

'Maybe we should wait. We don't know each other yet.'

The sharp blue eyes above hers held laughter. 'I see what I want. Don't you?'

'Yes.' She acknowledged his look with her own soft smile; he knew she adored him. All his faults were in disguise for her. 'I do.'

Dickie was the first to see them as they walked up the lawn hand in hand. The family were grouped for coffee around the swimming-pool. All conversation stopped as the two of them made their procession forward. As they came closer, Dickie's eyes swept over Olivia's glowing face.

Jim was glowing too, as he introduced her.

'Olivia, I would like you to meet my family.' He listed them from left to right around the pool like a ringmaster, with a sweep of his hand. She was silent now, feeling their eyes upon her. If she could have run, she would. Her cheeks flamed.

'And family, everybody, I would like you to meet Olivia, Olivia Charleswood, my bride-to-be!'

Such an introduction was calculated to shock. He made no allowance for Olivia's sensibilities. But the reaction was not what he had expected.

Kay was the first to her feet.

'Well, that's terrific, Olivia. May I be the first to congratulate you?' Her face was set in a delighted smile. She planted a kiss on her cheek.

Jennie was pulling out a chair to welcome her. Beside her Max was leaning to catch a quick word from Dickie, his face still staring at the newcomer, but pleasure standing on it too.

Jim tagged behind. He had expected an adverse reaction, shock and surprise, but they were being so nice about it, so welcoming, as if they had known her for ages, expected this. They had known he had a girl, of course; but had never met her. Now they were drawing her into their midst. He was already forgotten in the background as in his mind the family took over.

But it was Dickie who he saw turn in a whispered aside to Max.

'Is she pregnant? Doesn't look like a Bennett type to me.'

'Keep your voice down, Dickie.' The wind covered the words but Jim knew they were being said. It may have been only his imagination, because it was true. Olivia was pregnant. But the damage was done. As Max pulled himself from his chair, to come towards him, a smile in his face and his hands outstretched to embrace his son and congratulate him, Jim's ears rang and his heart pounded.

He seethed inwardly. Olivia seemed swamped by the huge personalities, by the rude, healthy and egocentric behaviour of each one of them. They seemed to eclipse her as they returned to their noisy chatter of a moment ago, including her in amongst them, the new and silent addition to the family.

Jim felt his father's arms around him, the bear hug.

'Congratulations, Jim old chap. I hope you'll be as happy as I am with your mother. She's a lovely girl. We've been waiting for this. Come on, have a drink.'

Not his mother. Not a surprise. He felt himself dragged into the group. It was all wrong, not the way he had planned it. They were trying to make a fool of him, trying to be nice and show him up when he had wanted to shock them, outrage them. Well, he would show them. He would show them.

'What do you think of Jim's girl?'

'Olivia . . . she's sweet, isn't she? Very pretty.'

Dickie and Kay walked out onto the balcony after dinner. Olivia was staying the weekend. The evening was balmy and warm; a hot sun had followed the windstorm of that afternoon, baking the land still and silently.

'I'm not so sure she's as fragile as she looks. She'd better not be anyhow, with Jim in charge.' Dickie wrinkled her brow as she raised expressive eyebrows.

'Oh, they'll be fine,' said Kay, rounding the corner of the

207

terrace. 'They love each other. Love conquers all, didn't you know?'

Dickie paused. 'No.'

Kay smiled at her and sat on the low wall. 'Did you know Dad said I could start in public relations and press? Probably thinks it's a good way to keep my feet on the ground,' she said lightly, but she was pleased; Dickie could see that.

'No, I didn't. When?'

She lifted her shoulders. 'Right away. Said I could test the market, offer any advice I can come up with as to market trends and likely expansion. He said if I had a head for business, I would prove my aptitude there.'

'Well not too many good ideas please, or we'll all be on the street.'

'Actually, I won't be staying in for long.'

'Oh?' Dickie sat on the wall beside her. 'Why's that?'

'Not really my cup of tea,' said Kay casually, folding her arms and staring off down across the shrubbery beneath them to the long lawns, dark and smooth in the soft evening light. 'I want to do something with more flair, more individuality, eventually. But not right now.'

'What did you have in mind?'

'Oh, I don't know. Though perhaps travel, yes, something to do with travel. That's been the only aspect really of the aviation business, bar flying itself, that I've been interested in, and it's alerted me to other countries, other ways of life. Perhaps America, I might go there.'

'You could always work for Bennett's in LA.'

'Uh-uh.' She chewed thoughtfully.

'It would be a pity not to get involved with the business side, Kay. I know you'd suit it.'

Dickie felt the silence weigh on her. America. She would miss Kay; Dickie had imagined her eventually working in the family business. She had given her so much support, been so involved in her ideas for building the kit, taught her to fly. It was very hard to believe she really was not interested in joining the company. But it was Max who had done it, put her back up, challenged her.

'I heard from Robbie.' Kay's voice fell into the silence between them.

Dickie's eyes darkened. 'Poor Robbie. Hope he doesn't get called up.'

'Well no, he won't,' she said. His letters had been her first knowledge of the reality of the war in Vietnam. Robbie had a gift for telling a good story and painted a picture of the horrors of the call-up. 'He says he's been classed S2 – you have to be A1 to be called up. Did you know in Washington, apparently they spin their birthdays in a barrel? If their birthday comes up, they have to be called up.'

'How crude . . . how *awful*.'

'Yes. I think he's been safe enough in Oxford.'

'Perhaps that's so.' Dickie looked across at her. 'Is he coming here for the summer again?'

Kay avoided her eyes slightly. 'No.' She remembered the last time. 'I think he's going back home for the summer. Says he's tired of PPE, wants to become an actor.'

'Oh, does he? Now that sounds more like Robbie! Does he know the business?'

'Oh yes. He's got loads of contacts over there. He's grown up amongst the stars. I expect he'll find it quite easy to get in.'

Dickie smiled. 'Well then, it's not a bad idea. What else does he say?'

'Oh, not much else.' She slid her legs over to the ground. 'Just sends his love to everyone.'

Dickie nodded thoughtfully, her eyes moving to the girl. She stood up. 'Well, I'm going in to get a drink. You want one?'

'No. I'll just sit out here for a bit. Enjoy the evening.'

Her voice was distant. Dickie left; stepped inside into the soft peach glow of the drawing-room.

Out here, it was quiet, the twilight darkening the hedgerows and the distant hills. Everything was slowly turning a dark shade of lavender, the peculiar light that only comes on a hot summer's evening, when white is blue-white, and skin is dark and lustrous. Kay stretched out and sighed. There had been a piece at the end of the letter especially for her. She was saving it. Robbie was dropping out of college, but he had invited her to America next summer. She was going.

'Alexander, I wanted to have a word with you.'

Alexander took just one more moment to finish writing up his ledger, the page before him immaculate, not one mistake. He was a perfectionist. He blotted it carefully, closed the book and looked up. A slant of sun fell across his dust-free mahogany desk. The chairman's office was in occupation now.

'Grandfather.' He smiled and stood up, his winter-green eyes remaining cold, though a glimmer stood in their depths. 'What a nice surprise.' He came around the desk to pull out the chair for him.

Rupert surveyed him, ignoring the chair. Then he crossed the room to his old familiar view, looked out at the river, and turned, his back to the light. It was an effective ploy, one he had used often before, causing the other to look more nakedly into the light. 'I hear that Robert Hewdon-Vassar has left, Alexander . . . or more exactly, you gave him no other choice.' He waited, watching.

Alexander looked nonplussed. He lifted his shoulders briefly. 'You're right that I received his resignation, but on the other, actually, it was entirely his choice.' He went back around the desk, trailing his fingers lightly over its polished surface. 'It was a board decision, a fair vote. The others are more visionary than Robert, that's all, they saw a modern way of thinking to corner a market, as I did. I put it to them all. I think Robert's problem is that he would like to have been chairman, to be honest. I don't think he can accept that you've given the post to me.' He kept his face averted as he spoke, wanting to hear Rupert's confirmation. It would mean everything, right now. 'The trouble is,' he said carefully, 'Robert's not *direct* family, like you and me. We couldn't let the bank go to an outsider, probably sits ill with him, that knowledge. Man's got a chip on his shoulder – for some reason,' he added casually, now looking up from the corner of his eyes to see his grandfather's profile lifted in thought as he looked out again through the window, listening. 'Seems to be more than just not being in control, somehow. Besides that, he's old, ponderous, and he won't move with the times. Added together, it's not only bad business thinking, it's dangerous too. A recalcitrant old man on the board is not what we need. We need unity, all pulling together. It works. You've seen the figures.' He tapped at the leather-bound ledger, and sat on the edge of the desk.

Rupert nodded. The figures were good, climbing well. Alexander certainly had flair. He had pulled off one or two coups that were quite outstanding. It was all lining his, Rupert's, own pocket too. He had come in here, after a telephone call from Robert, prepared to read the riot act, but . . . perhaps there was something in what Alexander said. Alexander in the hot seat was very inventive, yet manageable. Robert Hewdon-Vassar had become a royal pain of late; he remembered him grumbling pompously on the telephone about his 'position'. He'd become a real old bore – come to think of it – hadn't he always been. Yes, he, Rupert, had got him to do what he wanted over the years, but at what cost. It had been hard work having the complaining old fool as his confidant to all the moneys he had secreted away for his personal use. Hewdon-Vassar had been the only one of the board members both weak, stupid and greedy enough, to go along with him, *and* keep his mouth shut. Rupert suddenly realised he was actually rather pleased the man had gone, but what about his knowledge – what about, revenge.

'You shouldn't have sacked him though, Alexander,' he said, thinking out loud.

Alexander folded his arms, seeing the tide turn. He went with it. 'But I didn't,' he said, his voice light. 'He went of his own accord.'

'Effectively you did. Reading the man's character, you knew you had him in a corner.'

Alexander shrugged. 'Do you really mind? I mean, what does it matter? He's no loss. He can't do anything to us in retaliation . . . can he? He's getting a damn good pension,' he added, knowing the last was hardly heard by the man standing at the window. He had delivered his dart and seen it hit its mark. Rupert had braced himself slightly, his hands pushing into his pockets. Would he admit anything? It would be interesting to see. Alexander felt a skim of power pass over him for the first time.

'Oh no,' Rupert muttered. 'Can't do anything. Pass on a bit of gossip, that's all.' His mouth lifted in a swift smile as he looked over to his grandson. He saw the smile returned and felt reassured. His secrets were still safe, wouldn't do for Alexander to know what he had been up to. The younger man wanted power too badly; he read it in his eyes. Knowledge was power. It belonged to him as long as he kept them all in their places, and useful. But what about Robert Hewdon-Vassar. Would he keep his mouth shut – that was what was worrying him. It was what was worrying Alexander too; and now he knew that Robert Hewdon-Vassar had not revealed Alexander's findings. It was all he needed to know. As he spoke, he seemed to read his grandfather's mind. His voice came across the room to him. 'You know,' he said. 'If you handled him carefully, grand-

father, you could easily lay it all on my shoulders, make me out
to be the baddie – that way,' he shrugged expressively again. 'If
there were any grudge against the bank, it would be directed to
me – not to you. You could still be his friend, be understanding
– but put it this way: "it's a fait accompli, out of your hands . . .
it was he who resigned . . . that he'd look a bit of a fool coming
back now, even if you were to take a hand in it." Turn it around,
make him look the one who's right. The one with the pride
enough to walk out, make me out to be the fool who's lost a good
board member. That way you'll appeal to his pompous opinion
of himself. He'll be easy to handle then . . .'

Rupert looked at his grandson with not a little respect, and
certainly some amusement. Well, well! He was right! It was
probably what he had wanted to happen for years. He had got
rid of his albatross, and he had not even had to lift a finger.

CHAPTER TWENTY-THREE

Summer 1972

The sun was coming up over the sea, a red ball that streaked the lemon verbena sky and tainted the lilac above with the blush of another California morning.

Sabrine Hamblin reined in her horse as she reached the edge of the bluff looking down over the ocean. David came galloping up behind her, his horse's hooves thudding to a halt beside her.

'Isn't that beautiful?' she said. 'I've never grown tired of it.' Together they looked down over the view. The desert hills rolled down to the sea, dark and sulphurous, the calm surface of the ocean gilded peach on a smoky-blue grey as it reflected the sky above. As the sun rose, the tiny clouds became suffused with a smouldering crimson. A soft smell of sage was borne on the wind. 'I'll take you up to Big Sur, David, then you'll see something. Mountains stretching down through the mist to the sea, smells you cannot believe, beautiful nights. I have a cabin up there I bought last year to get away.' She smiled appreciatively at him as he took in the scene before them, silently enjoying it, sitting easy in the saddle. 'Well, you fitted right in, didn't you?' she said. She laid her gloved hands on the horse's neck, holding the reins casually. The horse moved restlessly, but her thighs were strong. She was a good horsewoman. 'You took to horses well.'

'It's in our blood. Yours too.'

'Yes.' She reflected a moment, enjoying the wind on her face. 'That girl called you again . . .'

'And . . .'

'She wants to know why you haven't called back. That's the fifth this week. You seem to have all of them after you.'

David did not answer for a moment. He seemed to be looking out over the canyon. 'Do you see that hawk?' he said suddenly. 'Watch . . .'

The hawk was lifting on the current of air. They watched together from the edge of the canyon. 'He's using the air current to keep himself aloft,' he said. 'Amazing how they can keep so still. He's seen his prey.'

Sabrine followed his gaze. The dawn ride had become part of their life together. She had become very fond of him; since his arrival he had fitted right in to the Californian life of sun, sea and sex, quickly adjusting. She teased him about the girls who constantly phoned him, not a little jealous of them.

'Well, are you going to call her back?' she persisted.

'Is that any of your business?' He looked at her, the dark eyes strong.

She could not tell what expression they held, whether he was teasing her or telling her to steer clear of his private life. David was not easy to control. At first she had treated him like all the other men in her life, even her twin brother, putting him to the test. David, however, had learned enough about survival to deal easily with Sabrine. He had given it straight back to her. In her view that made him a worthy adversary, and from then on their friendship had blossomed. She had watched the way he handled himself and the Malibu crowd. Even at this age, the girls were aware of him, and the women. He was definitely a sexual animal, but with a cool arrogance that held him apart from the superficial beach crowd. She sensed that David would not be a man to give himself to just any girl; she would have to be very special. He was the sort of young man she would like to have loved in her youth, and that feeling made her very possessive of him.

'Well,' she laughed. 'Maybe it's not, and maybe I don't mind as long as they're not serious! At least that way I still have you to myself.'

'I believe you really mean that.'

'Oh, I do!'

'Well, be careful. One day I will be serious.'

'I can't see it,' she retorted, uneasy. 'You're a hard man to pin down.'

'Not for the right woman.' He turned his horse's head away.

Sabrine drew a breath. She would hate to lose him. That coldness and certainty made him so attractive. It made every woman long to be the one to break it, to break him in. Tame him.

She turned her horse to follow him. They headed back to the path.

'You know there's a beach party tonight for Tessa Maxwell.

Everyone's going to be there,' she said. 'You should come along. It'll be fun.'

'No thanks. It's not my scene. I might take a ride down the coast. It's going to be a full moon tonight. I was thinking of taking a pack and going out into the desert, walking for a few days. I'll clean up the tack before I go.'

'You don't have to take care of that, David. Or the horses. I've got guys to do all that.'

'I want to. You shouldn't have so many people taking care of everything, Sabrine. It makes you lose touch.' He eyed her. 'Instead of going to that party tonight with that crowd of yours, why don't you come to a drive-in with me? *Easy Rider*'s playing in Malibu. We could take a ride up the coast together afterwards, to Neptune's Net. Have fish and chips. How's that?'

'Fish and chips on the beach!'

'Sure. With a full moon, they'll probably still be surfing. We could walk down and watch. Have you seen how when the waves break, the phosphorus lights the crest? It's extraordinary. Imagine surfing on that. I might give it a go tonight.' He raised an eyebrow. 'Do you want to come with me?'

She hedged for flattery. 'I'm sure one of those girls would love that invitation.'

'I'm asking you.'

Sabrine gave a merry laugh. 'I wouldn't let the public see me visiting the local fleapit. How would it look?' She was pleased, however.

David fell in with her. 'You won't have to. I'll drive you down in dark glasses and a wig. We'll stop at Fino's and have a milk shake. Just like you're my date. I'll even buy you some popcorn.' He fed his horse around a jutting rock, bumping her leg slightly with his own. 'You've got to see what it's like out there, Sabrine.' They had dropped the 'aunt' from day one. 'Get out of the ivory tower. I'll pick you up at six in my battered old pick-up. No one's going to know who you are. They only look for stars in smart cars. You're not going to stand me up, are you!' There was humour deep in his eyes as he grinned sardonically at her. Sabrine laughed, feeling quite girlish.

He did not give a damn about social status. It was so refreshing. He treated everybody the same, sounding out the counterfeits and exposing them. And he protected her quite touchingly, having no reason to think ill of her. He had not listened to rumour, judging her only by what he saw. He wanted his information firsthand and she had never treated him badly. Sabrine had given him a crack at the life he wanted and he responded accordingly. She remembered how well.

She did not commit herself either. 'David,' she said. 'You just reminded me. I wanted to thank you for something.' She looked at him, his sun-blond hair ruffled in the offshore breeze as they picked their way across the bluff. 'I heard you stood up for me the other day,' she went on. 'Edward let me down dreadfully with the things he said to the papers after our divorce. I know at that party people were talking when I came in drunk,' she said, referring to a party to which David had escorted her the previous week, a party she had had to attend, a party to which he had taken her once he realised she was not going to make it on her own. He had stood by her, trying to take the pressure off her by his presence. It had not worked. Sabrine in her inebriated state was impossible to disguise, but David had done his best. 'I know you defended my honour,' she said laughing self-deprecatingly, a little sadly. 'Thank you for that.'

'Better you shouldn't do it again,' he said drily. 'Just don't give them anything to talk about. You don't have to have those people in your life, Sabrine. You're a finer woman than that. They admire you, that's why they try to cut you down. Just don't give them any breaks and they'll have to find someone else.'

Sabrine looked quickly over at him as they rode, to see if he was mocking her. It was what she deserved. But no, he meant every word, that was what was so special about him. He was a strange boy, so assured in some ways, yet so naïve about her.

She spurred her horse forward to rid herself of the sudden pain in her chest. She knew how much she had come to love David, and she was scared. Love was a luxury she had never been able to afford. She did not want him to see her face.

It was time she got back into the party circuit full-time and divorced herself from too much time spent with him. He had brought out a new protective element in her himself. Though with others she was still selfishly manipulative and flamboyant, needing to constantly provoke at a whim, and on the set even more impossible, when David visited her there she was like a lamb. And take that party: she had been wrong, but David had come to her rescue like some old-fashioned knight, braver and more mature by far than men there who had doubled his age. He had escorted her out with such style she had felt like a princess dying both of her own shame heightened by his trust in her, and of love for his caring.

Lately too, her succession of admirers had been finding second place to him. More and more she had found herself asking his opinion, valuing his straightforward wisdom, looking forward to returning home in the early hours and finding him waiting on the step, the horses reined in at the fence, that easy grin on his face lighting up at sight of her, ready to take an early morning canter through the hills or along the beach.

'No way you can get drunk with my cure,' he would say. 'You'll need all your wits about you!'

And then they would saddle up, and she would race along beside him realising that she needed those people less and less. The fresh air, the sunrise over the sea, the soft Santa Ana desert winds that blew in bringing the sweet smell of sage with them. All this David had shown her so that now she saw it too. Oh, how jealous she would be when that special girl came along for him as so surely she would. She could not stand it. She wanted to lock him up all for herself.

She lifted her head and turned to him, the challenging look in her eyes.

'I'll race you to the boundary.' She pointed ahead to where the land ran flat along the mountaintop, and rose up again, intersected by a stockade fence.

David swiftly tightened his reins, ready for the challenge immediately.

'If I win you come out with me tonight!'

'You're on!'

Her horse sprung forward and she galloped ahead instantly. Laughing, he dug his heels into his animal's flanks. Full tilt, he was after her, gaining. He pulled alongside her, an excellent horseman, tipping a wink at her as he passed, his white teeth flashing in his sunburned face.

Sabrine's own face was wild with excitement as she faced the challenge, spurring her horse on to follow the chestnut flanks and tall young figure in the saddle ahead of her.

He reached the boundary face with yards to spare, and turned his horse to greet her as she galloped up behind him.

'You're supposed to let ladies win!' she said, laughing.

'Bollocks! I win a night on the town with you! Potato chips in the back row and a moonlight swim under the stars!'

'OK!' she said, delighted. She had never known she could be this happy.

'Well, Kay, you've done very well in the past three years, I must say. I think it's time you joined us in management. I'll be glad to have you!'

Max's smile was paternal as he stood by the open window of the drawing-room. It was a lovely summer's evening. The year had gone well, business was very good and his family were working alongside him. They sat around him now after dinner, Dickie on the sofa, Kay standing by the fire with her brandy, Jennie coming in with the coffee tray. A strong, good-looking family. Jim followed in from the kitchen. Max felt himself to be a lucky man.

Jennie put the tray down on the coffee table and sat beside her mother-in-law. Kay looked over at them both, smiled, and then lifted an eyebrow as she looked across to her father.

'Actually, Dad, thanks but no thanks.' She put her brandy glass on the mantelpiece. 'I'm leaving.'

Max's picture of happiness dissolved. 'You're not serious, Kay.'

'I am perfectly.' She saw all their faces, the disappointment and surprise. She had expected that, but it made no odds, she was going. She'd already stayed longer than she had meant to. 'It's flying I want. I told you that. I've never seen myself tied down to the family business for ever. It was only ever temporary for me, I think I said that in the beginning. There's a wide world out there, and I for one want to be in it. There's a lot I want to do yet, before I settle down. If I ever do!'

She had expressed her feelings eloquently. And Max, shocked for the moment at his own misjudgement of his daughter, realised his mistake. He had thought that once Kay had tasted the security of the business, she would not be able to relinquish it. But his daughter was not like him, not even like Jennie, certainly not like Jim. He knew who his daughter was like. Kay was an adventurer, a free spirit. Perhaps he could change her still. He sought the words to do so but found himself unable to find them. An unreasonable anger took hold of him.

It was Jim who stepped in and spoke. Standing in front of his half-sister, he reached out to kiss her.

'I think that's great of you, Kay. Very courageous. Wish I had the time to travel the world and find out what I wanted from life.' Jim's voice was encouraging. 'Good for you.'

He had rarely felt so uplifted. His own plans for independence were coming to fruition. In his capacity as a pilot for Bennett Air he had been approached to do a lucrative drug deal, on the European runs. The money would buy him freedom, and with Kay out of the way he would be in a much stronger position within the company. Max and Dickie did not keep a close eye on him; but Kay knew him better. None of them were prepared for Max's annoyance. Kay was too like her father and had meant precisely what she had said. The confrontation was inevitable.

'I think this is a remarkably irresponsible attitude, Kay. You could do well with the company. A secure, interesting job. You're going to give it up for what? Bumming around the world?'

'Oh, I don't know.' Kay was unruffled. 'I'd thought about travelling, yes, but eventually I'll end up in LA.'

'LA? Wherever did you get that idea?'

'Robbie. I'm going to go and see him this summer.' His next words surprised her.

'Robbie's in Vietnam.'

Her face moved swiftly to that of her father. It was true that she had not heard from Robbie in ages. 'In Vietnam?' she said, her voice hushed. 'How do you know?'

'Your mother had a letter from him,' said Max, off-handedly. 'Apparently he dropped out of college, went back to the States suddenly, and got classed A-1. He was flown out almost immediately. He wrote and said for us to keep our chins up.' Typically Robbie. 'Asked us not to tell any of you, and I wouldn't have unless you'd mentioned joining him in LA.'

Kay was silent. He hadn't wanted her to know. She felt a pit open in her heart, cold and clammy. She had not forgotten how he had woken her that night, shame and guilt written all over her face as she realised she had no memory of the previous evening. He had behaved like a gentleman, never mentioning any of it, but ushering her home, telling her he was a friend she could always count on in times of trouble. He had saved her honour and her pride. She had kept the flame alive all this time. Dear Robbie.

'I'll still go,' she said defiantly. 'He'll be back.'

Max crossed the room. 'Kay, you're an idiot. That wretched war is blowing away the youth of America.' Kay flinched, her mother's eyes upon her suddenly suspecting something, and lifting to try and warn her husband. He did not heed her. 'That foolhardy boy.' His fear fed his anger. 'Knowing him, he enlisted just for the fun of it. You're both children, just children . . . you haven't any concept of what war does to a man, have you? Even if he survives, he'll never be quite the same again.' Kay looked at her lap. Jennie stared up at Max motionless. 'And you should be thinking about getting married. How are you going to do that by drifting around the world?'

'I'm not going to drift, Dad,' She defended calmly. 'And if I did, surely it's up to me. I'm free and I'm single. I may not be for long as you say, so right now I just want to do my own thing.'

'Your own thing? Do you know how juvenile you sound?'

'I imagine you were never juvenile, father.'

Father and daughter stared each other down. Max, loving Kay as he did, was capable of being deeply hurt by her. She was the chink in his armour, and she was going to disappoint him the most. He had come to hope that Kay, innovative and strong, would join the company. But Kay had her father's obstinate pride.

'That's quite enough from you.'

'It's true though, isn't it,' said Kay, her cheeks flaming. 'You followed in Dickie's footsteps, and yes it was tough, but you were also lucky. It was what you wanted too. We know you made sacrifices for us, but it doesn't mean we have to do what you say. We can't be what you expect, and I want to do something entirely different. And surely, that is up to me.' The free and easy Kay was gone. 'Thank you for the opportunity of working in Bennett Air,' she said stiffly. 'But I never said it would be for ever. I want to go out and take my chances.'

'And get into debt.'

'Sure, get into debt.'

'You don't know the half of it. You've always had it so easy. I've been wrong, I've mollycoddled you. Both of you!'

'That confirms it then. It's high time I found out.'

'And don't come back until you have.'

'Believe me, I won't.' Kay strode across the room, leaving her place beside the fire. Her normally sparkling eyes were now hard and direct. 'I definitely won't.'

Jennie came to her feet, lifting her hands. 'Darling, stop. Please sit down. Max?' she pleaded. 'Let's talk this thing through.'

'There's nothing to talk about, Mum.' Kay was hurt now and

angry. 'Dad wants a kid with guts. Well, he's just under some strange form of illusion as to what that is. Jim, who does what he's told . . . ?' Jim's eyes darkened at her words. 'Guts are standing up for something you believe to be right. It doesn't matter what it is, it's just believing. Now, I'm going out.'

Max did not stop her, furious at her stand. But Kay too, had her own obstinate pride, and neither was going to give way. She was the only one who would stand up to the autocrat Max was capable of being when giving an ultimatum. The ultimatum was here. Horribly, the conversation had suddenly escalated out of all proportion into a stalemate where neither would back down, the two fiery characters in direct opposition. It was a trial of strength. The small argument had bounded out of all control.

Kay had reached the door. Max swung round.

'Kay. You are not going to walk out of here like this. If you turn your back on us now, you needn't come back.'

'Max!' Jennie tried to stop it. 'For goodness sake!'

Kay turned instantly. 'Fine. I'll be going right away.' She accepted the challenge immediately. 'I'll just go and pack.'

'This is ridiculous, Max,' she said as Kay's footsteps retreated across the hall and began up the stairs. 'Go after her. You can't just throw your own daughter out of the house!'

Max stood behind the sofa, his hands braced upon its back, his eyes hard. 'If you remember, Jennie, she chose to leave. I was not the one who made an ultimatum. She will soon find out she has made a mistake. I don't want to hear another word about it.'

He turned away and went to stare out through the window. Behind him, the family sat in silence. Sensibly, Dickie had kept her peace, not interfered. It was unbelievable that this small thing could have blown up like this. Jennie crossed the room towards him.

Two solid walls. Both hurting, both angry, too close. Jennie knew her husband and she knew her daughter. Both stinging with wounded pride, both wanting their own way. Neither would give in before the other. She stood behind him. 'Max?'

Max spoke over his shoulder. 'I refuse to discuss it, Jennie.'

Kay came downstairs with her suitcase, a tennis racket tied to the grip. She had a winter coat thrown over her shoulders. Her green eyes were as cold as the sea. Dickie came to the foot of the

221

stairs. Kay was not focusing on her, as if her thoughts were too far away for her to reach her.

'Kay. Kay, for God's sake.' She gripped her granddaughter's arms. 'What will this solve? Will you listen to me for a moment?'

'What?' She had said goodbye to her mother in her bedroom.

'OK, so he's not backing down and you're not backing down, and you're both being ridiculous, but would you do me a favour. Would you keep in touch with me? Please?'

'Dickie, just let me go.'

'No. I won't. Not until you promise me.' Her green eyes were steely determination.

'All right, I promise. Now will you let me go?'

She relaxed her hold, her eyes on her granddaughter's face. 'Promise me you'll let me know if you get into any trouble. Anything I could help with. Don't just go and disappear. It'd break your parents' hearts. And mine. I'm going to miss you very much. I love you.'

'And I love you too.' Kay's eyes swam glassy green in the pallor of her face. She held her grandmother tight for one moment. Dickie tried to hold onto her but she was gone, running past her and out of the front door towards her battered little car.

Spring 1973

The family sat at supper, for once quiet as they ate their meal. They were a smaller unit now. Jim was in London with Olivia, married and in their new house. Kay was gone without a word. Dickie had come out for supper.

The telephone rang in the hallway.

Max looked up. Jennie laid down her knife and fork, pushed back her chair. 'I'll get it.'

Max and Dickie did not start a conversation as she answered it, both waiting to see who it was. They listened to her distant voice.

'Foxhall Green 781?' A pause. 'Yes, this is Mrs Jennifer Bennett.' A longer pause. 'Oh my God, no.'

They both turned at the note in her voice, went quickly from the room towards her. Jennie's green eyes were wide with pain, her hand to her face. Her skin was icy pale beneath her freckles.

'Oh, my God!' She was sinking to the chair.

'Jennie!' Max was beside her, his hand on her shoulder. 'What is it?'

'Yes, Mom, we'll be over as soon as we can,' she was saying hardly above a whisper. 'Goodbye.' She replaced the receiver slowly, and stared sightlessly at first, before burying her face in her hands. She sobbed once, then again.

'Jennie darling, tell me.'

Max's heart froze beside her. Jennie was crying now, but then she pulled her head up, her hands pulling down her face as she looked up into theirs.

'It's Robbie,' she said. Max steeled himself, suddenly cold as death. 'He's dead. He was killed almost instantly at the front of an attack.'

Dickie sank into a chair; her thoughts had all been for Kay.

Max took Jennie close into his arms. 'I can't believe it's true,' he said. 'He was so alive.'

It was not surprising he had gone to fight, yet impossible to imagine that spirit squashed. For him to be cut down, dead, it brought it home to them all the more. He had been so bright, funny and loving. So like Kay. The thought struck her as it struck Max, looking down into her face and sharing her sorrow. Robbie could never have been pinned down, by Kay or by any other, but that had been his charm. Had been. He had always been up to something, always good-natured, footloose, at the forefront of every activity. 'We must go over. Poor Wiley . . . and Kay,' she said softly.

'I wonder if she knows,' said Max. 'Wherever she is.' They'd still had no word from her.

Dickie stood up, catching Jennie's eyes.

'I think I might know where to find her.'

Both turned towards her.

'Where? You know where she is?'

'Maybe.' She said no more. She sighed. 'I know where to start looking anyway.' She'd had a postcard.

Jennie came over to her, laid her hands on her.

'Bring her home, Dickie.'

Dickie patted her hands. 'I'll try.'

Max left the two women, and went outside alone. It was dark and it was as well; his eyes misted. It was a beautiful spring evening. He walked further out onto the terrace. A full moon glowed in the sky, a perfect night. Stars winked over a twilight landscape, an English spring evening at its most lovely, England at its best. Still, warm and velvet soft. Robbie would never see it again.

Max pulled a cigarette from a pack and smoked, needing it. He thought of Kay. Nine months had passed and not a word: that girl's pride. In the light of a life taken, a life they had all loved, what did anything matter? Foolish pride. How he wished his daughter back again and the silly argument dissolved, but it was not to be. Kay had gone; the wounding words with her. He thought of his daughter quietly and alone, and missed her more deeply than he could ever have imagined.

Jim heard the news in London with little feeling. Robbie had never been more or less than competition to him. Of much more interest was the state of the market, now that he was to be in control. His father had announced on the telephone that he would be taking Jennie away to California for a while to be with Wiley and his family. His grandmother, Dickie, was going off to try and find Kay. For the moment, it was all his.

The market was falling. With jets the airlines had become big business, but the need for massive injections of money had forced all the airlines to approach their banks and financiers who drove deals that required a city-like approval for any changes from the normal way of business. There was no room now for the old school, the mavericks of the air, like Howard Hughes, Eddie Rickenbacker; or even the Bennetts, mother and son.

The old guard who had been at the forefront of the industry had made way for the new, the young blood. Flying was now a business, not a dream of a risk. Thousands of airlines lifted millions of passengers every day of the year between major cities all over the world. Now the heads of the companies were anonymous faces in the crowd, not the characters and tough pioneers of the past. One of the new young blood was Jim Bennett.

It was an organisation to his mind, a computer-like organisation that was under his control. Everybody knew their place, and that was beneath him. Jim had no truck with innovation and excitement. He just wanted money and power for himself.

The old ways were gone for ever, gone was the novelty, the fun and the fear, the old bangers that groaned their way across the sky. Now the jets streamed by every second. Jim looked for a deal to prove himself; he saw the miracle of flight as something dull and boring, but something that he could capitalise upon for his own benefit.

The adventure was over, for them; but for him it was just beginning.

CHAPTER TWENTY-FOUR

'They're being remarkably difficult about going, Alexander.' The voice on the telephone held a northern burr, but its comfortable tenor gave the lie to the man who owned it. Harold Matheson was a sharp operator, and entirely unemotional.

Alexander leaned back in his chair. 'They refuse?'

'Yes.'

'Well, can't say we haven't tried to be nice about it, Harold.'

'Time to put the builders in?'

''Fraid so. What are you doing for lunch today, busy?'

'Yes. Want to meet at the club later?'

'Yes. Fix things up, meet me there around five.'

He put down the telephone as Guy came into the room. Alexander had a nice little sideline going, buying up rows of old houses and turfing the people out. Property development was in its boom years. He did not personally get involved; he had been clever enough to appoint a particularly ruthless developer, namely Harold, to run a private company and do the dirty work for a salary. He owned shares in a company in Jersey called Third Edition (Nominees) Ltd, and it in turn owned shares in the property company but nobody would ever trace it to him. The property company had offices in Piccadilly. Alexander knew damn well what was going on, but he used Harold as a cat's-paw to winkle out the tenants who became a nuisance and refused to move for the very decent prices they offered them to go. Having given them their chance he considered it reasonable to use other methods. Harold got them out by various forms of harassment. He could not put the rents up because of the Rent Act, but builders noisily swinging cranes and bulldozers that shook the foundations as close as their back yards generally made them see the point.

It was already off Alexander's mind as he leaned forward to look at the brochure that Guy had laid down on the desktop before him.

Guy tapped the glossy cover.

'Verney's. The fine art dealers in Cork Street.'

'Yes, I know who they are, Guy. I'm not a complete ass.'

Guy bridled. He was becoming so like his grandfather. 'They've run out of money. Coming up for sale. They've got a stock of pictures some of which are virtually unsaleable and a bunch of directors who've run out of money. They are tired and old and can't go on buying pictures because they lack capital.'

Alexander turned the pages. 'Breastfed on old ideals, new failure. Fair game, don't you think?' He raised an eyebrow at Guy and smiled.

'Quite.' Guy eased himself into a chair.

'Tell you what. Instead of having the bank buy them out, lend them money or whatever. I'd like to personally go in and take a controlling stake in the company. I'll take it over in effect. Make it a private investment of my own. I'll bring you, and perhaps Harold, in as shareholders. I'm quite interested in art.' He leafed through the brochure. 'It'd be nice to have my own cultured corner of London.' He closed the book, leaned back, his long hand caressing its surface, before giving it a push across the desk.

Guy pared his nails. 'And of course it is a very valuable property. All of Mayfair is becoming hugely profitable.'

'True.'

'There is one other thing.' He watched the careful interest in the other man's face. 'My moles tell me that much more property is coming up in that area, in that street. If we tread carefully, we could buy it up like a chess game and sweep the board when it all comes together. No one will know it's all ours, until it's too late to stop us.'

'Sounds about right for us. Go ahead with it. It'll be a personal investment.'

'It'll cost you. You're going to have to borrow to the hilt this time.' The years were repeating themselves; he had done much the same with Rupert but with a difference. Rupert had never brought him in or repaid him; Alexander did. He had taken the place of Robert Hewdon-Vassar.

'Nevertheless, I feel lucky today.' Alexander stood up and stretched. 'I'll be seeing Harold later. Anything else?'

'Oh yes, I almost forgot.' Guy was standing too. 'Your grandfather's in and he wants to see you.'

Alexander's complacent air dissolved immediately.

'For once. Just when I want to get out. Why couldn't he stick to the polo field like he usually does? I thought he wouldn't be bothering us for a while.' It was with a sense of irritation that he realised he would never be truly in control until the old man stopped interfering, or died gracefully, leaving him in charge.

'Oh, I think there's still quite a bit of fire in him!' quipped Guy. 'I heard him shouting at Jasper Motmore just now. You're next.' Guy still enjoyed stirring it up between them. It gave him the edge he needed.

'Still thinks I'm a junior,' muttered Alexander, checking his tie in the concealed mirror at the other side of a corner wardrobe. 'Time he knew different.' He knew what it was about.

Guy watched him. 'When are you going to let him know you're following in his footsteps like a true Redfield?'

Alexander took one last look, smoothing his hair and flicking at his immaculate jacket before coming back to his desk. 'When it suits me.' He picked up the folder and handed it to Guy. 'And that's not yet. I've run this bank for the last ten years, whilst everybody else was busy being a socialite or playing polo and attending garden parties.' The cold green eyes bored into Guy's as he took the brochure from his outstretched hands. 'But at least they've left me alone and for that I'm grateful.'

Guy knew what he meant. 'You've made a lot of money, appear to be doing rather well. That benefits them after all. They don't know what big risks you're taking or how dangerous they are. It's lucky that they've pretty well all come off.' Alexander had taken some real chances and won.

'Nothing ever comes to the faint-hearted, Guy. I learned that long ago.' He straightened his blotter and fed a fountain pen into the inside pocket of his jacket, looking up at his fellow director. 'We understand each other on that.'

They did. Guy had taught him everything. He was an avuncular figure for Alexander, an old-fashioned dealmaker who had seen it all firsthand. He had taught him what kind of things he could do in the way of making deals in the market, how he could play with takeover bids, how he could dabble in the gold market, how he could do entrepreneurial deals and make money that benefited both himself and the bank. His student had outstripped him, but Guy was very proud of his protégé. In return, Alexander had given him a great deal. Guy's advice had been a godsend, because Alexander was still the poor and embittered relation amongst the Redfields, Bryn-

Parrys, Lancings and Rees-Hulberts, all of whom had benefited from his clever deals and had greedily stuffed away their shares and proceeds in their own pockets and made off for social venues leaving him to do the work for them. Rupert had still not given him the promised shares, and he knew why and it still smarted with him. There had been no chink in the Bennetts' armour into which he could stick the knife.

Alexander knew just how vulnerable he was. He ran the bank but with such a small shareholding as to be useless. The moment he did anything wrong, the sleeping members of the family would all give up playing polo, band together, come back in and he would be out despite all he had done for them to make them wealthy.

Rupert, for example. He still summoned him like an office boy. It smarted with Alexander. The old man was sitting there waiting to strike like a viper in the grass.

He had no power. Guy Prudham watched him, sensing the younger man's hatred growing as he left the room and went to find his grandfather.

The waiter brought a tray laden with sandwiches. Jim picked out salmon and cucumber.

'I wanted to meet you here away from the office.'

Dickie gave him a quick smile as she poured them both a cup of tea. Tea at the Ritz had its advantages, quite apart from being just across the street from the Bennett Group offices.

'In our private office canteen you mean!' she said lightly. It had become home from home.

'I just wanted to talk to you privately. Quietly,' he added. And then she realised it was more than just a break from the office surroundings he wanted. 'You've stood back, as it were, for a while, let Dad run things,' he said. 'What do you think? Now he's taken over, do you have any ideas for improvement?'

Dickie was amazed – and amused. She reset the teapot carefully back on the table amongst the assortment of china. Then she sat back and crossed her legs. She was elegantly dressed in a silver-grey suit, creamy open-necked shirt and black pumps, her silver hair caught in a black velvet bow.

'Why, Jim!' she said. 'You're asking me?' It was a first; normally Jim played his cards very close to his chest. Especially since he had been in charge. Max and Jennie had already gone to California to stand by Robbie's family for a while and Dickie was flying out on her own mission that afternoon. Also, Bennett Air's domestic line in the States had not had a family member at the helm in some time. It was no distance in flying hours, and they were in constant telephone communication. Max was satisfied that his son could work on everyday projects without his physical presence. Dickie smiled at her grandson; he was a complex character, but she had always coped with him. She picked up a tiny sandwich. 'You're the hot shot around here these days, aren't you?'

'No, seriously,' he said. He ignored the plate of sandwiches before him. 'Sometimes an ol . . . fresh eye can spot things. Come on, tell me . . .'

She had thought he was joking. Now the teasing smile cleared from her eyes. She surveyed him. 'Well, as a matter of fact, I have got one or two ideas, yes.'

'I thought you did. Fire away.'

She put down her sandwich, rubbing her fingers on the pink linen cloth spread across her knees.

'I was thinking we could do with a new regional airline for domestic services in Britain.'

'Oh come along, Dickie!' He threw up his hands in exasperation. 'We've only just dispensed with domestic in the last decade!'

'Well, you asked . . . I know it seems controversial, but there's a bit of a slump. There simply isn't the demand to fill the Jumbo. All of us are feeling the pinch. The scouts tell me a couple of the smaller airlines are deep in the red. The industry seems to have over-reached itself.'

'Well, to maintain public interest we've either got to go for something gimmicky, or bargain fares, not recreate a domestic line.'

'I think we'll lose money on bargain fares.' She picked up her cup. 'Trouble is, one passenger paying a few hundred pounds to fly to LA sits next to a passenger who's walked on and paid half fare, and starts to get annoyed about it. You can see his point. It would be better to have a whole planeload flying charter than half and half, as it were.'

'Only the smaller airlines can afford to operate that way, Dickie.' He hunched over the table and drank his tea.

She sat forward, her eyes on him. 'Well, why not set up an offshoot that does just that, charter only? Make it a separate enterprise.' She palmed her hands open. 'It's just an idea. But I personally think we need to brighten things up again. Trouble is it's become old hat to fly. It's so everyday now, no longer an adventure. You could set up an air circus like the old days. It'd be publicity for one thing, and fun for another. You could have demonstrations, side-shows, trips for the kids, just like we were going to a few years back. I think the young would go for it. Or, as I said, a domestic operation; set up a new regional airline for the service, use a commuter-type airliner up and down the country. It could be an expanding area of air activity during the recession.'

'Far better we should cut our prices instead.'

'Jim, this isn't the time to cut, or to take chances. And it's sensible. Max has always been prepared to take risks, you know that. He's always been gutsy, but this is not the moment to lower prices. "In times of stress, build . . . don't divide." The domestic route would bring in a regular amount of money.'

'Regional work would be like taking Bennett Air back to its prewar operations.' He thought about his father, tough, risk-taking, yes, he was known for that, wasn't he. It irked him that they never showed him the respect he was due. Wherever he went and announced his name, Bennett, they expected his father; only wanted to deal with the old man himself.

'I disagree,' she said. 'Post-war everyone wanted to get bigger and faster and the industry outran itself. We have to use whatever fill-in methods we can come up with for the moment. I think an airbus service up and down the country to all the major cities. It would be a good thorough money-maker.'

She had always wanted to take chances herself, to do something with flair, but a steady influx of money was also a good thing, until they thought of a surefire winner. The times they were in at the moment were difficult ones. Chance undertakings could backfire badly. It was where many of the other airlines had fallen down. The small airlines had an advantage in that they could keep prices low, whereas major airlines could only offer low fares when forced to do so. Of course they could afford to operate at a loss for periods if necessary, perhaps even carrying a single customer on a scheduled service, whereas the small companies had to try and keep their aircraft at least half full. Maintenance or last-minute mechanical setbacks were also less of a problem for them; they had to contract out maintenance. But the smaller companies were biting hard into their profits.

'I think we're going to be forced to offer cut-price fares to compete during the holiday seasons,' he said. 'And hope that the winter low-traffic months will bankrupt the newcomers.' He eyed her now as he sat back. This was what he had been leading up to. Whatever he planned to do, he needed Dickie to sign as co-director. He wondered just how gullible she might be. 'I was thinking of trying for some new routes.'

'You know that's impossible. Scheduled air routes and prices are governed by the CAA.'

'Not if we negotiated in secrecy.'

'You're not serious!' She stared at him. She was not going to bite, damn it.

'Holiday charters are not scheduled as such,' he began. 'They're governed in an entirely different way from scheduled passenger services. You see, I think we could link up with an expanding holiday company, or buy up fifty-one per cent of its shares to force it into accepting Bennett Air as its transport operating partner. That way we would get into the holiday market. Entirely revamp all our publicity, our advertising campaign. Make us the new airline, for the pop youth as you yourself said. The airline for youth, the airline for the people, the airline that understands. Not some snobby organisation that only takes the elite. We should downmarket ourselves.'

'No, Jim.'

'Just listen,' he interrupted her. 'We could promote tourism in a new venue with new routes. The Middle East, for example.'

'You need your head examining,' she retorted. 'The Middle East is about to erupt. The tension there between the Arabs and the Israelis is mounting. Look what happened at Munich last September, at the Olympic Games,' she reminded him. 'The terrorist element. Air piracy is a problem that's going to affect us all.'

'Oh, that's just a flash in the pan. It's going to die down,' he said. 'I think we should aim for the unusual destinations just at a time when people are fighting shy of them. We'd be first off the mark.'

'You're crazy . . . and besides Max would never go for it. It would mean a terrific amount of new financing, plus if it didn't work out . . . you're talking about undercutting, Jim?' she said, leaning forward, elbows on her knees. 'What would happen if the big boys all ganged up on us and lowered their fares in unison? They could do that and swallow up a lot of our traffic. If we were to take the idea of cheap holiday flights, the absolute basics and keep the prices way down which is what I think you're getting at, we'd be in a very dangerous position. That idea could only be implemented on huge credit facilities to be recouped fast and repaid. If the others decided to undercut us we'd be stuck and the bank might call in the loan, at which point we'd be left high and dry with a stack of debts. I think that's what Max is afraid of. He'd rather we played it safe right now.'

'Dad's getting old. Look, Dickie . . . you and I understand. He disagreed with you once, didn't he. We all had to go along with what he wanted. I bet you agree with me, it'd be great to take a chance and pull it off . . . what a coup, eh? What would Dad think of me then, eh?'

She looked at him silently for a moment. 'Not a lot, Jim. And don't think about it. Whether I agree or not, we can't do anything without asking him.'

'I remember you as having more nerve than that,' he said caustically. 'And why can't we? Why don't we set it up? I've got signing power, so have you. First come, first served, pay on board. All extras to be extras and paid for, and if we overbook we could offer them a seat on a following flight . . . we could cut salaries by having people swop jobs within the company . . . make it a workers' cooperative. It's the American way. Call everybody a manager, give them a slice of the profits and they'll all work like they're self-employed . . . twice as hard. Longer hours means less staff and more profits. I reckon it'd be brilliant . . . it's unorthodox, and we'd win out over the others.'

'The others would cut our throats.' She looked worried now. 'The only way you could do that, Jim, would be to set up an alternative airline. Your own. Not use Bennett Air.'

'I'd like to, believe me,' he said through his teeth, his eyes cold. 'One day I'd like to set up on my own. Get away. Prove that I'm not a flunkey.'

'Oh, Jim, is that what this is all about? Proving yourself? You're not a flunkey! You're the one Max trusts with the business now. Can't you see that?'

'Of course I don't see that. I only see that Kay can choose, whereas I seem to have no say in the matter.'

'And you think Kay chose?' she said quietly. 'You think she had a say. Kay has gone, Jim. You are in charge. Max has given you the responsibility. How can you think of abusing it? What you're suggesting is out of the question. I won't go along with your ideas. You simply cannot flout his wishes.'

'Didn't he flout yours once? I heard he argued with you in that board meeting. You were dead against stand-by and you said so. Perhaps you were right, perhaps wrong, but he's as stubborn as a mule. Well, now I'm the new generation. Why shouldn't I have my say. Time moves on.'

'No reason why not, Jim, if it's done properly and with an eye to the company's benefit and not because of some grievance, or hurt pride.' Her green eyes were clear and wide as she regarded his brooding expression. He worried her. 'And don't you do anything off your own bat, Jim. There'll be another way . . .' She leaned down to pick up her bag. 'Now, think about the regional line. I've mapped out a report, having studied the market. I've got to go now.' She looked hard at him. 'Was there anything else?'

'No.'

'Goodbye then.'

'Where are you going?'

She surveyed him for a moment. 'First to enter an air race . . . and then to join your parents in California. See you in a few months' time, Jim . . .'

He tipped his head in acknowledgement. Felt the brush of her cheek as she bent to his, the quick tap on his shoulder as she left, stepping down off the dais to cross the hall to the swing doors and out into the afternoon.

He had thought she would not go for it. But he had hoped. Together they might have pulled it off, made some radical changes together. Now he would have to tread much more carefully; now he had alerted her. She was no fun.

Challenged she might like to be, but she was obviously not going to put any decent new ideas into the company. Well, he didn't need Dickie. He never had. He'd go it alone. Good thing he hadn't told her everything, just sounded her out lightly. What was it they said? 'Never take a partner.' It was good advice. She'd be sorry later she didn't come in on it with him. Yeah, he'd go it alone, and he'd reap the rewards.

He would set the whole thing up. He had plenty more ideas where that one came from. Max, all of them, would soon find out that they had badly underestimated him. The shareholders would see that he was the one with the bright innovative ideas; they would back him and he would run Bennett Air his way, and not just his father's way. He just needed finance, someone prepared to see things his way, someone with modern thinking.

He paid the bill and went out into the street. He headed down towards his club; he needed a drink.

CHAPTER TWENTY-FIVE

Alexander Hamblin walked into the exclusive gentlemen's club at the top of St James's Street. It was modelled on a country-house drawing-room: armchairs, seats around the fire, daily newspapers and faded magazines spread on the tables, stuffy old men and ancient retainers.

The customary low hum of voices was broken by a roar of laughter from the direction of the bar. For Harold, with his humble beginnings, his membership was a badge of approval; for Alexander it was a place to play poker and to get a decent drink.

He saw Harold almost immediately in the far corner and threaded his way through the room towards him. Harold was comfortably seated in a high-backed leather chair. He was nose-deep in a copy of the *Financial Times*.

He saw Alexander as he approached, folded the paper and smiled widely. He liked the younger man. He was from a different background, but they were of the same ilk. 'Alexander –,' he greeted him warmly, taking his proffered hand into his own. 'Sit down, sit down. What'll you have to drink? Brandy?'

Alexander nodded. He sat down, his eyes took in the scene around him. At the bar there was another roar of laughter; a man rocking backwards, drink in hand, surrounded by a small group of friends. He pushed a glass heavily across the polished bar.

'Get me another!'

Behind the bar, the older man stopped polishing the glass and put it down. He looked into the belligerent face in front of him. 'Sir, do you think . . . ?'

'Don't argue with me, damn you. I said, I want another drink.'

The barman's normally expressionless face tightened. Without another word, he turned and pushed the glass up under the nozzle of the litre bottle of Famous Grouse, but his eyes caught those of another across the room. He brought the glass down again.

'Make it a double,' the voice demanded from behind, and then faded into a loud mutter amongst his friends. 'Don't know how to serve decent drinks in this place.' He placed his hands squarely on the bar.

Harold had summoned a waiter, who was following Alexander's earlier course across the room towards them. In the same eyeline, Alexander watched the exchange at the bar.

'Who's that loudmouth over there?' he said.

Harold bent around the approaching form of their waiter to look.

'That?' He gave a chuckle. 'That's Jim Bennett.'

'Jim Bennett,' he said slowly, a small crease appearing between his eyebrows. He picked up suddenly, like a guard dog sensing an intruder.

'Yes, two brandies, please.' The waiter disappeared back the way he had come. Harold leaned back in his seat, his portly body well framed by the big chair. His brown button eyes were bright. 'You know,' he said, 'son of Bennett Air. Left in sole charge now that Daddy's out of the country. He's a pain in the arse, quite frankly.' He looked casually in their direction. 'Always getting drunk and carrying on. Seems to have a real chip about something. Can't think how they gave him membership.' His own chip showed as he spoke; he would not have dreamed of behaving like that in such an exclusive club as this, but Jim had gained automatic entry through his father, Max. It was a world of haves and have-nots.

Alexander had not taken his eyes from him. 'Looks like he's about to lose it,' he murmured. He raised an eyebrow in the direction of a dark-suited manager discreetly making his way towards the bar. He rubbed a long finger across his lips, watching. 'He's in charge of Bennett Air, is he?'

Harold gave another short laugh. 'More or less. I think they keep a pretty close eye on what goes on, mind you. They'd be mad not to.'

The drinks arrived, and Harold leaned forward.

Alexander was listening closely to the distant conversation. 'Where's the rest of them? The rest of the family? The father and er, the one who started it, whatever her name is, Dickie?'

Harold lifted his glass and swirled the liquid. 'California.

Looking after the rest of the organisation, I imagine. Taking a breather. The old lady's about to go over, as far as I know. I think she more or less handed over to the son a while ago. Still keeps her hand in though. I saw her going into their offices quite regularly last year. The daughter was even in for a while. Word has it she's a pretty bright kid, quite a looker too. Well, Alexander, here's to our deal today. The boys are in, we'll soon have the buggers winkled out of these slums!' He laughed roundly and raised his glass. 'Have to tell you a good story I heard . . .'

'Shush, Harold. I'm listening.'

Harold stopped mid-sentence, frowned and was silent. Alexander was indeed absorbed, his interest trained on the group at the bar. He did not appear to move a muscle. There were few people in the club and so it was comparatively easy to overhear the increasingly loud conversation that came across the room towards them.

'I want to escape his control, Dan. D'you understand that? Damn man –,' he slurred, 'thinks he controls ev'ybody. I'll prove I've got balls, though. I know the worst thing for him would be if I cheapened his precious airline – serve him right if I did. The others agreed, but Max Bennett, oh no, not him. Bloody autocrat. I've got plans, Dan.' He poked at his friend. 'Plans for a deal that'll undercut all the other airlines and prove to that old bastard that he was wrong.'

The manager had reached him. 'Sir, would you mind keeping your voice down a little, the other members . . .'

Jim swung round aggressively. 'Push off. I've paid my membership.' He turned back, his idea worth sharing. 'All I need's a little bit of capital to set the thing in motion. He'll soon see who's king.' He downed his drink. 'Anybody want to make a fast buck?' He grinned at them.

Dan laughed; the others did not answer. They all knew Jim. He was great to drink with, but business, no way.

'Sir . . .'

'Are you still here?' Jim turned, his mood becoming ugly. Around him, the faces registered it. One of his friends was downing his own drink, preparing to quit. Jim could get really out-of-hand once he had had one too many.

'Let me handle this.' The new voice was suave, smooth, magnetic. Jim's circle of friends parted to let the newcomer through. The slim and authoritative man had the air of one who was exceedingly rich and used to power. He smiled charmingly at the bleary-eyed Jim.

'Thank you, Mr Hamblin.' The manager inclined his head, and backed off.

'Who're you?' Jim slurred.

'Someone who'd like to talk to you. I've been listening to your conversation. It was hard to miss!' He smiled again, disarmingly. 'I think perhaps we could talk about it!'

'You mean *you're* going to lend me some cash?' Jim swayed a little, and laughed.

Alexander raised a mock eyebrow. 'Well, we'll have to see about that. First things first.' He opened his hand wide, to indicate he should precede him. 'Let's find a corner first where we can harmonise over a glass of brandy.'

'OK, old chap. Lead the way!' Jim winked at his associates. His voice was a mock whisper. 'You fellows are going to wish you were quicker off the mark!' He gave another wink and followed the elegant figure back to the corner table from which Harold was now conspicuously absent. Two large brandies were being placed side by side.

Alexander sat back, elbows on the arms of his chair, finger-tips touching. His voice was easy. 'My bank are in the market to loan out to enterprising new ideas, yes.'

Jim laughed. 'This is enterprising, believe me. Cheers . . . down the hatch.' He half emptied the brandy snifter, gritting his teeth as the fiery liquid burned satisfyingly. 'Aah!'

Alexander was close to his prey. He sensed it, smelled it, needed it. He could trap two birds with one stone if he was clever. His grandfather had infuriated him that day, questioning his every move. He was now running the bank, it was his, but when Rupert returned he was effectively nothing. Publicly he was respected, privately he was a nonentity, and would remain so despite the money he was accumulating through his own entrepreneurial deals. His grandfather had reminded him how easily he could gain those shares for himself, dug into him with the knowledge like salt in an open wound. It hurt him. But fate had played him an ace; he had known it was his lucky day when he had spoken to Guy earlier. If there was such a thing as premonition, he now believed in it.

He lowered his eyelids. 'If you were to set out your plans on paper and pay me a visit at the bank, perhaps I could accommodate you,' he said.

Jim grabbed at the bait. 'Want to hear a bit about it now?'

Alexander opened his hands. 'An outline, yes. Go ahead . . .' He signalled for another drink. He had not touched his own.

'Well.' Jim began, and then looked more closely at him. 'By the way, which bank?'

'Redfield's.'

Jim looked more alert. 'Redfield's! And you are?'

'Chief executive. I run the bank.'

Jim was observing him even more closely now.

He felt himself starting to sober up. His eyes narrowed, and he spoke more slowly. 'The Redfields would never have anyone but a relative at their head.'

'Quite correct. My grandfather, Rupert Redfield, is the official chairman. I'm in control.'

The short silence was like a month.

'I see.'

Alexander looked straight back at him, cool humour in his eyes. 'You've seen Redfield's this close up before, I take it?'

'Mm-hm.' A smile came into Jim's eyes. Business with a Redfield. With Redfield money. What a hoot. He did not care at all: in fact it quite enhanced the idea. He leaned back in his seat, his arms along the armrests. 'Well, let's talk business.'

Alexander felt the pleasure trickle through him like a cool stream. He never changed his expression. 'Fire away.'

It wouldn't have mattered what it was, thought Alexander, as he watched the other man talk his head off in his office later that evening. He had sobered up faster than he had expected; he could not wait to get down to Redfield's office in the city and tie the thing together. He had seen the amusement on Guy Prudham's face as he had left the office for the weekend. A Bennett at Redfield's: it had to be a first.

'. . . the most commercial, basic flights,' Jim was saying. 'Walk on, walk off, cheap mass advertising, pop music in flight, cheap picnic meals. No frills at all. The other giants won't be able to compete. Undercutting them all, we'll make a fortune. It was my grandmother's idea, inadvertently, of course. She talked about the old days, the way it was then, and I thought how far we'd come, overstretching ourselves, far enough for people to forget how it used to be and to see basic flying as something new!'

'Yes, I see. And how would you finance it?'

'Through a leasing arrangement on the purchase of the extra planes we'll need. It has to be charter. The routes and prices we have on the line at the moment are regulated, so I can't do anything there. But I could set up this offshoot.' His face was eager.

'Very enterprising.' Alexander, in contrast, was quite casual. 'I did much the same thing myself once I'd got the hang of the bank. An investment portfolio. It worked very well.'

'Did it?' Jim looked pleased. 'Yes, well that's the sort of thing I had in mind; an offshoot of the main company.'

Alexander nodded as if in agreement. 'Of course,' he said, leaning over his desk and idly touching the papers strewn there, 'if we were to do this we would have to lend money against an already established collateral. Perhaps that of Bennett Air itself, or . . . property to the value of . . . ? I take it you can sign for that, can you?' He looked down at his hands.

'Oh yes.' The words were like magic. Alexander briefly closed his eyes and smiled to himself. 'The internal rules of the company specify only two directors' signatures on any contract are necessary, not the whole board. It's one of the quirks in the way that the company is run. Any deal, however large, only two signatures are required.' He rested his hands along the smooth wood of the chair.

Alexander raised an eyebrow. 'That's fairly unusual.'

'Yes. But it's a curious thing left over from the days when Bennett Air was founded and nobody thought very much about it because there was only one woman, my grandmother, running it. She fixed the rules. They've never been changed.'

'Good, good.' Alexander played idly with his pen. 'So, can you get another? Your sister, perhaps?'

'Kay? No.' Jim pulled a face. 'She's no longer in the country.' He shrugged. 'But I think our stockbroker would. He has an eye to the main chance.'

Alexander eyed him. The admission was on the table now. This deal was a personal project. Well, he knew what that was. It was personal for him too. 'All right,' he said. 'Let's talk about it then.'

'Do you have to get other authority?'

Alexander shook his head. 'No. People have a misconception about the formality of banks. We're really just one big haphazard family, pretty informal. We sit around in one big room and simply discuss things. A lot of them don't even go down on paper.' He smiled. 'A lot is done on trust. If we think an idea is good, we go along with it. I'm the only one you have to convince, Jim. Like another drink?' He made as if to stand, indicating the cocktail cabinet in the corner.

Jim swallowed, his mouth suddenly dry. He had to do the best sales job of his life on this chap. Yet he seemed very amenable, seemed to think his idea a good one already. But, he would impress him further; keep a clear head. He wanted to keep his ideas straight right now.

'No, thanks,' he said. 'Later, perhaps. Once we've talked it through.'

'Very good.' Alexander sat down again, straightened his folder.

'So this won't have to go through official channels then,' said Jim. 'I won't have to sign a contract?'

'Not initially. Eventually yes.' Alexander's voice was friendly. 'That's not the main point though, is it? Main thing is to give you that money to get you going and quickly, isn't it? I gather there's a bit of a time limit to prove yourself.'

He knew more than Jim had thought. He felt a light sweat break out on him, and shifted slightly in his chair. 'Well, yes, actually that's right,' he said. Max would be back before the end of the year, perhaps even sooner. He wondered just how quickly he could get this thing sewn up.

Alexander went on, breaking into his thoughts. He seemed to understand. 'Later we'll detail up the contract,' he said. 'Hand it over to lawyers and accountants, and boring things like that. We people sort of rather superciliously don't worry about that, you see, Jim. We leave it to slaves to burn the midnight oil!' He leaned back comfortably, his manner bringing Jim into an elite sort of brotherhood that Jim liked the idea of. 'Merchant bankers at grand design don't worry about details,' he went on. 'We leave that to minions.' He waved an airy hand. 'We'll forget about it for now.'

Alexander's razor-sharp brain was alight, but on the surface he appeared casual, bluff even. He did not want to frighten off this weak individual with such an obvious axe to grind, yet from a powerful family who had given him so much trust they had more or less handed over the company to him in their absence. What a difference there was between their situations. Alexander disliked him intensely. He was a fool, and a lucky fool. Well, a fool and his money were soon parted, he thought. This would be easy. He lowered his pale lids to keep the light out of his eyes.

There would be all sorts of clauses in that final contract; all sorts that Jim couldn't adhere to. He was in a hurry, and that was making him blind to caution. He would never be able to fulfil their terms, and if by chance he looked as if he might make it, a fact that Alexander seriously doubted, he would soon break their chances by dropping a few hints in the ears of their competition. When the date came in they would be in default. Bennett Air would lose terribly. He would get his shares. *Fait accompli.*

'The sort of thing you could do of course,' he suggested, 'would be to buy the aeroplanes from an American aeroplane company and therefore, because the American company would want to be paid in dollars, we might advance you a dollar loan. Now, this would make a lot of sense,' he went on. 'All the revenues on the package tours you have in mind would come in in sterling, whilst the payments of interest on the loan would go out in dollars. Simple. We can do that, Jim.' He made a steeple of his fingers. 'I think if you paid interest half-yearly for the sake of argument, that would suffice. Well, what do you think?'

'Sounds pretty good.'

Alexander allowed himself a mental pat on the back. So far so good. He knew full well that all that would have to happen would be for the dollar to rise and for sterling to collapse to wipe him out. It was a very risky deal, but the man was greedy and he wasn't being careful. Alexander had an unbelievable nose for prophesying the state of the market long before anyone else. The likelihood was that sterling was going to decline. By encouraging Jim to mismatch his sterling income with his dollar outgoings he would put the man out of business.

'How long do you think it might take to purchase the aeroplanes?'

'Oh, a matter of months, before we start to kit them out,' said Jim. 'We could have them ready to go for the summer traffic.'

'And fly to the Med and the Middle East?'

'Exactly. A few exotic spots, unusual places like Beirut. We could advertise a package with luxury hotels, a long weekend with flowers in the room, swimming-pool, breakfast in bed with an Arab minaret outside, that sort of thing. We could take in the usual: Spain, Italy, France, and include the Canaries, Portugal,

North Africa, Seychelles, Egypt. You know the sort of thing. Hot and exotic, everything the English are not!' he laughed. 'Later we could draw it wider, the West Indies, for example, Bermuda. Students are going to love it. Set up charters through club association memberships. Fill the planes and let 'em go. We'll make a fortune.'

Alexander nodded. 'You mentioned another idea I rather liked the sound of when we were in the club . . .'

'Ah yes. Well, everybody's in a state about the airline industry at the moment, wondering how to woo the public. Could be that it would also be an idea to go to the other extreme. It's odd that in a recession people spend more money at Christmas and in the sales than at other times, so what about a really flashy airline? Power flying! Make it really exclusive. Get them in the air doing business, knowing that everybody else they rub shoulders with is somebody, see what I mean? Prestige. Money talks. And you can only fly Empereur if you're rich rich. Gold and leather stand-up bars, rich coloured carpets, mirrored walls, very elegant flight attendants. We could get a Boeing 727, convert it, put in around thirty seats instead of the usual one-twenty and make it look like a film set. Triple insulation to drown the noise of the engines, cut glass for the drinks and real marble in the loos. Unlimited booze, gourmet meals, a first-class chef on board, real china. Even in-flight services such as a hairdresser, or a secretary, a masseur. A limo to pick them up from home and drop them at their destination, and no waiting for baggage. An airline for celebrities. Bring back the excitement for the jet set: they're plagued by the also-rans nowadays. The big star sits up front, and beyond the curtain the fans are all slavering for his autograph. He's got the money, he'd like to pay for exclusivity. Let's take it off him!' He lifted his hand and pointed at Alexander. 'You know the trouble with Britain? Middle-class mentality. Everybody goes for the grey area. Well my plan is to go for the two ends of the market that need attention – the lowly student who can't afford the frills, wants adventure, wants to travel but can't afford the Bennett Air sort of price, doesn't mind how he gets there as long as it's cheap – and the film star or executive who minds very much, wants to get there on time, in style, and in privacy. And he's got the money to pay for that. I want to go for them both.'

Alexander stood up and smiled. He came around the desk. The man had good ideas, but he was going to fail. Alexander would see to that. It was a pity really: he would have liked to travel Empereur.

'Mr Bennett. Jim. You go home and work out how much you need. I think we have a deal. Redfield's can help you.'

Jim stood up and grinned. He shook his hand. 'You're onto a money-maker. Just watch.'

'I intend to.'

Alexander slid into the seat opposite his grandfather. He had arranged for them to meet at the end of the week in the pub down the road.

'Take a look at this.'

Rupert pulled it across. 'Bennetts!'

He read it quickly, leafing through the pages. 'My God, you got them. . .'

'No, *you've* got them, grandfather.' He was a sly judge of character, banking on these two men's need. This was his bait for Rupert. 'You sign. And by signing this document you herald the future ownership of the Bennetts' ancestral home,' he added mockingly. 'Longbarrow is owned by a holding company. Jim Bennett can sign for it all with one other, and that one other is a bent stockbroker willing to do anything to butter his bread on the right side. He thinks this Jim Bennett is going to be heading up the company within the next ten years, so he's going with him.' Alexander teased his grandfather's acquisitive nature. 'There is no way this fellow can get this together. The pound is collapsing. Within the year I predict real problems. He'll be bankrupt within two years and the family with him. There's a lot of unrest in the Middle East, as you know. Flying out there is a bad mistake, but he wants to do it. Exotic, he calls it. *Hot spots!* They'll be hot, too hot for him. He's a fool, and I don't like fools.'

Rupert mused. 'Still, his ideas are good. Pity.'

'That's what I thought. Fleetingly. Maybe we could put the idea to someone else, one of their competitors, and let them do it properly, with a decent amount of time and advice.'

Rupert nodded. 'Perhaps so. This is brilliant, Alexander. I've waited for this moment.'

'Yes, I know. So have I.'

Rupert looked at his grandson with new respect. 'What if somehow he pulls it off, though? If sterling doesn't collapse? If this brothel in the sky works out for a lot of randy businessmen and casting-couch directors, what then?' He tapped the papers with the backs of his fingers.

Alexander rested against the high seat, his cold eyes holding the glimmer of a smile. 'We alert the other airlines just in time. They'll band together and force them out of business. Either way, Bennett Air are going to lose. They can't win. You've got them. With a huge loan like this, they'll go bust.'

Rupert was delighted at his grandson's cunning. He swept the papers open to the last page, ready to put his name to the contract. He took out his pen and signed with a flourish. 'How's your shareholding, Alexander? Think it could do with a little topping up, eh?'

You old bastard, he thought. Still treating me like a nobody. He kept his feelings concealed.

'That would be delightful, grandfather.'

'I'll see to it – once we've got the Bennetts on the run.'

CHAPTER TWENTY-SIX

Dickie looked around her with growing dismay. The street was one of many in an area notorious for its criminal element. Venice was a hangout for drug pedlars, pimps and prostitutes. On her own, cruising slowly, she did not feel at all safe even in her locked car.

It was to here she had come, looking for Kay. The last postal address she had given her in Los Angeles was a post box number. There was no way the post office would give her a residential address, so Dickie had gone along to the one Kay had previously written to her from. It turned out to be a rickety old brown clapboard rooming house the other side of Venice, down a narrow street leading to the beach. Up a flight of wooden stairs to the second floor, hearing people shouting at each other and the blare of television, she had found the room. Dickie had knocked on the glass and curtained window of the door and was answered by a youth in cut-off shorts, very obviously in the middle of an evening getting high with friends. Stale air heavy with the smell of grass reeked from the room behind him, a barely discernible group of dark faces gathered together on low cushions around a low table spread with paraphernalia and illuminated by a single warm red candle. Cautious at first, the boy held the door on the chain, and then when she had explained who she was, he had opened the door wider, though not much. People of her generation did not venture down to Venice, especially those of her obvious wealth. Anyone older than twenty-five was suspect. He did not know where Kay had gone to, he had not heard that she had any work, and she had not even been able to pay rent for the room. Kay had left without a forwarding address. Dickie pressed for more information, any information. There was only one thing she could try: the boy thought he had seen Kay working in a mobile diner the other side of Venice. He could not be sure – it certainly had looked like Kay, but he had been in somewhat of a hurry to get home and had not stopped. She could bet why, thought Dickie, to herself. Some friend this was. The boy told her she would have to wait up until eleven: the 'munchies' did not start until after the movies were all out, the crowd had got home and got high before looking for something to eat. That's when the café trade would pick up. The door had shut and Dickie had turned and made her way back down the dangerous flight of stairs, aware of the search ahead of her. She had merely an area to cover after eleven o'clock at night, and no street address.

It was that very item that had been the one to worry her. Kay had kept in touch with her alone as she had promised, making her swear not to tell anyone of their correspondence or she would stop. Faced with such a threat, Dickie had kept it to herself, even though she longed to share the stories Kay had related with the family.

The last letter had come with no address. And then the letters had stopped. She knew there had to be a reason.

It was nearly one in the morning before she saw it. The street was empty, the white van halfway down it, back doors swung open to the warm night air. The lights were bright inside, a man still serving and a girl backing outwards, scrubbing down the floor. They were obviously about to close up.

Dickie parked and watched. She could not believe this was Kay, and did not want to leave the safety of her car unnecessarily at this time of night. She switched off the lights. The girl on the street stood up, put a hand to the small of her back and turned to look up the hill.

Kay.

Dickie forgot all else as she fumbled for the door catch, let herself out, closing the door behind her, her eyes never leaving her granddaughter's slender figure as once again she bent to wipe down the steps.

The first thing that was obvious was that she had lost a tremendous amount of weight, the second was that things were maybe not going so well. Dickie knew her granddaughter well, knew Kay would never have asked for help, for money or aid. She had far too much pride. Her letters had glowed with confidence, but there had been that missing element that Dickie had picked up on.

Dickie slowed her walk. She had great respect for Kay, for trying to stand on her own two feet with absolutely no help from home. Her pride was tempered with sadness: the sight of her standing there alone on this dark and alien street thousands of miles from home, the mop in her hands, moved her greatly. Kay was sorting it out on her own, probably would succeed in the end. Dickie almost dreaded what she was going to do to her, but there was no going back now.

She came into the light.

'Hello, Kay.'

Kay turned swiftly. Her look of recognition and shock, followed by a mixture of hurt and embarrassment, was almost too much for Dickie to bear. She could see instantly the knock her pride had taken, how exhausted she was, despite the California tan. Kay covered it up fast.

'Dickie.'

Dickie gave a small laugh. 'I've been looking all over for you.'

Kay said nothing for a moment, just held the mop between her hands.

'Want something to eat?'

'Oh, Kay, darling.'

'I can do you a great hamburger and chips, double thick milk shake, crispy french fries.'

She had laid her mop against the door and opened her arm theatrically to indicate the inside of the rather greasy van. Kay had seen her grandmother's turmoil, and sprung straight into action. Like the Kay of old, her pride had taken over the situation, treating her grandmother like a customer, acting out her role as if everything were fine.

Kay flicked the brick wall alongside with her dishcloth. 'Here we are ... best seat in the house, where all my favourite customers like to sit.'

She drew up a cardboard box, laid the cloth on it, the truth poignant for both of them. Dickie had found her out. There had been no air races. She was still trying to save towards her first aircraft, unbelievably expensive with no contacts, no finances. Max had been right. It was hard in the real world, without privileges. It made her even more determined to go it alone, somehow to succeed. The harder it had become, the less she had felt like contacting home. But Dickie, dear Dickie, had known, read between the lines, and she had come.

Kay laughed, let Dickie take her into her arms. She burst into tears, and laughed again.

'Oh, Dickie,' she said. 'However did you find me?'

'I imagined it was me,' she said simply. Kay smiled at her

stupidly through her tears. Then her expression broke and she hugged her as if she would never let her go again.

Dickie crossed the sitting-room of her suite at the Beverly Hills Hotel. Whilst Kay ran a hot bath, she had ordered room service. She answered the knock at the door.

'Good evening, madam.' The waiter pushed in a trolley laden with food.

'Just leave it there. Thank you.' She fished in her purse, handed him a tip, and he left the room with a small bow. The door shut behind him.

'It's here!' she called to the bathroom door. She went over to the small round table and two chairs, laid their places and took the plates from the trolley.

Kay came out of the bathroom, wrapping herself into a white towelling dressing-gown. She lifted the lid of one of the silver dishes. 'Smells marvellous,' she said.

Dickie looked at her. 'And you need it. Look at you – you're so thin, Kay.'

'But fit.' Kay sat down at the table, pulling her chair forward. 'I might not have been eating a lot, but I've made sure it was healthy. And I run every morning.' She picked up knife and fork.

'Very Californian,' said her grandmother drily. 'And tell me then,' she said, sitting down opposite. 'How's everything been?'

'Fine.' The word was defensive and light. She cut into her steak. 'God, this is good, Dickie. Thanks. You arrived in the nick of time, just like Batman.'

'Kay,' she began. 'You know I could have helped. You could have stayed at the old house up the coast, for a start.'

'No.' Kay's eyes warned her. 'Is that what you did when you started out?'

'No, of course not. I found my own place, but . . .'

'Exactly.'

'Kay,' she said, leaning forward. 'I had no option.'

'And nor did I.' Kay laid down her knife and fork, chewing more slowly, as she spoke. 'I thought you understood that.'

'Yes. Do Ed and Dory know you're here?'

'Mm-hm,' she nodded.

'They never said anything,' she mused, lifting her glass. She had spoken to Jennie's parents often on the telephone.

'I asked them not to. They respected that. They understand

I'm trying to make it alone. I see them occasionally, that's all. Bum a meal.' She smiled. 'Incidentally, I have entered an air race now, you know.' Her voice held a tinge of pride. 'I've managed to save quite a bit, not enough for my own aircraft, but . . . a friend's lending me one. It's tomorrow, as a matter of fact.'

'Yes, I know.'

'How?'

'It's my aircraft you're borrowing.'

Kay's eyes flew to hers. 'Dickie.'

Dickie shrugged her shoulders and smiled. She started to cut her food. 'You said a friend,' she said. 'Don't I count?'

'Of course you do, but I want to know how it came from you.'

She had stopped eating, waited now.

Dickie sighed. 'Kay, sweetheart, after you left, I understood totally what you planned to do, what you were up against. I knew because of who you are, that you would move heaven and earth to fly, and to do it in your own plane. I knew too,' she said more softly, 'that you'd have the devil's own job marrying those two desires together.' Her eyes held those of her granddaughter, seeing the truth there. 'Now darling, whilst I admire your ideals tremendously, I could not just stand by totally. I decided, that if the time came that you should ever manage to get to one without the other, then I would do what I could to help with the second. I merely alerted a few people that I know, and don't forget flying is a very incestuous business, I do know everybody out here,' she said, raising her eyebrows. 'I told them that if you ever needed help, and asked, that they should let me know.'

'And Bentley's let you know.' Her eyes were heavy-lidded.

'Mmm. Chuck let me know too that you were spending your early mornings flat on your back in his hangars, working with his engineers, to pay for the loan. He also told me you were way too thin. And lonely.'

'He was wrong,' she said quickly. And the subject they had both had on their minds was there between them.

'You heard, then,' Dickie said softly.

Kay nodded. A muscle moved in her jaw. 'I heard shortly after it happened.'

Dickie stretched out a hand. 'I'm sorry, darling. I know he meant a lot to you.'

Kay wrinkled her brow. 'Well, yes he did. And he didn't.'

She looked directly at the table. 'He was my first big affair, I suppose. The first time I'd fallen for someone.' She smiled ruefully, remembering. 'He was good to me, Dickie, kind, despite his . . . reputation. He asked me out here, and I wanted to come. To be with him.' She thought a minute. 'I really thought he meant it, that he was serious. And then when Dad . . .' she hesitated a moment, recalling her father, her mother, home, that night. 'When Dad let go at me, and said all those things about him, I really hated him, Dad and him, I felt they'd both let me down, both hurt me. That was why I got angry, that was why I left.' She let out a deep breath, Dickie silent as she went on, hands in her lap. 'I felt the two men I loved hadn't come up trumps. Dad was telling me I couldn't have my own mind, and Robbie couldn't face telling me the truth. He led me on, then couldn't go through with it. He deserted me.'

'Robbie Fairfax wouldn't have settled with anyone, darling,' she said gently. 'He was exciting, but unsettled himself. He had to go off and do what he did, probably the way he did it too. He thought he led a charmed life, he needed that sense of freedom and adventure. Have you thought that maybe you got too close to him, and that was why he couldn't face saying goodbye to you?'

'Yes.' She looked up. 'Yes, I have thought that. I think he didn't want to fall in love. Yet it was so easy to think oneself in love with him.' Her voice trailed. 'Oh, I wasn't the first,' she said, half laughing. 'But I'm quite over it now.'

Dickie heard the quaver in her voice. 'And how about coming home then?'

'To work for Bennett Air?' The quaver had gone, there was a wry humour there now. But yes, she did need home. She missed them all.

'Why not?' said Dickie carefully. 'We need you,' she went on. 'We need all the help we can get. I'm staying out here until the end of the year. Jim's running things in England, and frankly, he worries me. I'd like to know that you were there with him. To help, share the load. You'd be a valuable addition.'

'You're trying to manipulate me.'

'Not trying, darling.'

'And Mum and Dad?'

'They don't know anything about this. Or where you are. I'm asking you to help us, that's all. I need family in my company, Kay, whilst I'm not there.'

Kay surveyed her for a moment. 'All right,' she said softly. 'For you, I'll go . . .' She lifted a hand. 'But it's only temporary,' she warned. 'Just until you get back from LA, and then I'm coming back here, just as I planned.'

'Thank you, darling.' Dickie smiled, and lowered her eyes so that Kay should not see her expression.

'And you needn't look so pleased with yourself.' Kay's own green eyes matched hers look for look as Dickie lifted her own to those of her granddaughter. 'I mean what I say.'

Dickie's green eyes darkened with humour. 'Yes, I know you do.'

'I need to carry on believing in myself despite the setbacks I've encountered since I've been here. I'd like to make it on my own.'

'I respect that,' said Dickie cvenly. 'There is one other thing too if we're being this straightforward. How about your parents? They miss you very much. Couldn't we tell them now where you are? Your mother would be so happy.'

She saw the need fill the girl's eyes. She had missed them dreadfully, but pride had held her away. Now, now she was going home.

'Yes,' she said quietly. 'Let's tell them. Can I phone from here?'

'No need for that. We can see them after dinner.' The hint of humour in her eyes now filled them. 'We'll drive down as soon as we've finished dinner. They're staying out on the coast. I should think by now your father would agree to anything you want!'

Olivia climbed the stairs to their bedroom, Alice sleeping in her arms. The newborn baby was a darling child, Olivia's strength. She gazed into her face as she reached the galleried landing, the evening sun spilling through onto the polished boards of Russian pine. She could not recall that life was at all interesting before this sweet creature came into her life. She found her child absolutely absorbing.

The small Chelsea house was beautiful. Interior decorators had split the high sitting-room with a gallery, a small staircase in pine leading up behind it. On the gallery itself they had their bedroom, a huge studio window throwing the light in from above. The walls were antiqued yellow and the room full of books, tapestries and paintings. Above the fireplace, there was an oil painted by Olivia, two girls standing in a glade lit with a deep peach light. There were comfortable chairs and needle-point footstools made by her, and an iron chain chandelier with glass lanterns threw a soft light over the sitting-room beneath. A spray of flowers stood as always on the low table, and magazines were spread over the old black oak sea-chest. The room glowed with love and soft tones. It had taken Olivia two years to achieve this home the way she had envisioned it to be, and with the birth of her child she was supremely happy.

The telephone rang softly from beside the bed.

'There, darling,' she cooed softly to the sleeping child. 'Mummy'll just put you down and answer the telephone.' She laid the child, wrapped in its shawl, in the middle of their double bed and sat down, lifting the telephone. As she did so, she heard the front door slam down below.

'Hello –?'

The voice was brusque. 'Jim Bennett there –?'

'Er, yes – I think so.' She turned, her hand holding the phone to look down into the sitting-room, expecting to see him. 'He may have just come in. Can I ask who's calling?'

'Just say it's personal. He'll know.'

'Oh, oh I see.' Her eyes widened slightly. 'Well, wait a moment then.' She put down the receiver on the bed, looked into the quiet face of the sleeping Alice and went over to the banister. She looked down.

'Jim?' she said, her voice hushed. 'Jim, is that you?'

There was no reply. She heard noises from his study beneath the stairs. She went across the landing and down a couple of steps. She did not want to leave Alice lying there alone.

'Jim?' she called again into the well.

He came out of his study. His eyes were bright; he looked keen. He came towards her under the stairs, and she went down a few more steps to take his kiss. Unexpectedly, he pulled her in closer.

She smiled as he let her go. 'You're in a good mood!'

'I've got a great deal happening today, Olivia. A great deal! Just wait, we're going to really make it, you and I!'

He still held her fast. She enjoyed his boyish enthusiasm; so much of the time nowadays Jim was in the doldrums, but today he was euphoric. She kissed him again, almost forgetting the man waiting on the telephone upstairs.

'Oh, goodness,' she said, pulling away. 'I entirely forgot.

There's a man on the phone for you,' she pointed upstairs. 'Says it's personal. Wouldn't give his name.'

Jim's expression changed; his eyes darkened dramatically. 'I'll take it in my study. Put the phone down upstairs.'

He went immediately under the stairs and back into his room. Olivia climbed the stairs, passed her still sleeping baby, and went to pick up the receiver. She listened for him to talk.

'Hello. Jim Bennett here.'

'Jim, are you all set for Sunday?'

'Hold on a moment. Olivia?' She was already putting down the extension line as they spoke. She had heard the exchange, and thought nothing of it. Someone from the airline probably; Jim was off to Amsterdam on Sunday. A last minute hitch? She sat on the bed and gathered her baby up into her arms, and softly hummed to herself as she rocked the tiny bundle. She stroked the soft dark hair from Alice's forehead, and kissed the delicate skin. Downstairs, she heard Jim close the study door.

'Yes,' he said. 'I'm all ready. Where do you want me to deliver?'

The distant voice gave him the address. Jim nodded as he memorised it in his head. There were to be no scraps of paper to be lost and used as evidence. The deal was not his first. Jim's own habit was becoming expensive, and the drug dealers had singled him out quite quickly. As a pilot he was in a prime position to be approached for the European run; it had not been hard for them to see the weakness, the fatal flaw in his character. The rewards were lucrative, and Jim was after money. It was a meeting of minds.

255

CHAPTER TWENTY-SEVEN

In Mexico, Max walked out of the huge factory and into the brilliant sunshine. The foreman walked beside him.

Max strolled towards his car. 'I think we'll order another ten this coming spring, Wally,' he said. 'We need to step things up a bit. I'll be going home for Christmas. Talk to you before then.' He opened the door to his car.

'Right, Mr Bennett. That's to add to the others on order. Four left to go, I believe. 727s, yes, that's right,' he said, quickly consulting his book.

Max frowned. 'What four?'

'For your company. We got four out already.'

'Not for my company you haven't.'

'Well, a subsidiary then.' The man smiled apologetically.

Max felt a warning bell somewhere inside. 'No. Not that I know of. For Coastline, do you mean?'

'No. For the new offshoot in England.' Even Wally was beginning to look worried now. He had authorised the purchase of the aircraft through the usual channels without consulting Max. The normal paperwork had come through from Bennett Air in England, and he had gone ahead. It was only by chance that Max had visited today, on business at their new Tijuana hotel; normally he left the ordering of the aircraft to one of the executives. Only by chance had he mentioned it.

Max was very still, staring at him. 'What offshoot?'

'The package, charter line.' The foreman's voice was thin. 'AvanceAir.'

'AvanceAir? Is this a joke? You must be wrong, Wally. What are you talking about?'

Wally turned the clipboard around to show him the order. 'I'm not joking, Mr Bennett,' he said. 'I think you'd better check it out.'

*

Jim threw the crumpled telex at the waste basket. It missed the top and skimmed across the carpet. He put his head on his hands.

'Oh, Christ.'

He thought he was going to be sick. Disaster followed disaster, and now this. He had surmounted the first one, just: a cholera outbreak in Spain had put back their starting date. It had killed the tourist market. Not perhaps for the established airlines, but for anyone branching out for the first time it was pure poison. Suddenly all his potential custom had evaporated. He had decided to wait for the early autumn but still they had been left having to pay huge outgoings on the aircraft with no incoming revenues.

The door opened but he did not look up. Kay came into the room.

'Jim, have you heard?' She stopped, saw his look, the telex on the floor.

'Oh God.' He pushed the heels of his hands into his eyes.

Kay picked up the telex and straightened it out as she came to the desk. 'Oh, I see you know. That's what I came to tell you.' She sat in the chair, clad in jeans, one leg over the arm. War had just broken out between the Arabs and Israelis in Beirut. Everything was cancelled. 'Thank God it doesn't affect us.' She stretched, pushing her hands through her hair.

He took a deep breath. 'Yes. It does.'

'How?' She was genuinely puzzled. She let her hair drop to her shoulders again. 'Bennett Air doesn't fly to Beirut.'

She saw his face then.

'Jim. What's going on?'

He braced his face against his hands, running his fingers over his temples. His eyes were hollow as he began to tell her. Kay listened aghast, as the story unravelled, his plans exposed. '. . . we were set to go this month,' he finished. 'Oh, I know it was the wrong time of year to set up, but I thought I could start with winter exotic tours. I got the summer holiday market all right before the Spanish thing. Then this had to happen. I wanted to keep it quiet from you until it was away.'

Kay sat square on the chair and stared at him, her voice low.

'Jim. You couldn't have hoped to keep this thing quiet.'

'I already have,' he said, suddenly vehement as he looked at her. 'It's been running two months! If it hadn't been for that cholera scare it would have been go. I wanted it quiet, wanted it full swing before any of you knew it was my company. But you didn't, did you?' He seemed almost pleased with himself. 'Not much of a jailer are you? You didn't realise.'

Her eyes travelled over his now downcast face. 'Is that what you think I am?'

'This place is like a prison,' he growled. 'Always has been for me.' He bared his teeth and sighed. 'For once I thought I'd broken out.' He spun a pencil on the table.

There was silence for a moment. Kay sat looking at her half-brother.

'What finance were you using, Jim?' Her voice held a different note.

'Bennett. Our money.'

'Our money?' She sat up slightly. 'But there isn't any, Jim. We're borrowing all the time at the moment to keep the fleet going. There is no money. Certainly not for this kind of operation.'

'I borrowed. Borrowed from a bank.' He looked up at her. 'I knew you wouldn't go for it, so I co-signed with Thomas, as directors of Bennett Air.'

'Jesus Christ, Jim. You signed us as collateral? This means they can come after us?'

'Yes . . . No. I don't know,' he said, ill-temperedly, rubbing at his forehead again. 'Leave me alone, Kay.'

She leaned over the desk, her green eyes brilliant. 'Think now. What were the terms of the loan? The call-in date, when is it?' Her voice was urgent.

He laid his elbows out on the table, hanging his head. 'Interest paid half-yearly. Because of the war money will have to be refunded. I'll have no money to pay the interest. It's due this month. The loan will become callable if they wish to make it so. I'm in default on the terms of the loan by failing to pay the interest.'

He clutched his head and threw himself up out of the chair, walking to the window to stand with his back to her. 'I bought the planes from an American aircraft company too. They wanted to be paid in dollars. I got the thing financed on a dollar loan. All the revenues were coming in in sterling.

'Have you seen sterling . . . ?' His voice was almost a cry. 'It's collapsing by the day! The dollar's rising enormously. Sterling collapsing spectacularly. Oh God, I'm wiped out, Kay. Wiped out! The bastard knew it. He took me!'

'You damn fool,' she said coldly, standing up and coming round the desk towards him. 'Stop thinking of yourself. It's us you have to think of. We have at least got a good reputation with the bank. Now, you didn't go to Hammond's obviously. Who did you go to?'

He licked dry lips. She turned him round by the arm.

'Who?'

He looked into her face, her brilliant eyes commanding him.

'Redfield's.' So quiet, she hardly heard it, but she knew anyway, her skin chilling.

'Oh God.' She whirled round. 'We've got to get Dad back right away.'

'No!' He grabbed at her wrist. 'I'm not going to have him know!'

She threw him off. 'Stop acting like an idiot, Jim. We have to call him now.' She reached for the telephone. It rang under her hand. Jim jumped. 'Pick it up,' she said.

Slowly, he did, dreading the voice. It came.

'You're in breach of your obligations.' Alexander's distant tone was silky. 'You've got to repay here and now, I'm afraid.'

'I can't do it,' he threw into the mouthpiece. 'You know I can't, you bastard!'

'Well, sorry to hear it!' There was a laugh in the voice. 'We'll simply have to impound your planes. And of course you remember that you staked Longbarrow as part of your collateral. I trust you'll inform your family.'

'Give us a little more time,' Jim pleaded, desperate. 'I can work something out.'

'Oh, I doubt it,' drawled Alexander gently. 'Terrorism's going to escalate now, so they tell me. You *have* seen the news, I take it?'

'Even so, we can work something out, can't we?' Kay watched him, his eyes burning, his face white.

'Sorry, old chap,' he said. 'I already did that. Remember after the Spanish fiasco. I think we've been very patient. You're in default of the loan by failing to pay the interest due. The loan is callable, Mr Bennett. There's no room for manoeuvre.' The line went dead in his hand.

Jim slowly put down the receiver. Kay looked into his face. He shook his head. She lifted the receiver quickly. Dialled the number. She did not look at Jim as she listened to the telephone ringing way across the Atlantic. She closed her eyes, imagining

259

her father crossing the room, picking up the phone for this news.

'Hello?'

'Dad? Kay. Bad news, I'm afraid.'

She heard the echo on the line. His voice was calm, controlled.

'I already heard something,' he was saying. 'I was about to call. Someone just told me Bennett Air have been buying up aircraft out here. Is that right?'

'Yes . . . but it's far worse than that.'

'What's going on, Kay? Who put in this order?'

She paused, looked across the room at Jim's back. 'I can't say right now. Look, Dad, I'm coming over.'

'Can't you handle it?'

'Not this one. We need you. I'll be flying out in one hour's time before the press get to you.' She checked the time on her watch. 'I don't want to talk on the phone. Just act as if you know everything, but aren't talking. I'll brief you on the way home.'

Jim listened emptily as they finished their call. She was acting as if she was already in control. She put down the telephone and her voice reached him across the room.

'You'd better pull yourself together,' she said to him. 'A lot of people are going to ask a lot of questions. You'd better have your answers ready.'

He whirled round. 'How was I to know there'd be a god-damned war? Or that the money market would virtually turn upside down?' He glared at her. 'It's all very well to judge me now, now that it's failed, but what if it had succeeded, eh? What then, huh?'

'Jim, it would have failed anyway. You couldn't have hoped to succeed. If you'd kept just one eye on the financial market instead of ignoring everything in your bid to beat Dad, you'd have known that right at the beginning.'

'He said it was all informal,' he said defensively. 'Said it was good old boys and all that, there'd be no red tape about it. I signed as a mere formality. He acted so casually!' His blue eyes were wild.

'Of course he did,' she said, her face grim. 'Don't you see what you've done? Rupert Redfield's been waiting years for this moment. He's been trying to break us ever since the beginning!' She remembered from childhood the face in the forest. The horror of the man. 'Now you've caught us in his trap.'

'He said we'd forget about all the formalities, said it wouldn't matter . . . ,' he repeated. 'We didn't even sign straight away. It was all so easy.'

She looked at him with disgust. 'Didn't you read the fine print?'

'Well, yes.'

'You saw the call-in date?'

'So did Thomas,' he sulked.

'But you were convinced you'd make it,' she accused. 'And with a snake like Alexander Redfield. Give me the contract to take to Dad.'

He did not correct her mistake with the man's surname. He said nothing; he had never seen Kay so angry, or so cold. He opened the drawer of his desk, pulled out the duplicate paper-work and handed it to her.

'What did you promise Thomas?' she said into the silence, taking it from him.

'A partnership.'

'You arsehole,' she said quietly. 'You should be shot.' She paused for a moment, arms around the folder, before crossing over to the door. 'I'm catching the first plane out to LA. You get on the phone to Olivia and say you're coming and get back there as quickly as you can before this thing breaks. The press are going to be breaking your door down. You went ahead alone, and you blew it, Jim.' She reached the door and opened it. 'Let's just hope Dad can get us out of this one.'

He looked up, his expression nasty. 'Going to save the day, are you Kay?'

'Don't be more of an ass than you are already, Jim. We're all in this now, and you'd better start thinking of a way out, of working as a family for once,' she said, pointing a finger at him. 'If we don't the Redfields are going to own us lock, stock and barrel.'

She ran down the corridor and out into the street, hailing a cruising taxi. The taxi stopped at the kerb, and she jumped in telling him to take her to the airport; there was no time to go home and change. She sat back. She had the duplicate paper-work in her bag. She would study it on the flight out, look for a loophole. By the time she saw her father she must have worked out something. It was time for the whole family to come clean. There must be no secrets if they were to fight the Redfields and win.

CHAPTER TWENTY-EIGHT

Anthony Nightingale, the company lawyer, sat back with a sigh. 'There's no way out. It's watertight.' He pushed the contract back across the table.

Max tapped his fingers on the surface. The lines were deep in his face. Anthony had never seen his chairman looking so old. 'Are you sure, Anthony?' he said. 'Have you looked at every possible angle?'

At the bottom of the boardroom table, Dickie watched, a crease between her brows, her white hair pulled severely back from her brow. She was silent, as worried as they all were, the family gathered in strength now around the table.

'Every angle.' Anthony assured him. 'We'll have to sell off the remaining assets of AvanceAir and Empereur. Pool the remainder. That'll take time.' He gave a sigh and shook his head.

'We don't have time.'

'No.'

There was a short silence. Max appeared deep in thought. He could not believe his son's stupidity, or for that matter his own blindness in giving him so much potential power whilst this resentment was harbouring inside him. But one believed in one's offspring and was frequently blind to the reality of their natures. Beside him now sat the strong ones: Kay and his mother. Jim had not been invited to this particular meeting. He had fallen apart on his father's return: he was scared and he showed it. The boy had no backbone. He had faltered and stuttered and looked as if he would be torn apart by the reporters that had converged on the family as they had come out of their house. Max's eloquence had helped to save his neck as they piled him into the car and sped him off to a hideaway address. For the moment, Jim was just a liability.

Much of the bank loan had been spent buying the new aircraft, but equally it had been melted away on advertising, tour operators and influential officials who had been bribed to guarantee extra daily flights to the destinations for quick turnover. With no revenues, they could not hope to pay the half-yearly interest. It was a bad time for the business. They could not pull together a few million pounds; it simply was not there.

'Jim signed in good faith, I'm afraid, Max,' said Anthony. He tapped the edge of the contract. 'It's all there in black and white if he'd bothered to read it. Signed by both parties. Thomas too.'

'Well, I've sacked Thomas. He has no more part to play in our business,' Max said coldly. 'Right now we have to come up with something. And pretty fast. Rupert Redfield's not going to let us off the hook.'

'Yes. He didn't waste any time going to the press, did he,' Kay said drily. The papers lay on the table before them. They had all read the articles: soupçons for the press and the public to nibble on, early articles well within the body of the paper, but dynamite. Soon, if Rupert Redfield had his way, the story would break explosively on the front page as the Bennett dynasty crumbled for the world to see. 'We have to do something, and fast.'

Her father sighed. 'I agree, Kay, but what, for the life of me, I cannot think. If this contract is fair, as Anthony says, we haven't a leg to stand on. The bastard's got us unless we can come up with something. Something against him. He set out to get us, unfairly we know that, but he's coming out squeaky clean, according to the press.' He indicated *The Times* newspaper topping the pile. He gave a short laugh. 'He's making out the Redfield bank are simply acting honourably: on behalf of their shareholders they cannot afford to put good money after bad.'

'It's just what he would like, to humiliate us publicly.' It was the first time Dickie had spoken. She had flown back with them from California into the midst of all this. 'He's waited for this moment a long, long time. There's no way he's going to let us go. No, there really is only one solution.' Her eyes held them all as she leaned in to the table. 'Some way, somehow, one of us is going to have to find a way to fight dirty. It's the only language that man understands. We've got to get something on him.'

Anthony turned to look at the founder of their company. 'You think there's no point in even trying to call a meeting with him? Perhaps work something out?'

'With what he's got on us?' She gave him a look. 'Anthony,

you don't know this man as I do, as Max does.' She caught Max's eyes at the other end of the table. 'He wants to destroy us, and if we're not quick about it, that's exactly what he's going to do.' She stood up. 'Max, what are your plans?'

'Sell off the assets, realise some money. Perhaps try to dig up more from other sources. I don't know how successful we'll be, I'm afraid. He knows that we'll be trying to come up with the money and he's not going to let us. He's going to force this issue as hard and as quickly as he can. I have to say you're right: we have to find out something about him, something we can use to stop him.'

'Yes.' Dickie crossed the room to the interconnecting door to her office. 'I'll call George. Get him to put his ear to the ground. See what he can find out.'

Max stood, and looked across the room to her and then to his family. 'You two, see what you can come up with. But one thing you can be sure of, we're fighters, all of us. One way or another, we're going to win.'

The Times had run a short, succinct piece:

AvanceAir, the cut-price new holiday package firm, has gone bust before even starting to operate its planned exotic and stress-free holidays.

Combined with the luxury airline Empereur in the States, a lavish idea for celebrities, Jim Bennett, the eldest son of chairman Maxwell Bennett, had planned a spectacular deal to grab both ends of a floppy market. However, the difficulties in the Middle East have put paid to the branch offshoot of Bennett Air.

The recent drop in sterling has also had a salutary effect on many businesses with dollar loans. Mr Bennett bought his new fleet from aircraft manufacturers, Boeing, quite separately from the already huge fleet belonging to Bennett Air.

Bennett Air is a part of the Bennett Group, a large conglomerate incorporating many other transport divisions, property and engineering companies and aircraft assembly factories. However, at this time in the industry, it would be difficult for them to repay such a loan as they are responsible for both AvanceAir and Empereur.

Mr Rupert Redfield of Redfield's Bank has stated that he is

concerned, but his first concern must be to his shareholders. Mr Maxwell Bennett has refused to comment.

Meanwhile, Redfield's have impounded the Bennett Air fleet until the matter has been sorted out. Solicitors for both parties are meeting this week to discuss a satisfactory solution. It is thought that the Bennett Group would be very hard pushed to find ten million pounds in this short space of time.

Rupert closed the newspaper and laughed to himself. He felt revitalised. He had them on the run. He stood to gain a great deal financially, but more than that he would see Max Bennett and his confounded mother publicly humiliated. It had not hurt his cause to leak the story to the press. The Redfield bank were simply acting honourably on behalf of their shareholders.

He picked up the *News of the World* and shook it open. Their journalist was more insidious. She had been down to Foxhall Green and spoken to a few villagers obviously very ready to talk. She portrayed a story that involved the beginnings of something far more than a mere loan and a possible bankruptcy; a story along the lines of a personal feud. It was the stuff of soap opera, a story about rich, secretive and glamorous people exposed for what they were underneath. A very different angle.

Rupert chuckled aloud. They would not uncover the truth: who was going to tell them? Certainly not the powerful Dickie Bennett. She would not want a story of rape and incest to hit the headlines any more than he would. His chuckle subsided as he thought of what they had done to his family, Jessamy and Sabrine, and his blue eyes grew cold and malicious. No, they could not get anything on him, as he knew they would like to, without exposing themselves. On paper, it was a fair deal and that was the only way they could fight back. There was no fight. He had them, and he was going to screw them to the wall.

Kay found Frederick as she hoped she would, down by the bridge, pausing to watch the clear water rippling over the boulders in the autumn afternoon. A weak sun filtered down, illuminating the silver hair and stooped tweedy shoulders.

She walked up past the church green, cutting across the grass by the crossroads and up the small incline onto the bridge. The glare of the sun sliced into her eyes, making her narrow her eyes against the light.

She came abreast of him. He turned to see her there, saying

nothing at first. The knowledge was in their eyes, sadness in his.

'You've heard what's going on,' she said at last.

He looked back into the river's silver flow. 'I couldn't help it. The press arrived on the doorstep.'

'On ours too.' She shook her head. 'Jim's gone to pieces. Dad and Dickie're holding up.'

'They would.' Elbows leaning on the stone sill, he turned his head into the sun to watch her. The wind blew her hair across her face, the waves summer-lit, streaked with light. For the moment she did not retrieve it; she was too deep in thought. Her eyes had a curious glow in this light. She wore jeans, cowboy boots and a cream Aran sweater, a man's denim jacket over the top. The up-turned collar framed her face. She looked un-bowed, but concerned. Proud. 'You've held up too,' he said. 'You always would as well. A true Bennett.'

Her eyes searched his face. 'What do you mean?'

'You know what I mean. We've been friends for years now. I know you, Kay. I know what you're made of. In a crisis you'd come into your own.'

She did not answer immediately, but stared out over the river.

'This isn't just personal, Frederick. This is my family now. And yours. But basically it's your brother out to take revenge on us for God alone knows what cruel reason of his own. This thing was set up, you know that, don't you.'

'It's possible. Probably, yes.' He linked his fingers together.

She leaned over beside him. 'Then I count on you as a friend to give us a fighting chance. A way out.'

His eyes met hers. 'What do you mean? I don't know how I can help. I've rarely managed to hold my brother off once he's dead set on something. Something such as this, anyway.'

'You know him,' she persisted. 'There must be a way. He must have a skeleton in the cupboard, something we could negotiate with. A man like him.' She stared up river again, into the sun, thinking about him. 'I don't mean something personal. Just in business.'

He listened to the sound of the river babbling over the stones beneath them. 'You're asking me to shop my own brother to you.'

'Frederick,' she said. 'I know what happened in 1913.' She saw him stiffen as she spoke, even though her voice was soft; she saw the shame pass over his face. He had not known that she knew; she had never said. 'Look, it was a long time ago. I don't know the absolute circumstances but it hasn't made any difference to the way I feel for you. You've always been my friend, the one who understood me. Remember that day with the privet moth?'

He met her eyes but did not speak.

'Of course I didn't know then,' she said. 'You just helped me when I needed it. It was when Jim's grandmother, Katherine, came to see us.' She saw his expression alter, his surprise.

'Katherine? She was here? I didn't know that.'

'No. She said she wanted you to remember her as she was, a reasonable wish for a beautiful woman.' The wind stirred her hair, the sun's warmth on her uplifted face.

He looked off at the distant hills. 'She was still beautiful?'

'Oh yes. Very beautiful. Gracious. She said you loved Dickie better than anyone in the world, that she's known it all along.' She looked at him, saw the tension in his profile. 'She loved you though, Frederick, she said you were wonderful. She told Dickie how you'd lost Foxhall to Rupert. I think that's when Dickie started to feel differently towards you. She realised her only adversary was him, not your family. Until this thing with Alexander,' she added. 'So please, help us. There must be something that would redress the balance. We can't lose everything we own and my grandmother and father have fought for all these years just because of one man's hatred. It would be wrong. You would be wrong. You have the weapon to stop this, Frederick.'

She had spoken eloquently. He had not moved, listening to the soft voice slightly blurred by the strong wind blowing in over the river. It fluttered their clothes and burred in their hair. He stood up and away from the stone wall. He pushed his hands into his jacket and stood tall. 'Yes, I see,' he said. 'I see what you mean.'

She watched him.

'She was right about your grandmother.'

Kay smiled. 'Yes.' Her eyes sought his. 'You do know something, don't you, Frederick.'

He sighed. 'Yes, perhaps. But Kay, where will this finish? I don't want to lose Foxhall any more than you want to lose your home.' His dark blue eyes looked into hers, both compassionate and kind.

'I know. But whatever you tell me, I promise I won't ever let Rupert know what you do. And we will use it just enough to stop this. Not to try and retaliate. There's been enough of that. Let's put an end to this bitterness.' She held his look.

He nodded. 'Well yes,' he said slowly. 'There is a way I can think of. Through the bank. Years ago I realised Rupert was not being straight. There was this chap, a cohort of my brother's. I liked him, actually,' he said, wrinkling his brow in thought. 'Whenever I used to visit the bank he was always decent, if a little pompous. But I believe he might have done some private dealing with Rupert. I remember him mentioning it. Alexander forced him to resign, and Alexander is very like Rupert,' he said, a warning in his voice. 'Strangely enough though, Rupert never tried to get him back. He let him go, and that in itself was odd. An old trusted member of the bank being pushed out with no redress from Rupert. It's possible he might have seen him either as an embarrassment or a threat, not wanting to have done it himself but condoning it whilst leaving it as Alexander's decision. The dirty work was done for him. That would be like Rupert.' He looked at her, his trust in her showing in his face. 'He might tell you something. His name is Robert Hewdon-Vassar.'

'How do you know this?'

Max looked at his daughter as she stood there. He had been in conversation with Dickie in his study before she entered.

Kay stood where she was, still flushed from her long walk home. Her russet cheeks emphasised the colour of her eyes.

'I know, that's all,' she said coolly. 'Just get George Reilly to talk to him, to ask if he will cooperate with us.'

'First of all, Kay, I want to know.' Max swivelled round in his chair, his voice stern.

'All right then.' She eyed first her grandmother and then her father, came across and sat down with them around his desk. 'It was Frederick,' she said. 'Frederick Redfield. He told me. And I promised him it was merely an eye for an eye, no more,' she said, warning them both. 'No more. No more revenge.'

Max looked incredulous, his blue eyes dark. 'How do you know him?'

'I've known him for years. What does it matter? The point is that he has given us a lead. He's a kind and decent man. I've often talked to him outside the family as someone who under-stood me.'

Max stared at her. Again he realised just how little he knew his own children. He was more amazed at the apparent friendship that had gone on right under his nose than at the information they now had to work on. He looked at his mother. 'Did you know?'

She shook her head slowly, and closed her eyes. Little surprised her. 'No, but Kay's right. We should follow any lead that will help us.' She remembered Katherine's talk to her, Frederick's feelings for her and her belief in him. She looked at her grandchild and saw that knowledge in her eyes too.

She saw the gratitude in Kay's eyes. She stood up, and patted her granddaughter on the shoulder.

Max shook his head as he looked up at them both. 'Frankly, I find this all quite astounding. Kay with a secret friendship with Frederick Redfield. Kay, I don't want you seeing him again, and anyway, how do I know this is genuine?'

'Will you stop being ridiculous,' she said, rounding on him. 'Of course I'm going to see him again. Why don't you ring George instead of wasting valuable time, Daddy? Frederick has told us something, maybe this man will too. Something that will stall Rupert Redfield so that we can repay honestly. It gives us a fighting chance, that's all, without resorting to dirty tricks and bringing ourselves down to his level.' Her spirit showed as she defended both her friendship and her decision and stood up for Frederick. 'Of course it's genuine. And I gave him my word on behalf of the family.' Her eyes were commanding. 'If you betray that oath, you betray me. Please remember that. You too, Dickie, though I'm sure you know what I mean about Frederick. He is a decent man, and whatever he did to you was long ago. When this is over, couldn't you both give a thought to putting all this hatred behind us? Maybe then it would stop. It's high time that it did.'

She gave them both a last look, crossed the room and went out, shutting the door behind her.

Dickie reflected a moment as the footsteps retreated down the hallway. A smile came into her eyes, a pride in the girl.

'Make that call, Max,' she said. 'It's all we've got. Let's use it.'

He was already dialling.

CHAPTER TWENTY-NINE

The intercom rang on Rupert's desk. He leaned over and depressed the button. 'Yes?'

'A Mrs Josephine Latimer here to see you, sir. Shall I show her in?'

'A Mrs who?' Rupert frowned, trying to recall such a name as he turned the pages of the newspaper on his desk. 'I don't think I know her.'

'Mrs Latimer. Just one moment, please.' Rupert heard a muffled conversation. His secretary's voice returned. 'She says you might know her better as Dickie Bennett.'

Rupert sat back slowly, releasing the paper. A glow of pleasure warmed his face, his blue eyes sharpening. 'Aah!' he said. 'Yes, I will see her. Show her in.'

The moment that passed was decidedly pleasurable, as fine as the first sip of a good cognac. He sat ready to enjoy the meeting and to humiliate her at last. He had known she would come. She was that calibre of woman, who would not allow her son or grandson to come for her. She was not one to back down and let her grandson take the blame. He had counted on her nature and he was right. Here she was, in person. His eyes on the door, he heard his secretary's voice growing closer as she guided his enemy across the room to his office. The big oak door swung gently open against the thick carpet.

She came in. She was exquisitely dressed, still slender. The green eyes lanced through him as if she was the one in control: not an ounce of shame or withdrawal on that haughty face. Too much pride, she'd always had too much pride. He remembered those eyes in the wood when he had taken her, the same eyes commanding him to get off her land. He remembered how she had made him want to tear her apart. This time he would.

He did not invite her to sit down, nor did he stand. But she made no move either, ignoring the insult. As the door closed behind her, she stood there. Max had argued against her going, but this was hers.

She advanced a few slow steps before speaking.

'I'll come straight to the point. Your bank has insidiously tried to destroy my company behind my back. I am well aware that this is no straightforward default of loan as much as you are. I am also not totally unaware of the foolishness of my grandson, of which your grandson was able to take advantage.'

'If this is your way of pleading your case . . .'

'Be quiet. I haven't finished with you yet. As I was saying, your grandson designed this to happen. He put the whole idea of mismatching sterling against the dollar into my grandson's head, and urged him to go ahead with what was a hazardous and unviable venture from the outset.'

'The contract was quite straightforward.'

'Any bank dealing above board would not have presented such a loan. It was bound to fail.' She stood behind the visitor's chair and stared down at him. 'The press have already shown interest in the situation, no doubt alerted by you. I don't doubt they'll dig further. Do I have your understanding?'

'Oh you do, yes.' His smile was cold. 'But you won't tell them anything, now will you?' His smile was allusive.

She ignored the insinuation. 'Is this what you wish?'

Rupert leaned back in his chair, his eyes on her, hard now. 'Frankly, I shall be delighted to see you back in the gutter where you belong, Miss Bennett. I know you cannot hope to meet this loan. I know the state of your finances. You cannot produce that kind of money at short notice. You are finished, madam. And I, for one, am delighted.'

Dickie remained expressionless. 'That is your final word?'

'Yes. It is.'

'You are not prepared to cooperate, to let us find time and a way to make good our debt?'

'You are joking, are you not?'

'I could of course go to court and let this whole thing come out in the open,' she said. 'Show how you set us up.'

Rupert laughed unkindly. He stood up and walked away from his desk.

'Go ahead,' he said turning. 'Nothing would give me greater pleasure than to see you and your family in court.' He would relish the fight; one they would never win. 'A contract is a contract. I don't see you proving otherwise, do you?'

'Your reaction is exactly the one I had hoped for,' she said. 'You leave me, as they say, no alternative.' Rupert frowned and stepped back behind his desk, the rosy glow diminishing. She was digging into her handbag, bringing out a tape and a typed manuscript.

She held them both aloft. 'This is a typed and signed letter from a gentleman you used to befriend, a Mr Hewdon-Vassar. And this . . .' She threw the tape across and onto his blotter. 'This is the tape recording of our conversation.' Rupert stared down at the unmarked tape, sitting squarely there. 'I think you'll find that everything is there. Oh, and incidentally, I gave you your chance, which is more than you would have given me, but as you have not seen fit to play fair, nor will I. You see,' she said, her eyes extraordinary now in the dark of the room, filled with the light of battle. 'I no longer intend trying to repay the balance of the debt. I believe that you can take care of that personally.' Her eyes were full of meaning.

He knew immediately what was on the tape and who had been talking. She would know all about his deals, his private cuts, the bribes. All about everything. If Hewdon-Vassar had squawked his resentment he was lost. If he called in the loan she had the ammunition now to expose him publicly. Rupert had a strange code of ethics: a rape in a wood was nothing, stealing from his bank and having the world know was unthinkable. He stood to lose far more than money.

'Do you want to hear it?' she asked him, watching his face.

'No.' He was dismayed. He would personally have to make good the bank's losses. It was the only way out. 'You cannot prove this,' he said. 'A tape recording is no evidence in court.'

She had tucked the letter back into her bag and closed it with a snap. 'I'm willing to give it a try. Are you? We're talking about something between five and ten million dollars, Mr Redfield. Now, are you going to play ball, or not?' She stepped forward and retrieved the tape before he could stop her. 'I believe that is only a fraction of what you have salted away over the years. Do you really want us all to find out just how much? Not only me, but the *News of the World*? Of course, they'd love it. You've already given them the lead. They're champing at the bit now for more. If you wish it to be that way I just have to walk out of that door. The Bennetts have nothing to hide.' She held her head up, and her eyes challenged him.

'You are blackmailing me into covering up your grandson's idiocy.'

'Now we understand each other. Do I have my answer?' She

was uncompromising, as he had been. 'My silence in return for the contract.'

She waited calmly. Rupert tried to think quickly, realising he was cornered – for the moment, anyway. Her information could be lethal. On tape or paper or not, it was true, and once out in the open he would have the devil's own job keeping it under control. It was blackmail, but he had no option. Stalemate. Just when he had tasted victory. He still had the blood on his tongue.

'You don't leave me any alternative, do you?'

She smiled for the first time. She opened her handbag once more and dropped the tape inside. 'You will have the papers drawn up to the effect that the loan has been repaid, and at my Piccadilly offices within the hour.' She looked at her watch. 'It is now ten. If they are not on my desk by eleven, I shall be telephoning the press, the same press you alerted a week ago.' She turned to leave. 'I think that is all, Mr Redfield. We are even now.'

'We shall see.'

She gave another tight smile and walked to the door.

'Wait,' he said.

She turned.

'How do I know you will not let this out once I have signed?'

'Because I have given my word.'

'Your word?'

'Not to you, but to a member of my family,' she said coldly. 'I shall sign away my silence as my half of the deal. I will give your messenger the tape to bring to you. Apart from that, you'll just have to trust me.'

She reached the door, opened it and went out.

Rupert sat down again slowly. It wouldn't be personal. He would lose the debt within the bank's finances somehow. He could juggle them once again to his benefit. That bit wasn't too bad, but she . . . she had got him, hadn't she. He put his head in his hands, unable to think clearly for the anger that obliterated all rational thought. Guy. He would call Guy. He always knew a way round a situation. Beat her. He had to beat her. He reached for the telephone.

Dickie walked down the corridor, shaking. He had not known how right he was. She did not have proof. It had been a bluff, and it had worked. If he had listened to the tape he would have known; Mr Hewdon-Vassar, despite his resentment, had been enough of a gentleman not to dish the dirt on them. But now Dickie knew by his reaction just how deep his dealings had gone. He was a scared man. Without a written confession from Hewdon-Vassar they had nothing, but she had banked on the little she knew, the tip of the iceberg, and it had worked. Certainly the bank could have been put under a search, even so. She wondered. Had she been prepared to stop it here as she had said, out of loyalty to Kay, to her promise, or was it for less honourable motives than that?

Faced with that man again, knowing how much, how very much she hated him, how she wanted to destroy him – would she have done so if she had the power despite Kay?

She did not wait for the lift, but headed for the stairs. It was not over yet, not until eleven. She would be glad to get out into the fresh air again, out of this building. Her anger had primed her for the confrontation, but it had taken its toll. She would like to have carried it further, liked to have seen his face when she could have said she was taking his home from under him: Foxhall.

She remembered how she had sworn she would get that house, that feeling that she would never rest until she had it, and he was made homeless as her family had once been. She wanted him to know that feeling. But she had promised Kay.

They were all gathered in the boardroom at five to eleven. Dickie looked up at the wall clock.

'He's certainly leaving it until the last moment.' Jim stood up and crossed the room once more.

'Sit down, Jim.' Max's deep voice was a command. He studied some papers in his hands. 'He'll be here.'

The knock at the door startled them although they had been expecting it. Dickie's secretary came into the room.

'It's come,' she said. 'The messenger just arrived.'

Max came to his feet and took the newly typed contract from her and found it accompanied by the original contract that Jim had signed, and a covering letter 'Personal – from the desk of Rupert Redfield'. He scanned the pages swiftly as Dickie stood beside him, reading as he did.

'It's all there.' He handed it to her. 'You'd just better check, and you too, George,' he said to George Reilly. 'And Anthony,' he called the company lawyer forward, 'read it through carefully before we let go of the tape.'

Dickie handed the sheaf of papers to Philip and went over towards Kay. The younger woman sat beside the window in a deep basketweave armchair.

Her eyes met those of her grandmother. 'All right, Dickie? Has he done it?'

'Yes.' Dickie sat down beside her and looked out over the stone terrace, bleak now and shut off during the winter months. The distant view of the rooftops was one she had always enjoyed. 'He's signed it.'

'Thank God. We can all recover from this now. It's over,' she said.

Dickie did not answer for the moment, just laid her hand over that of her grandchild in a gesture of thanks that needed no words. They sat together.

At the desk, Anthony stood up straight. 'It's all straightforward. You're off the hook,' he said. 'Doubtless your man will now repay the loan himself.'

'He can well afford to.' Max reached into the desk drawer and took out the tape. He handed it to his secretary. 'Put this in an envelope with the letter from Hewdon-Vassar, seal it and send it back with the messenger.'

The girl took them from him and left the room, shutting the door quietly behind her. The room was silent for a moment, each deep in their thoughts. At the window, Jim's face was damp with relief, his eyes losing the haunted look they had held for days. It was the first time he had been back with the family since he had been sent off to his hidden address. Now, he felt a part of them again. For the first time, he wanted to pull his weight.

Max crossed over to Dickie.

She was still looking out over the scene before her, the grey skies and dark red chimney stacks breaking the unremitting winter gloom. 'I'd love to see his face when he gets them,' said Max, laying his hands on the back of her chair.

'Yes.' Dickie's eyes darkened. There was some information but little on the tape that would be incriminating in court, and the letter was simply a letter inviting them down to Hewdon-Vassar's country home for lunch. It would infuriate Rupert once he knew how he had been tricked.

Jim came over, brushing a hand through his hair.

'Thank you for intervening, Dad, Dickie.' His look included Kay. He had found himself out of his depth. Had silently watched as Dickie, Max and Kay had fought to pull them back from the brink and onto a firm base again. He had realised their ability, and his own lack of it. He stretched out his hand to his father.

'Thank God it's over,' he said.

But it was too soon for Max. 'And not with any help from you.'

Jim was left standing, his hand still outstretched as Max turned and strode from the room. Jim turned away, ashen.

Kay looked up at his face, feeling for them all. She had taken it all in. It was her first taste of how to fight a battle, and a realisation of what Rupert Redfield was capable of. But at least the battle had been fought clean and won, despite the bitter feelings remaining in her father's heart. It was time for her to go now. She would tell them only that she wanted to return to try out a new life in California, picking up the reins of her independence.

She followed her father out of the room. She found him down the hall in his office, staring out of the window. She went and put her arms around him. 'Daddy, have you time to talk?'

He seemed relieved to have the contact. He returned his daughter's hold, his arm around her waist. 'Yes, I'd like to walk a bit. Want to come with me, have a spot of lunch somewhere?'

He took it very well, she thought, but she had not beaten around the bush. Across the table from her in the restaurant, he had listened and understood. They were all learning, it seemed.

'I think you've earned it, Kay. I was in fact going to ask you if you'd like to help run things out there. You've proved yourself, a tactician as well as an excellent pilot. It's what we need in the company.' He paused and smiled. 'There's plenty of chances to try out there. You'll have access to the airfield.'

She laughed. 'All right, but flying comes first. I'm going to try for some new record, something that hasn't been done, if possible.'

'Good luck. Oh, and you can use our new house.' He and Jennie had bought a low Spanish-style hacienda on a bluff overlooking the ocean a mile up the coast from Malibu.

'Thanks, Dad,' she said. 'But I'll find my own spot. Something I can tuck away in, with some privacy.' She saw the disappointment on his face. He wanted to look after her, make it easy. It was not going to be her way. 'It'll be the first time I've had a place of my own.'

Back in the office, Dickie had had lunch sent in. She took a break from her work and lifted the napkin from the tray. The smoked salmon was from across the road, Fortnums, the best in town, and the half bottle of white wine perfectly chilled. She cut into the fish with her fork and took a bite.

By now, Rupert Redfield would know how successfully he had been conned. She felt some satisfaction in that, but not entirely. She was over seventy now. She should have given up fighting, gone into retirement like an old warhorse, but she could not rest. There was a different emotion now: Rupert Redfield was off the hook again. It was a small victory. She knew he would bury the loss in the gigantic financial embrace of the Redfield bank. In giving her word to her granddaughter, she had also inadvertently given her word to his brother, Frederick. It was a strange irony.

But something told her it was not quite over. And she hoped it was not. There were still loose threads. She had stood by her word to Kay, but only that particular word; that deal. If there were to be repercussions, any grumblings she might hear with her ear to the ground, she would unearth them. It would be a battle out in the open, with no restrictions, and she would be free to fight. There were weak links in the Redfield camp, that she knew; and it was his and his grandson's greed that had shown them up. George was already following a lead for her; a name that had come up in conversations over the last few weeks, and a man he suspected could be bought at a price. Well, she had money: she would buy Guy Prudham.

CHAPTER THIRTY

January, 1974

There was a deep orange moon hanging over the countryside. It lay in the sky calm and still, as if it knew its beauty, just beyond Cobbold's Wood as it sloped down the horizon. The wood, the firs on the opposite bank were black wedges against the sky. The moon was reflected almost perfectly in the river, just a ripple to elongate it like a Chinese lantern glowing in the dark water.

Kay crossed the gravel driveway and rang the doorbell.

She heard the footsteps approach, and pulled herself deeper into her coat. The door opened. Edward Callow looked out at her, a small figure on the doorstep.

'Is Mr Frederick Redfield in?' she asked.

'Whom shall I say is calling?'

'Miss Kay Bennett.'

The butler did not move a muscle. 'Please, come in.' He knew who she was all right. She stepped into the warmth of the huge hall with a smile of gratitude. 'Please . . . wait here,' he said, closing the door behind her. The cold evening was instantly forgotten in the soft glow inside. Kay stood and looked around her, bemused.

Edward crossed the hall to Frederick's estate office. He knocked and entered. The man was bent over his desk working by the light of a single goose-neck lamp. 'A visitor, sir.'

Frederick looked up. 'Who is it, Callow?'

'A Miss Kay Bennett, sir.'

'Kay!' He dropped his pen, surprise and a smile illuminating the severity of his features as he had gone over the books. He got to his feet immediately. 'Kay!' he called as he came around the desk and crossed the room. She had already heard him and was coming swiftly across the hall, her boots echoing up around the staircase and silence.

She came around the doorway as he did, almost bumping into each other. Edward Callow discreetly retired, heading for below stairs. This was a turn up for the books all right. Wait till they heard this one!

'Kay!' he said again, his arms opening to embrace her, and the sleepy blue eyes alive with amusement. She came into his arms quite naturally, though she never had done before.

'I thought it was time we got braver. All those meetings on towpaths and me cooee-ing out from behind a bush in the fields!' she laughed. Her eyes were aglow.

'You're lucky. I'm all alone here today!'

'Well yes, I knew that actually. I did wait until I was certain. I may be determined but I'm not foolhardy. I know he's up in London tonight,' she said, referring to Rupert.

He did not ask how she knew, merely led her into the drawing-room.

'Come in here and get warm,' he said. A huge fire crackled comfortably in the grate. Only one single soft standard lamp had been switched on. He went to the tables beside the fire. 'I'll get a bit of light on.'

'Oh no, don't bother,' she said. 'It really is quite beautiful like this. What a room, Frederick. What a beautiful house.'

She looked around her at the galleried drawing-room, the long mullioned and leaded windows, the woodblock floor strewn with plaited rugs, the glowing rosewood grand piano in the bay of the window, the family portraits adorning the panelled walls.

He refrained from switching on the light, instead went to poke up the fire. 'Is that an acquisitive remark or an aesthetic one?' he said, with humour in his voice.

Behind him, she threw herself down into the sofa. 'Oh definitely acquisitive!' She laughed with him as she pulled off her gloves and pushed them into her pockets. 'Thank goodness that's all over and it's worked out, Frederick. The tape had enough on it to frighten your brother if he'd started to listen, but luckily the bluff worked.'

He straightened, turned to look at her and came across to the sofa. 'I'm glad I could help.' He sat down beside her.

'Yes, thank you for that. I know it wasn't easy. But at least it's over now. They're quits.' Her eyes gleamed like a cat's in the firelight.

'Even though Rupert's like a bear with a sore head.'

'I don't doubt it,' she said drily. 'I'm sure he hates to let go of a single penny.'

Frederick nodded. 'Are you staying a bit? Would you like a drink?'

'Actually no.' Her face softened as she looked at him. 'This is a flying visit. I wanted to tell you I was leaving, that's all.'

'Leaving?' He frowned slightly. 'For where?'

'California. I'm going to work out there . . . fly a bit, whatever.' She looked down at her hands.

'Congratulations. Your father must think a lot of you.'

'Yes.' She paused. 'I just wanted to say thank you and I'll miss you. I'm sorry the row between our families flared up like this, and that I had to ask you to get involved, but it's turned out all right in the end.'

He gave a little smile. 'I'll miss you, Kay. I haven't got too many friends like you.' His eyes warmed as he regarded her.

'You've got Charles,' she said. 'Is he a nice man?'

'The best.'

She understood him. 'It's often easier to talk to strangers though, isn't it. Families can be so judging and they know so much.' Her eyes lit. 'Pity you can't come with me.'

'Had I been any younger I'd have jumped at that offer!' He laid a gnarled old hand on the cushion between them, the heavy gold signet ring winking in the light. 'You paint an exceptional picture of what's possible, Kay. Seeing it all through your eyes I feel quite optimistic.'

She smiled. 'I must go.'

She stood up, and he pulled himself to his feet beside her. She looked at him for a moment and then impulsively put her arms around him and kissed him on the cheek.

Then she turned and was gone.

'That damn woman. She found a way out.'

Alexander stared hard at his grandfather. *You don't mean we've lost it?*

'Yes, that's what I mean.' Rupert's eyes lifted up, regarding him coldly with their blue gaze, almost as if it was his grandson's fault: he had led them into this humiliating situation. 'I had to deal with her,' he said accusingly. 'She had me by the balls!'

'How?' he said.

Alexander stood in front of the massive desk in his grandfather's old office. His annoyance over the last few months of having his grandfather back in the driving seat was eclipsed by this news. He had thought his presence only temporary, that once his object was achieved Alexander himself would be back in power – and with the accompanying shareholding he needed.

Rupert eyed his grandson. 'Never mind,' he said. 'Let's just say it didn't work out.' He did not want to have to admit to Alexander any of the details of his dealings over the years. He had no idea he knew about them anyway. He looked back over his paperwork. 'Now, what's on the agenda for today?'

Alexander could not believe it. Rupert still was not going to confide. 'So I assume my increased shareholding comes to naught,' he said, ignoring Rupert's question.

Rupert laid down his pen. 'Naturally,' he said caustically. 'You didn't get the Bennetts for me, did you. That was the deal. You'd better come up with another if you're that keen to get higher up the ladder.'

He went back to his writing. Alexander stood for a moment, listening to the scratch of his fountain pen on the heavy vellum. No other sound filled the room but the fury lancing through his head, making it pound. He turned on his heel and left the room.

He marched into his own office and slammed the door so hard behind him that it swung open again. He threw himself into his chair, his eyes unfocused, his knuckles pushed against his teeth as he leaned on its leather arm, his thoughts full of impotent hatred.

He had been so certain.

Guy came quietly into the room, a half-smile on his face as he looked back at the door. 'Well, what's got into you today?'

Alexander stared up at him. 'You know of course.'

'Know what?' Guy strolled over pulling at his cuffs. His eyes still held their look of amusement.

'About losing out to the Bennetts. We had them, Guy, we had them, right here.' He slammed a fist into his palm, his teeth clenched. 'And then somehow, she got away, and I lost out. I wonder what the hell she did,' he murmured half to himself.

'Oh, that's easy,' Guy said airily. He came across and sat down on the corner sofa Alexander had had installed. Beside it was a small square marble table with a Chinese lamp and an onyx cigarette box. Guy pulled out a cigarette, without asking, and lit up. Alexander watched, still waiting.

'Well, come on,' he said. 'What do you know?'

Guy narrowed his eyes against the smoke, pleased with his knowledge.

'She went to Hewdon-Vassar.'

'No!' he breathed. 'Who told you that?'

'He did.' He took a drag. 'Thinks I'm still his friend. Your grandfather called me in to help. Told me about it, but it was too late. I do know that he talked, but luckily not on paper, and little on the tape she produced when she came to see your grandfather.' He tapped out his cigarette. 'Thank God. Otherwise we would probably all have been in at the deep end. Very messy as it was,' he went on. 'She conned him. Pretended she had more than she did – smart woman!' he said almost with respect. 'By the time Rupert called me in and I tried to talk to Hewdon-Vassar he'd gone. On a visit abroad, his housekeeper said. Probably on a Bennett Air flight, if my hunch tells me correctly.' He drew in a breath. 'Point is, she had us then. We lost and she won.' He laughed, relishing it all.

Alexander stared, his green eyes unblinking. 'You knew all this, and didn't tell me, let me go on thinking . . .'

'Oh, Alexander, come on. The battle was over before it was won. There'll be others. You had an axe to grind with your grandfather, and now he's had to cough up his private finance to make up the loan.'

'Is that what he's done?' he interrupted.

'Well, no, of course not. Not that quickly. It's a lot of money, but he's in the process of shoring up the leaks, yes.'

'How long will it take him?' His eyes bore down on the other man.

'I don't know. Weeks, perhaps, maybe more.' Guy stubbed out his cigarette. 'But you and I both know he's got enough stashed away to make up this difference *easily*,' he said, emphasising the word with raised eyebrows.

'But not immediately, huh?'

'No.' Guy watched him. 'No one's going to know though, are they, Alexander. I mean, your grandfather has been, shall we say, "cooking the books" for a long time. He's an old hand at it. A little shuffle here, a little shuffle there, and Bob's your uncle, the Swiss bank account looks all fine and dandy again and the bank's books balance too. Quite a sleight of hand!' He lowered his eyelids and watched Alexander carefully.

He had fanned the flames beautifully. Alexander was taking it all in. Guy examined his perfectly manicured nails. 'Robert's axe to grind is against Rupert, but you'd better watch out too. He doesn't like you very much either.'

Alexander gave a short, barking laugh. 'Hewdon-Vassar's got absolutely nothing on me. You forget, he was out before I was in. No, he doesn't know what I have been doing in the last few years, nor does my grandfather and equally, nor does my grandfather know that I am aware of precisely all the deals he has ever done,' he said softly. Then turning to Guy again. 'He doesn't know that I know all about him, does he? Hewdon-Vassar didn't tell him?'

Guy shook his head. 'No.'

'Good.' Alexander's eyes now held a faraway gleam. He leaned back in his chair and let his thoughts drift as he gazed off into the distance through the window. 'I'm not letting this rest, Guy. Bastard promised me a shareholding. I'm not going to wait until he's *dead* before I gain control of this company and get what's rightfully mine anyway. He'll probably live until he's a hundred.' His voice slowed. 'I set this up for him and by rights we should have had Bennett Air in our pocket right now, signed, sealed and delivered. I was looking forward to moving into Longbarrow.'

'There'll be other ways.' Guy's voice was encouraging.

'You're dead right there'll be other ways.' He turned to look back at Guy, and leaned once more over his desktop. 'That man shows one face to the public, one face to his family. He couldn't stand a scandal. I'm not waiting any longer, and you're going to help me.' Years of hatred festered in him. Now it was his turn to hunt and corner Rupert.

Guy pursed his lips. It was the ideal situation for him; playing his cards carefully he would always be the winner. A divided camp was always healthy for the third, the manipulator; despite his prime loyalty to Alexander. It did him no harm to set the one against the other. He would have the ear of both. He thought of the approach that had been made to him that morning by George Reilly, on behalf of a private client. He knew damn well who that private client was. It was all developing into a very interesting pattern from which he could only benefit. 'What did you have in mind?' he said.

'One very persistent lady reporter I know,' he said, picking up the address book to one side of his desk and flicking through, looking for a recent number. He found it. 'Loves smut. She's been after me ever since she prowled around Foxhall Green trying to find out some dirt for her rag. She's sniffed it out already. With what I know I can bust grandfather from here to hell.' He picked up the telephone and started to dial. 'He'll be out on his ear by the time I've finished with him, and I'm his natural successor. I want that chair for my own. I'm going to put his head on the block and he's going to need you.' His eyes locked onto Guy's with a dark smile. A voice answered and he broke the contact immediately. 'Ah yes.' he said. 'Lindy Bunter, please.'

Rupert recalled her face as he sat alone in his room, reflecting on their confrontation. He sought a likeness in that memory, transposed it to the face of his grandson, Alexander. No. No, there was nothing. Could not be.

Yet that question had been uppermost in his mind, despite everything else, when she had walked into his room in that haughty way of hers. So like Sabrine, so like her son, Max. Damn them. Was there something there, or wasn't there? He could not rid himself of wanting to know. It had been the question he had been dying to ask her, the question about his daughter and her son. She knew, he could bet his life on that, but she would not have told him, would she? It would have given her so much pleasure to know how the lack of knowledge made him suffer. He could not ask. Alexander would have told him, but Alexander did not know, he was sure of that too. Only Sabrine. And his granddaughter was cruel, he knew that too, despite this new cute relationship between her and the boy which everybody else in the family seemed to sanction. He knew her too; knew she would never give him the relief of knowing whether it was bait or trap: she would enjoy his mental torture. Besides, to ask would be to admit: as long as it was in his mind alone he could choose to disbelieve it, make it fantasy . . . Did he really want to know? Yes.

He gave a deep sigh and put his hand against his heart, feeling its rapid and irregular beat. His fingers squeezed and pushed against the fine warm cotton of his shirt. He leaned forward with a grunt of effort and pulled open the top left-hand drawer of his desk, uncapped the small bottle inside and shook out a couple of pills. He threw them into the back of his mouth, picked up the silver jug on the table beside his desk and poured the cool water into a glass tumbler. He drank it back. A couple of heart pills was all it took: not bad for an old man of eighty-four. No, there was life in the old dog yet! Enough life to vanquish that woman. It had been a battle of wills but he had survived. He always would.

Rupert stood up, stretched his long heavyweight frame like a cat. He had put the financial re-reckoning in process: it would take a little time to gather that kind of money, but he could realise it in terms of property alone. The West End freeholds were already on the market. Yes, he would shore up his problems there with ease and no one would be any the wiser. A little topping up from here and there, and all would be square financially, even though the losses would be heavy to him personally. Far more of consequence to him was her delivery of that tape and letter that had proved her ability to fight back, and dirty. Well, she would see what dirt was by the time he had finished with her. It was high time to put on the gloves. If that idiot, Alexander, was unable to set them up, or if there were no other way, he would simply frame them, he had people who would lie for a price. Pity the weak link, the son Jim, had gone. He would have been useful, especially with a chip on his shoulder to work on. But there would be others.

Lunch at the club. There were eyes and ears there who knew everything that was going on in the City. He would put out feelers. He went over to his private lift, pressed the bell, the doors slid open and he was hummed swiftly down the six flights to reception.

The girl was at his side before he had even seen where she had come from. Behind her, the commissionaire was lifting an arm to stop her, but she had slid by him with ease.

'Mr Redfield?'

'Yes, but . . .'

'Mr Redfield, your contract with Bennett Air? Why was it withdrawn?' In her hand the small tape recorder was like a gun pointed at him. Running.

'I don't think that's any of your business. Excuse me.' He stalked past her, heading for the steps.

She ran alongside. 'I've heard you took the loss yourself, personally. How did you make good those losses, Mr Redfield . . . ?'

'Jackson!' He called the commissionaire. 'Remove this woman.'

Jackson was coming over. Rupert was heading for the street, his car outside waiting beyond the swing doors. The girl was like a terrier. The red light on the tape recorder gleamed in her hand. He pushed at it, but she was quicker. 'I'm sure your shareholders would like to know . . .'

He started to run. Jackson was right alongside, grabbing for her arms. 'The private Swiss account . . . insider dealings . . . maybe even lining your own pocket at the expense of the bank . . . a handout here and there for services rendered . . . would you like to comment on this . . . ?' The machine was thrust into his face.

He batted at it like an angry wasp, ran quickly down the steps and strode across the wide hall. People were looking at him, stopping, staring.

'Now come along, miss.' Jackson was useless. The girl's thin black-jacketed arms freed themselves from his grasp. He would be fired tomorrow.

'Prop Finance, Jersey. Penn Activities. Eclipse, Luxembourg. Could you comment on these? It seems . . .'

My God, she knew it all. His head was fired with shooting pains as he ran for his car. She had broken her silence, the bitch had broken her word. He would murder her for this! Jackson had the girl now, pinned in his arms. She was calling from behind, the names ringing out for all to hear. The faces stared at him; they would all know. The sweat broke out on his forehead as he pushed on the glass, pushing hard against the vacuum in the swing doors, and out into the street. The photographer's flash was right in his eyes, and again.

'For God's sake, Martin, open the fucking door!'

The chauffeur was already coming around the bonnet of the gleaming Rolls. Now his face held amazement. The photographer had leaped from out of the covering shadow of the building. He ran to open the back door, pushed at the man's chest. He tumbled to the floor, the flash exploding again.

Rupert shoved his way into the back of the car. The door slammed behind him, and Martin was in, car in gear, moving out and away. The man was up off the street, coming fast for them, camera lifted again, aiming.

'Drive on!' he shouted. 'Fast! drive!'

Martin roared the big car up out into the road, swerving back onto the straight and away. Rupert sat back, his face a deep ugly red, his eyes chips of blue, bulging with fear and exhaustion. He was shaking. His hands on the seat each side of him were wet.

'Where to, sir?'

'Just drive.'

Through the streets of London, just getting away. He did not see where. After a few minutes, he took his white handkerchief from his pocket and mopped at his brow, his cheeks and neck. He pushed it back into his breast pocket, and leaned forward for the telephone.

Guy took the call in Alexander's office.

'It's your grandfather.' He put his hand over the mouthpiece. 'What shall I say?'

'Just tell him you'll be with him. I'll fill you in. Act surprised.'

Guy nodded, listened a moment. He nodded again. 'Good heavens! Yes, Rupert, of course. I'll be there.'

He put down the telephone.

'Wants me to meet him at Eaton Place.' It was the Redfield family home in London. 'Wants me to bring his files.'

Alexander put down his pen. 'The fish bites,' he said. 'Let's reel him in.' He smiled. 'I've still got a way to get them both.'

Together they sat down at the dining-room table. They spread the files between them. Guy had been his confidant a long time, totally aware of his double dealings both with shareholders' money and with his own private use of the bank: attacking failing companies, asset-stripping, insider dealings, harassment of his tenants as a landlord, bribes and handouts. The list was lengthy. A great deal of money had been secreted away over the years; he had never known quite how much. Now they would find out. He was about to be publicly exposed unless he could get his hands on the few million pounds he would need within the next few days so that they could keep the press at bay. He did not think that she was the last of the journalists that would hound him. It would spread like a mushroom cloud. His earlier juggling of the bank's finances had been something of a problem: it was as nothing compared to this.

'I'll have to shore it up somehow, Guy. I can't get my hands on that kind of money quickly though.' His eyes were still staring, searching for a way out.

'The only way to do it is to tie up the books, Rupert. That means actually feeding back the money so that there's no proof the bank did not receive it. With the accrued interest over the years, of course.'

'That's a colossal amount!' His eyes swerved to those of Guy.

'True, but I see it as the only way.' Guy reached out his slender hands to move one of the papers aside. 'Unless of course you don't mind the exposure. You could say something along the lines of a voluntary admission before the press crucify you. Sort of: "Certain things have unfortunately gone wrong in my empire, without my being aware of it, and therefore in the best traditions of the City I am going to repay x amount of money to the shareholders.' You know as well as I do, Rupert, that what the City has been about for decades has been ripping people off. Possibly everyone would just laugh it off.'

'Don't be ridiculous. You know I'm not going to say that.'

Guy smiled quietly, and reshuffled the papers. 'Well what are you going to say then?'

'That's why I called you. To help. Not ask me damn fool questions!' said Rupert irritably. 'You know perfectly well there's much more to it than "mistakes". Everything's bound to come into the open, if I'm not extremely careful. No, our only hope is to quash the rumours now, so that there won't be anything to discover were the bank to institute a search. Hopefully, they won't.'

Guy leaned back in his chair, one arm still resting on the table, flipping his pencil. 'Oh, but you know they will,' he said smoothly. 'You have committed fraud, after all, Rupert. The Department of Trade is bound to be called in to investigate your companies. The Bank of England, too, might well be quite offended. Even though they operate on their traditionally informal basis, they do expect the head of discounts to be reliably informed so that they feel they are keeping at least an eye on what is going on.' His mouth thinned into an infuriating smile.

'I know it's all based on "nods and winks",' he went on airily. 'But they have been known to get quite shirty when they're literally kept in the dark. And as you rightly say,' he added, 'there's more. If we really get into trouble, they might not be very cooperative.'

'No. Stop playing with that goddamn pencil, Guy.' Guy laid the pencil carefully down on the gleaming tabletop as Rupert frowned his disapproval. The man was running scared and irritable. He knew why.

Rupert had a strange code of ethics. He could not bear the thought of exposure. His dual character showed one face to the public, and another behind the scenes, as Alexander had said. He could not bear the thought of his public image being tarnished. With the same mentality that made him go to church every Sunday to show himself superficially as a worthy man, he viewed the destruction of that image with dread. He was honour-bound to protect it, despite the fact that in private he had dealt despicably with people all his life. To Rupert, the image was all: it had to be protected at all costs.

'That woman,' he said into the silence. 'She swore . . .'

Guy had been party to the rapid deal struck between them that other morning. He had seen the paper swearing Dickie to secrecy on the matter of her conversations with Robert Hewdon-Vassar. He had seen her signature. He knew what had transpired between them more or less, the rest he had guessed at. He regarded the man for a moment.

'How can you be sure it's her?'

'What?'

'Well, she's not the only one with an axe to grind, Rupert,' he explained. 'Let's be fair. You've crossed an awful lot of people,' he went on, enjoying himself. Him included. 'If you start accusing her, she might really go into battle, especially if she's innocent of your charges. And I think she well could be. You have seen how she can fight.' He watched as Rupert's bear head jerked up, listening to him, as he spoke in her defence. 'And you did listen to the tape. There was nothing on it in the context of what that journalist was saying: no names. I don't think Robert told Miss Bennett anything substantial. I don't think she has any ammunition at all. It was all a bluff on her part.'

That made him angry enough too. 'Well then where did that damn journalist rake up her muck from?'

Guy shrugged. 'I don't know. But the bottom line is, she knows. I would advise lying low until you're sure of who's at the bottom of this. Miss Bennett could be pretty ruthless if what I've seen already is anything to go by. And if it is her, we can deal with her later. Let's get you in the clear first, that's our main objective. You've got enough on your plate right now.'

Rupert nodded, calming. 'You're right.'

'Good. Now, let's get the money out of Switzerland, get it moving. Now, it's lucky that all those years I fixed the books for you. If we can just get the money back in where it's supposed to be, and very quickly, no one will be any the wiser.'

Rupert looked both grateful and worried. 'Yes, yes, I see

that. But I can't get it that quickly! Not before the bloody press come hammering on my door and everybody else's screaming for blood. You know that.'

'Well.' Guy was maddeningly slow. 'Then I suggest you borrow it from someone else who can get their hands on quick money.'

'Well. Who? For Christ's sake?'

Guy pursed his lips. 'I don't know, but you have plenty of friends. I would suggest perhaps someone close, family perhaps. And definitely discreet. That's essential,' he added. 'You don't want that escaping too.'

'Deeper and deeper,' moaned Rupert.

'It's the only way.'

CHAPTER THIRTY-ONE

Her body was magnificent. Her head was balanced proudly on strong shoulders. He could see the curve of her full, uptilted breasts, the long lean torso and thighs that were full and firm. In the high-cut swimsuit, her long legs tapered to fine-boned ankles and narrow feet.

David was sitting up on a rock, just back from the beach. Latigo was one of the few beaches still free from crowds, and it was not as socially structured as Malibu or Broad Beach. Lying in a cul-de-sac off the highway, the beach houses were braced with beams against the powerful seastorms. He thought he knew all the regular joggers by sight. He watched her. Beside him, Jack Weatherby mended his fishing boat. Jack was one of the richest men on the coast, but he drove a pick-up truck and he looked like a hillbilly. His family had lived on the coast for generations, picking up lots for sale as and when they came up. They had made a fortune in accrued property speculation over the years. But Jack's main passions were fishing and riding. He was a deceptively easy-going old fellow who was on first name terms with all the big names around. David had met him one day shortly after he had discovered for himself this small curved and quiet bay and they had fallen into easy conversation. Jack's house was a low-lying dark wood house, unpretentious and nestled in against the rocks, its wide deck blending in with them just where the boulders were at their heaviest. The steps ran right down onto the beach. Often David came down to the beach just to sit and talk out on Jack's porch as the sun went down.

He watched the girl run up the beach, a small dog following. 'Who's that?'

Jack pulled at the brim of his tattered straw hat. 'That? That's the girl who's taken the old May Rindge place for the summer . . . they made *Mildred Pearce* there, you know . . . the movie . . .' He went back to his boat.

David had never heard of *Mildred Pearce*. He looked briefly at the low house that Jack had mentioned, set back behind a wall, steps leading privately down to the beach. It stood alone, away from the others.

The girl pulled into sweat shirt, pants and an eye shield. The dog chased seagulls, then sat. She set up a fishing line. First the pole, thrusting it into the sand, then she set the line in. She tested it, walking into the water to fling the line, then back. She fixed up a low beach chair, a towel over her knees, a thermos by her side, and pulled out a script. She began to read. An actress: and he had thought she was somehow different. He felt a sense of disappointment. He'd met a dozen.

Kay, unaware of the scrutiny, absorbed herself in the script before her. It could be a good property for her cousin, Joleen. She had asked her to give it a look. She was happy to be involved in something so different to her life and curious about the film business. The line lay taut in the water, the gulls dived and screamed overhead and the water crashed at her feet, the spray on her skin. She wriggled her toes into the sand. It was wild and peaceful: the sort of day she loved. She was soon deep into the story.

As soon as he could, David had excused himself from Jack. As chance would have it, this was one day he had offered to help mend the boat. It took time. From the dip where the boat was lying, he could not see her. He wandered down onto the beach at last, but as he rounded the corner of the rocks, he realised she had gone. He looked up at the windows of the little cottage, but there was no movement. The stone sea wall was quite high, built for seclusion.

The sea frothed in, a sudden brush of lacy white against the dun of the day. The grey rocks were piled against the stilts of her house. He could see tubs of terracotta, bright with geraniums, a barbecue, and a lounging chair in green and yellowed sailcloth.

He wondered briefly at his curiosity. He had not even seen her features. And then he walked on, the girl's image almost dying from his mind.

Rupert sat back in his chair. A fine film of sweat had broken out on his forehead. Surely they had not heard yet? But whether it was some sort of early bush telegraph or not, one thing was certain: every associate with the kind of money he needed was either out of the office or not taking his calls. So far not one single person was going to help him.

He rubbed his fingers over his top lip. Who, who would help? It was urgent now. Lindy Bunter had broken the story, a scoop that the other nationals would soon pick up on; the thing would escalate out of all proportion. She had not named names, probably scared about libel for now, but that would not last. Rupert panicked: now it was only a matter of time.

Gilbert Rees-Hulbert, *of course*! Never in the City, probably didn't read that rag paper, and rich as Croesus. Let's hope like hell he hadn't smelled anything yet – Rupert's fear burned in his head as he dialled Gilbert's number, listened to it ring way down in the country.

'Hello.' The deep voice was slow.

'Gilbert. Rupert Redfield.' Now he would know.

'Rupert, how nice of you to call!' The voice was certainly not unfriendly, more curious. Rupert offered up a silent thank you, and closed his eyes briefly. He stared up at the ceiling.

'Gilbert, any chance of meeting up, old chap? In a spot of bother. Could I see you?' He hated to ask, hated this servile position he was in.

'Certainly, Rupert. Friday, do you?'

'Er no, I mean real bother.' He laughed roundly. 'Today, if that's possible.'

Gilbert hesitated, seemed concerned. 'Well, all right. Say my club in an hour's time. I could drive up, could do with a nice long lunch with all my old pals . . .'

'No, actually, I'd prefer to come to you, if that's all right . . .'

'Well of course, that's all right, old boy. See you here about one then? Have a spot of lunch?'

'Yes. Thank you, Gilbert.'

'Not at all, old boy, not at all.'

They sat out in the conservatory, surrounded by dark plants and the view of the fields stretching out snowy and soft before them.

'It's the devil of a day,' said Gilbert. 'Must be jolly important for you to come driving through all this snow, Rupert. Go on, have another.'

He pushed the plate of quiche over in his direction.

'No thanks . . .' Rupert moved away. Henrietta's cooking was appalling; he wondered why they didn't sack their ancient old cook and get a new one. She wouldn't have lasted a day with him. 'Gilbert, it is important. Believe me, I would not be here, would not be asking for your help if it was not.'

'I see. Go on . . .' He picked a handful of grapes from a bunch laid out on a silver dish.

Rupert sighed, wondering where to start, wondering what to lie about. Better just to say what he wanted, get it and get out.

'I need to borrow a lot of money. Very quickly. I'm in trouble. I can borrow the amount I need to survive with time, but I don't have time. A loan of such magnitude will take a while. I need quick money, Gilbert. That's why I've come to you for help.'

Gilbert nodded. He stared out over his land. 'Well, as you know, I can get my hands on a fair amount of money pretty quickly as you say.' He thought for a moment. 'What sort of money were you thinking of?'

Rupert drew a breath. 'Ten million.'

'Pounds or dollars?'

He was amazed at the man. He had not turned a hair. 'Pounds.'

There was silence for a moment. 'Well, that is a lot,' he said quite calmly. 'Are you going to tell me what it's for?' It was the first time he had looked at Rupert.

'It's . . . to do with the bank,' he said slowly and carefully. 'Nothing I can't handle, but this particular journalist – well, she's got a story on me and she's ready to stick the knife in.' Gilbert was watching. 'It's a story that if it caught fire, it could ruin the bank. We could have a run on the deposits, shares could fall at the stock exchange, that sort of thing. Could be quite dire.'

'Is the story true?'

'Oh well, you know, one or two things yes maybe, but nothing that anyone hasn't done before.' He tried to laugh, but coughed instead. 'The point is that, well you know how we do things in the City, bit of insider dealing . . . It's common practice, but the Bank of England might decide to be difficult, could make an example of me, just to prove a point, you know how awkward they can be at times,' he stumbled.

'Oh, just general run-of-the-mill banking perks, you mean then,' said Gilbert. 'Nothing fraudulent.'

'Oh no!' Rupert gave a grim smile. 'No, no, nothing like that . . . just the usual kind of inside information we all capitalise on.

Normally, of course, I'd be able to tie things up right away. Trouble is, I was already suffering some losses. Can't make it good right now, but I need to, Gilbert, for the bank's sake,' he said pointedly. 'To quash this rumour fast, today even, before it starts. What do you say?'

Gilbert appeared to be quite relaxed. In his own right he was an extremely wealthy man. 'Well, of course, old boy. If that's all it is, I'll help you. I can let you have eight million. Would that help? Can you find the other two?'

'Absolutely. An immense help.' He could realise the other two from the sale of the West End freeholds that had sold immediately he had put them on the market. Pooling his resources he could squeeze through. He felt a sense of euphoria that was close to orgasmic. 'That's marvellously kind of you, Gilbert.'

'Don't worry about it.' The other man raised an airy hand. 'I'm sure you'd do the same for me. What are friends for after all . . . ?'

Yes, what are they for, thought Rupert, remembering the unanswered phone calls of that day. Just wait until he was back in a power position again.

'How shall we set it up?' he asked. 'Can we do it today?'

'Yes, of course. I'll organise it.'

Rupert, coming down off his high now, was fascinated. It all seemed so easy. He was going to be off the hook; he was almost laughing.

'Gilbert, forgive me for asking, but where can you get your hands on such an amount of money at short notice?'

Gilbert chortled and rocked back in his chair. 'I've got my own personal little bank, didn't you know? No, I suppose you didn't. I keep it fairly private. And that's what it is – a private bank which I run, a licensed deposit-taking bank. I happen to enjoy running it as a sideline. It's a little financial outfit that I've built up. Quite proud of it actually. I lend money on commercial property development generally, that sort of thing. Built up quite a nice little business. Run it as a hobby, really!' He wrinkled his brow, looking like a contented old gnome.

'Good God!' Rupert breathed. 'I had no idea.'

'Yes, well, come on now,' he brandished a finger at Rupert's half-full plate. 'Eat up and then we'll go and sort you out.'

*

295

Kay lay on the grass, enjoying the sun. She had inherited her new position successfully. She had chosen to work hard, flying in every possible spare moment whilst keeping the low profile she wanted. Her American grandfather, too, was a good sounding-board. She spent some time down at the Colony, enjoying the company of Ed and Dory McVey. She was forming a reputation as a powerhouse of energy within the company and something of a loner when it came to socialising. Far better were the evenings when she would relax at the end of the day; she would sit out on her deck and listen to the sound of the ocean as it pulled her in a constant rush of movement, the long rollers sweeping down the coast to flood the rock pools at the eastern end of the beach. Or she would get in her car and go down to Ed and Dory's, and watch the Californian sunset sink over the mirrored ocean, the sky aflame, and talk to Ed, telling him of her new discoveries and challenges, her eyes shining. She had wanted to fly more than anything, and this week she had set up her own air show.

The first competiton was about to start. She sat up, ready to go and judge. Until now she had been just another spectator, mingling with the crowd sitting and standing out on the grassy field.

'Don't I know you?'

She looked up at the speaker.

'You'll have to think of better chat-up lines than that one,' she quipped, coming to her feet. She pushed the weight of her hair back with one hand and looked into his face.

She missed classic beauty by a hair's breadth, he thought: she was not breathtaking, but she had a look about her that was perhaps even more so because it was so unusual. It moved him emotionally; he could not say how, but her beauty did not make him catch his breath. He had seen plenty of those out here in California, where every waitress was an aspiring actress, the beauty and bodies garnered from every corner of a mixed-race nation. The results could be, and often were, extraordinary. Hers was more unexpected than that: like coming upon a beautiful view when you thought you knew the landscape, like a sudden discovery. The green eyes taunted him: a smart-arse rich kid, too used to pick-ups and coolly amused.

For David the mistake was genuine. He really had thought he knew her. But he was wrong.

'Sorry, I made a mistake.' He turned away.

'Oh, I . . . that's all right.' She had expected a few moments' more pleasant company, but he was already planning to leave. Intrigued, she wanted him to stay just a moment longer. 'Are you flying today?' she asked.

He was different, she knew that right away. A touch of arrogance about him that was intriguing. Recovering from his mistake, he appeared uninterested, had dismissed her already. He looked up at the sky.

'Perhaps,' he said. She noticed the strength in his face, the aquiline nose, the mouth firm-lined with deep dents at the corners as if it would pull into a roar of laughter. She could see it, wanted it to happen, but it did not. Eyes that were slightly hooded, very dark. 'It's a good day for flying, a wind to make you want to walk, to get out of bed early and ride out over the hills.' He talked as if to himself, looking up at the hills behind them. At the crest the white clouds climbed up a wide blue sky. Pale grey clouds were laced with sombre yellow. A fair brisk wind ruffled across them. Then he seemed to remember her. 'Yes, I'm going to fly. Friend of yours entering?'

'No, actually *I* am.' She felt slightly stung by his attitude. He was so dismissive, had not even assumed that she would be flying herself. Now he looked at her, saw the flare in her eyes and was amused.

'We're competitors then. I wish you luck.'

For the first time in her life she wished he knew who he was talking to. 'I wish *you* luck. I was raised on flying.'

His eyes narrowed. The crest of his blond hair was ruffled and unbrushed, his broad shoulders planes of light beneath the sun, his body fit and brown beneath the open-necked shirt he wore.

'Pretty pleased with yourself, aren't you?'

'I might have reason. You'd have a job beating me,' she said hotly, amazed at the strength of her reaction. What on earth was she doing this for? 'You're not a flyer,' she said. 'I haven't seen you around before. I know all the good ones.'

'Maybe.' He watched her, keeping a cool distance from her. 'But this particular one's important to me.'

'Why?' She felt she was asking too many questions, but could not stop.

'Because I aim to win this competition on behalf of my uncle. He wanted to fly but he was turned down from joining an airline by some English asshole.' She knew the name before he said it.

'Max Bennett . . . the guy who owns this outfit. There, does that suit you?'

He was laughing at her. She felt herself blaze against him. For a moment earlier she had warmed to him, felt something. Now her hackles were up; she was ready to take on this challenge. She wanted to beat him more than anything. He was so cold, almost fiercely arrogant; giving nothing of himself away. Perversely, she wanted to find out more.

Now he was turning away again. 'I've got to go and get ready.'

'I'll see you at the finishing line,' she called after him.

'We'll see.' His laughter mocked her as he strolled away. He'd see her – but not the way he expected.

'I gather your bank's for sale.'

'Are you in the market?'

Gilbert Rees-Hulbert looked with some extra interest at the woman who sat across the restaurant table from him in Les Ambassadeurs. She suited the elegance of the dining-room, in black Chanel, a white silk open-throated blouse and ropes of lovely pearls. Two excellent square-cut matching diamonds sat in her ears where her still dark hair was swept up with creamy-white waves. Her green eyes were level and well balanced under dark brows, and her skin soft and clear, despite the fact that she had to be well into her seventies by now. He knew the legend of Dickie Bennett, and was struck not only by the forcefulness of the woman, but by an element of emotion in her that he had not expected. He liked her, very much. Had liked her from the moment he had walked into the fashionable restaurant to meet at her invitation for lunch. She had waited until the coffee had arrived, banking style, before approaching the subject of business. The rest had been light, pleasantly informal chatter. Now there was a different edge to her voice.

'Yes,' she said. 'But first I want to tell you something. You remember that we used to bank with you?'

'A while ago now. You pulled out.'

'You know the reason?'

'No. Please tell me.'

'Rupert Redfield,' she said.

Her finger traced the edge of her coffee cup. 'At the time you went into the merger with Redfield-Strauss, he tried to break me with it. Obviously he didn't succeed . . . but there was no way we could remain after the merger.' He nodded as she went on. 'He's been after me a long time . . . still is . . .' Her eyes were expressive. 'It's my turn now.'

'I see,' he said slowly.

'Now I would like to buy your bank.'

He watched her carefully. 'I thought you had your own troubles lately.'

He was more shrewd than she had been led to believe. She liked that; it made it easier. 'Only in one area,' she said. 'The main Bennett Group is sound as I'm sure you're aware. Privately, I am a very rich woman quite apart from the company: that runs under its own steam. I have gathered a nest-egg, you see, for a day such as this. The irony is,' she said, with a half-laugh, 'that I have managed to salvage four million from my grandson's foolish venture, and that is now mine.' Her eyes were brilliant as she spoke. 'A fine irony, indeed!' She thought of the use to which Rupert's money was going to be put. 'For the purchase of your bank, Gilbert, I can put my money and company money together to buy you out. The City's going under,' she warned him. 'It's a good time to get out.'

'So why are you taking such a risk?'

'Oh, it might seem that way to you, but not really. It won't be the first time I've gambled on something I believed in. My personal instinct has always been reliable.'

'You must want it very badly.'

'Yes.'

'May I ask why?'

'Not really, no.'

'For you personally, or for the airline?'

'For me personally.'

Gilbert Rees-Hulbert drank his coffee in one quaff and replaced the cup in its saucer.

'Yes, Miss Bennett. I will sell to you. And for my own reasons, which will also remain personal.' He stretched his hand across the table to her. 'It's yours.'

She was in control.

The awards for the winning contestants of the air show were later that afternoon. The winner of the major event of the afternoon, the race up the coast, was to have the prize presented by Miss Kay Bennett, of Bennett Air.

As David walked up to the rostrum to collect his prize, she came forward to greet him, balanced on Wiley Fairfax's arm like a lovely ornament, her glorious chestnut hair lifting in the wind, and she was laughing. She had changed into a pretty summer dress that swung and clung to her hips, her tiny waist held tight by a wide belt.

The first thing he knew was that he had been wrong about her: she *was* beautiful. The second was that she was some English asshole's daughter: Kay Bennett.

It was clear that she had been waiting for his expression and was highly amused. As she handed over the silver chalice and shook his hands, paying him the usual winner's compliments, she whispered quietly:

'*An asshole, huh?*'

David was shocked. He had never realised she was a Bennett, but he had made it his business during the course of the afternoon to point her out to a casual acquaintance of his.

'What do you hear about her?'

'*Her?*' The reaction had not been reassuring. 'Oh, brother, you must be kidding. A pain-in-the-arse rich kid, likes to compete and win. A lot of guys have been burned by her; she's known for it! The original ice maiden, teasing and not giving in! Just watch yourself if you're interested in her.'

'Not interested, no. Just curious,' he had said softly, watching her laugh with a tall, red-headed young athlete over by one of the tents. She threw back her head, showing her throat. The wind caught at her hair making it shimmer with red and gold. The boyfriend, he had thought, as the man put his arm around her and gave her a kiss. He felt a little knife go through him.

'By the way, what's her name?' He had turned to the man beside him, but he had gone.

Now he knew. He caught a glimpse of spectacular legs and a wonderful smile as she handed him his certificate. He was supposed to back off, return to the steps and join the crowd that was now dissolving as the air show came to an end, but he did not move.

'Too scared to compete against me, huh?'

He saw the smile wipe from her face, the quick hurt in the green eyes and wished he hadn't spoken. But it was too late.

'Well, I would have thought you would have realised by now why I couldn't fly,' she said. 'I ran this show, I couldn't compete. What I meant was I'd race you when it was over. And I will. Choose your weapon. I'm no coward.'

He shook his head. 'Weather's too bad.'

'Afraid I might win.'

'Afraid you might lose and you couldn't take it.'

The green eyes shot sparks. 'Oh, I'll win.'

'In that dress?' He stepped off the dais onto the steps, holding his certificate. 'Don't be ridiculous.' He did not want to push this any further, wanted to stop her. It was why he had turned away.

'I can fly in anything, Mr . . . Hamblin,' she said, remembering the name on the certificate. His eyes caught, but the name meant nothing to her. 'Now you've got your rocks off against my father, you're just going to walk off, are you. Well you've still got his daughter to reckon with.' She ran down the steps alongside him. 'I'll take that one,' she said, pointing at the small yellow biplane quivering in the wind at the edge of the field. She headed off towards the plane.

'Look,' he went after her, grasped her arm and turned her. 'You'd be foolish to fly in this. Look at the storm coming up. No-one else is going up, not even to go home!'

'Nonsense,' she said, shaking her arm. 'Let go of my arm. I've flown in far worse weather.' The wind whipped her hair across her face, scalding her eyes. She did not give him the pleasure of letting him see he hurt her. She would not let him think of her any more as a silly feminine creature as he obviously had done right from the start. She would not give him an inch.

He let go of her arm.

'Then you're either a fool or a selfish child who can afford to write off a valuable and beautiful machine without a thought,' he said coldly. 'Either way it's not the behaviour of a responsible person as you so obviously wish to be seen.'

'You're afraid of losing. I'm not. I'm going up, with or without you!'

She ran across the grass. She resented his chastising her; his nerve, his interference, and the fact that he was right: normally she would never fly in such weather. She was simply as irresponsible as he had said, but he had challenged her and she had risen to it, like the child he had intimated she was.

She took the little craft up, and as always, the deep-throated throbbing of the engine, its optimistic roar as they flew off down the runway and lifted up high into the clouds, filled her with a pleasure and commitment that she never felt on the earth. It was the soaring away, the lack of boundaries and the challenge of one to one that enthralled her, coupled with the beauty that was given only to those who flew alone. It was a wild day up there: the wind buffeting her so that the wings dipped and lifted, and it was harder to keep her on course than she had imagined. But she never felt a flicker of fear: she trusted the machine she was with, murmuring to it as she headed out over the ocean as she might to a child or animal. Over the ocean, the wind was much rougher, right behind her then switching suddenly to throw her to one side. She righted the plane and pushed her nose up, climbing into the blue ceiling of the sky above California, blue and electric, the wind cutting her skin like knives of ice as she soared upwards, the roaring in her ears. She banked and flew back towards land. There was no other small aircraft to be seen. The wind was in her face now as she headed back over the beach, seeing the heavy rolling swell pounding in to the coast way down below her. She found the field and flew down, keeping her wings as steady as she was able. The other competitive aircraft lined the runway like colourful butterflies. None had left the airfield. She brought her down carefully, hit the runway with a little bump and another, and coasted her in. She had made a perfect circuit. It was foolish, but heady, and she had returned triumphant to a collection of worried faces, but she did not see him. Had he already left?

Kay drove home later in the day. The sky was turning to fire, the sea smoothed and silver like mercury, heavy and flat. The wind had long since blown itself out.

Fool, she thought. Wanted to show you could do it, didn't you. Wanted to show him you weren't just a Daddy's girl given a company to run, show you were a girl with brains and brawn. Well she had shown him just the opposite.

He was a nobody, a rich kid surfer, idling his days away: forgettable. She remembered the mouth that didn't smile, how she had wanted it to pull into that roar of laughter she knew was there. He was the one she couldn't have because he didn't want her. She had sensed something though under the coldness, the biting words between them, though the flippant words and arrogant attitude were everything she disliked in a man.

Obviously she was definitely not going to wind up with someone like him.

She closed her eyes briefly and his image was clear: It mocked her weakness. Cold, handsome, lean; she saw again the aquiline nose, the high planes of his cheeks, the full and sensual mouth that held both humour and cruelty in its line, the dark reproving eyes. It was clear he did not trust her emotions. And why should he after what she had done. God, how stupid, and how unlike her. Whatever had possessed her to challenge a windstorm like that in a paper-thin craft? It was only her absolute knowledge of the structure of the plane and how it would respond, that saved her. She was an expert. But then, so was he. She recalled admiringly how he had handled the Gypsy. She wondered what other talents he possessed, what he did, where he lived. She remembered how she had seen a glimpse of him in the car park five minutes after she had come down, a hot blonde leaning up against him. They had both climbed into his car and driven away. Kay had hardly been able to think straight. What did it matter who he was. She had not meant this to happen and with a man so clearly uninterested. The whole day had been a disaster.

She pushed the image from her mind and gunned the fast little car as she sped up the coast for home.

David dropped the blonde off at her house with a kiss on the cheek and headed back up Pacific Coast Highway. He wanted to be alone, to remember. That cool look, the long sea-green eyes shot with blue just like the ocean, and the smile that curled slightly at one corner, the brush of golden-chestnut hair that fell across her forehead, her chiselled features, that mouth. Then the anger in those eyes as he had challenged her.

His interest had been ignited too. But there could be no more. Once she knew who he was it would be over before it was begun.

He drove off the highway, over the familiar bump in the road, cut the engine and coasted down into Latigo. He felt like having a quiet drink with Jack. He parked the car out on the dirt road, went down onto the beach and climbed the wooden stairs. The windows were dark, the door locked. For once, Jack and Sissy were out. It was odd, David had never felt lonely until now. It was an unfamiliar and disturbing feeling. He turned, and walked out towards the balcony. The sound of the ocean was soothing. He listened for a moment, looking out over the beach.

It was then that he realised where he had indeed seen her before. She was the girl from Latigo Bay.

Kay was aghast. 'You must be joking, Dickie.'

'I'm not, Kay. This is the chance for which I have waited a lifetime. Much as he did for me. I cannot and will not let it go.'

'But you swore to me it would go no further!' She pressed the telephone receiver to her ear and walked over to the window. It was a glorious day outside, hot sun baking the deck, the sea glittering in the distance. 'You can't break your word.'

'This is a different matter. Nothing to do with what went before.'

'But of *course* it is!' she said, lifting her hand to rub at the pane of glass at front of her. The other side was misted with salt spray. 'You didn't honour your side of the contract. If not you, who told the press?'

Her grandmother had telephoned to talk to her; now all of this had come out. Kay felt sick.

Dickie's voice bridled. 'I would have thought you knew me better than that, young lady. A fighter I might be, underhand I am not. Unlike Mr Redfield I fight clean when I can. But fight I will, whether you like it or whether you don't.'

'Dickie, this is not the right thing to do,' she challenged her. 'After all, whatever lead it is you're following now, it stemmed from the beginning of all this, from Frederick. You cannot do this now. We promised him. I promised. I said that would be an end of it if he helped us. This is not fair. Tell me you'll drop it. Let it be.' She held the receiver tight, with both hands.

'No. No, I'm afraid I cannot say that to you, though I know how you feel about it.'

'I won't be a party to this,' she said evenly. 'I wish that in the event of this trouble I had not gone to my friend for help. He will feel betrayed, and it'll be me that will hurt him, because now I can't get in touch with him, can't tell him the truth.' The truth that it was one of his brother's own directors that had given her grandmother the information, had betrayed the Redfields behind their backs, not them. 'I won't forgive you for this, grandmother,' she said, her voice icy.

'I once was betrayed and nor can I forgive that,' said Dickie with a sigh in her voice. 'And I am going ahead. I've already bought Gilbert Rees-Hulbert's private bank. Rupert's loan is now mine, his future in my control.'

There was now no time to talk to Frederick. She had tried to stop it happening but it was something that was out of her control, and had been, long before she was born. It had come to a climax and had its own momentum.

Sadly, though through the best of motives, it had been she who had set the final ball in motion, she had been cooperative in fighting back with her family against Rupert Redfield. Despite her friendship with Frederick, it had been she who had inadvertently found the way to get the revenge her grandmother had so long desired.

'It's wrong,' she said. 'You should stop it now. Someone has to.'

'No. You can't stop it, Kay. Much as once upon a time we could not stop you when you wanted something badly. You understand now. We are too alike. In the same situation, neither would you have let go. I promised myself that one day I would own Foxhall. And I will.'

CHAPTER THIRTY-TWO

It had been George whom she had appointed as her emissary. Rupert had not suspected a thing as he invited the elderly banker into his study. He was a man who thought himself to be in the clear.

George did not accept his invitation to sit. He stood before his desk and dropped the contract onto its leatherbound surface.

'She's sticking to the letter of the contract, Mr Redfield,' he said formally. 'She wants the money repaid now.'

Rupert's blanket bewilderment held a needle that pricked him, even now. 'What are you talking about?' he said as he drew the contract towards him. He recognised it at once. He held it between his hands. 'This is a private contract with Gilbert Rees-Hulbert. How on earth did you get hold of it?' He was annoyed now. And yet, what had gone wrong? Something.

'It was between you and the owner of the bank, Liberty's, was it not?'

'Yes.' Rupert tapped at the cover sheet. 'As you can see. Now kindly tell me what you mean by this, and then get out. I'm growing tired of this game.' He rose to his feet.

'The owner of this bank is now Mrs Josephine Latimer.'

Rupert was half out of his chair. 'Mrs . . .' His brain became horribly clear. 'No.'

'Yes.'

Rupert bent quickly over the contract, leafed rapidly through, saw the new deeds attached to the back, saw the signatures, the truth, the dreadful truth. 'It can't be true.' He sat heavily in his chair.

'It's true.' George's voice was clipped.

'She broke the terms of our agreement,' Rupert muttered emptily. 'I'll sue.'

'It wasn't her. As you'll find out if you do. And very expensively, too, I might say. I wouldn't recommend it.'

'Who then?' His eyes lifted to that of the other man.

George was old now, more severe. He was a City man, and

Dickie was his friend. He knew what had transpired in this man's life, both in business and personal terms. 'You have many enemies, Mr Redfield,' he said.

Rupert bent his head. The lettering on the contract swam before his eyes. This simply could not be happening to him. He struggled for a way out. The long-term contract he had set up for repayment of the loan could not possibly come through within the time allotted. Just at the crucial moment, as he was about to come into the clear, she had caught him. He was in her trap.

'Now George,' he said, his voice reasonable. 'You and I are both sensible men. Mrs Latimer surely understands the situation. I cannot pay this immediately, but if she were to wait, well then, I could pay her the few million pounds with interest!' He tried to smile, his hands lifting wide off the desk. 'Greater interest, how about that?'

'Sorry. I have my orders. That is not acceptable.'

'Damn you, Reilly. And damn that woman!' He slammed his fist onto the desk so hard that the papers jumped. 'You don't have a leg to stand on and you know it. I will take you to court, all of you, expose you for the blackmailers you are. By the time the case comes up, I'll be in the clear.' He came to his feet again, glaring.

George retained his cool. 'I suggest you make a visit to Mrs Latimer. She is expecting you at the family home, Longbarrow, around about five.'

He left the room.

In the drawing-room of Longbarrow House, Dickie awaited her visitor. She had asked the family if they would go out for the day. She knew he would come. She stood at the lovely bay window that overlooked the sweeping lawns down to the river. It really was the most idyllic view, the house so perfectly balanced in the palm of the land, protected by the gentle hills behind. She remembered how she had first seen it, she and Sam, those early sunrises before the day had started when two small children had scrambled up onto the grassy hill to look down over the splendours of the valley in the morning, couched in mist beneath the blue sky, feeling the stillness of the day before the world awoke, listening to the early doves cooing, a distant farmyard cockerel crowing on the silent air, the early peach-soft view of Longbarrow lying above the meadows beyond the river. She had never dreamed one day it would be hers. And nor had he. Rupert had wanted it too; it was the first of her victories, but as nothing compared to what would happen today.

She tried to assess her feelings. Nervousness, exaltation, anger? No, none of these, not even anger. She felt an overwhelming sense of calm. If anything she was cold, the sort of cold that came with a lifetime of hate followed by the moment one had waited for: the perfect revenge.

The door bell rang in the distance. The house was full of flowers and warmth. He would see it at its best. She heard George's footsteps as he went to the door, the distant voice, and the door shutting. She smiled. The footsteps approached. She had been right. Now she did feel emotion: she felt it in her eyes as she turned.

George let him into the room, closed the door and left them together. She made no move to approach him or greet him, just watched him. He had come to her humiliated, she saw that at once. He would ask for her help. It was the worst thing that could have happened to him. She wondered what he would say.

His blue eyes bored across the room.

'How did you do it?'

'It hardly matters. Have you come to repay your debt, Mr Redfield?'

'You know I have not,' he growled. 'How the hell could I find that sort of money in days?'

She nodded. 'I'm sticking to the letter of the contract, of course, as you did with us. You know of course what that means, I take it. If the money cannot be paid fast then I must seize your assets. I own Foxhall as security for my loan to you. I have no option but to foreclose on the loan.'

'Why did he sell to you? Why did he betray me to you? He must have known something.' He took a step forward. 'Tell me, what did he know?'

'I have no idea.'

'I'm not going to give you Foxhall. Hell'll freeze over before I do.'

'You have no choice.'

'You bitch. I should have done more than rape you there in that wood – a rape you enjoyed, I've no doubt about it,' he said cruelly. Dickie drew herself in as his venom exploded. 'I should have had you dealt with like the trash you are. That never changes, despite your money and your house. You've got them all fawning over you, haven't you, and I bet you love it. Oh yes, but you're still nothing. Nothing!'

Her eyes were as hard as emeralds. She kept silent, though a tremor lanced through her as she watched her enemy turn.

'. . . you may think you've won this round, Miss Bennett, but I'll come back and I'll hurt you like you've never been hurt before. I damn nearly lost everything because of you, did you know that? You. You . . .' He lifted a disgusted hand. 'My father saw fit to take your side, but it made no difference in the end!' he said, his eyes gleaming. 'I kept what was mine, and I will again. You'll never get Foxhall . . .'

'I already have.'

His eyes stared hard into hers. 'I have until the end of the month. It says so on the contract. I can do a lot by then.'

'You should have read Paragraph 13 (b), the default clause, a bit more closely. If interest is not paid by close of business today, you're in breach of contract.' She looked at her watch. 'Business closed officially one minute ago. Foxhall belongs to me. I want you out of there by the end of the week. I shall be gutting the place and turning it into a home for the retired and needy. That is all, Mr Redfield.'

She turned her back on him. Heard him come across the room towards her, pushing the tables aside. The flowers crashed to the floor. Dickie turned swiftly, his face looming at her, his hands outstretched to grasp her. He was like a bull, red and charging, blindly angry, roaring his rage.

The door flew open behind him and George came running in, accompanied by two younger men, strangers. They caught him and pinned his arms just as she could almost feel the sweat on him touching her.

Her breast rose up and down as she stared at him.

'Now Mr Redfield,' she said. 'You will learn what it is like to be vulnerable and defenceless. You will learn what it is like to have your home taken from you, to be unable to fight back. You have tried to destroy me and my family far more than I could ever have attempted to destroy you.' Her face was carved and cold. 'There are many ways to hurt me, but only one way to hurt you, and I have always known what that was. It was you who showed me.' She paused a moment. 'You thought you could destroy me through my home, through the money I had accrued, through my business. But you see,' she said softly.

'There is only one thing that truly matters to me, and that is my family.' She turned away and walked to the window, looking out for a moment, and then she turned to look at him once more. He was standing there, pinned between the two men.

'It was your mistake. You thought that I could be destroyed through the image I had built, and through my home. But you forget, I had no image to protect. You already destroyed that when I was barely fourteen years old, and as for my home, the only one that I ever cared for, you took that from me when I was little older. So you see, there was nothing you could do to me any more, except hurt what I loved, and luckily, because you are so blind to love, you did not understand. What you understand is where I am going to destroy you. For good. There are only two things that you would protect at any price: your image and your home, your ancestral home. I am taking both of these from you today. You made a mistake, Mr Redfield. You thought I had the same base values as you. Well, I don't,' she said with an almost pitying smile. 'And now for you, it's too late. That's all. You can go now.' She turned her back on him once more.

The two men held his arms. He threw them off, straightening his sleeves. He would not be thrown out like a dog.

'You won't have the last word, Miss Bennett . . . you won't. Just wait and see.'

'Throw him out,' she said, not turning.

They took his arms, propelling him protesting to the door. She heard them thump into the furniture, his furious cursing, knew how it would hurt his pride. They dragged him across the hall, the front door opened, and Rupert was unceremoniously hauled down the steps and pushed into his car. She heard the two cars start up in the distance. They were to escort him off her land, for good.

She still did not turn. She felt the trembling cease inside her. It had been an ordeal, but she felt the pride surge back now. She had done it.

She thought of the house, that big dark house she hated. She knew it so well. Downstairs particularly. She remembered that hot kitchen, scrubbing black lead into the fireplace on her hands and knees, the baby growing inside her and straining at the heavy clothes she wore to conceal it. In the heat of summer, she had stepped out into the cool to recover, faint. Even now, the perspiration rose on her skin in memory. In that garden that had been the pride of Rupert's wife, Caroline, the stone maiden had stood, no feelings, cold and beautiful, no way to be hurt. She had not wanted to remember it when Katherine had come to see her, recalling the past. But now she could. She let herself relax and remember how she had made her oath then, to be like the statue, cold and unfeeling until she had her revenge.

That other had ruled her life, coloured every judgement, every move. Some had been sad, some had been happy, but they had all been towards one end. This was the last. Now she was free at last.

George stood at her shoulder.

'It's mine now, isn't it,' she said.

'Yes, Dickie. Foxhall belongs to you.'

CHAPTER THIRTY-THREE

Kay had arranged to meet her friend at the Baja Cantina, a bar and restaurant in the centre of the Malibu shopping mall. Many of the locals, young and old, stopped off there in between shopping, playing tennis, or on the way to or from the beach. The terrace outside held a few tables and chairs, and beyond the low wall one could play spectator behind dark glasses and watch the crowd go by.

Kay sipped at her Strawberry Daiquiri. On the table in front of them were deep fried prawns, two orders of guacomole and some tangy corn chips. She had mentioned the young man she had met to a girlfriend, a young blonde sculptress. She had a small studio up the coast amongst the hills and looking down over the ocean. They had met out jogging on the beach and formed a friendship.

Now she looked out casually from under her eye-shade in the direction that Kay had pointed.

'Not him?'

They watched the man who had swung down from the seat of the open jeep. It was dented and dusty amongst the Cadillacs and BMWs, painted a sun-faded orange. He hefted a bag over his shoulder and strode towards the store. Kay watched him, the lean stride, the surety. She felt herself prickle.

'He's a strange one,' said her friend, Tina. 'Sort of silent. Doesn't give anything away. Loves his horses, though. We all had him picked out one time or another, but none of us made the grade. Very picky. No one's good enough, I reckon. Wouldn't I have liked to be the one!' she said, a little dreamily. Then she shrugged and sucked at her straw.

'Family?' pressed Kay.

'Lives with his aunt up beyond Point Dume. Sabrine Sydney, you know, the movie star.'

'Oh . . . yes, yes I do know who you mean. She's very beautiful.' Then she remembered. 'My cousin's up for a part in her new film.'

'Better watch out for her, then. She's apparently a jealous lady.'

Kay smiled again. 'All right.' Then she raised her eyebrows at the man who now re-emerged from the store, empty-handed. He came towards them. Kay's face was half-hidden by her glass: she watched him over the rim. 'Don't you know anything else about him at all? Is his family rich? What he does?' she said softly. 'Does he work?'

'Oh yeah, he works. He's an excellent horseman. He runs the stud for his aunt. Horses seem to love him. They do anything he wants . . . !' She laughed. 'I don't think he's got any money though. He doesn't act like a guy with money. I mean look at that beat-up truck for a start!' She gave a snort of laughter again. 'In the land of status symbols too!'

'Maybe he just doesn't care for that sort of thing.'

'Oh dear,' she said in mock surprise. 'Defending him already. A very unhealthy sign.' She leaned over and patted Kay affectionately on the arm. ''Fraid I can't help you any more than that. Most I know his family are English. He came over here a few years back. Apart from that, nothing. He keeps himself to himself. No gossip.'

His eyes met hers, she was sure. Dark, narrowed, they lanced through her in swift recognition and then dismissed her almost as quickly. He grabbed open the handle of his jeep and threw himself up onto the high seat, kicked it into a roar of sound and slammed the machine into gear. He had not missed the girl whose hair was like a banner of light on the small terrace. It drew him like a beacon. It had stopped him for only one moment. He drove away and out of the parking lot. Kay felt a sinking disappointment.

'Want to go to the beach this afternoon?'

'No.' Kay unclipped her purse for money. 'I have to get back to the office.' She laid ten dollars down on the table and stood up.

'Catch you later then.' Tina was staying awhile, her eyes both curious and observant. 'He's not worth it, you know,' she said. 'Don't break your heart. Ciao.'

Olivia pushed the last of Alice's cotton sweaters into the big holdall. The telephone started to ring in her bedroom.

'Get that, would you, Jane?' she shouted out.

The telephone continued to burr insistently.

'Good heavens,' she said. 'Does no one answer telephones in this house!' She ran into the bedroom, picked up the receiver. Jane was coming up the stairs, holding Alice's hand.

'Sorry, Mrs Bennett, Alice wanted to go to the lavatory.'

'OK.' Olivia smiled at her. It was just that they were in such a hurry. 'Yes,' she said into the mouthpiece.

'Jim Bennett, please.'

She had heard that voice before, its guttural quality as if it was not the man's own; that was it, that was what was strange about it. She did not bother to ask for his name this time.

'Hold on, please,' she said. 'Jane, shout at Jim, would you? Tell him there's someone on the telephone for him whilst you're there.'

The nanny, Jane, leaned over the balustrade.

'Mr Bennett! Telephone!'

Jim came walking across the drawing-room below. He had been out in the front hall. He looked up at them as he came across, his face harassed.

'Get a move on, would you, Olivia. Hang up when I've got it.'

He strode into his study under the stairs and closed the door.

Alice had raced over to the bed already ahead of Jane and had eagerly pulled at the new and fascinating array of colour there. She tugged at the carefully folded and stacked clothes, tumbling them all to the floor, and climbed up onto the bed.

'Oh God . . .' said Olivia, still hanging onto the receiver. 'Those were the clothes I'd put aside to go in our trunk for the ship. Grab them quickly, Jane, so they don't get mixed up with my air baggage. We're in a real hurry now.'

She heard him pick up downstairs. 'OK, Olivia, I've got it.' He waited for her to put down the receiver. She did, then went quickly across to help Jane pick up the shamble of clothes on the floor and start packing again.

He had not confided in her and Olivia had not known she was to keep quiet about their accompanying him. On the other end of the telephone, the man's voice appeared more guarded than usual, that was all. Jim agreed almost eagerly to meet their contact in Rome the following morning, an appointed destination he had no intention of keeping. Rejected and incensed by Max's treatment of him, he had decided to do another bigger and final drug deal and pocket the money for a new life for them all in Spain. He believed they would never find him there in hiding. The family had withdrawn all his responsibilities and now he had no authority at all in Bennett Air. He was little more than an errand boy.

At first he had refused the men when they had approached him. But they had remained persistent and they had something on him now too. It was the lesser of two evils.

It was dawn as they reached the Bower Hill field. Olivia and Alice waited in the car as Jim brought the Rockwell Sabreliner onto the runway. This airfield was less conspicuous than Heathrow. He would head out for the Channel and France.

'Come on, hurry up,' he said as Olivia climbed out of the car with a sleepy Alice in her arms. She climbed up the steps to board the small company jet as he went back for their luggage.

'Jim, where are we going?' Her voice stopped him.

'Never mind. Come on, we're late.' He pushed her up the steps quite roughly.

She turned to look down at him. 'Is it something to do with that man?' She was worried now. Jim was acting so strangely. And why were they doing this early-morning flit? He had given her explanations about there being less traffic, how it was pretty at that time of day. She did not buy that. No, there was much more to this. And now she knew as she saw his reaction that she had had reason to doubt him.

'Which man?' he barked.

'That man that called last night.' She looked into his grey, strained face, the dark hair whipping over his forehead in the early morning light, the blue eyes sharp and pale. Alice stirred uncomfortably in her arms.

'I've asked you, Olivia, not to ask so many questions. Now, I've got a job to do, and I'm taking you along. We're simply going to live in Spain for a while. Now is that so terrible?'

Alice gave a small cry and woke up, whimpering as she did so, and struggling to see where she was. It was unfamiliar and cold. It wasn't her bed, and despite her mother's arms, she was scared.

'Mummy, where are we?'

'Sssh, darling. Just going to have a lovely aeroplane ride with Daddy.'

'Now see what you've done,' said Jim. 'Woken her up.' He stepped up behind them. 'Can't you do anything right?'

315

Olivia moved into the narrow aisle, setting Alice down on the seat. She was wide awake now, looking around her.

'Daddy, are you going to fly us?'

'Yes.' He ducked his head as he came in, leaning back to talk to her. 'Now be good and quiet and sit tight when Mummy tells you.'

'I will.' She scrambled straight into her chair, sticking her legs out ahead of her. She let Olivia clip her in. 'Are we going far, Mummy?'

'Not very far. And at the other end we'll be able to play on a lovely beach and make sandcastles. Would you like that?'

'Oh, yes!'

'Then be very good, and we'll soon be there.' She sat down beside Alice and strapped herself in. Jim went out, down the steps. The wind blew into the small passenger cabin and Olivia was silent for a moment. Then Jim was back, loading their bags on board, shutting the door and pressing them into an airtight compartment.

Soon the engine was turning over, roaring into life. He checked his instruments, took his time and cleared his departure on the radio. There was nothing odd about the early hour: he often flew early in the morning on private flights to the Continent. The early arrivals amongst the ground crew lifted a hand from the radio tower as the small aircraft sped down the runway and up and away into the dawn sky.

Jim's six-foot frame was pressed back against the seat as the machine gained speed and climbed above the houses. He banked south-east and flew placidly towards the glistening thread of water ahead. He dipped down slightly to see it. It was early morning, the light exquisitely soft as the sun came up over the Channel.

He would hang onto the dope and sell it himself, maybe even sell the aircraft too if he could do so without being caught. He would be rich and free for the first time. They droned out over the Channel and the engine died. Suddenly, and without warning.

From behind, Olivia felt the catch in the plane. She looked up from the book they were reading.

Jim struggled frantically to start the motor. The plane dove for the sea. He panicked, forgetting all the rules. Nothing happened: they were going to die, none of the instruments would work. He pulled on the wheel, desperately trying to lift her nose, to glide. They pancaked into the cold black waters of the Channel.

The plane started to sink, swiftly. Horrifyingly, Olivia found she could not move. Her arm was broken, the seat belt jammed. She was strapped in, imprisoned.

The water was up to their chests. They were going down fast. Alice was crying. 'Mummy! Mummy, help!'

Olivia screamed at her. 'Get your belt undone! Get your . . . Alice! Pull the buckle, pull the . . . Jim, where are you? Help us!'

But Jim was unconscious and silent, the plane floundering, going down fast. And the little girl did not know how to unstrap herself. Jim's cock pit door burst open as the waves slapped against the hull of the aircraft. He floated upward, felt the dash of dark water, came to, blinded, disorientated. He thrust himself upwards over the wave. 'God . . . Olivia . . . Alice.' He tried to get back in but the waves cast him back.

'Mummy, help me!'

Olivia's eyes were wide with fear. Jim had gone. She knew it, felt it. 'Darling, pull the buckle! pull the buckle! oh God!' She fought with her buckle, tried to force her way out. Her eyes were wild as she sought her daughter's hands, tried to guide them. The small fingers scrabbled uselessly with the buckle that she had fastened tight for her own safety.

The plane yawed and slewed deeper. The current was impossibly strong, the water bitterly cold. With a last effort, Olivia clawed herself from her buckle, never stopping her cry: 'Flip the top up, darling . . . flip it, flip it . . . that's right!'

Olivia fell across the seats as her buckle suddenly snapped open. The water was up to her chest, closing over her daughter's head. Under the sucking water her frozen fingers took twice as long to snap it open, searching frantically, finding the clasp, pulling her child into her arms to struggle through the escape hatch and out into the desolate early morning sea.

The aircraft had crashed into the sea about three hundred yards from shore. It had been seen. Immediately local fishermen and auxiliary coastguard put to sea. A helicopter whirred out over the Channel.

It was bitterly cold, the waves seemed huge. Alice, only four, did not even struggle in her mother's arms. Olivia saw Jim, bobbing over the waves. He tried to get to her. And then the waves lifted between them and he disappeared from view. In her one good arm she held her child's head above the water, murmuring to her all the while, telling her to hold on, though Alice never said a word.

The helicopter poised itself overhead. They could see them now. The rotors swept a film across the waves. The water was bitter, but it was a particularly calm day, otherwise there would have been no hope. They saw the man, clinging to a wing of the plane. They saw the woman: she was grey and shivering over on the other side of the hull. She was trying to swim and hold up the baby at the same time. As rescue came, she slipped down into the water herself. None of them could have lasted many minutes more.

She had tried to save her child, encouraging her to hang on with a hitherto unknown strength. She was numb with cold and shock and barely alive as they were winched up onto the helicopter. She floated into unconsciousness on the way up, the child still clutched in her arms.

The man was unconscious also, though coming round as they lifted him. His jaw was broken in two places, he had a nasty cut to his temple and his nose was half torn from his face; he appeared to be unable to see. He mumbled and slipped away from them again.

The crew gave the little girl the kiss of life as they flew them to the Haslar Naval Hospital at Gosport.

She was coming round as he bent over her. His face contorted at first, then blurred. Jim? She did not remember where she was at first, and then . . . oh God. She clutched at his shirt, as he leaned over her bed. She opened her mouth but no words came.

'Don't talk now,' he said. 'Try to rest.' Jim had heard the story of her tremendous courage and somehow it had not surprised him at all. He had always underestimated Olivia's strength; he realised that now. Realised too just how much he actually loved her.

Her eyes closed and then fluttered open. They were filled with pain. He had never seen anything like it and could not look away. He had to bend to catch her words, so faint. Her fingers touched his shirt and slid away.

'My baby. Alice.'

He tried not to show in his eyes what he had heard but found himself unable to conceal it. Her eyes, like that, demanded the truth.

'She's alive, Olivia, but she hasn't regained consciousness. She's in intensive care, I've seen her.' He had: it was awful. His eyes showed it. 'She's going to be all right, I'm sure of it. Try to rest.'

A sob escaped her lips.

'Oh no.' Olivia, so close to her beloved daughter, could not bear it. 'Alice, my darling.' she trembled. She turned her face away in grief and silence.

A nurse hurried into the room behind him.

She touched his arm. 'You've got to go,' she said. 'She's not well enough to be upset. Come back later. I'll take care of her.'

She leaned forward over the woman. Stroked her hair, held her wrist. 'There, there.'

He left the room, leaving her with her grief.

'Damn,' he said. He punched the wall. Hot tears scalded his eyes. He stood in the soulless hospital corridor. It was empty.

'Damn.'

CHAPTER THIRTY-FOUR

The image of them all was in her mind as Dickie spoke on the telephone line from England, telling her the story as Kay listened, horrified.

'. . . I can't believe it . . . Dickie. What can I do to help? Shall I come home? There's a flight out this . . .'

'No, of course not, Kay,' the voice interrupted. 'There's nothing you can do here. What about the business over there?'

'Well it's fine. I have got a big day tomorrow, a couple of deals to tie up . . .'

'That only you can do, right? The business needs you on the spot, Kay, that's what I mean. You can be sure I'll let you know if the situation gets worse. Then you can get right on a plane and come home. Meanwhile, I think you should sit tight and try not to be too upset. I'll keep in touch . . .'

'All right. Please make sure you do.' Dickie was right. Pressure of business would keep her here, at least until the weekend.

'I will,' came the voice. 'Call me tonight if you want. Goodbye, darling . . .'

Kay put down the telephone, and tried to concentrate on the work that was on her desk, but pictures of the family kept coming into her mind. Jim, Olivia, little Alice. She saw them in the hospital. Images of David too came unbidden into their midst. She could not rid herself of him. The conflict was tearing her apart. It was too hot in the office. She could not relax or concentrate. Outside her window the sun blazed down. She put down her pen with a sigh, packed up her files and pushed them into a drawer. There was too much on her mind. She wanted to go off on her own, somewhere. She walked out through the glass-partitioned office.

'Stephie, I'm going home. Take my calls, would you?'

'Yes, Miss Bennett.'

Kay kept the top down on the ride home, letting the fresh wind lift her damp hair from the nape of her neck. She felt restless and awkward; useless. She had been told to stay put, yet she could not put them from her mind. Maybe a swim would help.

She arrived home and looked down onto the cove. She stepped out through the French doors onto the deck in front of the house. The soft beach curved round towards the rocks on the far corner. The tide was going out, flooding gently into the rock pools. There was no surf to speak of. She suddenly wanted something else, not a swim, not her habitual jog up to Paradise Cove. Pulling on her jeans, sweatshirt and trainers, she started to walk up the beach, heading north.

She rounded the corner past the rocks, meeting Clay on his palamino pony. He was a regular rider on the beach. His dog ran beside the horse, the little patchwork puppy that often followed her down the beach; a roamer.

She bent down to scratch his head.

'Morning, Clay.'

'Morning. Where you off to?'

'Oh, I don't know.' She stood up. 'Just felt restless.'

'Want dinner at the Sandcastle tonight?' The horse shifted and turned on the spot. He smiled down, trim and strong, a handsome young chap, tanned and blond. He had asked her before, though only once.

Her answer was the same.

'No thanks, Clay.'

She never gave more explanation, did not see the need. No wonder she had the reputation she did, he thought. Never let a guy feel better. Always left him feeling ashamed of asking. He called the dog.

'I'll see you then. Come along, Fred.' He spurred his horse forward, the dog following.

She watched them go thoughtfully. She was aware of his interest, but today she simply did not feel like giving anyone an explanation. She just wanted to be alone.

Further up the beach she saw the stream trickling down to the water. She decided to follow the river bed. Climbing up the bank, she crossed over the highway and started up the incline towards Sycamore Canyon.

At its head, the waterfall twisted together in a stream of water and exploded forty feet out over the canyon wall, falling a hundred feet down to the pool below, from where it snaked down the hill towards the highway. It was quite a hike for anyone to come up here, and few did.

David reined in Alabaster, laying his hands on the pommel of the saddle. The leather creaked beneath him in the silence. At the head of the waterfall the swallows took advantage of the breeze and curve of the canyon's mouth to dip and swirl above the crashing water.

He rode towards the head of the canyon. It was a favourite place for them both, horse and rider. Alabaster, his own Arabian stallion, the only one he had bought for himself, skittered along the path, picking his way through the sage bushes. They were alone, enjoying each other, the expert horseman and the perfectly tuned animal, highly intelligent and in perfect tone. David controlled his gait, collecting him, practising his equestrian skills to take his mind off his thoughts. The animal responded beautifully. They had almost reached the waterfall, their turning point. It was hot, midday, and time to turn back before Alabaster broke too much of a sweat.

He looked down briefly into the canyon. The spiralling birds always pleased him, as did the powerful strength of the water as it thudded in crystal sheaves down the dark walls of the canyon. It was rare to find anyone else up here and that was a part of it too. Way below, the pool widened out, reflecting a greeny-blue from the clear hot California sky.

He recognised her immediately. The distance did not matter. This time there was no mistake. All the thoughts he had held in check came together in the forefront of his mind as he saw her turn, lazy and contented in the water, kicking her long legs out before her. On her back, her eyes closed against the brilliance of the sun, Kay was naked.

David did not move. The thunder of the water was all he heard. As she pulled herself up out of the water, shaking the droplets from her hair, he drew in his breath, his dark eyes intense. She stood up to her waist in water, and then as if by some remote antennae she smoothed her wet hair over the crown of her head and looked up.

He could not turn away now: she had seen him. Even at this distance their eyes locked, and she was still. She did not change her expression or try to cover herself. She merely stared; he could feel the power of those green eyes far below.

He turned the head of his horse and started to pick his way down. All thoughts of returning to the stable were gone for now.

At the least, he told himself, he could say hello, meet her again, examine his feelings. He was already halfway down the canyon, more curious than ever that she should choose this place he deemed his, before he fully realised how he had been drawn towards her without even thinking twice about it.

When he reached the foot of the canyon and guided his horse forward around the last clumps of sage, the pool was empty. He looked around for her, down the hill, shielding his eyes from the sun. Alabaster threw his head up and down, impatient to either get going or drink. David quieted him.

'Hello.'

She was still there. Squeezing the tail of her hair at the nape of her neck, green eyes squinting in the glare, freckles standing out on her skin, her head domed like a wet spaniel, her white cotton shirt thrown over her, already dampening on her wet skin to show the shape of her breasts and her body beneath.

'Hello,' he said. 'Do you know the trails around here well?'

'No, but I'm learning them.'

'Keep your eyes open for snakes. They come out with the heat.' He looked down at her bare legs. 'Want a ride down?'

She laughed. 'My jeans are over there. You don't have to rescue me, you know. I'm not a damsel in distress.'

The cold, almost fierce look on his face relented suddenly.

'Do I look like a knight on a white charger?'

'A bit.'

'Did you know I came this way a lot? I've seen very few people here. I've never seen you here before.'

She felt the rise of irritation again. What was he suggesting, that she had looked for him, found out somehow that he came here?

'Could it be something as simple as that we like the same things?' she asked, her eyes lighting up again.

'Perhaps.' He laughed, warmly now. And remembered. 'Where's your dog?'

'Dog? Oh, Fred, you mean.' She looked harder at him. She only ever ran on the beach with the dog. 'I didn't know you lived at Latigo,' she said swiftly.

'I don't. I visit Jack Weatherby. Sometimes we fish together. Maybe you'd like to join us for a cook-out tonight,' he found himself saying. 'It's just private. Hamburgers and beer on the beach. Perhaps a bit of bonito if Jack's been lucky.'

She was aware of every breeze, every bird, and every waving

piece of grass; the sage filled her, the sun touched every sense in her body in that moment as he asked her. Her whole body seemed to come alive.

'I'd like that,' she said.

Kay was all too aware of the drama unfolding at home as she hung up the telephone and went back out to the beach. She sat and watched David build their fire. She had not checked back into the office but had gone down to return the script to Joleen. They had spent the afternoon together playing tennis, a way of taking her mind from the evening ahead. She had been late returning, swiftly changing into shorts and a thick sweatshirt, her hair brushed out after the exhilarating feeling of a long shower.

'What did you think of her?' said Jack to his wife, Sissy, as they watched the two on the beach.

'Prettiest smile I ever saw. Quite a gal. And what were you doing going out buying bonito for David tonight? I saw you.'

'Well . . .'

'I thought you were invited to this dinner,' she said.

Jack scratched his head, pushing back his hat and laying it on the deck beside his chair. 'Me play gooseberry?' he was offended. 'You ever known me to do that?'

'Yes, I have. And quite often. You're curious as a cat, Jack Weatherby.'

He chuckled. 'Well, not tonight. David sure is a lucky fella.'

'Sabrine ain't going to like it though. She loves that boy to death. Couldn't have her own, they say. Sad thing, no kids. Fill your life up.' She watched the couple on the beach. They had fifteen, a mixed bunch, every one special, every one living close on the land they had bought for them all the way down the coast.

'Oh,' he growled, 'it's no big thing. David keeps his life private anyways. She'll probably never even get to know.'

Sissy pulled a doubtful face. She said no more, rocking in her chair on the porch and watching the sunset as they had done for fifty years or more.

'That was a beautiful horse you were riding today. What's his name?'

David bent over the fire. He turned the fish onto its side. The fat sputtered and the flames darted hungrily upwards.

'Alabaster.'

All the tension had gone out of her now that they were here on the beach. She let the moments ride. 'I'd love to own a horse like that.'

'Well perhaps you could. But it's an expensive business.'

'How much?'

'We paid 1.5 million dollars at Lazlo Fair for Jubilee, his mother.'

'Good heavens.'

'It's a pretty fancy affair. You should see for yourself some day. Carpeted barns, classical music, drinks beside the ring.'

'I never realised. I'd like to see it.'

He nodded, split open a beer for her. Kay took it, feeling his fingers brush swiftly against hers, warm against the ice-cold of the can. Her nerves fluttered and a trail of fire laced with ice sped up her spine. She lowered her eyes as the spark reached there, and drank the cold beer. She did not speak. She listened to the crackle of the fire, aware of the strength of his legs, of the breadth of his tanned and golden arms beside her, the strong wrists and the deft sensitivity of his hands. She remembered what Tina had said about his control of a horse; she shivered.

He looked at her. 'Are you involved with anyone?'

The question was direct and it shook her. She covered up.

'I thought you did your homework better than that.'

'I do. I'm asking about the past.' He scooped the fish from the fire onto a plate, and started to bone it expertly.

'Everyone has a first love,' she said, thinking about Robbie. 'He died in Vietnam. It was nothing serious really. A crush more or less. He was almost like family. We'd grown up together. Infatuation!' She laughed softly. 'First loves don't last.'

'They do if you want them to.'

She stopped laughing at the tone in his voice. 'Who was yours?'

He looked at her, but did not answer. He handed her the plate.

She felt silenced, unnerved by him, by what he didn't say. She took the plate and the fork he gave her and set it on her crossed legs. He had even brought a cut lemon. She squeezed it onto the fish and took a bite. 'Delicious. Where did you learn to cook?'

'A long time ago. I've always cooked for myself.' He started
to eat too.

'In England?'

He nodded. 'Yes.'

'Is that where your uncle comes from?' She took another bite,
picked up her can of beer.

'Who?' He glanced over at her.

'Your uncle,' she smiled. 'The one who thinks my father's an
asshole.' She took a drink of the beer, her eyes dancing.

'Oh. Yes,' he said. And looked away again.

Kay let the silence build a moment. 'And whereabouts is
that?' she asked. 'Where do *you* come from?'

His eyes were dark and direct. 'Nowhere that you would have
heard of, just a small place.' He looked back at his plate, his
appetite suddenly gone. 'What about you?'

'Oh,' she said. 'My family live just outside Henley, a little
place called Foxhall Green. It's beautiful, the Thames Valley.
Have you ever been there?' They were making small talk,
disguising what they really wanted to say.

'No. Can't say that I have.'

'Actually we're one of the old Malibu families,' she was
saying. 'My grandparents are the McVeys. They live down in
the Colony. They came out here in '21. It was the village then.
It was all starting. Do you know them?'

'Yes, I think so.' Two houses away from Sabrine's beach
house. He knew the McVeys. Would they make the connection?
Malibu was an incestuous village where everybody knew everybody, and if they didn't at first they sure as hell soon found out.
There was little danger actually of her discovering his real
identity through them. Sabrine had effectively cut all ties with
her family except for him though he was unaware of the reason.
She had refused to discuss it, or them. Now it would work to his
advantage.

'I had no idea it could be so beautiful out here,' she said,
leaning back against the sand. 'The nights are so warm, and the
sound of the ocean. I've never known anything like it.'

'The nights are the best,' he said. 'Do you sleep out?'

She looked over at him. 'On my deck? No, I haven't actually.
Not yet.'

'You should. Sleep out under the stars. Look up.'

She did. The sky was a blue purple dome way above them,
the stars clear and sharp against it, thousands of them. She had

never seen anything like it. It was beautiful. The sea frothed in, a line of lacy foam on the dark sand, and then pulled out again, to return in rhythmic thunder. She felt warm and safe, mesmerised by it. By him beside her. They both listened for a moment. She was acutely aware of him; the silence far more sensual than talk. Talk which had been exploratory, about nothing as was usual, covering what was not being said.

'Why don't you sleep out tonight?' he said.

She looked at him. 'Here on the sand?'

'Why not?' He had made the decision. 'I'll be right back.' He left her, went back up the beach. Alone, she felt the imagination of his touch. He would come back, he would lean over. She would feel the brush of his skin, his thigh, his arm, and then he would turn her face very gently and he would kiss her. And soon he would not be gentle at all. Nor did she want him to be.

He was back. He sat down beside her on one knee, laying out the rug he had brought.

'It's Alabaster's rug. Quite clean.' He smiled, his teeth flashing so white in the darkness that her heart lurched. 'Here . . . lie down.'

She went to him, lay obediently on the rug. Now, and she waited. He folded the rug gently over her, tucked her in like a child. He brushed her forehead with his fingertips.

'Go to sleep,' he said.

He lay down on the other side of the fire.

He was extraordinary. She would never sleep.

'Wake up, Kay.'

He was bending over her. She woke up immediately. His hair was roughened by sleep and he had a slight beard. His skin was more freckled than she had realised and the dark brown eyes more like chestnut in the early morning light. He smiled his sharp white smile, the collar of his blue sailcloth shirt standing up against the wind. It was day, the light blinding.

She sat up. It was dawn, fresh and new, a lovely crisp smell in the air. The sea held glimmers of a curious light in the folds of the waves as if lit from underwater, reflections of a hidden sun. The rollers came in, foam flying, wild and heavy.

'Sorry I had to wake you,' he said. 'I didn't want you to wake up alone on the beach. It's five. I have to go and take Alabaster out. An hour from now and he'll be kicking the door down.'

'Can I come too?'

He paused, thought of many things. Discarded them all. 'All right.'

He had watched her while she slept, since the sun had come up. She had lain free of her blanket, her haunches sharp against the light. The set of her sleeping mouth spoke of many things, some good, some bad. There was a strong look to her face, a quiet pride, a hint of something atavistic in her far flung ancestry, perhaps something noble. Her hair framed her face in red-dark tangles, which as the sun lifted over the sea, turned to golden shards in the twisted curls. Her skin was lovely, her mouth a deep dark pink, and soft like a child, like a woman. He had ached to kiss her. He had not.

Now she stood and stretched, going up the beach ahead of him. Some private joke of her own made her laugh, or maybe it was just pure happiness. Her chuckle was as free as a child's. She had long brown legs, a neat bottom and a smile that broke his nerves. Strong shoulders, an hour-glass figure and level green eyes, sea-pale; and as changeable. Kay. He wondered when to tell her as he followed. They had found out about each other, skirting around the edges of their real lives. Their time together would come to an end soon. And he still had not told her. He knew this was one girl he would not give up, and one that would not forgive him for avoiding the truth. The longer he did it, the worse it became. She would wonder why he had said nothing in the first place. Yet he had wanted her to stay. And now they were on their way back home. To the ranch.

CHAPTER THIRTY-FIVE

The Bank of England had not known. Potentially they would have been involved in organising a rescue, their rescue taking the place of a merger with another bank being prodded into taking over the bank that was in trouble. But they had not been told what was going on.

It was Lindy Bunter's story that had broken the news, a scoop that the other nationals soon picked up on. It appeared that Redfield's were deeply involved in all sorts of dramatic transactions in which they were buying shares. The can of worms was opened. Not only was Rupert in trouble, but it transpired that his grandson, Alexander, had followed in his grandfather's footsteps. Alexander was a surrogate young banker who had taken risks, and it had all gone terribly wrong. Redfield's suddenly found themselves with shares in all sorts of companies they were hoping to do deals on, the value of the shares had first collapsed in 1973 when the stock market went down, and collapsed even further now in 1974. The City was coming apart, British banks collapsing. The Heath Government had precipitated huge inflation, expanding the money supply and encouraging the banks to lend far too much money. This had sparked a boom in property which had now got out of hand. Banks were left having lent money to these property companies and the companies were collapsing in value. They could not repay the banks. The City was heading for a financial crisis.

Alexander had borrowed bank money to put into his personal investment property and the art market. He had made Rupert responsible for his debts and now they were left in a very exposed and vulnerable position.

Almost immediately the shares had started to fall on the Stock Exchange. There was no real proof but the suggestion was enough. There was a run on the deposits at the bank as people became panicky and pulled their deposits out. The directors of Redfield's, the members of the family from the collateral branch, suddenly saw that the bank they owned was losing them money rapidly. They returned to the head office from their country homes to question their chairman and chief executive, both of whom were refusing to admit liability. As one for the first time ever, Redfield and Rees-Hulbert directors had gone to their main clearing bank and said they needed stand-by lines to shore up their deposit base. But the clearing bank had seen them going down the spout and denied their help.

It was then that they had gone round to the Bank of England to tell them that their deposits were being pulled out at such a rate that they would lose their complete deposit base, or at least three quarters of it, within three months. They asked for support. The Bank of England apologised but was adamant: they had heard a rumour regarding their chairman and had decided to make an example of Redfield's. They were going to let them go bust.

The press were like ants as they swarmed over the Redfield building. Rupert was visibly shaking as he heard the news. It had all happened literally in days: a spectacular collapse. He had been hoping for a miracle, but there was none. He had not even told the family about the loss of Foxhall simply because he refused to believe this was happening.

Shuddering as he put down the telephone to one of the directors of the bank, he immediately called Alexander. He found him at his London home and told him to get down to Foxhall immediately.

Dickie took the telephone call from George Reilly as she sat at her desk by the French windows of Greatley House. Outside in the orchard the cherry trees spilled over with blossom. The blue sky above was unpatched by cloud.

'Redfield's is collapsing,' he said. 'There is no way it can be saved.'

'Good,' she said. 'It should collapse. Do you think Gilbert Rees-Hulbert might rebuild it? He's in control now, isn't he?'

'Might do,' said George. 'except that everybody is falling around in tatters. There's a general banking crisis. The disease is spreading to other banks. The City is in trouble. It's getting worse daily. Most will survive intact, of course. They'll pull out in time.'

Dickie looked out over the garden. The roses were in bloom; a blackbird sang, and charged the other birds to match his rousing song. On the step a cat shook himself quickly with the sound of rapid birds' wings. He licked a leg ardently, enjoying the warmth of the sun after winter.

'An apocalyptical end,' Dickie murmured.

Rupert was in his study as Alexander entered. He turned immediately and it was clear the toll this had taken on him. His skin, normally jowly and a ruddy-red, was now slack and grey-toned. His eyes were bloodshot and abnormally blue, and he was stooping. Alcxander had never seen his grandfather stoop before.

Rupert crossed the dark book-lined room towards him.

'I should take a stick to you for the mistakes you have made,' he said, thrusting his finger at him. 'The humiliation of this whole affair. Have you seen the papers! You know what they are saying about you, Alexander? That you've run the bank into the ground!' He approached him, the blue eyes burning like turquoise. 'It was at your instigation that this whole charade with the Bennetts began. In trying to beat them out of their land, instead we have lost Foxhall!'

'We've lost Foxhall?' He had never meant that to happen.

'Yes! What did you think you were doing, trespassing on bank's money? You had no authority.' He still believed he could have survived, kept Foxhall. Now, with Alexander's games come to light, there was no chance.

'You of course are blameless in the whole thing.'

'That is not the point.' Rupert came and stood over him. 'It is my bank. I'm going to see you bankrupt, Alexander. I won't save your neck, nor will any of the others. I'll instruct them.'

'You may find them more obtuse than you imagine,' he said lightly, his eyes narrowed now. 'Don't forget that for the last ten years I have effectively run the bank while you let me get on with it. And get on with it I did. I pulled off some mighty good deals, grandfather, deals they won't have forgotten. Now if we have any chance of resurrecting Redfield's, who do you think they will rally round, eh? You . . . or me?' He gave a short laugh and turned, moving round to the back of the chair. 'Oh, admittedly this collapse in the property market has favoured neither you or me, but not through want of trying. I merely followed in your footsteps and did rather better, I feel . . .' Rupert understood immediately.

'How much *do* you know, Alexander?'

'Everything.' He smiled. 'I went through Hewdon-Vassar's desk when I sacked him.' His mouth twitched pleasurably. 'So you see, I think I can properly resurrect the bank when this is all over, pull off some excellent deals in the future, and you may find me rather harder to get rid of than you think. They'll forget this, it's a flash in the pan. The City'll pick up again, and what they are going to want is a bright young whiz-kid like me. Not you. After all, you're out, aren't you?'

'You young fool,' he said slowly. 'Do you think yourself so high and mighty? I will simply remove what few shares you have, any influence you have. Why do you think I never gave you more power, eh? Because I knew then what you are, know what you are now, Alexander, knew how you'd use it . . . against me! I was right! I only have to pick up a phone to be back. Redfield's is not dead yet. The City may be collapsing, but as you so rightly say, we'll pull through somehow. I have a lot of friends.'

'Conspicuously absent of late, so I hear.'

Rupert hesitated. 'Who told you that?'

'Guy Prudham.'

'*Guy Prudham*, he would never tell you my personal business. He's my adviser, my right-hand man. Always has been . . . the one man I could . . .'

'The one man you never rewarded,' Alexander interrupted. 'The one man who you should have. He deserved it. But you wanted to keep him in your power too, didn't you? Under your control.'

Rupert lifted his head.

'Guy would never betray me, Alexander. I don't care what you say. He helped me recently when this thing broke. Came straight over, told me how to get out of it. You didn't know that, did you . . .'

'On my instructions.'

'Your wha . . . oh, don't be ridiculous, Alexander.'

'Guy is homosexual, grandfather.'

Rupert's eyes flew open. 'I don't believe it. Guy?'

'As I say, homosexual. You know what that means in your terms, don't you,' he said slowly. 'We understand each other.' He watched the other man's face. 'I set you up, grandfather. And you fell for it like the old fool that you are. No, it wasn't just the Bennetts I was after, though they might have been an

interesting feature. It was you.' His thin face tightened percept-
ibly as he stared his grandfather down. 'I wanted that bank,' he
went on. 'I've loved it. It's the only thing I've ever cared for,
and I meant to make it mine. Not you or anyone else will stop
me. You've ruled my life, treated me with contempt, offered me
shares and then taken them away when I didn't perform, forced
me to marry a woman against my instinct. You thought you
could cure me. What a pitiful idea that one was!' He spat the
words at him. 'Now I'm going to do the same to you, treat you
with contempt. You have only yourself to blame, you nurtured
this in me. I asked you to sign that contract knowing your
consuming greed and hatred. I banked on that. I'm a good
judge of sadism, you know. It amused you to play with my life,
didn't it?' He smiled maliciously as he came around the chair
and advanced on his grandfather. 'Well, I've got more to tell
you. Oh, much, much more.'

'Alexander, stop!'

'Oh, no!' He laughed. 'Want to know why Gilbert sold the
bank to the Bennetts, huh? Because I told him,' he said softly. 'I
told you had forced me to marry Verity, I told him what I
was. That's how much I hate you, old man. But what I didn't
tell him was this. Verity was leaving me, she found me in bed
with another man, she threatened to tell you everything, and I
was frightened. Yes, in those days I was, but no longer. I
thought I was going to lose everything, and I would have if
she'd got to you, but she didn't. When she came to the house,
she taunted me for not being a man, and I raped her.' He
laughed again. 'I made it. Do you realise that? I made it with a
woman without having to pretend like I had to with her when
you forced me to marry her. Do you know how disgusting that
was for me?' His eyes were fierce and staring, their vision filled
with an unholy light as if he could not truly see as he came after
Rupert, stepping slowly forward. 'Well, in the end I lost
nothing because she was so distraught she did not know what
she was doing when she left the house. And of course I played
the grieving husband to the hilt, didn't I?'

'You bastard!'

'No more than you. I'm only interested in myself, as you are.
Now I will have the one thing I wanted, the bank. I am the
natural head. There is nothing you can do about it. I made no
mistakes. I set you up. Set you up for ruin, public disgrace. And
that's what you have to face now. You can't, can you?'

He put back his head and roared with laughter, manic, pointing his finger.

'Look at you, you're finished, ruined.'

'I will leave you nothing.'

'Well,' he said. 'That's not an awfully big threat, now, is it? You don't have a lot to leave. Except perhaps that Swiss bank account and the companies in Jersey.'

'It was you,' said Rupert with a dawning realisation. 'You did set me up. It wasn't her.'

'Of course. Haven't you listened to a word I've been saying? We planned the whole thing, Guy Prudham and myself. He's a smart fellow, I have to give you that. You taught him well, and in turn he taught me. And now I'm going to have it all. I'm sure you've left it all to me in your will, haven't you? I am, after all, the one who knows the bank as well as you do?'

Rupert coughed, clutched at his chest. 'I've left everything to your son, David, you bastard. And to Charles.' He bent over, his hand grabbing the back of the chair. 'Think I'd leave anything to a poof!'

'You know what?' Alexander stopped elegantly across the room. 'I don't believe you. And now, you'll never have the chance to change it.' He pushed at Rupert's shoulder suddenly. Caught off guard the old man staggered back, losing hold of the chair. He could not get his breath.

'What? I'll leave nothing, nothing. Just let me . . .' Rupert stared at Alexander, his words sinking in. There had been no mistake. 'I'll tell Gilbert about Verity. He won't help you then. He'll ruin you.'

Alexander's eyes lost their merry laughter and snapped cold. He went to the fireplace, grabbed the stick that had beaten him as a child.

'Oh, will you?' he said. 'I don't think so.' He strode back.

He brought the stick down on Rupert's shoulders. On his head. Rupert fell under the blows.

'God, Alexander, for God's sake, no!'

He cowered on the floor. Alexander rained the blows down.

'See how this feels, you sadistic bastard. It's my turn now . . .'

He did not know how many times he thrashed him, he hardly heard Rupert's cries. But then the blood stopped thundering in his temples, and the red mist of hate cleared from his eyes, and with a sound of disgust he broke the hated stick in half and threw it in the old man's face. He turned and left the room, leaving Rupert clutching his fingers against the blood-red pattern of the Persian carpet he lay upon.

The door slammed. Rupert moaned and struggled, pulling himself up onto his knees, onto his haunches. He had tricked him, tricked him. He was not as weak as Alexander had thought! He would get up, go after him, tell everybody. He would win again. He would pay for this. He clutched at the back of the sofa, pulled himself up, and dropped.

He stumbled onto his knees, he could not catch his breath. He grasped again for the sofa, missed, grasped air and fell. He opened his mouth, shouting. His cries were nothing more than a weak groan.

No one was there. The door remained shut. His grandson's betrayal had finished him, and now a heart attack had brought him to his knees. He could not believe it. He was not going to die, not alone, surely! He grasped at his chest, at the terrible pain, his arm useless now, dangling. He crawled on his knees towards the door, slowly, his mouth open, eyes bulging.

But Alexander was gone, and the house was empty. He had left him to die. Rupert fell against the carpet, his mouth drooling. Downstairs, the kitchen staff had heard the roars and now the banging around upstairs. They had heard it all before, the roars for attention, the demands, the lack of consideration. They were playing a good game of Snap. They drowned the sounds, pretending they had not heard. They all laughed and cheered as Edward Callow beat the new cook faster and faster to the finish: 'Snap!'

Rupert's arms were spread out before him, his hands still clawed with pain, his legs up in a foetal position as if he was trying to get once more onto his knees. His eyes stared out sightlessly.

In the drive the Jaguar roared away, heading for London.

Rupert's genes had finally surfaced in a future generation. It was his own flesh and blood, and not Dickie, from whence came the final revenge.

CHAPTER THIRTY-SIX

Gilbert needed to be present at the reading of the will. Not only because he was family, but because he had a special reason for being there.

The butler showed him in to the drawing-room. Charles came across towards him, took his hands warmly.

'Gilbert, I'm so glad you were able to come.' They had called the family in for an emergency reading of the will before Rupert's funeral.

'I wanted to say how sorry I was about your father, Charles. And to say I never meant you to lose your home.' He shook his head. 'I was angry at something I had heard and I wanted to hurt him, as he had hurt me. Believe me, I never wanted the rest of you to suffer. I would like to offer my help in retrieving it for you, if that's possible.'

Charles smiled. 'I want it back too. It's our family home, and a family thing. Frederick has agreed. We are pooling, selling our shares in return for liquid cash to buy back our home.'

The two men walked over to the window. 'Let me be the one to buy them from you, Charles. I'm willing to pay you good money. That way I could make good use of them.'

Charles looked at him. 'Are you going to try and salvage the bank?'

'Yes, indeed. Why don't you join the board?'

'Me? I know next to nothing about banking. I'm a farmer,'

'You were a doctor once, but you changed from that too,' Gilbert observed shrewdly.

'I was younger then.' He turned slightly. The others were beginning to filter into the room, the lawyer amongst them. 'I think Father's will is about to be read.'

'I'd like you to join us at Redfield's, Charles.'

'It's good of you, Gilbert. But I've a feeling that if my father's will holds what I think it does, then Alexander will be in control. If he gets Rupert's shares, nothing will hold him back. He's a very determined man, despite his recent troubles. I truly

336

believe he means to climb back on top. With the power of those shares behind him, he'll do it.'

'That's why I wanted to talk to you,' said Gerald, concern in his eyes. 'I need your help to keep him out. A family show of strength. Alexander's like Rupert. He only thinks in terms of the singular. He'd destroy it . . . I want to resurrect it. The banking world is in a state of absolute collapse. Only Alexander would survive if left at the helm of Redfield's. That is clear to everybody.'

'Did you speak to him about this?'

Gilbert nodded. 'He believes as you do. That he will inherit those shares. He seems quite cocky about it.'

In the distance, Alexander came through the drawing-room door. He looked excitable, on edge. Charles looked over at him. 'Did you reach David?' he called across the room.

'No, he's out. I left a message.' He sat down in an armchair to the side of the fireplace.

'He accused me of selling the bank to that woman, as he called her, Dickie Bennett,' murmured Gilbert, catching Charles's attention again. 'Said I had never taken an interest in Redfield's, whilst he had built it from an acorn into an oak. He's right, of course, but equally I would not have lined my own pockets at the expense of others. Thankfully, I retained enough of a hold on my shares to have some control. The other members of the family are backing me. We'll fight him off somehow, if it comes to it.'

The lawyer was coming over, Frederick with him.

They shook hands with him. 'Charles, a word,' he said, drawing him aside. 'Your uncle has been telling me about your plans to talk to Mrs Latimer . . . Miss Bennett . . . Charles,' he went on, 'whereas I applaud your wishes to stop this feud, it is early days yet. Too early. Let the wound settle a bit. I think things may be different from now on. After all, she hasn't exactly booted you out, has she? She could have done. It's been a week since it officially became hers. Play a waiting game, is my advice. Don't go rushing in.'

Charles looked to his uncle standing alongside.

'And what would you advise, Frederick? You're head of the family now.'

Frederick paused. 'I think we should make her a straight financial offer. Pull together, and show family strength. It's something I feel she would both understand and respect. Show

337

we are down, but intact. Rupert's gone now; she may feel very differently.' And here his thought wandered slightly to a far-off picture; would she forgive him? The decision she made would show her answer. 'I think our lawyers should approach her, say quite honestly that we would like the return of the house. I think I know that she will exact her price. But equally, we can do no worse than to ask.'

Alexander was amused as he sat by the fire and watched them first talk, consternation on their faces, and then take their seats for the reading of his grandfather's will. Of course it would be his. It was unfortunate that they had lost Foxhall to that woman. He had not meant her actually to get hold of it; he had meant for his grandfather to be only in danger of losing and for himself to come in at the last moment and save the day both for the bank and for himself. The damn banking crisis had been a blow, an unforeseen blow. But all was not lost. Foxhall might be gone, but he still had the house in Hanover Terrace, and he would soon hold the shares he had coveted for nearly twenty years. Rupert had not had the chance to change his will.

He settled back, arms folded as the preamble started.

Soon he was sitting up in his seat, listening intently.

Rupert Redfield, for once as good as his word, had left Foxhall to his great-grandson, David, to be managed by Frederick until his own death. He had not cut his son from his will either. Despite their differences, and whether by tradition or because of his own father's rejection of him, he had left his majority holding in Redfield's to Charles, asking that he take over the running of the bank until a successor was appointed by him. To help him do this he had given him access to his Swiss bank account. It amounted to a small fortune. There would be no need for any selling of shares.

He had left Alexander nothing. Even in death, he had cheated him.

David's cottage was tucked back on the edge of the canyon, with a wide deck, and propped on long wooden legs anchored in the rocks below it. It was almost alpine, up amongst the tall firs, eucalyptus and pepper trees. A dirt road wound round and up to it and then went on down to the main house.

They walked up onto the deck together. The view filtered between the fir trees to the sparkling bay down below. There were no neighbours and absolute silence, around them just brush and sage, heavy green foliage and the dust and rocks of the lane.

The ranch could be glimpsed out on the point, white and low, spread out elegantly with a sloping red-tiled terracotta roof and adobe walls. The black-stained wood windows were long, set deep into the walls. Spanish wrought-iron gates closed the estate off, and repelled intruders who might wander from the highway looking for a way down to the ocean and the bay. Behind the house, between David's hill-top cottage and the house, lay the corral for the horses, more extensive than the house itself. Tall firs shielded it from the sea breezes. A swimming-pool was a strip of blue darted in amongst the white and green, semi-concealed by a low white wall and trellis covered with bougainvillaea.

She went to the balcony, then turned looking at him silently, a smile in her eyes.

He held her look; came over. His hand slid over her bare shoulder leaving a trail of sensation behind. They stood like that for a moment. She closed her eyes. He had been so quiet on the way back, a quiet born of pleasure in her company, anticipation. She hoped so. For her, that was what it had been. She felt lulled and soft and good, the fire in her smouldering like embers. She could wait now for the lingering moments before it happened, as she knew it would. She opened her eyes again, their expression smoky as she gazed down over the view. The wind was like the stroke of a cat. The sea was flecked with white, spray blowing as the rollers came into the coast. The smog had cleared and it was a hot day. The pepper tree shook over the deck. The air was dry and combustible, a shake of sea spray in it. All she thought about was his body, about making love. Out here, on the deck, the sun and wind around them. It filled her. Inside, she felt herself burn.

He was too aware of her. He had never meant it to come this far. The wind had got up in the last half hour but the sun was strong. There was a good smell in the air. He enjoyed the feeling it gave him, hearing the hollow sound of the wind, the beating in the trees, imagining the sound of the breakers down on the beach below. He breathed deep with satisfaction, all his sensuality alive in him.

Just beside him she stood, her tangled chestnut hair lifting in the wind, her profile raised to its caress, her eyes half-closed. He could see the down on her skin, the freckles, the soft gleam on her parted rosy lips. She was so delicate. He felt the feelings steal through him as he watched her dreaming, drifting. The sun was like a warm blanket that had settled on them, the rough grass around the deck inviting them to lie in it and make love there in the open, the rushing wind around them.

He pulled her to him in a moment. Unresisting, she was in his arms, receiving his kisses, warm and sweet-smelling. Familiar, though she was new. The sun was on his skin; she was in his arms.

Kay felt it all as if in separate sensations; the wind in her face, in her hair, felt his kisses and the warm cold of his body as their skin collided. White clouds scudded across the blue of the sky as she opened her eyes to see his dark eyes looking into hers. He was lean and sunburnt, his blond hair sleek in the sun, his eyes narrowed. His handsome face seemed naked with emotion, his fingers were hard as they pressed into her skin, his breathing quickening her own heartbeat. She closed her eyes, unable to see the awakening in his face without awe, and laid her face against his throat, without speaking, to let the sensation of him fill her. She wanted him to lay her in the rough grass, the wind blowing and blustering around them, smelling the damp sweet smell of the earth, the musk of his body, the warmth of his skin touching hers, everywhere . . . her lips came up again to his . . .

The telephone rang lightly from somewhere inside the house. It did not stop. David drew away. 'I'll be right back,' he said gently.

Inside, he picked it up, his mind still on her. 'Hello.'

Frederick's voice crackled distantly over the wire.

'David . . . ?'

'Uncle Frederick.'

'Didn't you get your father's message?'

His head started to clear as he heard the note. 'No?'

'He spoke to Sabrine.' Frederick sounded weary. 'David . . . I'm sorry to have to tell you this . . . but Rupert has died . . .'

'God, no . . . when?'

'Yesterday. We tried to reach you.'

'I was out all night,' he murmured. His eyes took in the girl now sitting at the table on the balcony, calmly waiting for him, the blue ribbon with which she had tied her hair in the open jeep now lying loosely on her shoulders. The sun cast a glow on her profile, on the skin he remembered, tasted still in his lips and hands. He saw her bare shoulders soft in the morning light.

'Well, I'm afraid he had a heart attack. No one was there to help. I think it could have been the news . . .'

'What news?'

'I'll come to that. David, we had an emergency reading of the will this morning. Rupert left you everything, but I'm afraid part of it is already lost.' He paused. 'You see, we've lost Foxhall . . .'

David listened as his uncle spoke on, his expression changing. He had wanted to tell her so much. Not now.

'They own the house?' he said at last, incredulous. 'All the land? Everything . . . ?'

He heard the answer clearly. Kay smiled at some thought of her own, ran her hands along her arms and leaned forward, relaxed. His eyes were drawn to the skin she had just touched. He frowned.

'Who was the instigator? How did it start?'

He listened and his face grew grim. Whilst she had been dating him she had been operative in helping to destroy his family. It was her. His grandfather had made many enemies. And the worst of his enemies was her grandmother. She was, according to rumour, just like her. They had sworn to ruin his family. Now they had. David felt he knew the truth. 'Will you be coming home?' asked Frederick. 'Funeral's the day after tomorrow.'

'Yes. I'll be home.' He put down the telephone and walked towards her.

She smiled warmly up at him as he came back out onto the terrace.

'I thought I'd lost you,' she said. The smoky look was still in her eyes.

He stared disbelievingly at her for a moment, as if seeing her for the first time. Kay's welcoming smile dissipated. Concern etched itself into her eyes. That cold, fierce look was back on his face.

'What's wrong?'

'My great-grandfather's just died,' he said evenly, watching her face.

She looked properly concerned. 'Oh, David.' So that was it. 'I'm so sorry.'

'Are you?'

341

'Yes, of course.'

'Come on, I'm taking you home.'

She felt the shock of his words. 'Well . . . all right. I'll just get my shoes.'

She had left them on the other chair, feeling a free and sensual delight against the sun-warmed boards beneath her feet. She pulled them on, tied them. Followed him wordless off the deck.

He did not speak all the way home, but dropped her with a curt goodbye. The look in his dark eyes said it all; this was all there was. His jeep whirled in the dry sand of the dirt path behind her cottage and was gone, burring furiously away up towards the highway.

Kay was dazed. She watched for a moment, then turned, stepping down to her front door and unlocking it. Then as she turned the key, her disappointment and tension welded into anger. He was as arrogant as she had originally thought, and she had imagined that he was beginning to care. She had seen a swift and dark light in his eyes, now it seemed it was only her imagination. It was she wanting him to love her, feeling that something was beginning. And now there was nothing. As she let herself into her house she somehow knew it was not his grandfather's death that had caused that coldness. It was her; but why?

The door of the trailer remained adamantly shut. The director sighed.

'All right, everybody, take a break while I sort this out.'

He made no secret of the fact that she was a pain, a right royal pain to be honest. Old fading stars were the worst. She was becoming a joke. If she did not pull herself together, he would break her contract on the next picture lined up for the summer. He had every reason. The others in the cast gave knowing smiles and wandered off in the sunshine to drink and chat under the trees, have a smoke.

Sabrine had thrown a mood on the set that morning, refusing to come out of her trailer until they found David and got him there. Apparently she had gone to his cottage early that morning before the unexpected, pre-dawn shoot and found it empty. So what, thought the director, as he approached the trailer. The lad was young and good-looking. Christ, this was ridiculous. He knocked wearily on her door. 'It's me, Sabrine.'

Her fears had come true. There was a girl in his life, a special girl, she knew it in her bones. David might have been a loner, but she knew his moves; he would confide in her, or she would find out. He had never stayed out with a girl before, always came home. He had told her he was seeing Jack. She did not believe him, could not humiliate herself ringing that damn fool Sissy and asking her. They didn't get on. Sabrine was feeling as much pain as a rejected lover. She had gone to his cabin that morning to ask him to drive her to the set. She could not say what scared her, except her instinct. She knew. And once he was gone, she would have no one. She could not bear it, could not bear to be alone; not after having known such happiness.

'The door's not locked,' she shouted. Idiot. She folded her arms, sulked.

It opened. Sid Longman peered in. He was young, early thirties, one of the new breed of avant-garde geniuses. She did not like him. 'Can I come in?'

'Where is he?'

Sid came up the steps and sat down on the bench settee. 'He's at home, Sabrine,' he said. 'I just spoke to him. I don't think he likes being questioned, he was not very forthcoming at all. Said he had to speak to you though. He's coming over.'

'He's coming here!' Her face warmed with delight. 'You see. David loves me.' She swayed slightly. 'I told you.'

Sid Longman sighed inside. This woman was the pits. She was either batty or drunk. 'Yes, well will you come back on the set now?'

'No. Not until David gets here,' she said flatly. 'By the way, did he say where he'd been?'

'Fishing.'

'All night?'

'All night. He slept out on the beach, like many a young man has done before him.' He braced his hands to his legs ready to leave.

'Alone?'

'What?'

'Was he alone?' She hated herself. 'You know, singular? By himself? Alone. Don't you speak English!'

The director sighed. Sabrine was like a big child. 'Sabrine sweetheart. I doubt very much whether he was alone. He's a grown man. One might expect him to have company. He probably had a young lady with him. Having seen your nephew I doubt whether it was a boy. Is that enough?'

'Do you think she was pretty?'

'I would think so. David's a good-looking young chap. What does it matter? Would you rather he was a faggot? Please, Sabrine.'

He opened his hands wide. His patience was at an end. He saw the quarter-full bottle slip from behind her pillow. She was a wreck; no longer at the age at which she could do this and get away with it in the morning. He would never use her again; he had made up his mind now. Old stars were definitely, very definitely the worst.

She looked at him then, sensing and seeing his disgust. A drunken woman was not attractive. She was digging her own grave, but she could not stop. She would demand David's attention, though she knew he would be cold and angry. She stood up suddenly.

'I'm going home.'

'But what about the picture?' He looked alarmed now.

'Fuck the picture.' She stalked out of the trailer, stumbled down the steps into the daylight. He came quickly down behind her, following her. 'Sabrine, what are you doing?'

'I'm going to find David.'

She reached her car, saw the faces of all those around her staring, those who had once looked at her with awe. Not now. One or two were laughing, hiding their faces.

'But I told you,' he said, coming alongside her. 'He's coming here! He has something to tell you!'

'Oh, yes, so he is.' And then she burst horrifyingly into tears. Around her she felt the laughter and derision rain down upon her from their eyes. She could not bear to look up. 'Take me back to the caravan, Sid,' she said, weeping, her hand shading her eyes.

He put his arm around her and led her back. She could feel the humiliation pinching at every part of her, exposing her. She had the girl to blame for this.

Whoever she was.

Dickie walked in the wood. High above, the canopy of green shifted and swayed in the breeze. Sunlight dappled through on to the acid-green fingers of sprouting beech leaves that layered and intersected the wood. The roof rustled against the sky like a taffeta petticoat. Memories. So many. She walked on, feeling the carpet of bracken and twigs crackling beneath her feet. The beech wood was at its most beautiful in early summer, the tall lean trees climbing high above, and at her feet the woods were deep in bluebells, a misty blue carpet.

With a lightness of heart, she felt the curse of revenge float away from her. She had owned Foxhall. At least for a few days. And he had known that before he died.

She walked on through her wood, enjoying it for the first and last time. There had been tragedy in her family too; it was not a time for more revenge. When she got back to the house she had to call Kay, to bring her home. Olivia was not improving. The family needed to be together now. This morning, she had accepted the Redfield family's offer. Mindful of Katherine's words she had told them the house was theirs again at the end of the week. It would belong to the whole family now. The fight was over.

CHAPTER THIRTY-SEVEN

Kay looked out at the ocean. There was a forty-mile-an-hour wind, and it was picking up even more, wrapping around the beach house in armfuls of gusts. A seagull balanced on it, motionless, just above the rollers that came in to rock the decks and suck at the rocks, surging around the backs of the houses on the beach, blasting back through the sea walls. It was a wild day. She thought of Olivia no better, Alice in a coma; she thought of David.

Max's voice was distant on the telephone. She had to ask him to speak up.

'I said "How's the business?" Got anything to contribute?'

'I thought I'd make up a report from this end. I've already mapped it out. Let them know what's happening out here. You know I always thought the basics of Jim's ideas were good. I think we should come up with a package, some new ideas to give the shareholders confidence. Not a lot's going right over there, is it?'

'No. The bottom's dropped out of property and banking's fallen flat on its face. They need to hear some good news. I'm not sure your idea's the right one but we'll talk about it when you get here. When will you come?'

'Tomorrow.' Her mind had spun elsewhere. She wanted to see *him*, however briefly, however he felt. 'I have a couple of things to tie up first.'

'Look forward to it. I'll let your mother know. She'll be happy. Safe journey, darling.'

'Thank you, Daddy.' She put the receiver down slowly. He had not called her. She wondered why. Every moment of her day had been filled with him. A powerful feeling like this was not one-sided, she did not believe that. He had to tell her why he had changed. But how could she go to him and demand that he tell her when that last look in his eyes had told her that he hated her. Well, she had the afternoon and the evening before she flew home. She could not just sit there in the cottage wondering. She went outside and climbed into her car, and headed for the highway going north.

A police car screamed past, siren blasting, then an ambulance forcing its way through the traffic. She looked up as the fire-fighting helicopter whirred overhead. The ranch! She gunned the car up the hill. She saw the fire immediately as she reached the crest. Her first thought was of him, and the horses.

She reached the long drive and turned in. Above, the mountains were dark and sulphurous, the flames leaping fifty feet in the air like a dragon's-back of flame as they swept down to the valley and the ranch. She parked her car by his cottage and could already hear the horses in the corral, whinnying and calling. She jumped from her car and ran down through the bushes towards the stables.

He was there. Leading Alabaster and a big chestnut out of their stables, talking to them, calming them. The chestnut was rolling its eyes, Alabaster more steady. He saw her as she ran into the yard and stopped.

'What the hell are you doing here?'

Gone was the night before, the gentleness of the morning.

'I've come to help.'

'Go home,' he said curtly. 'I can manage alone.'

The chestnut danced on the rein, jerking his arm. He quieted it. They could smell the smoke now; against the mountains it blackened the sky. The fire roared distantly. In the stables adjoining, the horses began to kick and whinny.

'You can't manage all of these,' she said. 'You need help.'

His eyes accused her, but he made a quick and necessary decision. They were short-staffed, only one stable boy remaining: Sabrine's staff had a quick turnover.

'All right,' he said brusquely. 'See the two over there. They're the easiest. Take their halters, you'll find them on hooks inside the doors, and lead them out. Follow me down to the beach. Down that path.' He indicated with a nod of his head a narrow path that led off downwards through the bushes. 'Can you manage that?'

'Yes.' She turned to go.

'Wait.' She looked back. 'Have you handled a horse before?'

'Of course.' The hauteur lit her eyes. She said no more, just ran for the stable door. She had never handled a horse in her life, but she had seen others do it, seen him and taken it in. She was no fool.

347

'Be quick,' he called.

She opened the door, clucked softly to the horse who danced on his straw to and fro, the whites of his eyes showing. She found the halter, slipped it on over his head as best she could, her hand caught at the rope just by his noseband and she led him out. She tied him quickly to the hook outside, then did the same with the other horse. Her heart raced desperately. So far, so good. Their hooves struck against the stones as they danced fearfully, smelling the smoke.

'Come on, good boys, good boys,' she said. 'Come on.'

She pulled gently and they came. He had already gone, down the path. She hoped the horses would not break away, that they would be easy. They were, following her down, seeming to understand, her voice gentling them all the way. The curve of the bay came into sight, the wind whipping up towards them, whirling and swirling, the perfect wind to fan a fire to its height, dry and hot.

She felt a real sense of joy as she reached the beach and saw him there, talking to another young lad. He had the horses penned behind a makeshift fence, and was leading David's last two in as they spoke. She came across the sand towards them, the two beautiful animals now following in her wake, as docile and obedient as two well-trained dogs on a walk.

He turned to look at her as she arrived, taking the animals from her. Their hands brushed as he took over the ropes and she could not help the sensation that darted up through her. She looked down, over-conscious of his strong, muscular arm, the dark blue cotton aertex he wore, the warm masculine smell that came from him, giddying her senses, reminding her of how he had leaned across to tuck her into the blanket last night on the beach under the stars. Her eyelids prickled with need of him, wanting him to suddenly take her in his arms and look so dark and deep at her again, the way he had, the way that made her heart race and her body tremble.

He did not. His face was cold and carved as he looked down at her, the face of a stranger.

'Thank you for your help. You can go now. We don't need you any more.' It was cruelly said. She felt the words bite into her as he handed over the horses to the other and strode back up the path towards the house, his long legs encased in riding boots and jodhpurs. He soon disappeared into the scrub and small trees that dominated the corner of the bay.

She did not move for a moment. Then she felt the eyes on her from behind. She turned to look at the lad, who was watching her with a mixture of sympathy and curiosity on his face. She gave a little smile, went over and stroked the nose of one of the horses, her mind not really there at all.

'Will they be all right now?' she said.

'Sure,' the boy answered. 'We set this up for the fires. Soon as the winds pick up they start lighting them up in the hills, those jokers. You gotta be prepared. This one's bad though,' he said, looking up. 'It's heading straight for the house.'

She looked up too. The pall of smoke crested over the sky, obliterating the blue. The boy saw her consternation.

'Highway's over that way if you want to get out.' He pointed down the beach. 'There's a path up.'

'No,' she said. 'I'm not going back.' She made her decision; he could be as dismissive as he wished, but she could be stubborn too. She turned and ran back the way she had come, pulling herself up past the bushes and heading for the stables.

A mile north, sheafs of orange flame lit the wind, dark smoke colouring the brilliant blue of the sky. Above her, the tan smoke already billowed across, reaching in a long tail far out to sea. To the east of the canyon, heading almost due south, came the north wind, crossing the canyon with swift ease, the flames carried in its embrace. The wind came whistling down Dume Canyon, tangy and sharp. She dashed up onto the bank and along the flat path into the yard.

He was already up on the roof of the stables. She came to a halt beneath him. A wall of dense black smoke backdropped the scene beyond, a dull red light behind. The fire was almost on them.

'I thought I told you to go home!' he shouted. He brandished an arm towards her car. 'Take your car and get out of here while you still can!'

'No!' She started to climb the ladder he had propped against the wall. For whatever reason he was angry, though he might hate her, she was still going to be there. If he thought she was too weak to cope with this, to rough it alongside him, he was wrong. She was going to show her mettle, to prove she could help defend the corral.

She clambered up on the roof.

'What the hell are you doing here?' he roared at her.

She stood up as straight as she could. 'Helping you!' she

cried. The rush of the wind and the billowing fire filled the air with noise.

'You've done enough damage already,' he said. 'Do you want to do more? Wouldn't you rather see us sink?'

She did not understand and did not want to. She grabbed the hose at his feet. He reached for her hand. The hooded eyes were cold, the mouth pulled tight, the crest of blond hair roughened by black smoke. His eyes were on her. His dislike for her was so blatant that she stepped back as if struck, losing her balance. She slipped from the roof, her arms flailing wildly.

His hand meshed around her wrist with a grip of pure steel. As he hauled her back beside him he was not gentle; she was so close their bodies were touching. She felt a fool, but her pride turned it to a furious anger.

'Look, if you want to be unpleasant to me, that's your affair,' she said. 'But you need help. When the fire gets here you need me back to back with you. You could do with my help,' she threw at him. 'And besides, it's too late for me to leave!'

It was. The highway had already been barred to traffic. In the distance the police cars flashed their lights constantly as they set up the road block.

'All right.' He let her hand go as if it seared him. He was looking at her intently; it could not be that he was thinking of her safety, only of what a nuisance she presented to him, she knew that. Wondered why she had ever thought of coming here, but now she was she would see it through. 'You can leave when it's all over. I just hope you can take what you're going to see,' he said. 'I don't think you have any idea . . .'

Her green eyes were defiant, her chin determined. He was not going to get rid of her that way.

'Just show me what to do,' she said.

'Like this,' he said, grabbing the hose in his hands. 'And not until I tell you; the rule is never to use water until it is essential . . .'

She nodded her understanding. And then they waited.

There had been a major brush clearance in every direction, but firestorms consumed the oxygen in the air itself. First the ashes spread over the house, the fields, the cars, settling everywhere.

The sun became blood-red as the black cloud covered it. Great tongues of red and orange flame licked high within it, devouring the hillside, fireballs of burning brush bounced and danced ahead of the main fire, driven by the wind, kindling new blazes in its path.

She could hear the roar and the crackle of the oncoming fire within the howl of the wind, the invincible wind. The wind and the fire were one.

It became dark, an urgent, smoky dark. The fire hid behind the smoke now in the canyon. Nothing between them and it but the Pacific Coast Highway. The four lane thoroughfare hardly slowed it down at all: the wall of smoke glowed blood-red, then the fire burst through and was upon them. It had hurdled the highway. It reappeared in a firework display of light a hundred yards away, brighter and hotter than any day.

Kay caught her breath. She had never expected anything like this. He looked towards her. She showed nothing of what she felt.

'Get ready!' he called.

Their faces were quickly blackened by smoke. A handle was set into the roof that she had not noticed before. Now he was turning it. Almost immediately the sprinklers that surrounded the driveway sprang into life in a shower of fountains that sparkled brilliantly against the oncoming fire. It was time to use the water as much as they could.

'Watch the house!' he grabbed her arm and shouted into her ear. 'If you see a spark turn your hose on it. Don't watch the fire . . . turn your back on it, watch the roof. If a spark catches, we're finished. I'm going to take the house, you take the stables. All right, I might have to leave you. Think you'll manage?'

The sudden concern for her made her catch her breath. She looked swiftly into his face. 'Yes, I'm fine,' she said and turned away.

The heat parched her throat. The canyon was ablaze all around them beyond their wall of water, but the fire could jump, she had seen that now. She heard the trees and bushes exploding in the heat as it engulfed everything in its path. She ignored the heat, the sparks, the smoke, responding less to the terror of the scene than to its magnificent and stark beauty. It was far too late to try and escape now anyway. She had to stand and fight. Her adrenalin lifted her up, enflamed her as she turned on her hose and watched it play. Maybe it was the unbelievable noise, the power of the fire, the flames now fifty feet high leaping overhead and sending showers of sparks even

351

higher as they roared through the trees that lined the driveway, maybe it was beacuse they were fighting the fire side by side, but she was not scared.

She almost forgot his warning to turn her back on the fire and watch the house. It was a sensational sight, terrifying and beautiful at the same time. She turned. A burning brand of wood had lighted on the rooftop, nestling next to the slate at the lip of a wooden junction. Quickly, she swung the hose, played it out. Turned to see another ember dance through the air and land beside her. She jumped back, braced her feet, pointed the hose. It was out.

Animals raced past the house, flying for their lives. She saw them all, tiny furry creatures. Some would survive, some would not. The birds had already gone, seeing it from afar. Now the bobcats, coyotes and raccoons were unearthed from their burrows and racing ahead of the holocaust. Rabbits, squirrels, field mice all flew for their lives, but even if they survived their safety was short-lived. After the fires would come the rains. With no sage to bolster the hills, the earth would wash down into mud, blocking the highways. The land would be blackened and burnt, all protection gone.

She doused the area all around her. The fire raged on. Sometimes he was beside her, sometimes he was not. Helicopters were whirring now through the dense smoke as the fire-fighting team quelled the fire. They were experts. The land could not be saved in the path of the fire, but the houses could. They blasted the ring of land around the compound with sheets of water.

It was a tough, exhausting job. Kay stood her ground, but she started to feel the strain. She showed no fear, only courage and a lack of self-centredness, a true survival instinct. David had come back alongside her. She stood right beside him and never let up. As he realised that the worst was over, he let himself relax slightly for the first time.

Could this be the girl who had helped destroy his family, this girl who was now fighting to save the corral right alongside him? At one point he had looked at her determined little face and knew she was almost enjoying it.

They shared the look, and laughed.

He knew he loved her.

*

Steam rose from the blackened stumps of bushes. The live-stock and buildings were intact. All around them stretched devastation, but the ranch was saved. The fire had moved on. It was over.

There was a smut on her nose. He brushed it away. His touch set off a thousand charms tinkling in her head.

He took her hand. 'Come on.'

They left the scene, his arm around her as he walked her back up the hill towards her car. He got in without a word, taking the steering wheel, spun the car around and down the coast. The wind in her hair was magnificent.

'Can I use your shower?' He looked across at her, meeting her eyes.

She nodded, smiled at him. Exhausted, but together. They had won, beaten the fire. And now.

Their words were unspoken as they drove. Nothing need be said. His hand found hers and held it. He leaned over only once during the drive and kissed her cheek, pulled her into his arm. Like that, they rode home together.

Down at Latigo the moonlight cast an irregular path upon the ocean. The blood-red setting sun had died with the fire and now the moon silvered the waves on the dark belly of the ocean. The rollers slid in smoothly, oily dark, the foam a line of white against the dense blue. The tide left a stain of silver on the beach beyond the dark shadows of rock and sand. The ocean was a dark milky blue scattered with sequins of moon-light. As quickly as the winds had come, they had died. Now all was quiet.

She had no idea how beautiful she was. She turned from the window and the ocean and looked back at him where he sat on the bed. Without a qualm, she shrugged off the heavy-duty jeans, the thin white shirt. Her skin was brown. She wore a pair of blue bikini knickers, cotton, that had ridden up high on her buttocks, the elastic slightly worn. Her legs were strong and limber, like a racehorse. As she turned her back to him and laid her clothes upon the chair, he was aware of the line of her buttocks and thighs in the soft light spilling into the room. It caught at his stomach.

She unhooked her bra, the swell of her breasts gentled by the opaque light from the lace-shielded window. The still shadows of her body enticed him, the light danced off her skin and

353

beckoned him more openly. She turned to face him. There was that look in her eye again as their eyes met, a look he had only glimpsed before, but now held his boldly. It was humour, depth, promise. Passion.

His shoulders were broader than she had imagined, seen only on a beach against the wide space of skies and air, not filling a room, a space enclosed now made theirs. So intimate. It breathed around them, silent. His body was longer, leaner. Strong. There was a gleam of blond on it. Their eyes caught and held again, familiarising. Here they were at last, ready to take what they wanted, what they needed so badly, at any time; the holding off the sweeter.

This time the knowledge pounded in her temples, up under her ribs. She wanted to move, but she found herself as if imprisoned, unable to do so. He did, he came and took her hand, pulling her to him, sat again on the bed, brought her in between his thighs. He caught at the elastic of her pants, pulled them down over her thighs. Her skin was like satin. The feel of her ran along his skin. He touched the crisp dark red hair that sprang under his fingers, stroked up around the curve of her waist to cup her breasts. He pulled her mouth down to his, his hands in her hair holding her face close, tight. She moaned gently against his lips and it set him on fire. He was full of her, she was full of him, the whole of her along him touching, sliding softly, rough and smooth, hard and soft.

Breath-catching, her sigh like a flame. He was no longer gentle.

She drove him back to the ranch in the morning in her car. The sight that met them was incredible: only the ranch left standing amongst the blackened hills. They drove up the drive and parked outside his house, climbed out and stood together looking down over the valley. She turned back to face him.

'I have to go home now,' she said. 'To England. I'm catching the flight later this morning. I need to get ready.'

He took her into his arms. 'Why?'

'My brother's family was in a plane crash, his wife is very ill, his little girl is in a coma,' she said, her cheek resting against the now familiar warmth of his chest. She closed her eyes and let herself go in his arms. She sighed, thinking of what she was going back to, what she herself had started inadvertently, the

354

acquisition of Foxhall, the death of her grandmother's enemy, the air crash. 'So much tragedy,' she said. 'Lately, there's been so much.'

The chestnut waves of her hair softly brushed his face as she lay in his arms. Now was the moment to ask her, to make her admit, or to find out her innocence. He so needed to know she was free of guilt. Or was she the instigator, a traitor to Frederick: it would be impossible to believe then that he loved her.

'What else has happened, tell me.'

'Oh, I don't want to talk about it. It's just family.'

'Tell me anyway.' His arms urged her.

'Well.' She paused for a moment. 'Just recently my family nearly lost everything. There's been this feud between my grandmother and . . . this other man.' She moved out of his arms, suddenly tense and unable to stay there. She looked over the hill down to the bay and the ocean. 'He tried to ruin us, he and his grandson. They set up a contract designed to trap us.' She looked into his face, her eyes worried now. The breeze blew a lock of hair across her face; she pushed it back. He kept his feelings to himself, but his eyes did not leave hers. He wanted to see all of it there, the truth.

'And did they?'

'No. We all put our heads together to find a way out.' She scuffed at the ground with the toe of her shoe.

His throat went dry. He pushed his hands into his pockets, still.

'Who found the way?'

She sighed, did not look up. 'I did.'

Briefly, he closed his eyes. That was it. She had betrayed Frederick.

'And then what happened?' He forced himself to ask. Her answers were vitally important. He wanted to tell her he loved her, but he had to wait, to wait because of this. He could not even tell her he too was flying home today – he would fly later now. She would ask too many questions if she knew that he was going to England too.

'Luckily we were able to sort things out.' She looked over at the sea again, apparently deep in thought.

'Was that an end of it?'

Now she tensed, frowning. 'No,' she said quietly, sadly. 'It wasn't. We turned the tables on them. It became them in danger of losing everything, and I . . .' She hesitated. 'Oh, you don't want to hear this.'

'No, I do.' God, if only he could believe in her. 'You?' he pressed. 'What did you do?'

'I . . .'

'So there you are!' The voice was slurred and hard. They both turned dramatically at once. It had cut into them. Sabrine stumbled up the path, her arm lifted. She was drunk and aggressive; it was at once obvious. Kay looked startled. David drew in a breath. He had almost known. Damn his aunt. 'And who is this?' she said, swaying to a halt, her eyes glued to Kay.

David swore silently to himself. Another moment, and now he still did not honestly know. 'Sabrine, this is Kay.'

Sabrine flashed him a glance that ran up and down his body and back to his face, the intimation obvious. She came to the side of the car, and leaned on it, her eyes like razors. 'I was all alone, and this . . .' she accused.

'You weren't even here,' said David.

Kay pulled herself together. 'Well,' she said. 'I really must be going . . . nice to meet you,' she said tightly. Her eyes caught hold of his. 'My plane is leaving . . .' So much left unsaid.

'I'll come to the bottom of the drive with you.'

'No, it's all right really. I'm sure you and your aunt have a lot to sort out.' She smiled apologetically as she stepped towards the car door on which Sabrine was leaning.

Patronisingly, thought Sabrine, standing back.

'Goodbye,' she said. 'Perhaps we'll meet again.' Her eyes swept back to his. Sabrine did not miss that look. She looked at him too; said nothing.

'When will you be back?'

'I don't know . . . maybe two weeks.'

His eyes held hers. 'Call me.'

She climbed into her car, turned and was gone.

Sabrine folded her arms. 'Who was that?'

'I told you.' He watched her reach the highway, pause and roar back off down the road. He felt cold and non-committal.

'Trying to avoid the issue?' she said.

He watched Kay go with a sinking heart. 'Will you stop being ridiculous?' he said. 'Don't you think there's more to worry about?'

She eyed him sharply. He was being super-sensitive, unlike

David. All her instincts went on full alert. There was something he was trying to hide, she had been right.

'Frederick wants you to call him,' she said slowly. She had heard the news about Rupert with equanimity. He had left her nothing, she had expected nothing. Neither did she care.

'I'll ring him now,' he said. 'Then I'll come back to the ranch.'

He walked straight up the hill to his cabin. Sabrine watched him go, a thoughtful look on her face. Then her gaze swung around towards the empty highway. To her jealous nature, it was obvious the two were in love, but the constraint was equally obvious: they had not told each other yet. Why had he not introduced her properly? She was very suspicious. She went back down to her house. She would make it her business to find out who the girl was.

David dialled through to England. Frederick came onto the telephone.

'David, where have you been? Been trying to get you.'

'There was a hill fire. I was out all night. What's up?'

He looked out at the bleak and blackened landscape.

'The Bennetts sold it back to us . . . Foxhall!'

'Oh God.' He turned into the telephone, straining to hear. 'Frederick . . . tell me something. What do you know about the daughter, Kay?'

Frederick's voice changed. 'I told you . . .? How do you . . . ?'

'Never mind. Was she operative in getting Foxhall?'

'Kay? *No!* She came to me, that's all, and asked for a legitimate way to get them out of a deal fixed by Rupert and your father. I'm afraid they set out to trap the Bennetts. I merely gave Kay the wherewithal to counterattack. Which she did.'

'But I thought you said she started it, started the chain that led to their taking over Gilbert's bank . . . that was how they got Foxhall, wasn't it?'

Frederick's distant voice held a laugh in it. 'No, no! Their own double dealings tripped them up, as the market collapsed. I'm afraid that Dickie Bennett saw her chance and went in for the kill. Can't say that I really blame her. Kay was nothing to do with it. Though I never spoke to her again, I can be sure of that. She would have tried to stop them. I know her. She'd

357

never lie. Very honourable, strong as a lion, my Kay,' he said fondly.

'*Your* Kay?'

'Yes.' He laughed again. 'Well, not really mine. I've known her for years, she just feels like mine.'

'I didn't know,' he said slowly.

'No, well, I couldn't say before, because of the trouble and all of that, but it's all over now, thank God. Sorry it had to be such tragic circumstances, Rupert's death.' He paused a moment; despite it all, he was his brother. 'But,' he went on briskly. 'Everything's fine now. I think she's even forgiven us for hurting her so many years ago . . . I'll tell you all about it, when you get home. I've got to go. Just wanted you to know. You've got everything.'

Except the one thing he wanted, his girl. Kay. Kay.

Kay hesitated as she pulled to a halt in front of the house. It stood back majestically from the drive, throwing a golden glow onto the wide sweep of gravel, the white walls glowing softly in the light. She had come straight from Heathrow to Bower Hill, driving herself home in one of the company cars there.

Most of the lights in the house were on. She paused, then stepped out and walked up to the front door.

It opened before she could reach it, throwing a shaft of welcoming light around her as she stood there.

'Mummy!'

'Kay!' Jennie threw her arms around her. 'How are you, darling!'

'I'm fine, but . . . is Jim home?'

'Yes, he's just arrived back.' She went in with her. 'He was getting in a night's sleep before going back to the hospital to be with Olivia and Alice . . .' She shook her head. 'He's going to be all right, his wounds were only superficial, but Alice and Olivia . . . they simply aren't mending, especially Olivia.'

Kay was lost for words. She slipped her hand into that of her mother's.

'. . . she saved the little girl,' Jennie went on as they passed into the hall and walked on together into the drawing-room. 'She held her in her arms despite the waves and the cold.'

'Olivia has amazing strength. I don't think anyone really realised it.'

'Least of all Jim.' Kay looked at her mother as she spoke the

358

words. 'He's taken it really badly. I don't think he ever knew how much he loved her, how much she meant to him. He's fallen apart. He always thought he was the one in control of the relationship.'

She slipped her arm from Kay's waist and went over to the tray that stood beside the fire, lit despite the warmth of the summer day; the evenings were cool. 'I left you out some supper, darling.'

Kay shook her head, and let herself relax into the sofa, her mind on the tragedy. 'I don't really feel all that hungry, thanks, Mum. Is it too late to go down to the hospital?'

'I'm afraid so . . . and besides, Olivia slips in and out of consciousness. Alice is still in a coma. Better wait until the morning, Jim'll be so pleased to see you. I expect he could do with your company right now.'

'All right.' Kay lifted her hand and took the brandy her mother had poured her. 'How's Dad taking it all?'

'Well. You know your father.' She sat down and crossed her legs, sipped at her drink. 'How are things going in the business over there?' she said, altering the subject. 'He said you had things to tell him.'

'Very well. We've managed to come up with extra dividends for the shareholders this year. And it looks like we might be going into the bucket shop market, after all.' She sipped her brandy, gazed distantly into the flames.

'After all that fiasco with Jim too.'

Kay nodded. 'Yes. The problem with Jim was that he didn't see all the problems through, didn't set it up properly, but of course, sensing the current trends, it was a good idea. We might do it for next season.'

'Who swung that one?' Jennie asked.

'I will I hope. Oh, and Dad and Dickie have already halfway agreed. So has everyone else. I've judged the market in the States and put in my ideas. We've got a very big fleet now, well over a hundred jets given all the companies, all the old aircraft phased out. Dickie says the adventure is over.'

'Well, it is really, isn't it?' She brushed her fingers through her hair, recrossed her legs.

Kay held her drink between her hands. 'No,' she said with a lift in her voice. 'That's an attitude of mind. You never lose your sense of the future, what it can bring. The element of adventure is relative.'

Her eyes warmed as she thought of the hill fire, of him next to her, loving her. They had hardly slept all night, he had reached for her again and again, touching her, kissing her, stroking.

Jennie saw the warmth melt in her daughter's face, the slow smile.

'And how is it in the States? Looks like you're enjoying it!'

Should she tell her mother. She was bursting to say, to tell someone. Not yet, not yet. It was still her secret, hugged to her.

'Pretty good.'

Her mother nodded, realising she would have to wait to hear about whatever or whoever it was that had transformed her daughter. Kay was glowing despite the concern in her face for what was happening here, and it wasn't all Californian good living and sunshine that was doing it.

She put down her glass, stood up and lifted the firescreen into place before the dying embers of the fire.

'Well, darling,' she said. 'It's been exhausting the last few days. I'm tired and ready for bed. If you're not going to eat your supper, I'll stick it in the kitchen. Daddy's running Dickie home, he'll be in in a bit. You gonna wait up to see him?'

'Yes.' Kay uncurled from the sofa and came to her mother. She put her arms round her. 'It's good to be home, Mum, despite everything.'

Jennie held her daughter, sharing the tenderness. They both felt for Jim and his family. In the morning, Kay would see what they all had seen, the tragedy of gentle Olivia, white as a ghost, the tubes that kept her alive trailing from her in that hospital room. And the child . . . the child didn't bear thinking about. The little girl's room, cards and flowers adorning the wall above her bed and the window sills. Cuddled into her cot with her was a small teddy bear, a pink satin bow adorning him and still immaculate, untouched by a little girl's eager hands. She looked just as if she were sleeping, her eyes closed, her dark curls spread against the pillow, her lips red and softly parted, her chubby arms arranged over the sheet. Jennie gave her daughter a tighter squeeze and kissed her cheek.

'Good night, darling.' She bent to lift the tray and went out to the kitchen. Kay sank back into the sofa. She was over-conscious of the elements of tragedy and happiness that mingled in her at the moment, two such opposing elements. She heard her mother rattle around in the kitchen, then the lights in the hall went out leaving only one softer light burning outside the front door. Her footsteps climbed the stairs and a distant door closed. The house purred.

Kay put down her drink and went across to the French windows to step out onto the lawn. She walked down the terrace and sat at the table and chairs that were always left out, winter and summer.

A light went out upstairs on the landing, darkening the terrace. It was better. A heavy moon hung in the sky, tranquil. It made the land so light, almost like day. It was very quiet, an English country quiet. Way above, a lone aeroplane blipped across the night sky. She watched it out of sight. Everything here was so quiet, so still. She drew it in, lonely. Their togetherness so recently made her lonely, for him. She missed the sound of the ocean.

She missed David.

CHAPTER THIRTY-EIGHT

Kay swam strongly towards the ocean, cutting through the rollers and out beyond. She was a good swimmer. She loved the water.

She flipped over onto her back and swam parallel to the beach for twenty yards and then back again. And then she trod water. She had tried not to look too often towards the beach. It was still empty. With a sigh, she started to swim in again. He was not coming.

She had left England the night before, having stayed home a week, a week in which Alice had come out of her coma. She was on the mend. Olivia too, seemed to have stabilised; the danger over at last. Kay had pressing matters on her mind, more personal than business. She missed David with all her heart. Making the family promise to let her know immediately should there be any change in either of them, she had flown back to America earlier than expected. Just for a few days. She had telephoned him early and reached his ansaphone, left a message to say where she would be, swimming at the Colony. There was so much she wanted to say to him.

Sabrine watched the girl from behind her storm glass windows. She had discovered the identity of David's girlfriend. It had not been difficult. And David was still in England. Perfect. Her eyes had been alight with malice as she left his cabin and made her way down to the coast. She was not planning to lose him, and to a *Bennett*! She had plenty of time in which to destroy their relationship before it even got off the ground. Neither of them would ever trust the other again. She could lay a ten-to-one bet the girl did not even know who he was.

In the hospital, Jim arrived late. Her door was ajar, the sheet over her face. He moved forward, pulled it down . . . he touched her, felt the cold. He dropped to his knees with a surge of pain inside him. Olivia. Oh, Olivia. There she lay, still as if sleeping, the white shroud pulled back off her face. Her lovely face like a doll's, waxy and white, the red lips prominent, the heavy lids pale and closed in sleep, forever sleep.

His face was pressed to that of his wife, lifting her into his arms. Now the tubes were all gone she was like she used to be, only such a heavy weight. Such a limp and heavy weight. He sobbed against her lifeless chest. He remembered her fear, her screaming: 'Jim, help us!'

He had not been able to help her. And now she was dead. He held the slender body pressed tight against him as if he would never let her go. All else faded. He no longer wanted to live . . .

Sabrine slid back the window, kicked off her shoes on the deck and went down to the beach. The wind whipped at her black hair and the sun burned her skin. Her smile was grim. Alabaster skin, these days she was proud of pale colour. Alabaster; David had named his horse after her. This chit would not have him.

Kay body-surfed in with the biggest of the waves, letting it carry her close to the shore. As it lost its strength she let it go, standing as it sucked back out again. She walked forward against the undertow, feeling the sun warm her. It was good to be back. It would be even better when his arms were around her again. She smiled.

'Hello, Kay. Little sister!'

Her eyes opened wide. On the sand in front of her stood David's aunt, Sabrine. 'Hello, Sabrine.' Her smile was not forthcoming; she knew something was wrong about this visit. 'Is David with you?'

'No. David's not with me.' Sabrine stood, her legs braced against the wind, her thin summer dress fluttering against her legs. Her eyes were narrowed and in her hand she held a cigarette, its filter stained with the red of her lipstick. 'This is private . . . between you and me.'

Kay came to a halt a few yards in front of her. She looked briefly up at the houses beyond, Sabrine's house. She knew which one it was. The patio doors stood open to the day, no hoped-for sign of David there.

'I don't understand,' she said.

'No, you don't, do you!' Sabrine gave a chuckle. 'I called you "little sister" . . . do you understand that?'

Kay stood still, her eyes calm. 'No.'

Sabrine's smile twisted the corner of her mouth. 'I'll let you into a secret then,' she said, the famous eyebrows arching cruelly. 'You and I are sisters!'

'What are you talking about?' Kay picked up her towel, wanting to be away. Was she crazy?

Sabrine read her mind. 'You think I'm potty, don't you?' She shook her head slowly. 'I'm not. I'm just going to give you a little history lesson . . .' She leaned forward slightly. 'You do know the history of the Bennetts and the Redfields, I take it?'

Kay had been towelling her hair. Now she stopped, the towel held between her hands, very still. 'Partly, yes,' she said slowly. 'Why . . . what's that got to do with . . .?'

'Look hard,' she said. 'Don't you recognise anything?'

'No.'

Sabrine laughed. 'No family resemblance, huh?'

'What do you know about our family and theirs?' said Kay. 'What's this all about?'

'Why, it's about you and David. What do you think? David's my nephew, has he never mentioned his father's name . . . my brother, Alexander?' Her smile danced on her face.

'Alexander. No.' The faintest shred was coming clear. The only Alexander she knew . . . the way she had said it . . . her eyes started to register the truth. Sabrine was watching as closely as a snake. She laughed delightedly.

'Oh, I see you're getting there . . . congratulations!'

'Alexander . . . *Redfield*?' she said slowly.

'Alexander Hamblin,' she corrected her. 'David's grand-mother married a Hamblin. There, I thought he hadn't told you,' she said, pleased. Kay's face had registered first shock and now disbelief. She had always thought of Alexander as a Redfield, had never heard him called Hamblin . . . they had all just spoken of him by his Christian name, and then the contract. The first had been in Rupert Redfield's name. The second. She had not seen the second, had not needed to. How ridiculous, how crazy. Why hadn't he told her? That was why he had acted the way he did. She stared sightlessly at the sand, unmoving, numb.

'Oh, I'm not surprised really,' she was saying. 'It's so complex. Even poor David doesn't know the half of it, but I'm going to tell you. You know of course what went on between my grandfather and your grandmother, now don't you?' she was saying.

'Yes,' muttered Kay miserably. 'I do.' Where was David? Why wasn't he here? Sabrine must have taken his message, come to find her instead.

364

'Why did you call us sisters?' demanded Kay. 'I'm not your sister, whatever you may say about the families. What happened was long ago.'

'Not so long, not so long!' Sabrine smiled. 'I'm coming to that. My mother was in love with your father, you know.' Kay's eyes grew wider. 'She ran away on her wedding day.' Sabrine's voice was slow and languorous. 'She found him in the fields. They couldn't resist each other. They made love. *Brother* and *sister*.' She clicked her tongue. Kay turned her face away. 'Shocking, isn't it!' she went on, mercilessly. 'Yes, I thought so too when I found out, and I found out the hard way, just as you're going to,' she said, suddenly cold. 'I found your goddamned father irresistible, just as she did, that was until I found out he was my father!'

Kay's hands leaped up as if in protection. 'Don't be *ridiculous*!' Her green eyes went wide with horror. 'What are you saying. You're mad!'

'Mad, huh! And well I could be with all that's been going on!' she said, her face contorting with frightful laughter. 'But I'm not. You will be if you carry this any further, though, *sister*,' she said. Thrusting a finger at her, Sabrine said, 'We're blood, and that makes you and David blood too. You're related, do you realise that? The relationship would never work between you and he knew it. That's why he never told you! Do you know where he is now? At his great-grandfather's funeral. He knows he can't marry his own blood!'

Kay was horrified. In desperation, she sought a reason, an escape. She did not break down, her character was too strong for that, but unbidden and frightful in her mind were those moments when he had seemed so cold. Moments when he had known what was happening and wanted to stop it. Oh God! Had he set out to seduce her for revenge, more revenge? This time for Jessamy Redfield and her father, Max? She saw the faces, saw his. She had never known what her father had done.

'How do you know you're his children?' she cried, trying to conceal the shake in her voice.

'Oh, really!' Sabrine's smile said it all. An actress, she fixed her with an intense look reminiscent of her own father. Kay saw the similarity and it shook her. Sabrine grabbed the moment fast.

'Be smart,' she said. 'Get out of the situation you're in. Tell

David you no longer wish to see him. If you love him, you won't break his heart by telling him the truth that I have concealed from him all these years. I love him, you see,' she said, pressing home her point. 'I wouldn't want to see him hurt; would you? Imagine if he knew the truth. David, with his pride, knowing he'd been sleeping with his own flesh and blood?'

She drew back.

'If you write him a note, I'll see he gets it. Drop it at my house. It's the best way.'

She turned and left her suddenly, dramatically and without a farewell. Just walking back up the beach towards her house. She went inside without looking back.

Kay did not move for a moment. The woman's presence still seemed to hang in the air like a repugnant aroma. How could David have lived with her and liked her? She was a snake. She pulled her towel around her neck, suddenly cold, and walked back to her grandparents' house. She felt as though she were tearing inside. Desperately, she wanted to see him. She loved him, it was a pure love that was not dirty, as Sabrine had suggested. Neither was she the sort of girl to back down from a confrontation, but Sabrine had caught her unawares. And he was not there to ask. It could all be a pack of lies. She had to talk to him. He was at Foxhall. She would call him, to hell with pretence any more. She headed for the deck.

Her grandmother came running out above her as she approached.

'Kay! Kay! There's an urgent call for you. From home, honey, quick!'

Kay ran up the steps onto the deck and went into the cool of the McVeys' drawing-room. She picked up the telephone.

'Hello?'

'Darling.' Her mother's voice was distant, choked with tears. 'Poor Olivia passed away last night. We're all in a state of shock.'

'*Olivia?*' She felt the choke in her throat.

'Jim has broken down. She was so brave. Oh Kay, that poor little thing. Everybody loved her.'

'Mum, I'll be on the next plane.' There was no question about her return. The other dark thoughts had been pushed to the back of her mind. Though it was only a day since she had left them, so much had happened. She was even still packed.

She put down the telephone and ran into the guest-room to get changed. Dory had gone off somewhere. She returned, polishing a glass, as Kay re-appeared, pulling herself into a white cotton sweater.

'Oh, Dory . . . Olivia has gone . . .' She threw herself into her grandmother's arms, and the old lady stroked her hair.

'Yes, I know, dear.'

'I have to go home . . . Dory . . .' She started to tell her grandmother about David, then stopped. It was too hard. 'Nothing . . . I'll see you.'

'Sure, honey.' She kissed her.

Was it as Sabrine said, he had been lying all along and now simply could not face her? She ran out of their house to her car. She would have to hurry to catch the flight. She gunned her car out of the Colony and up the highway to Latigo, bumping off and down the dirt path to her cottage on the beach.

With little time to spare she tried to call him. Her heart was aching as she put through the call to Foxhall, knowing there would be a misunderstanding unless she reached him. When she finally got through the butler answered, yes, he had been home, he was on his way to New York now; no, Mr Frederick was not in. She left a message, saying she had called. She could not say any more than that, it was too private. And then she called his cottage, left a message that she had been back and would he call her at Longbarrow if he wanted her.

She missed him all the way over in the plane. Like a cord stretching as the aircraft flew further east, the thinner it got the more it seemed to hurt her, the sharper it got. Like waking from a strong dream, it stayed with her; she could not throw it off, now she was able to give herself to her own crisis.

Kay had been brave all her life. She was not going to break down now. She pulled down the shade on the window and turned her face to it, so that no one should see her tears.

Sabrine slipped into David's cottage and closed the door softly behind her. In the darkness she could see the light flashing on the ansaphone in the corner. Holding her breath, she crossed the room and replayed the tape. It whirred in the silence, stopped and started again. That voice.

She listened to the message and then erased it.

Now David would never know the truth. Kay had left town and Sabrine could embroider on that to her heart's content. By the time she returned, if she ever did, the damage would have been done.

The door opened behind her, and David immediately switched on the lights and saw her there.

'What are you doing in here, Sabrine?'

She whipped round. 'Oh, David. I wasn't expecting you back so soon.'

'Obviously.' He put down his case and looked around. Frederick had told him so much more on his brief trip home. He had hoped that Kay had been trying to reach him. That was all he had thought about as he had flown back to be with her. His cottage might belong to his aunt, but it was off limits to her. She knew that. He wondered what she was doing in here.

'I was just looking for something,' she said. She turned and pretended to search, moving chairs and cushions. 'A piece of tack for one of the horses. Well, it's obviously not here!' She stood up straight, her hands clasped, and smiled. 'How was the funeral?'

'Depressing. How's it been here?'

He came across the room towards her. 'Oh, fine,' she said, and stepped back.

David frowned; she seemed so . . . nervously excited.

'Let's go out riding now,' she said. 'I've missed our rides. The horses have too.'

'Not right now. I have to make a call.' He was going to ring Kay straight away, to ask her to meet him, to tell her everything, who he was, that he loved her. He picked up the telephone, surprised to see no light. There were always messages, from breeders, friends. Not Kay? He frowned.

'Miss Bennett's private line, please . . .' He waited; his eyes roved to those of his aunt. She was watching, eyes bright. '. . . Is she back yet?'

'Well no, I'm afraid not,' said her secretary. 'Who is this?'

'David Hamblin.' Sabrine had turned and was roaming restlessly around the room.

'She's just left for England, Mr Hamblin.'

'Just left . . .? You mean she's been back here already?'

'Yes. But she had to turn right around. Her sister-in-law died. I think she's planning to stay over there for quite a while as far as I know. She had no immediate plans to return.'

He took a breath. 'She left no message for me to that effect. Did she leave a message with you if I was to call?'

'No, not here . . . but actually I thought she left a message on your machine,' said the voice. David turned to look at his aunt. Her back was to him now. She was touching the books on the shelf. 'She said she had.'

'I see. Thank you.'

He put the phone down slowly and looked at his aunt. 'Were there no messages on my machine?'

'What? Oh, I don't know.' She turned and shook a hand lightly in the air. 'Perhaps . . . obviously not.' She gave it a quick glance. 'David, why don't we take a trip together. I have an idea of going to Acapulco. How about that? Wouldn't it be fun, just the two of us . . . ?' She was almost girlish.

'Sabrine. What's going on?'

'I've no idea what you're talking about.' Her eyes flickered.

He went over, grasped her shoulders, suddenly understanding. 'What have you told her, Sabrine? Why did you erase the tape?'

Sabrine was shaken. 'Oh, you don't know, David, the awful truth of what I've had to live with!' she said tearfully.

'Stop this, Sabrine, and tell me the truth. What have you said to Kay? I'll find out, so you might as well tell me.'

So, tearfully she did, the whole story coming out; her discovery of Jessamy's papers, her own mother's admission, her shame.

'She hid her shame from all of us, David. Her affair on her wedding day. Max Bennett is my father! Kay and I are sisters!'

'What!'

'Yes, yes, it's true. Now do you see. I did it for you!'

'You told Kay this?'

The dark anger in his face was terrible, the hurt. 'Yes,' she said miserably. 'I tried to spare you, that's all. Now you must see the relationship is impossible! Mothers are cruel. Mothers are hateful! You're better without one. Mothers are bad!' She was crying freely now. 'She tried to kill me, David. Alexander saw her, saved me. She put a pillow over my face. She tried to kill me.'

'Mothers are not all like that, Sabrine,' he said. 'You need help. I'm going to find Kay now and talk to her father. Ask him the truth.'

'No!' She jumped up.

'Yes.' He pressed her back into the seat. 'I'm going to find out from him.'

'He did, he did sleep with her. You've got no mother, David. You need me. I'm your mother now. You're the child I never had,' she wept. 'Don't desert me too. Don't desert me, I need you!'

'Don't be ridiculous, Sabrine.' He knelt in front of her. 'Kay needs me. To explain everything.'

'You can't. I didn't think you would . . .'

'Didn't you? Then you don't know me very well. Something as uncertain as this would not keep me from her side. I'm going to find out, Sabrine.'

He stood up and grabbed his case.

'Where are you going?'

'Back to the airport. I don't care about some outdated feud. I want Kay, whoever she is . . .'

She had entirely misjudged him. She was hysterical with need, grabbing at his arm as he went to the door. He prised her fingers from him.

'Look, Sabrine, I care for you but I love Kay. I'm going to ask her to marry me.'

And he was gone, the door slamming, his feet running down the steps. Sabrine choked on her sobs. 'David!' She pulled open the door, tears streaming down her face. He was turning the jeep, wheels biting in the dust. She raised her hand. 'Stop!' But he was going, the jeep roaring down the track to the road.

She stood weeping on the balcony. She had enacted this scene so often before. This time it was real.

Kay's black veil fluttered in the breeze as she stood with her father at the edge of the church green. The hearse had arrived, both of them watching with the heavy weight of sadness in their hearts.

Max took a step forward. Kay held his arm.

'Dad,' she said. 'I have to ask you something.'

He turned to look down into her face. She tried to see something of Sabrine there, but could not. This was her father, a proud, fierce but loving man, who could also be incredibly gentle. There was nothing there of her. But she had to ask.

'What is it?' he said.

She paused a second. 'Dad . . . this is probably not the moment, but I need to know. Did you ever sleep with Jessamy Redfield?'

He was visibly shocked. A moment passed. Then: 'Yes.'

370

Her heart caught. 'Could her children be yours? Sabrine and Alexander?'

His face looked grey and old. 'It's quite possible.'

That confirmed it. She stared emptily at the scene before her, seeing nothing.

'Why do you want to know?' he asked her. 'More to the point, how did you find out?'

Kay, tight with grief, shook her head and did not reply. She took his arm. 'It's time to go.'

CHAPTER THIRTY-NINE

Sarah Redfield opened the paper, reading the newspaper article.

'How's the practice?' Charles's voice chipped into her thoughts. He thought she looked too tired these days.

She lowered the paper and lifted her legs onto the arm of her chair. 'Exhausting,' she said. 'Wonderful at times. I'm learning all about the real rudiments of marriage. When it comes right down to it, it's *my* bookshelves and *your* teacloths. You've no idea how people get when they're getting split up.' She raised an eyebrow; being a divorce lawyer was an eye-opener. 'I'm turning into an amateur pyschiatrist.'

'Not so amateur. I've always thought you to be pretty good at sorting people out.'

'Yes, look what I did for you all those years ago.'

'Exactly. I rest my case, m'lud!' He leaned back in his leather swivel chair as she laughed at him. He let the sun from the bay window spill onto his face. Foxhall was at its most beautiful in the summer, the gardens mellow and colourful outside. 'You don't feel like giving it up then,' he said then, mellowed himself.

'Giving it up!' she exclaimed. 'Whatever for?'

'I rather wanted you home. With me.'

A car door banged out in the driveway. Charles frowned and peered out. He could see nothing. The car drove away.

'You'll have to wait awhile yet,' she said, lifting up the paper again. 'I'm going to be made a partner next year. Who's that arrived?'

'Don't know,' he said. 'But congratulations, darling.' He heard the footsteps approach the door. 'Why didn't you tell me before?'

'Oh you know me, element of surprise!' she teased. The door opened. They both looked up. 'David! What on earth are you doing back here?'

He gave her a swift kiss. He looked at his great-uncle as he came around the desk.

'Uncle Charles, I have to talk to you.' He looked swiftly at Sarah. 'Well, it doesn't matter if you don't know about this, Aunt Sarah, it's time you should. Time we all talked about it.' He looked directly at Charles. 'I don't have time to beat about the bush, Uncle Charles, so I'll ask you straight out. Sabrine has told me that grandmother and Max Bennett had an affair, that it resulted in the twins, her and Alexander being born. Is that right? Are they his?'

Sarah did not look at all surprised. She knew the story.

'Oh my God!' said Charles. He sat down. 'Who told her that?'

'Grandmother. Is it true?'

Only now he realised his oversight. He and Jessamy had spoken at cross-purposes. He could have spared his sister her anguish over all those years. The truth returned to him from the night he had sat in David Biddy's surgery checking back through the old records. He remembered both sets of files, the Bennetts' too.

'No,' he said, shaking his head. 'How awful. That's what she believed, and Biddy never told her the truth.' He looked up at David. 'Max Bennett does not have the same blood group as the children. Their father, John Hamblin, did. They are definitely his children, not Max Bennett's.'

'Thank God.'

Sarah looked from one to the other.

'I can't imagine why he never told her,' murmured Charles. 'Except that maybe she never asked. She must have been so certain, so guilty, that she saw him there in their faces. What agony she went through, and I could have spared her.'

David's relief still held a catch. 'But there is a resemblance. I saw it once she told me. It was there in her face, very slightly, but something. How could that be? It's in Kay's face too, Max's daughter.'

Charles hesitated a moment, not knowing where to start.

'Well, you see,' he said. Behind David the door opened.

Frederick had seen the car arrive, come to find out who their guest was. Their voices had drifted across the hall on the quiet summer day. He had caught the gist of what was happening. Now he understood David's questions from California. He had met Kay. Somehow it seemed so inevitable; the two of them meeting. He could see it now; they were made for each other. If it were true and he were not imagining things, then he knew he

373

had to speak. He could not keep quiet if Kay's happiness was at stake.

'So you've met Kay, have you?' he said, coming into the room.

David turned and he saw immediately that he had been right. This was a young man desperately in love. 'Yes,' he said quietly. 'I've met Kay.'

'Sit down, all of you,' said the old man. 'I have a lot to tell you. It's hard, but it's time you knew . . .'

As he finished talking, the silence weighed heavily in the room. Sarah, staring at her hands, was the first to speak. She shook her head.

'So that's what it was all about.'

'I've been ashamed ever since,' said Frederick. 'How often I've wanted this all to end.'

David had not sat down with the rest of them, only leaned against the desk behind him. Now he straightened.

'Well that's exactly what's going to happen. Come on. You can help. We're all going to Longbarrow . . .'

CHAPTER FORTY

Kay walked slowly beside her mother in the gardens of Long-barrow. There was a summer fog that laid a glassy film over the land, the harsh summer colours softened and pearly. Speedwell and celandine were scattered in the long grass at the edge of the freshly mowed lawn, freckled with daisies. The sound of a moorhen tapped at the riverbank. In the distance, the fledgling fields glowed under the sun, and in the meadows the silver mist was still bathing the shadows.

'He needs help,' Jennie was saying. 'I've seen the doctor, the pyschiatrist. He has irrational fears, mostly that everybody's going to leave him. He needs someone's help to overcome that. The doctor says I have to be as firm and consistent as I possibly can with him. You see, he feels responsible for his mother's death as well. She tilted her head slightly. 'Now, of course with this extra burden of Olivia, his mind has snapped completely.'

'It's a heavy burden you're taking on, Mum,' she said, matching her stride to her mother's as they walked arm in arm. 'If you need any help . . .'

'Thank you, darling, but it's the least I can do. I don't think I ever realised just how bad he felt. Until the plane crash, he simply viewed the world as a chessboard in which he could manipulate the pieces. But I believe we can get him better. We have to alter his entire self-image, hold him completely responsible for his actions and make him feel total self-disgust, never pity him. And at the same time, give him absolute love and trust in us. He's going to go into therapy, start again.'

'At least having Alice pull through must have helped. He has a reason to go on living.' Immediately after Olivia's death, he had attempted suicide. From there he had sunk into a state of lethargy, until today, when within days of her mother's funeral, Alice had been allowed home. Her cries had brought a reaction in him. That afternoon they had found him kneeling beside her bed, rocking her to sleep.

'That's true,' said Jennie. 'We all have hope.'

Do we? thought Kay to herself. Her thoughts fled to David. Pain eclipsed her. Would she ever feel happy again? She hung her head, then brought it up again swiftly. She did not want anyone to see her pain, ask her questions. That she could not bear. To talk about it to anyone, her wound still so open.

Jennie took her arm from hers, and turned her daughter to face her. She had felt her body tremble.

'Darling,' she said. 'When you're ready to talk about it, I'm here. Don't forget.'

She kissed her swiftly on the forehead, knew she wanted to be alone.

She was gone. Kay could hardly contain herself. She turned away unable to face her grief. Her mother understood her act all too well.

A car was coming up the drive. In the back she thought she saw a face she knew, but her eyes were blurring too much to see clearly. She thought she saw the face give her a long look. Kay blinked and turned to run indoors. She saw him everywhere. The tears ran freely; she dashed at them with her hands. The car headed for the front of the house.

Kay was standing by the fireplace in the drawing-room by the time he strode in, her face resting on one hand, her thoughts far away. The rest of the family were seated, reading the Sunday newspapers. It was a quiet day, muggy and damp outside, the windows standing open. All of them had heard as if at once the commotion in the spacious and airy hall outside. Footsteps strode across the parquet flooring and the drawing-room doors were thrown wide.

She brought her head up fast as she saw him. His eyes found hers immediately. Neither of them moved, their eyes locking.

On the sofa, Dickie twisted in her seat to see who had come in. She did not recognise the young man as one she knew, and yet there was something. In the second that followed she looked over towards Kay. He quite clearly meant a great deal to her granddaughter; she was amused to see the collected Kay thrown right off balance by his arrival. Her long fingers touched her throat and her lips were parted, her cheeks flushed with shock, and love too for this young man, but also there was pain.

Dickie sensed almost immediately who he was. As the flustered maid appeared in the doorway behind him, she felt no need for an introduction. Now it was suddenly obvious as he stood and gazed at Kay, flustered and hesitant beside the fireplace. It was as if the tableau had been frozen. Max had risen from his chair by the window, and Jennie, coming in from the garden, her arms full of sweet, wet roses, stayed his arm. Their perfume seemed to fill the closeness of the long cool room.

A Redfield through and through, the manner reminiscent of another though different, the thick blond hair, the strong eyes intense and seeking, the lean and powerful height.

'Excuse me for barging in on your family like this,' he was saying, not hesitant at all as he came towards Dickie and stood before her. His eyes took her in before flicking quickly over to Max, the man he remembered from childhood, and Jennie, and back again. 'I had to come,' he said almost to her alone, as if she would understand. 'My name is David Hamblin, and my great-grandfather as you probably know was Rupert Redfield.'

Max moved at the door. Jennie held his arm as Dickie lifted her arm up onto the back of the sofa, watching him.

'I know who you are,' she said. 'Why are you here?'

'Mrs Latimer,' he said, 'I've come to straighten out this fight between us once and for all. And to thank you for giving us back our home.' He did not lift his eyes as more footfalls filled the hall; nor did anyone else, held by the power of his firm, young voice. 'Foxhall is mine now, and I've come to claim it,' he went on. And then turned back towards Kay facing him from the fireplace. There was now only two yards between them across the rug. His voice had softened considerably as if the next words were said for the two of them alone. 'And that's not all I've come to claim.'

Kay's eyes flew wide and tragic. She swallowed, her vision misting. God, he did not know. 'David,' she began.

He took a step forward, holding up his hand to stop her.

'Wait, Kay,' he said softly. He made no attempt to kiss her though his burning eyes drank her in with their need, his wish for her love. He just took her hands gently in his once and then let them go again, as he turned.

'I've taken the liberty,' he said, 'of inviting two of my family whom you already do know, to accompany me.'

Charles and Frederick stood at the door. Nobody spoke, as each stared at each other. What was this? Max looked swiftly at the men, his emotions strong on his face. 'What the devil?' he said. Jennie felt the tension of his muscles under her fingers. She saw the expression of her daughter's face and began to understand everything that had been troubling her. Of course!

'Wait,' she said, soft under her breath. 'See what they have to say.'

Charles moved forward now. 'I'm sorry,' he began, 'that this has had to wait until now for the full story to be heard. I only just realised it all myself, how many misunderstandings there have been. For a long time I've known that you, Max, were my brother.' His eyes held those of Max, though Max's were the Redfield blue, not his. Max's expression was unreadable. Dickie looked down at her hands, her expression rueful, thoughtful. Apart from that she was still, as still as everybody else in the room as Charles's voice went on: 'I know too, what happened between you and my sister.' At that pause, Kay's eyes lifted to those of David, their green now so sharp with tears that it was all he could do not to take her swiftly in his arms and press his lips to her face, holding her, tasting her again, protecting her. He steeled himself to wait until she too heard the end of her sentence, and then he could take her in his arms and feel her soft against him. Charles now looked at Kay. 'Kay, David has told me that you love each other.' Kay's eyelashes fluttered as she looked away. Everybody knew what this meant now, yet she did not feel as ashamed as she thought she would. She did love him, it was undeniable, could not be wrong. 'There is no reason why you should not do so,' he finished. Max looked at his daughter as her head came up listening; he was the one who had felt the shame. Now there was an absolute silence as Charles finished.

'You'll all remember I was once a practising doctor. David Biddy kept both our family records in the safe. One night, when he was out, I read them all, read the family medical records. I read my sister's confession to him. Jessamy was so certain the twins, Sabrine and Alexander, were yours, Max, but they were not. John, her husband, had a blood test run. I don't know whether he suspected something or not, but anyway, the end result was the twins had his blood group. I checked your medical records, Max,' he said, holding the man's eyes with his. 'Your blood group did not match.' He shook his head. 'You did *not* father them.'

There was a soft sob from Kay, her shoulders lifting as the pressure fell away. David's arms were around her as she sank in against his shoulder, tears of joy in her eyes, feeling his face against her neck, kissing her gently. 'Oh, David, David. Sabrine . . .'

'Yes, I know darling, sshh now. It's why I came. I love you.'

Dickie watched them for just a moment, seeing the clarity of their love. This young man was strong and decent. He reminded her of her brother, Sam. She smiled briefly to herself. At last the Redfields had bred something with balls, she thought, as she stood up. He had given a command performance, a young man right after her own heart. Now it was her turn.

She lifted her hands, as the hum of voices started.

'Before you all start talking at once, I too, have something to say.' She looked at them all, Kay in David's arms turning to listen, her eyes damp, a soft smile there. 'There's more to this than any of you know,' she started. 'It's time you knew it all. Knew the secret that I alone have carried for sixty years.' Her voice had trailed off, very soft. She turned towards Frederick, still standing just inside the room. For the first time her eyes were compassionate towards him, though their shining brightness remembered everything, every little detail. He almost flinched from her gaze, it was so full of emotion. For years, Dickie had been driven to hide her feelings, letting her energy forth in revenge, business, anger and need, with passionate love for her family. Now her gentleness and sensuality showed through, the eyes that he remembered from so long ago.

Her voice matched their gentleness.

'Frederick,' she said. 'Come and sit down. Have a chair.'

She went across to him herself, taking his arm to lead him forward. Everybody in the room knew the story. Startled and unmoving, they watched her welcome her old enemy, the one that they had known for years to be her adversary.

The old man let her lead him. He sat down gratefully into the chair she offered him. 'Thank you,' he said, his voice humbled.

She nodded, and stood straight again.

'Now,' she said. 'I'm going to tell you all something that will come as a shock to you. And Frederick, remembering your age, I want to prepare you,' she said with almost a flicker of the old Dickie humour. 'This old man,' she said, her voice evening out again, 'was once very foolish.' Frederick bent his head, ready to hear his condemnation in front of them all.

'But,' she went on. 'He has always had the reputation, I know, of a kind man in this village. What he did to me was not, but it was forgivable.' Her hands twisted slightly in each other, her chin lifting. 'I cannot say that he was entirely to blame.' Frederick started to look up to see the startled expressions on their faces. Dickie's eyes were lamplike in the pallor of the room. 'You see, all of you, when I was fourteen I was just a village girl. I had no hope of loving a man like Frederick Redfield, but love him I did. From afar. After all these years I know now the power of my own persuasion. I cannot rule out the effect that the power of my love might have had upon him, though what he did was wrong, terribly wrong. I have come to believe, through a talk with a mutual friend, Katherine Haslett, that he might not be totally to blame. I've thought about it since. I did want him, though not the way it happened. I can see that now. And,' she said, giving a long sigh of breath, 'I've been wrong. Carried it on too long, done too much damage to all of us. I want to ask all of you to forgive me.'

Frederick's eyes were on her, their dark blue mesmerised by her words. He started to get up. She put a hand on his shoulder, as the murmurs of assent started all around her.

'No, wait,' she said. 'There's one more thing you all have to know as well.' She drew in a breath. Her hand still lay on the tweed shoulder of the old man on the sofa. 'Rupert Redfield, who is the man I truly hated for starting all of this, chapter and verse, was the one to blame. But, rough and brutal though he was, too excited by his conquest of me, he did not take my virginity.' She let her words sink in all around her. 'No,' she went on more softly. 'I let you think it, all of you. That was what was wrong of me.' Her eyes absorbed them, then back to Frederick. 'He failed, and was not man enough to ever admit that to his brother. It was you, you, Frederick,' she whispered, 'who did it. Look around you. This is your family. Kay, this is your grandfather.'

There was absolute silence. And then tears, gasps, cries of joy. Max looked across at the old man, who, stunned, was coming to his feet, looking around him. His family? The look of happiness on his face was almost too much to bear. And Dickie's face too. Her green eyes were swimming as she smiled upon him. Max saw a frail old gentleman who had paid the price of one day's mistake in a lifetime of loneliness and regret. And Dickie had loved him. Jennie had already loosed her hold, smiling, holding onto her trug of flowers as Max crossed the room to join the others milling round him.

Kay did not hesitate. Slipping from David's arms she went to Frederick.

'Grandpa?' she said gently. And then laughing she threw her arms around him, hugging him to her. 'Oh, I knew I had a reason to love you!'

There were tears in both of their eyes. He patted her back, holding her close. Behind her came his son. His son. He could hardly believe it, as Max's eyes, so very like his own – why hadn't he known? – held his, his hand stretching out to take his in a firm grip. Kay turned as her father came forward, the strong smile on his face, his eyes brimming with feeling. He had no words. What could be said? He merely clasped the old man's hands in his, clapped him on the shoulder and then they were hugging each other. Neither had ever hoped for so much, such a discovery.

Dickie turned away. She had broken the ice for all the family with her words. She knew now why she had always felt so much for Frederick. She had loved him, with a child's naïve love, but the episode with Rupert had rolled into one hate, coloured all her life until his death. Now she saw clearly, and remembered. Now she felt her own sense of guilt for all the pain she had caused them all, all the things she had brought about with the feud, hurting her own family as much as she had hurt theirs. It was the love that Kay and David shared, two such strong and decent young people, that had wrought this moment, this happiness.

Dickie was moved. She sat down opposite, tired. Her revenge had always been against Rupert. It had ruined her life as much as his. She had been wrong, carried it on too long.

She felt the warmth of Kay's arms around her neck from behind. Then the girl slid down beside her.

'Dickie,' she said gently. 'Thank you. You can't believe how happy you've made me. Us.' She bent and kissed her.

'I'm sorry you had to go through that, darling,' she said. 'It was the two of you that turned everything around, made me realise I had to let you know the truth.'

'And I'm so glad,' she said. 'It's all over now. All this hate and bitterness. We can all start to get to know each other. See.'

She turned her face smiling to see Charles and Max exchange a word. The tension was high in the room. Framed against the light from the window the dark shoulders of both men held the same angle, something of the same strength. Charles said something and Max half laughed, then let himself laugh again. Charles smiled at his pleasure. Not brothers after all; free to like each other.

Dickie gave a small chuckle. David crossed the room towards them.

'Well, I acclaim that young man as a very worthy adversary for you, young lady,' she said, patting her hand. 'Quite a match.'

Kay smiled as David came to claim her, and she turned to stand and feel his arms around her again as he led her away. Dickie watched them go, out onto the lawns of Longbarrow, past Jennie, who kissed her daughter and then without the slightest hesitation the handsome young fellow who had taken her daughter's heart. She patted his shoulder as he firmly placed Kay's arm through his and made her his own.

Dickie stood at the window. She watched the young lovers stroll out across the lawn. A Redfield at Longbarrow. She had never thought to see it happen. Behind her, the room was still punctuated with words and laughter. She gave a deep sigh of emotional exhaustion. The family were together again. Jim would recover in time, a better and happier man. Kay would stay in the firm, she was sure of that now. And at last a young man with the qualities needed to run her empire. Or rather Max's. Albeit a Redfield. She chuckled at the irony. It had been Frederick's money that had started Bennett Air in the first place.

'Well, Mother.' The familiar dark voice was at her side. His arm went round her shoulders. 'You did surprise us.'

'Yes. I did, didn't I!' she said.

She turned in his arm to catch sight of Frederick. He was looking over towards her. His eyes showed his feelings, his gratitude. And then he smiled. Charles took him by the arm.

'They're leaving, Mother,' said Max. 'But we'll be seeing them.'

'Yes,' she murmured. 'I've no doubt of that.'

It had all come around full circle. Kay and David walked arm-in-arm up through the long damp grassy fields to Sam's Hill. She told him of its origins, how Dickie and her brother had sat out here as children dreaming of their futures, Foxhall to one side of them beyond the wood, Longbarrow, peach in the early morning sun, lying in the valley.

'Kay,' he said, 'will you marry me?'

Her smile was radiant. 'I thought you'd never ask.'

In front of the huge fireplace at Foxhall, Frederick settled in with the papers. He stretched his legs out before him. They were stiffening up with age; he felt the cold even on a summer's day. The fire had been lit. He wished he had a dog, lying there at his feet. He remembered the last time he had felt like this, a summer's evening and his dog at his feet, when Foxhall had been his for a short while. It had been the day she had come to call, asked him for the money to take her to America. She had been bold; she still was. He smiled and laid the paper down across his knees. He need not be lonely any more. He had family, and Foxhall was his until his death. He was weary, but with the weariness of sudden emotion, that was all. He closed his eyes to sleep. Now there were so many tomorrows to look forward to.